CRASHING INTO SUNRISE

The Emotional and Artistic Upheaval of a 1940s Youth

A Novel

by

Gerald F. Sweeney

For Eileen
Go Blue!
Happy Days
Jerry

THE COLUMBIAD—BOOK 3

A series of seven stand-alone novels about a family in the 20th Century

ISBN 978-1-60910-918-9

Printed in the United States of America.

BookLocker.com, Inc.
2011

First Edition

Dedicated to Barbara Brunswick, Mardi Christensen, Mimi Danzig,
Lois Dowsey, Barbara Fetzer, Bob Fiertz, Bob Guder,
Pat McKenna, Jeanne Marshall, Joe Scanlan
and Marylou Wilkinson

No life would have been complete without them.

Lost time. Drifting around back there somewhere in the cigarette smoke, its ghost swirling to curl alive. Watching its slow sinuous shapes resolve into a dance. Circling back on returning feet. Swinging out on moonlit melodies. Memory clarifying the shadows to reveal the dream of one's own puffed-up flesh with its smell of young love.

Old now, fewer left to care. Still some continue to churn back, searching for embodied heat until, slowly, a fog-enwrapped light begins to tumble back past the pickets of history to reveal remembered images sculpted by the sun. Arriving like a warm kiss, the memories of then becomes now.

BOOK ONE

Chapter 1

Jim Mahoney sensed that he was passing a milestone when he first walked onto the lawn of his high school as if his life had just veered off the country road of childhood and began chugging along the highway of adolescence, where posted limits were often ignored. At the same time, he was accompanied by an uneasy, side-mirror feeling of having already reached a distant destination, that the near and far were closer than they appeared. As if this section of his trip had already been determined and he was merely catching up with his hitchhiked future. Whatever the journey, he realized it was time for him to accelerate, to raise his performance level. God knows he had the combustion. If he were only better able to control the unruly sparks that exploded within him and map out a path that would allow him to find the right way. And locate the switch that could help him snap on his headlights.

In the shadow of redbrick Manhasset High on Long Island, and amid the commotion of back-to-class week, he noticed his brother sitting on the grass with a dozen friends in an irregular circle under a spreading maple known to this generation simply as The Tree. He approached the group with no sense of inappropriateness about trespassing into Matt's social territory. His brother, shorter than Jim, but three years his senior, was decked out in casual scholastic attire: slacks in the wide style, a yellow sleeveless sweater over a white Oxford shirt. The girls, quizzical at the nerve of this freshman, looked crisp in their summer print dresses. The day was September perfect. The year 1943.

"You all know my 'big' brother," Matt said as Jim, a six-footer, stood by.

"Isn't he the kid that rides around town on a mini-bike?"

"I've seen him setting up pins in the bowling alley."

The girls' plumpish, red-sticked mouths distracted Jim, who knew most of these upperclassmen as friends of his brother or from yearbook pictures and sports events. For Jim, these senior girls were flesh and moving icons, uncrated Venuses and catalyzed goddesses that moved among the lower species.

Bev, who was exceedingly blonde, greeted him, "We finally got little brother under The Tree."

"Freshman girls better watch out," said Ally, the beauty with a cameo face.

"Forget freshman. With what's left of the draft bait around here, maybe we could recruit him in an emergency."

"Can we make him the class mascot?"

"He's too big to be a mascot. We might leave him as a souvenir to later classes."

Jim, who hadn't said a word, smiled and lit a cigarette. He had never been very good at small talk. He had been bothered by a fairly severe stammer until he learned to kiss girls in the seventh grade.

"We should organize a pagan dance for freshmen. Have an initiation ceremony around The Tree," said Vince, the class clown. "Like a maypole."

"We could brand their foreheads."

"No need. They've already got plenty of zits."

Jim touched his face, but it was a good day.

"What's with The Tree?" Jim finally spoke.

"The Tree knows all," Bev added.

"Shouldn't it be an oak? Aren't they supposed to be sacred?" asked Vince.

The seniors appeared to be drafting in innocence behind the reality that the country was at war and that many of their friends were already overseas. Next June's yearbook would be dedicated to a classmate who died in service and would honor those military recruits who "left behind forever a few carefree years of their lives, the Saturday night dates, rattlin' jalopies, saddle shoes and all that falls into the pattern of joyous teenage life." The operative word was "forever"—the lost time that war sheared from their youth.

Yet there was a lack of adult repose among them. Fingers twisted other fingers. Feet jiggled. Hair was pulled at, inspected and patted down. Abrupt facial changes reflected a lack of confidence; there was an awkwardness of expression, an unfocused yearning and frightened looks that couldn't disguise unknown fears.

When the seniors turned their attention to someone else, Jim felt uneasy standing there and moved on.

Watching him depart, Ally turned and whispered to Bev, "I think he skipped a couple lessons at charm school."

"Are you kidding? He missed the whole semester."

Jim, green to sarcasm, hadn't heard the jabs. Intrigued by the casualness of their manner, he sensed there must be an art to lounging, the languorous way kids strayed in and out of conversations, adding a put-down here and a friendly insult there. They had a way of looking comfortable while totally engaged, leaning back nonchalantly while their blood thumped with excitement.

"Did you notice how sleepy he looked?"

"Probably needs a lot of shuteye."

"That's because his hormones are burning a hole in his Boy Scout resolutions."

Bev spotted a boy sitting in a car in the adjacent parking lot, one who had recently made an unsuccessful raid on her virginity. "That Saylor guy thinks he's so hot with girls. He came up to me and said, 'Are you a real woman yet?' I said that's my business. So he says, 'What are you waiting for?' I looked him in the eye and said: 'My equal.'"

Jim too noticed the kids hanging around the parking lot, crammed into cars. Most were enjoying a post-breakfast smoke, the tastiest of the day, dramatically articulating the air with their weeds, as if the tiny white wands they waved through their inadequacies were directing their personalities. Owing to Jim's interest in high school matters, especially football—his brother Matt was a team starter—and because of his faithful attendance at the raucous bonfire rallies on the nights before the games, Jim was familiar with most of the cars, many of them Model A's. He was accustomed to seeing these kids squeezed into souped-up buggies filled with purloined gasoline that had been wheedled out of near-empty pumps at the local garages.

It was the year car owners spent a good deal of time rotating their balding tires. Gas station owners arrived some mornings to find their slashed hoses had been drained during the night—gas prime-pumped by mouth. Matt's car, overflowing with a group of his friends, sat in a row alongside the other tin cans. His was a '29 Chevy, complete with rumble seat, lacking a windshield and featuring a passenger door fastened by rope. In winter Matt would wear a fur hat and goggles while driving.

Jim was reminded that George Hellas, away in the Navy, had reconstructed half the old cars in the lot. He was rumored to have loved his supercharged cars so much that he slept in them at night. One day George and his buddy Ray put on a display in the school parking lot. They poured kerosene into the filter of George's engine, then raced the motor, and an immense smoke screen resulted. That alerted one of the secretaries in the school office who called the fire department, believing the car was alight. The hooter downtown began to wail, and minutes later the fire trucks came screaming onto school property. But, of course, by then the smoke had disappeared and George was sitting innocently in his car fiddling with the choke.

Everywhere Jim looked, there were lively circles of students re-establishing school ties after their summer recess. Some girls jiggled in place as though bouncing on springs, unable to control their enthusiasm. Confidant suburban girls, still tan, many dressed by Lord & Taylor, appeared soft and graceful, gentle looking with quiet voices, some sitting in groups on the grass under The Tree or along the low wooden fence that outlined the lawn between the school and the row of stripped-down cars. They were touched by a trace of aloofness; the more popular the girl, the more cloud born. There were notable exceptions among these princesses of the realm, found mainly in the more mature senior girls, among them the luscious Frenchified bombshell, Valerie Des Pres. So confidently sensuous, how could she not feel superior to average females, mostly sub-debs struggling with their sexual selves? All those faithful female grandchildren, offspring of the good daughters whose mothers were Edwardian ladies, all these Vickys, in dread and filled with ambivalence in the presence of their laced-up grandmothers, frightened girls who were seeking liberation in the Swing Age just as their mothers had in the Jazz Era. Mother and daughter often in collusion against outdated morals.

Schoolmates melded into comfortable cohesion, eager to share themselves with each other, alive with fresh pulsing hormones that confused them and nurtured them at the same time. Their wide-eyed focus streamed outbound where they hoped to engage with others in social bindings that might offer them love and an environment to exhibit their creativity. There was a robustness about everything they did. Their fleshy bodies burst with excitement. Many gestured extravagantly. Some had known one another since kindergarten and had watched their bodies and personalities double in size. There were old secrets rummaging around their bookbags along with unbroken trust in each other. Not to mention little jealousies and small wounds. There had been sleigh rides and dancing lessons and a World's Fair where they had expressed their friendship publicly, steadfastly maintaining loyalties locked in the inner springs of their unconscious. Now it was time for them to widen their circle. Cliques from the different grade schools would refresh the pool. Jim's class would become an entire society unto itself.

Newcomer Jim's shock of black hair had been elevated with a hand-pushed pompadour. He recognized he had the advantage of being a curiosity, the new boy, the incensed one from the Catholic elementary across town. Around his neck he wore his faith in the form of a cloth scapula that honored the Immaculate Conception, a fabric neckpiece that sailed over his hairy chest that he displayed by keeping a top button undone.

Jim reached down and picked up a twig off the grass that had escaped the sacred maple. He fingered its rough texture for a moment and snapped it in two. Then he walked toward the school building ahead of his friend Mardi Bobbette and overheard her talking to a friend.

"Who's *he*?"

Mardi said, "Hi Jim," then, sotto voce, "New blood."

Jim figured that the teenage personalities that fascinated other youngsters were the ones that displayed breezy emotions in public—minor actors who didn't mind bleeding their feelings in front of a crowd. His cockiness aside, Jim couldn't understand why others moved out of his way as he walked toward school and didn't know that they might be laughing at him behind his back for his rooster walk. He only knew that he attracted people's gaze. When he peered out of his smallish hazel eyes, his imagination awoke to the prospect of two hundred and fifty new sweater sets. He had no conception that this was a seat of learning. To him, it was a venue where girls were designed to supply favors and theatrics.

Jim was actually a few days late attending school. He had been visiting his grandmother and his married Aunt Marge in Chicago and had misjudged the scholastic start date. The health and welfare of his Midwestern relatives, his second family, had been deteriorating and he had been instructed by his mother to report on their well being, but he proved to be no judge of others' problems. His maternal uncle and his uncle by marriage had both recently been scooped up in the military draft. As a consequence, money was tight and no one could foresee a favorable end to the war. Then news came that the Army had sent sickly Uncle Jack, his mother's brother, to a hospital for extended tests of an undiagnosed disease. Jim, visiting the women who had helped raise him in the years of the early Depression, chose to enjoy the holiday and ignore the family's signs of trouble. He preferred the less stressful home of his Aunt Mary Rose, who was bright and chipper and always managed to register her laughter in the mirth and foibles of everyday life. Mary and her pert and pretty daughter, his cousin, Tess, welcomed him in their rambling Victorian mansion, set in a middle-class neighborhood where mother and daughter like a team of good spirited vaudevillians, entertained. He enjoyed rambling through the city, attending a White Sox game and riding the Madison Avenue streetcar into the Loop to hear Charlie Barnet's band at the Oriental. He had even made a side trip to see family friends at a Wisconsin resort. He had smooched all his old girlfriends in Chicago. Up north in Delavan, he went out dancing one night to a lakeside ballroom.

He stood by the side entrance of the school and savored the moment. Appreciative looks were darting his way, glances that signaled that an interesting new specimen had arrived. Having spent the last eight years restricted by nuns, he felt a sense of freedom in his new environment, unweighted with church ritual and confessional guilt. He had a fleeting acquaintance with many of these public schoolers; it was a relatively small town of five thousand. Like himself, a pair of his parochial classmates had opted against Catholic high schools, so he knew his friends Frankie and Terri would be here. Scouting and sports interests ensured that he would know a few other tenderfoots and ball carriers. After he doused his cigarette, he walked through the door and made his secular debut.

Teenagers were scuffing along the halls. The worst offenders in this ricocheting contest for attention were kids like Jim who had the shoe repairman add metal taps to his heels. He sounded like Bojangles strutting on stage. As he trekked down the crowded corridor, he watched girls' eyes lift toward him.

After some effort, Jim found his homeroom and discovered Frankie wearing a sharp new outfit and Terri, conscientious as a librarian, in a floral-printed dress. Tall and clever Ben from Scouts was in the class. And Jim was happy to see his "Spin-the-bottle" partners Mardi Bobbette along with Bootsie Harding—Mardi with her perfect figure and smoldering eyes and Bootsie, blonde, thin and imperious. Satisfied that his entrance had been successful, Jim sat down next to Frankie.

"Watcha doing later? Working at the bowling alley?"

"Thinking about going up to the club before they drain the pool," Jim replied.

"You going for the record?"

Jim, with his swimmer's body, had an aggressive need to perform physically. He thought he could beat the pool record at the Village Bath Club, fifty-eight laps.

Frankie and Jim had been friends since fifth grade, biking together, wind-sailing with open jackets down Leeds Pond on skates, active teammates in three sports as they grew out of boyhood. Like Jim, who had had a serious ear operation as a child, Frankie had some physical problems and perhaps these ailments made both of them more sensitive than others to various forms of pain. Frankie had a wiry, athletic body and had been competitive in schoolyard sports. Now, he would employ his grace of movement to slide out onto the dance floor. He and Mardi could have been a ballroom dance team.

Frankie introduced Jim to a roly-poly guy sitting next to him, named Rocky from the Plandome neighborhood.

"You related to Matt?" Rocky asked.

"Yeah, a senior."

"My sister, too. Name's Ally."

"She cheers, right?"

"She cheers, all right. Ought to see her practicing splits on the living room rug."

Jim was crazy about cheerleaders. Michele, from last year's squad, caught in a conflicting time between losing her boyfriends to the armed services and the kidnapping of a Japanese friend who had been swept up by the government and interned along with her alien family, discovered Jim in a time of need. Michele had lingered with him one stressful afternoon in a shaded garden and out of physical necessity, taught him how to soul kiss.

Rocky, with a sense of humor that he inherited from his sharp-tongued sister, would join Frankie and Jim to form an instant trio.

After the homeroom meeting, there was a general assembly. Five hundred students crowded into the auditorium to listen to the principal, Mr. Leslie, commonly known as "The Beak." His austere presence and stern visage were new to Jim. The headmaster reminded him of a male nun in a business suit.

The introduction to the program began with the new national anthem, the one that replaced "Hail Columbia." Piano accompaniment was provided by one of the school's more accomplished musicians, while the violinist, a flat-chested freshman named Lucy, wore a corsage surrounded by bushy ferns, greenery that became agitated when she fiddled. It was her debut performance and her parents had arranged with the florist to celebrate the occasion. The duo played as their music teacher, Mrs. Chance, conducted from the auditorium floor beneath the apron of the empty stage upon which the principal would speak. When the music paused, Mr. Leslie lectured his pupils about their solemn duty to be studious and civic-minded, what with the war on and all. Everyone was being asked to sacrifice, but he was lecturing to kids who possessed so many advantages that the small amount of wartime goods subtracted from their comforts caused little pain.

The short event ended with the singing of “God Bless America,” Kate Smith’s radio song. As the pianist began to play, there was movement. The bulky musical instrument appeared to be in motion. The piano started to slide along the floor. It skidded away from the piano player’s perch and he had to scramble along to keep up, watching nervously as the departing instrument stuttered along the floor. Some of the audio-visual guys had rigged a rope that ran along the floor to the piano legs. From their nest under the stage, two burly guys were hauling on the line, pulling the piano away from the performer, who was now missing notes and trying to drag his bench behind him with one hand while he faked a melody with the other. He was literally chasing the piano. Totally perplexed by what was happening, the piano player looked like a person who had lost his pants on the middle of a dance floor. Meanwhile, nervous Lucy the violinist, as she watched the piano lumber away, became so dismayed that her ferns shook violently.

The students were howling as Mrs. Chance, her back to the instruments, continued to conduct the audience while Principal Leslie boiled like a Maine lobster. Jim reveled in this rebellious behavior. Terri, a piano player, didn’t appreciate the joke.

“Dismissed,” Mr. Leslie shouted before the hymn came to an end. “Leave!”

The students went rolling into the corridor. Signs were propitious for a rowdy year even though the AV Department would have to get through the term with two fewer members.

Jim's first class was with Senorita O'Hara, a frowlsed woman with a sly, dark humor, who commuted from Greenwich Village each weekday to rattle the complacency of her suburban charges. Jim spotted Frankie's friend Rocky and sat next to him.

"Who's that dark-haired girl over there?" Jim asked Rocky. "The one who looks like she's popping out of her dress?"

"Bonnie. How 'bout them bazookas?"

Bonnie was one of those small girls with a figure that was like a flashing light to fourteen-year-old boys, an illumination delineated in sculpted, voluptuous curves. Her breasts stood out prow-like and appeared to have a life of their own.

"OK. Pipe down. Looking over the roster here," said Senorita O'Hara interrupting their gawking. "I see a few familiar family names." Looking up, she asked, "Which one of you is *Señor* Southdown?"

"That's me," Rocky said.

"I hope you'll be as good a student as Ally."

"She's always been my role model," Rocky said mockingly.

O'Hara, arching her eyebrow, evaluated Rocky and mentally filed him in her instant classification system, arranged by years of teaching, as a potential wise guy.

"So, let's begin. *Hola*!"

No reaction.

"I said, *Hola*," the teacher said in a louder voice.

"*Hola*," they responded.

As they were separating at the end of class, Rocky said to Jim, "See you later, *Señor*."

"*Adios*, *amigo*."

Jim wandered in and out of classes for a few hours and then spent a free period in the library. He spotted some guys from Scouts lined up on one side of a long study table and he noticed as well that one of the beauties from the senior class sat reading at the adjoining table. Jim tried to sit down opposite his friends, his back to the girl facing the line of guys on the other side of him.

"No, no. Don't sit there. Come over here," they insisted, so he rose and took an empty chair alongside his in-line companions.

The girl opposite was near-sighted, wore a tailored shirt and a skirt many inches above her knees. Sitting, her skirt floated into dangerous territory.

"She's not wearing any underpants," the guy next to Jim said.

The six guys waited for her to cross her legs, uncross them, anything.

When she did, there was a lot of snuffling and snorting at their table. Jim was frozen with excitement and uneasy guilt.

Later, when it came time for gym class, he changed into shorts and sneakers and lined up on the football field for instruction. The small, burly athletic director announced that training this year would include close order military drill and the running of an obstacle course that had been built over the summer, designed to help students, some of whom were sluggards, prepare for military fitness. Off the boys went on a cross-country run that included rope climbs, wall scaling and trench jumping. Later in the month, the service recruiters would begin prowling the ranks of the senior boys, many of whom would be in uniform by Christmas. His brother Matt would leave for the Army Air Force in March.

After school, Jim revisited the gym area, picked up his football gear and deposited the pads and uniform in his assigned locker. Regular team practice would start the next day, giving Jim the chance to head downtown to the Greeks. There were at least fifty kids crowded into the Chocolate Shop's booths ordering soft drinks and grilled cheese sandwiches. They demanded ashtrays from the owners' two boys, classmates at school, who were frantically trying to keep up with the needs of their customers, jammed into sixteen booths. These were overflowing with teenagers sitting alongside large pocketbooks, texts strapped together by belts and sports equipment, mainly lacrosse sticks. Floating above the caramel-fudge smell hung a cloud of smoke and queening over the entire scene was the tall, slinky senior, Valerie Des Pres, whose sultry looks and droopy lids missed no sexual reference. Afternoons, she sat drinking black coffee, contemplating her moves. From the jukebox, Bunny Berrigan's trumpet glorified "Sometimes I'm Happy," a refrain that resounded in most of the kids.

Jim stopped for a pack of cigarettes at the front counter but had to wait for Alex to serve him. Chesterfields, Lucky Strikes and Camels, the three leading brands, had already gone to war so Jim had to settle for a lesser, harsher-tasting offering. Meanwhile he surveyed the crowd and saw Mardi sitting with curvaceous Bonnie from his Spanish class along with other freshmen. Lighting up from a new pack, he threw a lustful glance at Valerie and then sauntered over to greet his classmates.

"Come on," Mardi said. "Squeeze in."

Luckily, he had to push in next to Bonnie, feeling her thighs next to his, which jump-started something in his pants. She was wearing a sailor's pea jacket, a wartime fashion statement, over her slight shoulders. Jim was always quick to notice details about the Navy, especially anything to do with its aircraft carrier fliers. Every kid had a special attachment to one of the military branches, particularly when older brothers were involved. Jim was particularly inspired by the aircraft carrier engagements of the *Yorktown,* the *Enterprise* and the *Hornet*. He had begun researching and even writing about the fliers who fought in the Pacific battles where sailors either conquered the enemy or burned to death.

"Who has a ride to the Farmingdale game?" Mardi asked.

Ben, like Jim, was trying out for football, said, "Not unless they make me the starting tackle and I get to ride the team bus."

"Wait your turn, freshman. Lucky if you carry the water pail."

"You gotta grow them muscles a little," Bootsie chimed in.

"You mean I have to actually exercise?" Ben said, striking a Charles Atlas pose.

Ben was tall, broad-shouldered, double bright and shared a shy vulnerability that was appealing. His cowlick was in keeping with his aw-shucks reticence. He had about him a sobriety and sincerity of expression that demanded honest and careful response. He came from serious people, European-serious, though he and his brother were teaching their parents to loosen up in the American style.

Ben and all the guys, in order to make more room in the booth, had their arms slung around the girls' shoulders.

Jim's friend Mardi was mischievous and droll. A witty brother and sharp sister had helped instruct their sibling on the wiles and ways of scholastic life. Years more mature than her contemporaries, Mardi was ahead on their common journey to adulthood, as if she had prospected the way and knew the crash points and detours. Her perfect body was another siren call to the male population and her ability to role-play as one's sister made her one of the guys' favorites. In all her high school group pictures, Jim and Ben, feigning innocence, could be seen standing behind her in class photos, trying to goose her into a whoopsy-daisy look of surprise.

Frankie and Rocky were there, too. But it was Bonnie who was steaming up Jim's energetic libido. She had a popular older sister as well and knew the score. Small and dark, surely one of the most beautiful girls Jim had ever seen, she would become a fashion model in Manhattan before her junior year.

"Anybody going to the dance a week from Friday?" Ben asked.

"Whose band?"

"I heard the Club Packard Orchestra, with that guy Billy Baker on trumpet."

"What'll you wear if you go?"

"Think I better get a date first. Nudge. Nudge," said Mardi, poking Frankie.

"You don't need a date. Just show up."

"Are you kidding? My father won't let me out of the house by myself," said Maryjan, another attractive girl with soft blonde hair. Full-bodied and athletic, she was regularly forced to fend off jokes about her father, the kind of suburban handyman who actually painted his garage floor and was once spied mowing his lawn during a snow shower.

"Maryjan, I hear you need your dad's permission to go to the bathroom."

"You guys. Don't pick on my father. He means well," Maryjan added with a playful hurt look.

More than anyone else that Jim would know in his teenage years, Maryjan had the ability to extend her warmth to others. No one ever doubted her friendship. There was not a false note that ever rose out of her empathy. Jim wondered if the knack to embrace others was a feminine trait and concluded it was. Meanwhile, his attention focused on Bonnie.

They were all smoking except Maryjan and Ben.

"Pass me one of those coffin nails," Frankie said.

"Buy a pack of your own, moocher." was the reply.

"I called you last night but didn't get an answer," Mardi said to Boots, who had her own phone in the bedroom.

"I must have had the vacuum running." Everybody knew she was spoiled rotten and had a live-in maid to do her ironing and could barely turn on the radio.

Everything a joke.

Frankie noticed all of Ben's books.

"What are you? Some kind of budding genius?"

"Yeah. And if you're not nice to me, I'm going home to study."

Alex, the owner's son, came by wearing a long white apron, "You just sitting here or are you gonna order something?"

"Give us a break, Alex. How about a straw and glass of water? That way you'll look busy so your folks won't fire you."

"Wise guy."

"OK, Alex. I'll have a black and white soda. Will that get us more booth time? You know we all love you."

"You just saying that or you trying to tell me how deeply you care?"

After Alex had dumped the ashtrays and wiped away the debris off the black, marble-topped table with his smelly rag, he said, "Don't feel like you have to leave a big tip or anything. I can always skip college."

"I was going to leave you a nickel, Alex, but these guys told me I had to spend it on the jukebox."

When Alex moved on, Rocky said, "Bobby Dare's having a party Saturday night. Are you all going?"

"What'll we do? Dance? We're too old for Spin-the-Bottle."

"We could practice in case we do," Jim contributed.

"Let's hear it from Romeo," Mardi said. "Probably practices in front of a mirror."

"Mine kisses me back," Frankie added.

The conversation mainly dwelt on upcoming social events. The only time they thought about the war was when newsreels at the movies confronted them. Even then, they were so busy gabbing that they didn't see the bloodshed and the sight of all those bodies lying in fields and ditches in who-knew-what country. Their callowness was forbidding. They distanced themselves from the conflict, even though Jim had a fascination with aircraft carriers.

A year later in the far Pacific, his Navy mates were talking about George Hellas.

"You should have seen him when that rooster MacArthur came ashore at Leyte," one gob said to another sailor in the hammock next to the one where his buddy Seaman Hellas was sleeping. "George was running a big landing barge and was beached up right alongside where they were shooting pictures of Mac wading through the surf, sucking on his corn cob pipe, retaking his empire. There's George—all six foot five of him, thirty feet above the waterline at the controls of his beachwagon watching the brass come back to the Philippines. Standing up there like he was a prince of the sea. Now look at him. So frail he looks like covered bones. Lucky he's not a skeleton seeing as how he took all that shrapnel. How many operations has he had by now? Six? Tore his head open, split his back, and left iron in his gut. I was next to him, so close that when I caught some shit, our blood mixed on the deck."

Curious about the new girl, Jim walked Mardi home instead of swimming.

"Where have you been hiding that Bonnie?" Jim asked.

"She's been around forever. It's just that her folks never let her out for parties."

They talked about the kids they liked; the others they put down. The first were attractive on the surface; the others had mostly chosen a different path to grow. The popular kids tended to be gregarious, sassy and conventional within a confined code; the drones did squirrelly things like study and think about their future.

Footloose kids like Mardi and Jim were content to skip along through the storm of confetti manufactured in the glittering ballrooms of their juvenile imagination.

They all—popular or not—sought for guidance but had a hard time finding it. Some accepted their suburban traditions and others rejected them. Indeed the conservatives in most generations tended to be pliable and homebound, whereas the activists couldn't wait to stretch out into the larger world. Brother Matt often complained that their family was financially over their heads in this affluent suburb and consequently lived below the grade in what he called a money-mad town. Some searched behind the social façade and learned to play the game; others just rebelled against it, like Jim and Mardi.

They sat in her faux-Mediterranean home on Webster Avenue—red-tiled roofs, stucco arches that separated interior rooms that should have been painted white instead of a dull gray. A dark house that could have been Latin bright.

"Anybody else home?" Jim asked.

"No. My dad's out of town." She hesitated, "Thank god he's gone most of the time. I hate him."

"Same with my step-dad," Jim said. "I keep out of his way. Would be nice to have a father that said I did one thing right."

Mardi's anchors were her siblings. "But it's tough with Tom in the Navy and Gloria off at art school. I'm on my own for the first time. And my mom's no help."

"Mine either. She always sides with my old man."

Jim's commentary on his step-dad was conditioned on the fact that his natural father had died when he was an infant and his mother remarried a tough advertising exec named Bob Hill. The family conducted most of its activities at arm's length.

Mardi continued, "I'm tired of always scrimping. It's like a poorhouse around here. My mom never knows when she's going to get house money, so she had to go out and find a war job. My dad's always traveling. We never know where he is or what he's doing. Mom thinks he follows the horses."

She hesitated and said, "I keep looking for something that can unlock what I feel inside and sets me free."

"Yeah. It's like I'm filled with glue or something that keeps me choked up."

"Only when I dance something clicks. Lets me sail away."

"If I'm playing piano and listening to swing, I feel like that."

"You'd think there would be a teacher or somebody that could help," she said.

"Grown-ups don't know how to help. You'd think they'd know stuff—they have jobs and all. But they're so busy with their own bee's wax, they could care less."

"But it's hard to get things straight by yourself."

The two teenagers sitting on a fat-pillowed sofa were intermittently querulous and complaining. More perceptive adults would wonder if they were not intimidated by their environment and had to fortify themselves with defensive personalities and build an imaginary world to offset the reality surrounding them. A petulant pair, Mardi tended to wear a pout while Jim was showing signs of an unearned arrogance. The two were at their worst in her dark house. It took away their natural spark.

"So how do we make this a good year?

Mardi said. "I'm just going to keep practicing dancing so I can audition for the Rockettes someday."

"I just want to be a Navy flier."

The unguided dreams of two hopefuls.

"And I have to figure out a way to make a mark at school," Jim lamented.

"Do what I used to do," she said. "I'd try out a different personality every day until I got one that worked."

"What do you mean?"

"One day I'd be happy-go-lucky. Next I'd be mean. Then I'd be everybody's friend. Next a snob."

"Maybe I should try it."

"After a while," Mardi said. "You find the one that suits you."

High school—an arena of wet egos and false allure, a tryout of personalities as well as hairdos.

There was to be between Mardi and Jim only the possibility of romance, never the actuality. They became each other's personal advisor regarding the rites of growing up. They would learn together and heal each other's wounds. They remained bound-up friends who often stood in her doorway in a long embrace, taking strength from one another's arms.

Early fulfillment eluded them even though their bodily juices were boiling for answers. It wasn't that they were seeking some intellectual or spiritual completion. They couldn't even imagine such a journey. If they could only find a way forward that wasn't so complicated. Pinned down by ignorance and naiveté, maybe they could find a way to release themselves. Find the right path. They'd help each other try.

* * *

Jim, whose head was filled with melodies, often launched songs into the air. He serenaded his neighborhood while walking home from school, as he did after leaving Mardi's house. He would whistle loudly, and the reverberations that rang around the hills in the small valley in which he lived echoed back. His mother often heard him twittering a block away as she sat at her upstairs desk, fingering invitations and writing notes in her perfect hand. Grace Mahoney Hill was learning to interact socially in an effort to help her husband succeed, joining a host of organizations and benefit committees since arriving on the East Coast four years ago.

Jim entered the house and plopped his books on the up stairs.

"That you, son?"

"Which one?"

"The one who whistles."

'That must be the younger one."

"I'll be down in a minute. I'm answering Uncle Francis's latest letter."

Jim's grandfather Martin had just died and Grace, keen to retain her sons' family connections back to the Midwest, was corresponding with her former brother-in-law, Jim's Uncle Francis. She was reaching back through the streets of Chicago and out past the Mississippi to the Iowa farms where the patronymic O'Mahoneys had settled in 1840. After a long sea voyage from Ireland to New Orleans, the pioneers followed the big river up to

Dubuque. Jim knew nothing about these historical events. Neither knew nor cared about his father's family. The truth was that he could barely remember Grandfather Martin, who came by at Christmas with gifts of books. Though the boys' relations with the paternal side of the family were tenuous, Gracie had insisted, after her remarriage, that Matt and Jim keep their Mahoney surname and made sporadic attempts to keep up with their clan.

At dinner the five Hill-Mahoneys labored over Gracie's meatloaf, mashed potatoes and peas. The head of household, Bob Hill, was an account exec at a Manhattan advertising agency and spent overtime working and traveling the country when and if air flights, reserved mostly for the military, were available. Grace, nearly forty, had settled comfortably in Manhasset and was gaining respect in the community as an organizational volunteer. She was reliable and could maintain ledgers, owing to the business acumen she accumulated after her first husband's death. Grace Mahoney Hill had overcome the poverty of Chicago, the loss of a spouse and her oldest child, an emotional breakdown and an economic Depression and had emerged in feisty fashion living in one of the better places in America. She felt that she was now at the high point of her life. She had discovered the advantages of becoming a clubwoman and sharp bridge player, allowing her to interact with ladies resembling the big-hatted Hokinson women in the *New Yorker*. At the same time impelled to act like one of the "girls" in Claire Booth's movie, *The Women*.

Jim remembered some of the hard times and heard enough of the family history to know that there was a large amount of pain flowing through the generational narrative. What he had been able to do so far was resist the genetic hand-down of his parents' suffering. Jim either chose to ignore or blanked out the pain. He would not allow their problems to come down the chain and cripple his own growth. But, in compensation, of course, he lost his sense of compassion.

Also at the family table were brother Matt and his half sister Francy, age five.

"How'd it go at school today, Junior?" Pappy asked Jim.

"Went all right."

Mashed potatoes, clumps of banality, circulated around the table.

"Did you boys get the teachers you wanted?" asked Gracie.

"I guess one's as good as another," Matt replied.

"When's your first game?" Bob Hill asked him.

"Two weeks from Saturday. Farmingdale."

"I'll try to make it," Bob said. In the past few years, businessmen had stopped working Saturdays but Bob sometimes traveled into town to clear up the week's workload. He did take an interest in the boys' sports activities. Maybe his only interest in them. He had played both scholastic and college sports himself. Small but tough like Matt, Bob Hill had excelled at track and even played college football back in the Twenties when lightweights were not unknown.

"Does Farmingdale have a good team?" Bob asked, trying to keep up the conversation.

"Nobody knows." Scouting wasn't one of the Athletic Department's strong points.

"Francy, eat your peas now."

"Yick."

"Never mind about 'Yick.' Just scoop them up."

Bob looked adoringly at his only natural child. "Pretend it's a game," he said. "How many peas can you put on your spoon?"

Francy fell for the ploy and began counting.

Their dinner conversation never rose above the mundane. Aside from a few words about mutual friends, one would never know that literate New York was only eighteen miles away. Politics, ethics, art and ideas never weaved their way across the tablecloth and consequently the younger members were not aware of what they missed. As a result, Jim was never challenged by worldly issues, never grasped a wider view than the ones that interested his friends. In adult company, he was as boring as the potatoes. The parents couldn't be blamed, though. The Depression had forced the nation into worrying about basic existence and little else. The family had survived that battle but retained the scars of deprivation. Jim had no substantial fidelity to the family's greater mission, which seemed to be making money.

There was little love in the home. Sure Pappy and Gracie loved Francy, and Gracie probably did love the boys. They had been through such hard times together that the intercession of grief and poverty had worn them down to passing pleasantries. There were fractures in all their personalities, though there appeared to be no need to call an ambulance just yet.

After dinner, Jim descended into the finished basement festooned in knotty pine, and went to his upright and played for nearly an hour, strolling through his inventory of ragtime, boogie-woogie and swing songs. He practiced regularly; there was at least one discipline he subscribed to. Music was a treasured release from tension, mostly sexual, as well as from the ennui born of a lack of an understanding of the larger world and its needs and realities.

Late that night, he turned on the radio as he lay in bed to listen to the bouncy swing rhythms originating from Manhattan's supper clubs. These melodies stimulated his unconscious, raised his emotions, and allowed him to broadcast his own yearnings back out into the atmosphere, giving him an opportunity to inter-connect the blue-black night and his longings. And Harry James played "You Made Me Love You" and Sinatra sang "All or Nothing at All." The lyrics were his psalms.

* * *

Many kids had a good time growing up on Long Island during the War. Until Pearl Harbor changed the American temper, places like the North Shore spent the early years of the Hitler War in isolation. In 1941, when the suburbs ended at Roslyn, Garden City and Rockville Centre, each of the towns was a unique community with its own personality—all citadels of conservatism, bound together by their angst about FDR. Manhasset was new-rich and filled with advertising and radio people. Roslyn was both upscale and down-to-earth Polish. Miles of country separated each town, while somewhere to the east lay an unexplored never-land of potato farms and horse estates. Some families even had summer places twenty miles east in remote places like Huntington. Economically, the towns faced west toward the skyscrapers that were visible from the highest hills in town. Thanks to the Long Island Rail Road, Madison Avenue and Wall Street were less than an hour away. The Japanese attack solidified the communities by uniting them with patriotic zeal. Residents watched airplane factories spring up around them and soon saw a sky-full of fighter and bomber planes clouding-up their sky.

Food and gas rationing were the norm. Government-inspected horsemeat was now available for consumption (no coupons required). Other signs of war were the anti-aircraft balloons, like giant footballs, lofting over the defense factories. For Boy Scouts prowling in the woods in search of merit badges, the sudden overnight appearance of an anti-aircraft gun emplacement was always big news in the neighborhood.

Everywhere in America, Johnny got his gun. Older brothers joined the Army Air Force, or programs like the Navy's V-5. Two guys writing home from the tundra talked about the grueling conditions that faced them building the Alcan Highway. Others were sweating in the jungles. Once a kid reached sixteen, with his parents' permission, he could sign up as a seaman. One big hulk, who had been condemned to the eighth grade for three years in a row by the nuns, turned up at school one day in bell-bottoms on his way to Great Lakes. Younger guys joined the Civilian Air Patrol and practiced flying Link Trainers. Girls could join the Motor Corps and dress up like British ambulance drivers and learn how to strip engines. Volunteers collected "Victory" books to be shipped overseas; others sold War Stamps, or did Red Cross knitting or worked on the scrap salvage trucks. Everyone contributed.

Teenage fashions were also dictated by the war, although the first synthetic shirts that would melt near a radiator were still a few months off. Leather became scarce and one of the hallmarks of wartime civilian shoes were soles composed of a kind of cardboard substitute that tended to melt in the rain and crumble in layers.

The girls were bouncy balls of wool in plaid skirts and sweaters accented by bobby socks and loafers, their lipstick as red as a fire engine. Some shortages, like stockings, presented problems. With no silk or nylon versions available, girls began painting their legs with brown paste to imitate hose wear, but it also ran in the rain.

When girls' skirts rose above the knees, most boys deserted their scoutmaster. The fact that males turned so quickly from woodworking to juvenile misbehavior was startling. Scout troops turned into wolf packs, either barking at the cold-colored moon in pitiful sexual repression or howling through the double features at the local theater. Going to the movies proved to be a noisy match between cynical teenagers and the Hollywood dream machine, complete with rowdy outbursts and catcalls.

Teenagers, though enmeshed in the outer web of the global conflict, hardly moved beyond their own emotional cloisters to experience either the suffering or the disasters caused by the chaos of world war.

* * *

On his second day of high school, Jim defied current fashion standards and appeared for classes in dungarees, a white button-down with shirttails hanging out, loafers and white sox. He stood out like a lighthouse. Nobody ever wore jeans except on Saturday mornings and the sight of him on school grounds in such a scruffy outfit illustrated his non-conformity. However, he could care less what other people thought about how he dressed. The beacon that guided him radiated from his needs, wants and desires. Others could light their own way.

The school paper nailed him in the next issue of the "IMPpressions" column—"Jim Mahoney, '47. Dreamy-eyed girls, 'He'd swim a mile for a Chesterfield,' dungarees, moonlight nights, 'Set 'em up in the next alley.'"

The day's excitement was augmented by news of the opening of a teen canteen downtown called the Juke Box. If that wasn't enough, there was a rumor that a movie crew from *March of Time* was on its way to film the event. The genesis of the place was prompted by parents concerned about the national rise in juvenile delinquency, a war-related increase in bad, often felonious, behavior. Riots had been fueled by the unrest of young people in L.A., Detroit and Harlem earlier that spring. The war unlocked rooms in the American house where the cudgels and billy clubs had been stored, the ones that had come out for the old labor wars—the Homestead, Pullman and Haymarket Square riots. However, these 1943 uprisings were mostly race-based, more like the 1919 Chicago beach riot. Matronly suburban outrage had been stimulated by images in Manhattan's newspapers of zoot suiters—tough-looking young males wearing outlandish outfits with elephant-leg-wide trousers, oversize jackets with enormous shoulder inserts, porkpie hats, tropical-flavored fabric and dangling, floor-length metal chains—portraits that had frightened Manhasset ladies to build a "dry night club" to ward off these borough intrusions.

Local funds were raised to renovate a storefront on the town's main street, a haven designed to entice kids to come by and dance around a Wurlitzer stacked with recordings from the Miller, Goodman, Shaw and Dorseys' orchestras. After classes on opening day, the social elite from school wended its way downtown. There was a smell of polished floors, painted walls and the pungent fragrance of leather—belts, shoes, elbow patches and pocketbooks. The guys wore sports coats or lumber jackets; the girls were in cashmere sweaters and pleated plaid skirts or milkmaid jumpers. Some wore penny loafers. Others romped around in saddle shoes.

Responding to the music, the crowded dance floor was soon heaving. When the teenagers started swinging out Lindy-style, bumping and knocking ensued. Frankie began dancing with Mardi but an upper classman named Kenny B., who was fond of younger girls, soon cut in. Kenny, both good-looking and a fine dancer, knew from experience that the younger girls were receptive to his advances. Alert, he had quickly noticed the careless rhythm of Mardi's body as she swung recklessly out in twirling swift-steps to the rollicking beats of their favorite songs. They began "Stomping at the Savoy." They hopped to the "One O'Clock Jump", then the "Two O'Clock" and "Opus One." They swung their shoulders through "Tuxedo Junction," "Perfidia," "Song of India" and "Sing Me a Swing Song and Let Me Dance." Jive jumpers were called jitterbugs; slow dancers were snails.

With their feet pounding to the music, the thudding made the floorboards creak. Swing tunes sang in their blood. Their psyches had been invaded by the music of their time so invasively that many of them would never be excited about popular music again in their lives. When youngsters feel that their music is the best ever crafted, what need for newer noise?

When the film camera crew arrived to memorialize the event, the school's royalty was in attendance. Bibs and Bev, Ally, Trudy, Melissa, blonde Pat, Stu (he had skipped football practice to attend) and Leo, combing his hair, as well as Suds, Glenn, Yosh, and Conkey not to mention Frankie and Rocky. When the celluloid personalities filmed that day appeared on the larger-than-life local screen, the movie showed them as upbeat, energetic youths. The remarkable thing was that they all looked so casually joyous.

Jim, his brother Matt, and the entire football team were absent. Coach wasn't an advocate of fraternization, dancing or carbonated beverages.

It was five-thirty by the time Jim entered the canteen. The crowd had thinned out leaving three dozen kids still huddled around the jukebox and coke bar. He saw Bonnie dancing with Kenny B., the latter relying on his reputation as an elder studsman who favored freshman girls. Jim aggressively cut in. He was stiff from practice and moved with greater awkwardness than usual. Bonnie perked up when he began to lead her around the floor. She had the confidence to know she could win over this new boy.

"I was hoping I'd see you," she said.

"I was busy getting this fat lip." The more experienced players had banged him around. "The team doctor has the same remedy for all injuries, to soak their wounds in Epsom salt. But I don't think that would work on this one." Then he asked, "These older guys bothering you?"

"More likely I'm bothering them," she said with a twinkle. She was pert and had a sassy reputation. And lovely. He had been close to attractive girls before and her beauty had not swept him away. Rearranged his hormones a little perhaps, but he was confident enough to maintain his emotional equilibrium.

When they danced, he felt her breasts like fluffy balls of wool under her knobby-knit sweater. She could feel his wand rising.

"Did you get my note?" he asked.

"Yes. That's why I waited."

"I didn't want to come on too strong, but I wanted to see you."

"And, shazam, here I am."

"I figured you had some magic in you."

"Maybe the magic's between us."

"Where are all our girls?" he asked. In his conceit, he had already acquired them.

"Mardi, Boots and Maryjan were here and gone. 'Fraid they've deserted you, m'lord, but I've waited for His Worship."

The song on the jukebox was Sinatra's rendition of "People Will Say We're in Love" presented with a great deal of "wooing" and angelic harmonies. Recorded during the yearlong musician's strike that prevented band members from accepting studio work, backup singers had been called in to provide an "orchestral" sound for the crooner. There wasn't even a piano. Sinatra, taking time to unwind the lyrics, warbled at a slow sleepwalking speed.

The couple clung to one another, barely shifting their feet. The tempo required little effort.

"Slow motion Sinatra," Jim commented.

"That's the draggiest song I ever heard," Bonnie replied. "Any slower and they'd have to unpeel us."

"Maybe I'll get to walk you home," he said, before one of the other seniors cut in.

"So gal-lant. I'll even let you carry my books," she batted her eyelids, mocking every schoolgirl coquette.

"And you can carry my sweaty jersey," he responded.

"Too generous," she said as she slipped out of his arms and into another's.

He walked over and ordered a coke from one of the volunteer ladies behind the counter. Kenny B. and a guy named Saylor were observing Bonnie dance.

"Those freshman girls. They're a bumper crop," Kenny said.

"That one especially."

"Yeah. She looks like a fine breeder."

It was true that the freshmen girls ranked in beauty with the currently renowned line-up of senior girls. The sourness and stringy looks that had invaded women's appearances during the Depression were evaporating as if the wrinkles of despair had been smoothed out in this loose money, war-exploited economy. It was true that something else was nourishing women's complexions. Maybe it was the anticipated flashpoint encounters and sought-for sexual release stimulated by the war's uncertainties. Or maybe they were simply picking up where their frisky sisters from the Twenties left off.

Kenny B. was sunny and light, with a boyish grin that warmed coeds' hearts. Unkind words never struggled through his Ipana smile. A champion of womankind, he bolstered their self-esteem by attending to their comfort. A bon vivant who drove a spotless red convertible, he introduced many of these local girls to urban nightlife in Manhattan that opened up their prospects and vulnerability to more adult diversions. Jim was to learn a great deal from him about pleasing the other sex. Six months later, while he was on leave and wearing his naval officer's training uniform, Kenny's handsomeness would stun the girls. Bright white on white, with gold accents.

Saylor, on the other hand, was dismissive of most things, including females. He had a supercilious look that often imploded into a surly scowl. If he weren't so nastily good-looking, his appearance would have been less inviting. Some girls swooned over him while others loathed him, mostly for his acid tongue. Saylor, an only child, took an immediate interest in Jim as if he might have located the brother he was always looking for. Maybe he could sense the conceit of the younger boy.

Standing next to them, a pretty girl overheard them talking about Bonnie.

"Good taste. She's adorable," said Rocky's sister, Ally.

"Girls don't want to be adored," Kenny said. "They want to be listened to."

"So says the seer. Did you hear that?" Ally remarked, as she turned away to talk to one of her other friends.

Kenny continued, "Notice when some girls walk or dance? They have this confident look, heads high. It's because they feel good about themselves."

Jim said, "But a lot of girls walk around acting dumb."

Saylor said, "Just an act."

"Most of them are smarter than hell."

Saylor said, "They're mostly a bunch of Calamity Jane's."

Kenny said, "That's because they don't want guys to think they're smart. Here's the point. You have to keep their confidence up, then they don't have to play games."

An all-out jolly guy with a twinkly smile and personality joined them.

"Hey, Dumphy," Kenny said. "You know Jim?"

"This our brand new Lancelot?" Dumphy asked Jim. "Saw you at practice."

"If you mean freshman dollyrocker, yeah."

Jim smiled and wondered where the new arrival got his name.

Nicknames were a favorite way to humanize these uptight, inarticulate youngsters, who, like Jim, were in need of a social bridge to somewhere. Anywhere. Quite a few of these names came from the movies, some from Snow White's seven dwarves. There was Happy from Matt's class. An eighth dwarf could have been Dumphy Donovan, one of those guys, seemingly chubby, but a pillar of steel under a fleshy exterior. To match his physical strength, Dumphy displayed a masculine ebullience that bordered on brotherly love. One of the Alpha fraternity boys, he was an almost perfect member of any male club. There was a bright streak that ran through him enhancing the sharpness of his manliness, a readiness of mind that made his school counselors gasp. Last year, he had posted one of the highest Regents math scores ever recorded in the state. But one would have to be a diviner to comprehend such brilliance, because Dumphy never shared more than a broad smile and an easy disposition, holding in his ambitions and desires. Like nearly all his contemporaries, he was suffering some form of unrequited love. Sensuous Valerie Des Pres had dazzled him since the moment he laid eyes on her, and it was only in the last month that she had finally blown some smoke his way as a sign of recognition.

Dumphy said to Jim, "You know what you need? You need a nickname. I think I'm going to call the two of you," indicating Bonnie, "Duke and Duchess."

"Naw. They're more like Popeye and Olive Oyl," countered Saylor.

"You need glasses. Olive Oyl is a tube of toothpaste compared to her."

Kenny and Dumphy turned to talk to a bystander named Suds, while Saylor, evaluating Jim in his usual snide way, asked, "Any extra-curricular activity other than football, like the *Cub Reporter*?"—the high school paper.

"Hadn't thought much about it," Jim replied. "My home room class put me on the dance committee."

"Reason I bring it up is because I like to write stories," Saylor said. "This year they put me on sports."

"I'm writing a novel," Jim said.

"WHAT?"

"Yeah. About Navy fliers in the Pacific."

"That's weird. How did you get started on that?"

"I dug up stories about the Midway and Coral Sea battles, and got hooked."

"Funny subject, isn't it?"

Jim answered, "Who knows why? After a while, I felt like I was flying with those guys. I just wanted to be them."

Saylor watched the emotion rising in the new kid.

Jim continued, "Those dive bombers and fighter pilots went through a lot, like those guys from Torpedo Eight. I feel as if I'm pasted to them. Stuck to them."

"You got to let me read it." No one had ever asked Jim to read his writing before.

"Sure. I made a carbon."

In a while, Bonnie came up to Jim.

"Ready to go?" he asked.

"Just want you to know I turned down a ride from Kenny."

"Good for your leg muscles to walk uphill."

He didn't know, but that was a low blow. Early illness had weakened her legs.

"Let me grab my things."

He helped her into a pure white, perfectly tailored jacket.

Standing nearby, a neighbor of Bonnie's had been watching them. Who better to bother than freshmen? "Where did you find him?" the older, freckled girl asked.

"He's my new chum," Bonnie replied.

"I'd watch him," the upperclasswoman said. "He's got beady eyes."

Jim was stung by the remark. No one had ever insulted him before in public. He was more startled than anything.

Bonnie stood up to her, "What made you say such a thing?"

"Just warning you."

"I don't know where that came from," Bonnie said as they stepped outside. She was feeling bad because she wanted everything to run smoothly with this new boy. "I'll have to rethink liking her."

Their conversation was easy, which was an accomplishment for him. It was almost as if they knew they were to be connected. Bang just like that on their second day of meeting one another—the frightening awareness that they would open to each other, accepting the idea that mutual vulnerability was sensitizing both. Their potential closeness surprised them.

Bonnie thrived on gossip, like most of her girlfriends. Her older sister had been stirring her curiosity about the school's hi-jinx for years. Big Sis had warned Bonnie through cautionary tales—things like: Keep your mouth closed when you kiss and keep your knees together. Don't have more than one drink when out on a date. No wrestling matches—Bonnie's head was filled with shibboleths and juicy tidbits. Sharing stories about dating were part of her social education, not that she would ever remember which piece of slander she had, in turn, shared with others.

With Jim, she stuck to more familiar people and places. Did he like to ice-skate? (Yes) Did he play lacrosse? (No, baseball.) Would he be working during the school year? (Yes, at the bowling alley and at the Village Bath Club.) What was his favorite school subject? (He didn't have one.) Not even one? (Well, he liked to write.)

"Have you ever seen a Broadway stage show?" she asked.

"No, but I get into Times Square all the time to hear the big bands. I've seen about a dozen of them—Benny Goodman, Tommy Dorsey, Claude Thornhill. Even Cab Calloway."

"I wish my mom would let me take the train in."

Bonnie's mother, a former southern belle named May from Painted Rock, Alabama, kept a generous but firm grip on her two daughters' activities. But her hold was slipping. Her oldest, away at nursing school, had not even asked permission to join her beau for a college weekend.

Once home, Bonnie introduced Jim to Mrs. Cassidy.

"How come I haven't heard about you before?"

"I was at St. Mary's."

"A Catholic boy?"

"Yes."

The immediate linking up of their two personalities filled Bonnie and Jim with feelings of elation, as if they had both been victorious in their ability to extend their egos to one another. Both were a little reckless and eager to give away their affection. Actually, it was more like keeping score than uniting emotionally—their relationship to be read by others as a social match.

Bonnie was in the habit of spending hours on the phone every evening. When she reached Mardi that night, she confessed that she liked Jim.

Mardi said, "Just keep your eyes on him. He tends to waver. But when he hugs you, you'll know you've been hugged."

* * *

A few days later, his mother asked Jim if he had written a note to his Uncle Francis expressing his condolences on the passing of his dead father's parent, Jim's natural grandfather. Of course he hadn't.

"That's plain thoughtless," his mother said to him.

It wasn't that he had been such a bad kid up to now but he was beginning to show some uncaring streaks. So what, he said to himself, that he didn't spread a blanket of goodwill across his family and friends. It wasn't rampant selfishness that kept him from connecting with others; he was simply lazy. He *was* careless. It wasn't a matter of forgetfulness either. He instinctively knew the right thing to do and was cognizant of his own neglect of good manners. He knew he evaded the closeness that could develop from good deeds and actions. In the old movies, sometimes the front plane was actually frozen in place though the subject appeared to be moving because the scenery in the back was shifting. The person was stationary, but the illusion produced by a whirling background implied motion in the foreground. Jim often let the back noise of his hubris cover up his failure to make upfront choices. If he could stir up things around him, maybe he could escape responsibility.

* * *

At six-thirty on Saturday evening, he walked up Flower Hill to pick up Bonnie. They lied to her mother that they were going to the movies downtown but instead detoured to Bobby Dare's party. In Mrs. Cassidy's view, it was bad enough that Bonnie was going out on a date in her freshman year, but she had put her foot down when it came to parties where, heaven forbid, "feeling up girls" might be prevalent. However, she had succumbed to her husband's view that things had changed since 1925 in Dixie and that Bonnie was a sensible girl.

About sixty kids showed up at the party and the pair quickly mixed with the crowd, mostly freshmen and sophomores. For many it was their first party and their faces wore the flush of excited anticipation. Dancing had already begun in the dining room where the rug was rolled back. Upended, the carpet stood guard in the corner. A big pressed-board record player spun the latest hits. When it came time to Lindy the cutlery in the kitchen rattled in vibration.

Everyone was dressed up. The boys all wore checked jackets and cloth ties. The freshmen girls mostly wore dresses that celebrated the new fall fashions; they appeared crisp, blossoming into early maturity. Bootsie, the thin blonde, wore a red plaid jumper over a white blouse. Bonnie appeared in a flounced sleeveless black outfit; her overall look seemed slightly overblown, designed to match her exploding bust line. Mardi stayed with a skirt and sweater, indicating that in her reduced-income household, new clothes were an issue. Household financial problems often caused friction that showed up in her temper, which could heat with intensity. Maryjan wore a pleated tartan skirt and blue jacket. The girls, more developed and usually taller than the boys, wore flat shoes partially to compensate for their height, a problem that tiny Bonnie needn't bother with, especially with Jim. Their complexions, though sometimes bumpy, were shining.

Jim was proud to be with Bonnie. He wondered what they looked like together, what image they cast. He reminded himself to have a picture taken of the two of them standing close. He had already wheedled some photos of her modeling the dress she wore tonight. She and Maryjan had taken photos of themselves sitting on a boulder on Bonnie's front lawn—posing like magazine mannequins, unsmiling and aloof.

When tropical music emerged from the record player, the kids recognized the Conga rhythm and started jockeying for position. A line of dancers immediately took shape. Good-natured Frankie, dancer extraordinaire, was at the head of the line, and creative as always, he led the long, curving, single-file line out the front door and onto the street, in and around trees and bushes and finally into the backyard. A fifty-foot long line of high-steppers, each holding on to the waist of the person in front, twisted into the neighbors' yards as the song burst out of the open windows, a swaying string of kids, laughing and chanting *One, Two, Three, Kick* through the back gardens, celebrating their arrival into the social world. On parade.

It was a warm September evening and many of the guests sat outside. When the sun set and darkness spread across the lawn, the Dare boys wheeled out a half-keg of beer and tapped it. Most of the girls refrained from drinking while a majority of the boys indulged, Jim among them. During the uncorking ceremony and the first drawdowns, the guys stood in a circle around the keg telling sports stories. The girls chatted away under a trellis that ran along the back side of the property.

"I don't know if it's because it's their first party or what, but some of these girls have overdone it with their falsies," Bonnie said to Mardi, both voluptuous.

"Did you see Lucy? Her bra inserts are the size of seat cushions."

In a country where the contours of a girl's chest were as important as her manners, boosting the content of one's figure was normal practice. The only thing a girl had to do was look at movie posters, the pin-ups in *Esquire* (currently banned by the post office for its Vargas drawings) and two-piece swimsuit ads to understand where her appeal to males lay. Though the boys might not know the exact terminology concerning alphabetically delineated brassiere cups, they were aware that "forty" signified magical mammaries that would in all likelihood reappear in their dreams. Padded or stuffed bras were part of the sweater enlargement campaign to snare a male's attention. With Jim, the maneuver always worked.

As the party moved into the ten o'clock hour, urges brought on a change in mood. Some couples were seen necking behind the bushes as the beer loosened their inhibitions. Other kids, sticky with hormones, clung to one another.

Jim and Bonnie didn't stay for the emotional fireworks. They were one of the first couples to leave. She had promised to be in by eleven. When they reached home, Bonnie took him by the hand around to her mother's garden. Bonnie had years before decided that was where she wanted to be kissed for the first time. Electricity shot through them when their lips met.

* * *

Ken and Saylor from the upper classes were soon shepherding Jim around school, steering him through the gossip network and reputation-building process that stemmed from teenage competition. Ken, with his sunny disposition and slick manner, was known as a great flirt. His dancing abilities were celebrated every afternoon in the new teen canteen and to be chosen to dance with him was a signal honor that Mardi Bobbette, among others, enjoyed. Ken's knack for appearing at school dances with girls that no one had ever seen before had friends speculating on what beauty contest he would draw from next, choosing girls across Long Island and beyond. He was currently thinking about taking Jim on one of his ventures. Saylor, too, saw in Jim a kid with possibilities that needed polishing and planned to include him in the country club dance circuit that would soon begin, events that were the social highlights of the year. Saylor, smooth and egocentric, also intended to sweep Jim up into his fraternity's initiation process.

* * *

Word from the Midwest continued to rattle Jim's family. The Chicago branch had pooled their money to live together: his grandmother, his Aunt Marge and her baby and for a while, Jim's Uncle Jack. First Margie's husband had been drafted, followed by Jack. Marge was forced back into the job market to make ends meet because Army pay was only $21 a month plus a small living allowance for married GIs. Jim's grandmother had been enrolled as babysitter. Then disaster struck.

The bad news reached the East Coast. Jim came home one afternoon and found his mother crying. He couldn't remember the last time he had seen Gracie, who was at the zenith of her life's achievements, weep. Word had arrived about her brother.

"Jack's been diagnosed with TB. They've had him lying in that god-forsaken army hospital for months without figuring what was wrong with him. And now they say he's going to die. . ." She erupted in grief. "They can't get any of that new miracle drug to keep him alive."

Jim listened to her, embarrassed at her distress, but continued to build his barricade against pain.

* * *

High school gymnasiums are remembered for their basketball games and tumbling mats splayed across brightly polished wooden floors, but even more warmly recalled because of the dances held there, times of closeness and mounting sexuality. At Manhasset High, the gym was the site of the Soph Hop, the Junior and Senior Proms and the graduating class's Senior Frolic that followed the distribution of diplomas. The hard-reflecting surfaces that rebounded with sound during a close basketball game were softened on these special social occasions when creative attempts were made to lower the ceiling, humanize the immense cavern and prepare an intimate space that sought to mimic a ballroom or nightclub. Then cardboard palm trees blossomed and hedges of paper flowers appeared. Highly decorated gardens, even a pool, were constructed along with gazebos and wishing wells, transforming the barn-like setting into a semi-tropical rendezvous.

None of these decorations was on display at the regularly scheduled school dances held quarterly during the school year. At this first dance of the year, the gym loomed over the students in its pristine, boxy mold while the hard surfaces loudly reflected the sounds of a swinging thirteen-member band. The only concession to formality was that the school's caretaker, Mr. Sotz, was in a business suit instead of his usual overalls.

Jim's date was Bonnie. Frankie was there with Mardi, and Ben escorted Maryjan. The last two pairs had walked to school but Saylor, having taken up with Bootsie, drove Bonnie and Jim. On his way up the hill to pick up Bonnie, he was filled with a strong desire to hold her, with emotions so powerful that they seemed to free him of all his childhood angst. His own juices had helped cure a neglected childhood.

The dance crowd was buzzing with a rumor that was turning into a dark fact. Chattering teenagers are like early warning systems, youth news flashes through their community with alacrity. The information that was whirling through the youth network tonight was the story that one of the gasoline alley guys had actually ridden his motorcycle through the school's hallway after school. He stank up the building before Mr. Sotz, waving his hammer, started chasing the biker. As the teens entered the dance that night, there was still the aroma of burnt fuel wafting along the classroom corridors.

That wasn't the only piece of news. The latest centered on Frankie's brother Leo, the popular sophomore, who preened narcissistically to maintain his good looks and wavy blond hair. If he didn't look exactly like Adonis with his curly crown, he nevertheless acted as imperious as any god. That afternoon, a gang of car jockeys, all of them lying about town waiting to be drafted, cornered Leo in one of the gas stations. They held him and shaved his head, his leonine curls floating away into the oil stains. The samsonian action deflated Leo for months while his hair grew back. Tonight he was home scratching his itchy scalp while brother Frankie, with the humility of someone aggrieved, showed up at the dance to defy the sniggling auto rats, as if their actions gave Frankie an opportunity to display his own and his family's pride.

The band warmed up the crowd with a few swing standards that raised the audience to its feet. Then the music makers livened things up with the Hokey-Pokey ("You put your right hand in" and shake your tush all about). As the night progressed, the music slowed down and bodies clung closer together. That's when Mr. Sotz, who had a romantic streak in him, turned down the lights.

During an early music break, the four couples sat around one of the cafeteria tables that had been wheeled in for the occasion.

"Did you hear about one of the sophomores, Janet Juniper?"

"Is she the one with the big mouth?"

"Yeah. Nickname is Walkie-Talkie."

"She's dating some guy from King's Point."

The location mentioned was in a neighboring village across the bay where the government had established the federal Merchant Marine Academy on an old estate facing Long Island Sound. Keeping the Atlantic shipping lanes open was crucial to winning the war, and the Germans had been sinking merchant ships for a year and a half, leaving the government desperate for trained navigators. The toll on Allied shipping had been horrendous. Vacationers along the Jersey and Hampton shores were annually stricken with the sight of devastated ships erupting in fiery blasts out at sea, exploding into the night, death visible from their dune decks.

"Those Merchant Marine guys are all draft dodgers."

"Hold up," Ben said. "I hear they die quicker and uglier than in any other service."

"Janet always loved a uniform. She used to go home every day and iron her Brownie uniform."

"You can't blame her for dating out of town," Mardi said. "All the healthy guys are in service, and the rest, present company excluded, are babies."

"Pat Rodolfo, Mary's sister, she's only in the seventh grade and she's dating a sailor out in the Hamptons."

"Pray she doesn't get pregnant before high school."

Ben said, "Maybe she could get special credit in Home Ec."

"Or a blue ribbon in French." Sex and France went together.

"I feel sorry for the senior girls. Most of their boyfriends are away in service."

"That's why they're all knitting argyle socks and sweaters."

"And learning to bake cookies."

"And writing V-mail letters on that tissue paper stuff."

"I like it when they smooch the back of the envelope with a big red splotch."

"And mark it SWAK—sealed with a kiss."

After the dance, Jim knew that Saylor was thinking about driving out to some lover's lane, but on reflection, the sophomore estimated that the freshness of the relationships between Boots and himself and Jim and Bonnie might better stew a bit before adding too many sexual ingredients. Instead, they headed for the streamlined, all-night diner on Northern Boulevard. The first diners in the country had all been reconstructed railroad cars, so the theme persisted, but now these eateries were built to look like the sleek *Twentieth Century Limited*, shiny aluminum carriages. The windows were shaped like diner cars on trains, rounded on both ends. On Friday and Saturday nights, the Skyliner Diner with its indirect lighting became an art deco version of their daytime Greek hangout, and cheeseburgers became the choice of the teen realm instead of Mrs. Polapolis' grilled BLT sandwiches. The booths were packed after the dance and their voices echoed from the tile and glass surfaces. Eight of them squeezed into a curved booth built for six.

"I can't help thinking about the senior girls," Boots said. "Always going off to the Merchant Marine Academy dances to find partners. Some all the way to West Point."

"A couple of them go into New York to the big USO dances."

"Think of Laura. She took the train all the way across the country to become an army wife."

"Probably carrying her first piece of luggage."

"And wearing her first hat with a veil."

At her front door, Bonnie and Jim swelled with passion—his privates and her mons and breasts. His mind-body system was being jerked in spasms of sexual fantasy, but he couldn't act on his urges.

* * *

The "Jersey Bounce" was spinning out its easy-swinging rhythm from the Wurlitzer at the Juke Box the afternoon before the Farmingdale game. Kenny B. was gliding Mardi in and out of his arms when Jim entered after football practice. Slinging his books in a corner, he approached the soft drinks bar and found Saylor.

"I'm nominating you for the Alphas," Jim's new friend said. "But don't say anything. It's a secret ballot, but you'll get in."

"Sounds good." The Alphas had been recently formed to empower a bloc of roguish sophomore boys. His acceptance would mean that Jim would be one of the few freshman candidates to join the upper-class fraternity.

"All the regular guys are Alphas—Danny, Hunter, Dumphy, Stu. All them."

The news puffed up Jim's self-esteem. He was being recognized as a comer after only a few weeks in high school. He accepted this sense of belonging, which enlarged his conceit, not understanding that his only assets were his height, his attraction to light-hearted girls, and his easy, unafraid manner. He was being initiated for physical and superficial reasons, the transient appeal of appearance. There was little substance to him. Perhaps there was a small hint of generosity of spirit. Maybe a reverence for the figure of Christ. Or his literary incarnation of Navy fliers. Little else. He had a ready smile that would soon enough turn into a defensive sneer if he was caught short or felt uneasy. The balloon of his high school personality was beginning to fill with ego-stained air. There was the poison of self-delusion in those breaths.

Mardi and Kenny joined them.

"Hey Tree Top," she cozied up to Jim.

He put his arm around her until he could feel her softness. She looked up at him with glittery eyes.

"C'mon, Skipper," she turned and said to Saylor. "Your turn." And off they went to dance to the Ellington-Strayhorn standard, "Satin Doll." Saylor was as bad a dancer as Jim and she knew she had to accommodate both with slower tempos.

"A doll all right," Kenny said, watching the pair open their arms to each other on the small dance floor.

Kenny asked, "Do you have a ride to the Farmingdale game?"

Jim said he didn't. His brother would ride on the bus with the rest of the team.

"Why don't you come with me?"

Jim was elated by the invitation. About eleven the next morning, here comes Kenny B. in his '39 red Ford convertible that was polished up like a fire engine. Because Kenny never went anywhere without the company of attractive girls, two lively juniors were already on board. They rode south and east along the new Northern State Parkway. One of the best road networks in the nation, the parkway system spread to the Atlantic beaches one way, New York City another and east toward the Hamptons with their sparkling ocean beaches. The wandering road, designed to do the least amount of damage through the estate area of the Gold Coast, had been carefully planned so it wouldn't interrupt the course of the Buckram Beagle Fox Hunt. The parkway zagged through the old Mayfair estates that were feeling the stern privations of war—staffs decimated by the military draft, the flight of workers to defense plants and the imposition of higher taxes. Kenny's Ford flew unimpeded at 40 mph along the concrete highway bordered by luxurious plantings. From place to place immense mansions emerged from the woods that might have raised normal curiosity about the high-octane Twenties and the more sober Edwardian Era, former times that the young car occupants knew nothing of, nor cared to understand.

It was on this top-down car trip, the girls' hair frenzied by the wind, as the freshman and the two girls in Ken's convertible sped east, that Jim Mahoney found one strand of the new independent streak that would carry him to manhood. The ride changed Jim in ways he would have found hard to explain. It was as if he had finally ditched the wounds of his childhood—all the mental and physical pain of a lost father, debilitating ear infections, the isolation of boys' homes where he was sent after his mother's breakdown following her husband's death, the children's military school where he had been humiliated, then the arrival of a tough step-father who came to dominate the family—all that flew away in the streaming air. He felt strong now, showing signs of the energy that would amaze people all his life, self-confident and whole. He had become teenage sure of himself. Free. Emboldened. Ready for fun and laughter even though inhibited sexually. It was the ride of his lifetime. Blue air clearing out his fears and doubts that allowed him to float freely on the whims of youth swirling around him. Kay's long red hair—flames whipped up in a wildfire—swept across his face and he could smell her warmth.

Manhasset won the game and they raced back to town to announce the victory by riding down Plandome Road tooting their horn. Sitting on the backs of their car seats, the foursome waved at the waiting crowd in front of the Greeks' soda shop, kids that had patiently gathered to hear about the game's outcome. Riding with Ken, shouting out the score—"We won! We won!"

* * *

In October, twenty miles to the west, Duke Ellington played his new piece, *Black, Brown and Beige*, at Carnegie Hall, celebrating color. Jim had heard the Duke a couple of times in the palaces of Broadway but he didn't have a clue about the orchestral piece.

* * *

Jim and Ben were two of the four freshmen tapped to join the Alphas along with one of the lacrosse guys and another freshman class leader named Eddie Barns. On "Hell Night," the new inductees were warned to wear old clothes, advised they would never be able to don them again. When the novice quartet descended into Danny Devon's basement that served as the group's headquarters, they entered a hostile environment, as if the mischief planned that night might have a nasty edge. Initiation turned out to be messy. They painted Jim's body red, looked forward to whacking him on the ass with wooden paddles, spread jelly in his hair, gave him disgusting things to eat and forced him to take a pill that made him pee green for a week. The grossmasters for the evening's performance included Saylor and a couple other sadists who belittled the prospective new members by dripping globs of syrup and other concoctions all over them. The newcomers were harassed and insulted and then they were beaten.

Each member had constructed his own paddle. Depending on their woodworking ability, their swatting weapons were crafted to different levels of violence. Some were short, others were decorated with burnt-in symbols, and some were long and thick. Members got to use their handiwork by whacking the backsides of the new prospects. Jim was first up. He bent over and seventeen teenagers took their turn paddling him. Some were considerate, administering gentle strokes, lightly felt, but some of the more aggressive members were heavy hitters. Jim managed to get through the ordeal without sobbing though the pain was severe.

Ben was next to face the gauntlet and showed not only his courage but humor, ribbing some of the brothers about their gentle whacks: "What was that? A fairy kiss?"

But the real damage occurred when Eddie's turn came. In the interval between the time of voting in the new members and tonight, Eddie had begun making passes at Bootsie Harding, the girl that Saylor was dating. Word leaked out to Saylor and he was furious. Not athletic himself, Saylor, like most sixteen-year old boys, had sufficient strength to do harm when he approached Eddie with his long paddle. No one could have guessed the results. Saylor struck Eddie full force, eliciting a loud cry. Jim, still salving his own wounds, did not register the intensity of the cry of pain as he otherwise might have. Saylor pounded Barns again and again. The hitter's face turned red and his anger flushed into his hairline and throat. He struck repeatedly, madly. Eddie was bearing up well under the battering as some of the other members began shouting at Saylor to lay off, but he hit him again. Eddie by now had fallen to his knees onto the concrete floor, yet Saylor continued to beat him. Finally some of the watchers interfered and pinned Saylor's arms as he snorted, "The son-of-a-bitch."

Eddie was in great pain, holding his back where some of the blows had landed on his spine. The fraternal closeness of the evening dissipated and a pall radiated through the now fractured community. The next part of the initiation process included a planned ride to a distant location where the victims were to be dumped off in a remote spot. That part of the ritual proceeded but without Eddie's participation. Danny and McKnight, who were appalled by Saylor's behavior, drove him home.

After once more swabbing Jim with salad dressing, they blindfolded him, tied him up, drove him ten miles to the Bronx-Whitestone Bridge and dumped him on the Queens side along a dark side street. He removed his impediments and looked around at the black midnight scene, catching sight of the bright necklace that outlined the bridge. In the distance he could make out the distinctive amber-colored lights of the Cross Island Parkway and that gave him a bearing. A car approached with no headlights and slowed down. He thought he recognized the convertible.

"Hop in," said Kenny B. "Saylor told me to follow you here. But watch out with all that gunk on you. Sit in the back on that piece of canvas."

He was as prissy as an old maid about his car but he was a welcome sight.

Eddie's father was enraged at the treatment of his son and threatened to sue them all. When word of the battering leaked out, there was a negative reaction throughout the community. The Alphas' reputation was damaged and their members criticized.

A few weeks later, after Jim had been declared a member of the Alphas, he received his fraternity jacket and wore it like a peacock among his uninitiated peers.

* * *

Jim and Bonnie began double dating regularly with Saylor and Bootsie. The arrangement increased Jim's social mobility because Kenny B., on his way to join a Navy program in Pensacola, sold

Saylor his red convertible, so transportation became more dependable for the freshmen as a result of this new friendship. Wheels gave the foursome an option, if gas was available, to ramble through the dark and inviting tunnel of night to find a lonely road or one that petered out on the sands of the Sound.

In October on a leftover warm evening, Saylor collected his crew and they headed to a country club dance. It was one of those red sky evenings when the whole of Long Island simmered under a rose tent. The girls, Bonnie and Bootsie, wore cocktail dresses with fashionable jackets, both so beautiful that they would have taken most male adults' breath away. But these beauties need not be troubled that Jim or Saylor would spoil them with flattery. The guys took it for granted that their girls would be stunning. Nor did they bother to notice the affectionate way the girls greeted them with cheerful smiles and eyes filled with anticipation. Bonnie's eyes actually glistened. Jim had stopped by the florist, enabling him to tie a wristband of yellow roses around her thin arm. He wore the same flower in his jacket lapel

Their destination was the Plandome Country Club, a plantation-like eighteenth century mansion with five high pillars supporting the shade of a vast veranda. The rolling landscape reflected the bucolic taste of some tycoon from older times—the gilded days before the First War. Immense reception rooms greeted them, along with a clubby bar with dark wood paneling and round poker tables covered by green cloth. The location, not an ordinary one for a high school dance, was available because clubs like this had seen half their male clientele go off to war and were struggling with their budgets. Youngsters from a Bayside prep fraternity called the Geks, hearing tales of the club's problems, had booked the affair.

The two couples swept through the lobby and entered the ballroom and found an empty dining table.

"What'll you have?" Saylor asked, knowing there were no age limits on drinking within the confines of the club. "I'll put them on my dad's tab. I know the bartender."

None of the other three had ever had a cocktail before and were caught unaware.

Adventurous Bonnie said, "I'll have a Shirley Temple."

"Me too," said Boots.

"That's not a real drink," Saylor said.

"What do you suggest?"

"A lot of women like Singapore Slings."

"I've heard of a Gin Fizz," Bonnie said. "I'll have that."

"Me too," said Boots.

"How about you?"

"A beer," said Jim.

When Saylor left to retrieve drinks—the club lacked waiters as well as members—Jim pulled out a half-pack of Chesterfields that he had been saving, and offered a cigarette to each of the girls. He was surprised that they both accepted though he was aware that Bonnie had been practicing at home in front of her mirror. They lit up and surveyed the crowd.

The dance was well under way and the sub-debs and their beaux were slow dancing to music from the dozen members of the band that would play until 1:30a.m. About half of the revelers lived locally; the others were city people. Many Douglaston families chose to send their offspring to the suburban Manhasset school rather than Bayside High in Queens, so there was a passing recognition of many in the crowd. Cigarette smoke glided across the ceiling and the smell of hard liquor wafted in from the bar.

A couple of Alpha leaders and their dates joined them. Danny Devon and his sidekick, Hunter McKnight, the pair that had started the fraternity, escorted two freshman girls, studious Lucy and the other a bold-breasted Amazon named Barbara. Danny carried a pixie look about him, but appearances deceived because he was recognized as the best all-around athlete in school. Big-shouldered Hunter was marked by a slash of a scar that ran down his right cheek, a lifelong reminder of a crash with an automobile he endured while riding his bike down Munsey Park hill. Lucy was thin and more mature than her appearance would suggest. She and Danny could easily be underestimated. Barbara was nearly the size of Hunter and self-possessed. She was buxom and open and friendly with a big smile that reminded Jim of a younger version of his mom.

Alpha members occupied two of the other tables, guys named Stu, Nick, Dumphy, Gib and Mitch—the last had squired empathetic Maryjan. Jim was always struck by the vitality of these guys, how they were always wisecracking, chasing after the humor of a thing. And how they never talked about anything serious. All of which suited Jim fine. He had come to believe in the theory of natural guys. Tall, young men with physical grace, commanding looks and an easy way with other males, the kind he could trust to be normal. The object was to be loyal and circumspect, not flashy or showy, perhaps leaving things unsaid but nevertheless understood. And invested with spunk and a sense of daring but with no room for funny ideas. True, Jim had heroes in grade school: Ernie Johanssen who carried himself like a chieftain and Larry Stella whose loping stride and bright mind were charged with a flashing imagination. Those had been his role models. But not one adult led Jim. He was totally under the influence of these, his peers.

Jim watched them all. He noticed how people reacted to one another. He could tell more by their movements as to how they felt than by what they said. He was always observing, never leading.

"This is table Number One, Number One. Where the hell is Number Two?" one of the nearby groups chanted. Across the room, table number two responded. The chant song ended at eighteen.

Jim and Bonnie danced, neither of them light-footed, but warmly enclosed in each other's arms. Her beauty shone in a fragile Irish way while he was striking in his size and lusty carriage. They were growing closer. The impact of their initial attraction had given them confidence, as if building such self-assuredness might be the purpose of their coming together. Mutually buoyed, they exuded an attractive liveliness. When these kids danced, they were not performing solos amid a pack of people. Couples embraced each other with vigor.

The drinking became pronounced. A couple guys were beginning to float sideways when they walked, and there was some slurring of speech among the Alphas. This was the night when Jim became aware of the difference that alcohol could make in a person. Hunter McKnight seemed able to down his beverages with ease, showing no effect. Danny, on the other hand, got silly after one rye and ginger. The couple of beers that Jim drank made his head buzz slightly, but he maintained his footwork. Saylor was steady as a rock. The girls stopped after one drink. The only telltale was a heightened color in the girls' cheeks, but that could have been from excitement, or in Maryjan's case, excessive time on the dance floor.

"There's a girl outside drunk on the eighteenth green," someone announced.

McKnight, a golfer, half inflated with alcohol, added, "Let the chippies fall where they may."

"Did you hear about the swim party up at the Strathmore-Vanderbilt pool?" Barbara asked. The location she referred to was a refurbished mansion that served as a swim and tennis club for the residents in that part of town. "Seems like a bunch of guys were skinny-dipping up there one night when the manager, hearing the commotion, turned on the pool lights and they all had to run like scared rabbits."

"That's old news," Saylor said. "That happened a month ago."

"I just heard about it."

"You should get more friends."

"Did you hear about Joyce, that senior girl?" asked Maryjan, who had come over to sit with them.

"What happened?"

"Some thief broke into her house while she was upstairs and she surprised him messing in her father's study. The guy panics and starts to run away but she's right after him. She's strong as a bull— no, wrong gender— anyway, she tackles him down on the street and holds him until the police came."

"Recruit her for the team."

"She'd do better than some of you bananas," Bootsie added. Whenever she commented, Boots had the habit of pulling back her head, sort of cocking it, as if to say, "Take that."

"Let's do the boys' handkerchiefs," said Bonnie, who had a knack for sketching.

One of the minor fashion traits of the times required guys to wear handkerchiefs in their upper jacket pockets. They were sometimes in color, floral looking, but mainly plain white, stuffed in, with a few tails sticking out. The practice at these dances was to take handkerchiefs from the guys and illustrate them with pen drawings. Jim's once-white square went around the table, and was soon titled GEK DANCE and the date. The more creative among the crowd would draw pictures of themselves and their dates while others sketched Dopey from *Snow White*, or the Bugs Bunny movie character. Some of the girls simply left lipstick kisses. One wise guy burned a cigarette hole through the fabric. In other cultures, waving handkerchiefs would mean something different, goodbye or snuffled tears, but here they were dance souvenirs.

There was whispering among the males indicating that some mischief was abroad. A plan initiated by the golfers in the crowd, chiefly McKnight, began circulating. The idea was for the guys to meet back at the club after the dance about 2:00 a.m. They were alerted to bring flashlights.

The couples sailed across the floor as the band played on. Once, misjudging the audience, the orchestra started to play a waltz, but the groaning through the hall sent them hot-licking back to a bouncy swing number. There were perhaps seventy-five couples, half of them now high, exhilarated by their strength and lustiness. Many were emerging for the first time onto the public stage.

At 1:30, with every girl's head resting on her date's jacket lapels, they finished dancing to the quiet reverie of "Goodnight Ladies." Afterwards, Saylor steered the car toward the Sound and they found a beach parking lot where the two couples dipped into their libidos. Jim and Bonnie were in the rumble seat. Their kissing stunned Jim with its impact. The softness of her skin felt like a silk pillow. Their lips pressed together sealing the excitement that they felt for one another, feelings that had been spontaneous from the beginning. He kissed her throat and she closed her eyes. Both of them were churning with desire.

"I'm on fire. We shouldn't get this hot," Bonnie warned.

"It's OK if it makes us close."

But their bodies were already ahead of their words. They knew what they needed prior to any commentary. Their blood controlled them not their words. Their communion began with kissing, offering them the release they had been hoping for. Then, after five minutes of venting their steam, frustration took over again when they realized they didn't know how to proceed. Her lipstick went askew and he looked like a clown wearing hers. Maddened by what had lit them up, she lurched against him and threw her arms around him. When they broke to examine each other's faces, they were awash with desire, both frightened by the intensity of what was happening to them. Her mouth hung slack, her breathing as hard as his, amazed by their pounding hearts, seeking an answer as to where these primary emotions was taking them, their first real knowledge of shared sexual response.

"Oh, god, what have you done to me?" she asked.

"It's you who did it."

They looked into the car's front where Saylor and Bootsie were trussed together.

"Look. Her eyelashes are twitching."

They laughed, breaking the spell.

Later, after depositing the girls on their doorsteps, a group of Alphas returned to the darkened country club and McKnight proposed a game called Westhampton Golf. He explained the rules. First they broke into the pro shop and pilfered a half-dozen clubs and golf balls and lined up on the first tee. It was the first time Jim had stolen anything, aside from his mother's purse, since raiding the 5&10 back in Chicago.

"What we're going to do is hit the ball off the tee at the same time. But first we take a slug of this bourbon because there's no sense playing this game sober. The object isn't to get your own ball in the cup because you're free to hit any ball that you see on the fairway. Just run around until you find a ball and give it a smack and keep on going. The one who knocks the first ball in the cup wins. Got it?"

"What's the prize?"

"What we don't drink from this bottle."

Jim was already feeling a little woozy from the beers and now the swig of liquor sent his head spinning. He stood with a club in his hand, holding it like a baseball bat, and at the signal, took a swing at the ball and either through miraculous intervention or sheer luck, made contact. Six balls flew through the air. The guys started scampering down the fairway, each in a circle of light, knocking any ball that emerged from the dark. There was a lot of circling around looking for lost pellets as they progressed toward the green. Soon, fewer balls were in contention and shuffling and pushing began among the more drunken players, who were laughing outrageously and swinging for the moon at imaginary golf balls. By the time they reached the flag, they were rolling on the ground, wrestling for a chance to putt the last remaining ball into the cup. One guy stumbled into a sand trap. Another fell in the adjoining pond and was rescued by fellow fraternity members. Their hilarity, dampened by the ocean's night air, was muffled but contagious as they staggered toward the endgame.

When Jim finally arrived home, he was unsure of his footing but he managed to sneak upstairs without making a lot of noise.

* * *

The Alphas' clubhouse was located in Danny Devon's, their leader's, cellar. Every afternoon, a dozen or so brothers strayed in and out of the backdoor entrance and spent after-school hours playing poker and blackjack. The tolerant Devon parents, who seldom trespassed into their own rec room, did not approve of the way the youngsters decorated the downstairs with stolen goods: traffic signs (*One Way, No Exit, Park at Your Own Risk*), lawn decorations (a bird bath and a statue of Cupid) and a Manhasset sign purloined from the platform of the railroad station. Plus a Schlitz over-the-bar beer sign that once twinkled in their favorite pizza place in Port Washington. And a big gas station sign, the one with the winged Flying Red Horse. When Jim first saw it, something rang a bell in his memory but he couldn't spring the recollection loose. Didn't he once think when he was a kid that the Flying Red Horse involved some kind of myth about the Indians out West?

Among the cardsharps were a few football players, their season now over. Only the basketballers were missing.

"Hit me," said McKnight, with a five sitting on top of a nine.

Saylor obliged and turned to Jim.

"Hit me with the right pape." Then, "I'm bust," folding his cards.

"Argyle?"

Stu Argyle, a handsome blond kid with a dazzling smile and a strong frame, was one of the most popular boys in town. A natural, he would always be Jim's ideal high schooler. A tough lineman on the football team, class president and a sterling lacrosse player, he had a distinctive gait. Walking on the tips of his toes, he seemed to bounce as he glided along.

A derisive moan came from the other table.

"What happened?"

Dumphy, one of the players, said, "This numb nut filled an inside straight. Skinny, you're a lucky bastard."

"Blow it out our ass," Skinny returned.

"How many wild cards?"

"Just deuces."

At Jim's table, Argyle held fast while lugubrious Freddy, a seemingly mid-forties teenager, world-weary and cynical, turned over his ace to declare "Twenty-one."

Danny came home from basketball practice and scooted down the basement steps in fast tempo, his feet performing a glissando down the stairs.

"This place is a mess," Danny said. "Stop throwing your butts on the floor."

Because he was their leader and landlord, the card players shuffled around picking up their nicotine remains.

"What this joint needs," Saylor said, "are a few more signs."

"Time for another raid."

"We have enough stuff," Danny complained.

"Don't be a wet blanket."

"I know one just ready to be picked."

"Where?"

"Across the street."

"Which one?"

"The Munsey Park sign."

They all knew which one. At the various roadway entrances to the village within the larger community, an accomplished wood turner had created a handsome welcoming sign with embellishments that made the sign appear like something hanging in front of a colonial inn. It swung from a red-brick community entranceway that introduced travelers to the twists and turns of publisher Frank Munsey's subdivision, a neighborhood that was distinguished with art-inspired street names—painters from the nineteenth century—chosen by the Metropolitan Museum of Art, the district's legatee.

"Let's go get it. Bring some tools."

A half-dozen Alphas walked to the nearby intersection of Northern Boulevard, the old road to New York. There the soft-yellow sign stirred in the autumn breeze—*Welcome to the Village of Munsey Park.* In broad daylight, three guys climbed the entrance-gate wall and checked the connections that held the sign in place. Never mind that their older brothers might be scuttling up a wall somewhere in North Africa in an effort to hoist their combat ensigns. Here stealing was the object.

"It's heavier than I thought."

"Can you bend the thing it's hanging from?"

No one questioned the action. Things were meant to be hi-jacked. They got away with what they could. There was only one policeman for the entire town.

It took two of them to carry the sign back to Danny's basement, where it made an attractive addition to the other stolen items.

On his walk home through Flower Hill, Jim was unaware of how a bunch of juniors from this neighborhood differed from the Alphas. Members of the Flower Hill Gang fostered an exaggerated sense of fairness. In soccer, members would allow an opponent to take his time to set up a shot rather than crash in and try to disrupt a kick. There was a certain male thoughtfulness to their actions, a diffidence that was generous. They recently blocked the establishment of an antique automobile show in town even though they were all enthusiasts. They didn't want to institutionalize things, call attention to themselves, as if that would disrupt the equilibrium and privacy of their friendships. So different from Jim's group, breaking into pro shops, stealing signs, sitting around playing cards.

* * *

That fall the popular girls from the freshman year were initiated into one of two sororities that had sprung up recently. Bonnie, Mardi, Maryjan and Barbara opted for ATA, and Bootsie and Lucy for the other. The ATA sorority, with fifty or so girls, maintained a strong roster of outstanding coeds, dominated by its sophomores, Melissa, Pat and Vivien, as beautiful as the new girls in Jim's class.

As the cold weather set in, Jim borrowed his mother's Brownie and took a few pictures of Bonnie sitting under The Tree, her chin tucked into a white scarf beneath her black pea jacket. She looked up mischievously toward Jim and provided him an image that he would always carry with him of the perfect gamine with flashing eyes and a beauty that stunned him. Cameras loved her.

A week later, word began to circulate that one of the sophomore girls had attempted to commit suicide. As the story unfolded, it seemed that she had threatened her life because she had been blackballed by one of the high school sororities. Jim hardly knew her. His reaction was callous. He remembered she was short and blonde. With nice legs.

* * *

Then came word of his Uncle Jack's death. His mother was beside herself, detached as she was from her family in Chicago and unable to acquire a railroad ticket because of heavy military demand on transportation. Even her living brother, who worked for the New York Central RR, couldn't arrange passage for his sister. Gracie was forced to mourn alone, making the hurt deeper. The fact that Jim did not sympathize with her loss isolated her all the more. Luckily, Matt was more attentive.

* * *

Even though many kids in town were unaware of and ignorant of world events, headlines reflected the war's reality. Daily papers covered the terrible details of the war news. On December 6th, 1943, almost two years to the day after Pearl Harbor, Marines continued their payback for that treachery. Troops assaulted Tarawa in the Gilbert Islands and in three days absorbed and dealt out carnage on a massive scale. It was the quickness of the deaths that shocked the public. A thousand Marines lost their lives in a few days.

* * *

Just before Christmas, McKnight asked Jim and four other guys if they wanted to make some extra holiday money. A neighbor owned a public relations business in Manhattan that annually distributed bottles of liquor to his contacts in the media business, small reminders that the firm was grateful for any favors made on behalf of its clients by print and broadcast people. Given the scarcity of manpower, many companies turned to high school kids for part-time employment. The result was that educators, believing they were aiding the war effort, granted permission for student workers to skip classes the last week before Christmas vacation. That allowed the Alphas to earn some spending money hauling booze around New York City. They were all supposed to be eighteen and responsible, but none of them was either. McKnight, who had served in this capacity before and acted as straw boss, kept Jim, the youngest, under his control, hoping, among other things, that the neophyte wouldn't get lost in the caverns of midtown.

On the way to town on the train, McKnight laid out a plan.

"It's like a bonanza," he said. "And we're going to enjoy some of it. They'll tell us we have to deliver in pairs. We carry these containers of liquor around to newspaper and magazine offices. Radio stations too. Each bottle with some guy's moniker. The PR people will insist we give the bottle of hooch to the right person. Be sure it's the right guy because there's a lot of those balonies with their hands out, ready to snatch somebody else's booze.

"Here's the thing. Sometimes one of these guys has moved on, so we have an undeliverable bottle. What we do when we have an extra is rent a locker in Penn Station and stash the loot and pick it up on the way home. Got it? This is a five-day job so by the end of the week, we should all have a quart apiece."

Jim doubled his knowledge of Manhattan that week. For two or three years, he had traveled to Broadway to see the big bands—the likes of Jimmy Dorsey ("Helen will now sing 'Green Eyes'") and gentleman Duke Ellington—swing outfits that played in Broadway movie houses between shows. The intermission was more engaging than the accompanying film to the teenagers that streamed into the Greco-Byzantine palaces that dotted the wartime-darkened Great Gray Way to hear their favorite orchestras.

On task, McKnight and Jim, armed with their liquid souvenirs, began roaming around town delivering the goods. They were welcomed everywhere. They learned how to get by the receptionists that guarded the inner sanctums, moving directly onto the editorial floors, each office or desk marked by a nameplate. Or they'd step into a newsroom—one was the *Times*—where they were greeted by shouts of welcome and wisecracks. They were assigned to visit radio stations as well, and Jim was fascinated to see the equipment and studios. The pair lingered at one and was offered a tour by a friendly radio host.

"My ma used to know a guy in Chicago who was big in radio," Jim said. "Called himself the Wizard. I listened to him once."

They visited trade magazines and business papers. They subwayed down to Wall Street to distribute their booty among financial paper personnel. Scooting around, Jim finally got the hang of the West Side and East Side IRT lines with their crossovers at 42nd and 14th streets.

He enjoyed the solidity of the neo-classical buildings on Fifth Avenue and walking through the intersecting parks like Union and Madison Square, darkened treegrrouds that complemented the city grid. The bountiful space of Central Park also amazed him. He felt sloppy sometimes in his jeans among the fashionable people he observed along the shopping boulevards, but felt comfortable with the friendly editors that took time to inquire about him, asking where he was from and what music he liked.

"The usual," he would say. "Glenn Miller and Tommy Dorsey."

The world was motioning to Jim. What with his interest in writing and the favorable reaction he enjoyed among these media people, and the welcome he had received at the *Herald Tribune* when he was researching his Pacific Navy book a few years earlier, he began to warm to the print world.

When the young liquor messengers found someone had departed for the armed service or another job, they would heist the extra bottle and transport it to iron-sculptured Penn Station and store it in a locker. To cover their tracks, they would sometimes return an undeliverable fifth of whiskey to the PR office in an attempt to affirm their dubious reliability. Each night, housed in a sack, a bottle or two made its way back to Manhasset. On the last night, it was Jim's turn—Schenley's.

He didn't dare bring his loot home, so he stashed it with Frankie's help in a snow bank in the lot behind the Washington home. Afraid to domesticate the bottle, a group of freshmen boys that Saturday night built a fire in the woodlot and sat around the flames passing the cold bottle back and forth. Fire and ice. Though they hated the taste of the rye and despised the burning in their mouths, they got high. Smoke from the fire and their cigarettes combined to give them a heady feeling. When Jim arrived home, chewing Sen-Sen, he was able to slip by his folks, who were busy entertaining in the rec room downstairs. Then he got in bed and his head began to spin. He woke in the morning with a nauseous taste in his mouth, a queasy stomach and a loopy feeling in his brain.

* * *

The two big social events surrounding Christmas were the Knickerbocker Yacht Club dance, a fraternity affair, and the holiday party supervised by the mother of one of the sophomore ATA sorority girls, a matron who held high social expectations for her offspring, a perfect doll-like daughter.

Before dressing on the night of the party, Jim ducked into the shower. The water floated over him, the warmth shielding him from the cold air seeping in through a crack around the frosted window. His imagination opened to the possibilities of the night before him. Exhilarated by his youth and strength and excited by the prospect of a good time, the comforting water flowed over his body and he felt clean and alive. So young, fourteen, ready to challenge nature's and society's grip. He considered himself fortunate for being who he was. How few in the world had his advantages? Not many from what little he knew about other cultures. He lived inside a sumptuous enclave, within a teenage conceit that encouraged his sense of well being.

He was about to be catapulted onto the bachelor/deb swirl engineered by his community's social life. There were various strata in the town's pecking order: the chief one consisted of those with a New England educational backbone, as if these members held the right to lead others, illustrating Boston's higher sense of orderliness. There were also the New Yorkers who would rather be living on East 73rd Street, but temporarily parked themselves in the suburbs while their children grew. Then there were the Midwestern upshots, ambitious men like Jim's Pappy, Bob Hill, who came from a region that produced many of the best businessmen, because they were hungrier. Another group consisted of borough people moving east toward suburban life. Plus the homing pigeons who didn't know or care about any other community, but their own. Then there were the Whitneys and estate people who were on a whole other level.

Full of self-confidence, Jim dried himself off, dressed and walked toward the Shoreberry section. He would meet Bonnie at the party. Her mother, coiffed and primped for a holiday event of her own, drove her daughter to the party, fussing with her hair through most of the trip. Bonnie wore a patterned kerchief to keep her locks in place, poised to be stripped away at the moment of arrival, as if she were to be uncovered like a serving of guinea hen. The sorority beauty, Vivien, along with her parents, met their guests at the door, forming a small receiving line. The only one at the affair in a long dress, Vivien, posed as if she were anticipating the photos of her coming-out party. Her father lingered behind them in the background, wearing his prewar Bond Street outfit.

"Mother. Father. May I present Jim Mahoney. He's a friend of Bonnie's."

"How do you do."

"Hello. Thanks for the invitation."

"A pleasure, I'm sure."

"He's Matt's brother."

"A friend of Vince?"

"Yes."

There were some new male faces wandering among the holly plants, and Jim was curious to know who they were. It turned out they were private-school boys on holiday, one sporting a cigarette holder. They appeared to be wearing heavier-than-normal wools; as if the clothes were hand-stitched by Brooks Brothers tailors who understood the difference between various grades of textiles and grades of people.

The local boys wore slacks and a jacket, some spiffed up with a new tie or shiny loafers. A few looked so young they might have been manikins set loose from the boy's department of Fields' Men's Shoppe downtown. The young women were dripping in colors of satin, matching the festive illuminations: a ceiling-high tree with colored strings, along with twinkling lights around the mantelpiece. The girls wore green taffeta or red velvet dresses and featured their grandmother's jewelry, pieces that had come alive with art deco. Or Aunt Celia's circle pin. To Jim, each girl a work of art.

There would be no dancing here or games. This would be a decorous party even though the punch had an appropriately mild kick. The young people would mimic their parents' cocktail parties if Mrs. Applegate's plans succeeded.

Jim knew his invitation was essentially based on his relationship with Bonnie. He found her in a large circle of friends and she welcomed him with warmth even though he could see from the way her eyes pivoted nervously that she was on edge.

Ben was standing aside with a bunch of guys telling a story. "I got this job at Lord & Taylor blowing up balloons for kids visiting Santa. Left over from before the war. The balloons, not Santa. Last night I'm sitting alone huffing away in the back of the stockroom when two of the senior girls, Ally and Babs, on break, come by and say they want to wish me a Merry Christmas. So they sit on my lap, one on each leg and start covering me with kisses. I'm in heaven. Sitting there in a stack of balloons with lipstick all over me and in comes this supervisor who says, 'I thought I heard something popping back here. Must have been the buttons on your fly.'"

Jim laughed. Spotting Bonnie, he moved to the larger group.

"They're telling another story about George Hellas. You heard this one?" Stu asked. "About George and The Beak"—their school principal. George was the sky-high Greek boy who had been leader of the car pack before war and was now overseas in the Navy.

"It goes like this. George is awaiting reassignment behind the lines somewhere in Hawaii and he gets called down by one of his officers and they show him this letter, written months before, one that had been chasing him around the Pacific. It's on MHS letterhead from the Beak saying that George was undoubtedly the one who had stolen the clapper from the school bell and demanded its return, under the presumption that if any crime had been committed on campus, George surely was the chief suspect.

"George is flabbergasted. He says 'He found me way out here?'—The officer says, 'The clapper. Where's the clapper?'—'I haven't got any damn clapper, sir.'—'Says right here you stole it.'—'It's just they blame me for everything.'—'What do I tell him?'—'I know what I'd like him to do with his clapper, sir.'"

They all laughed, the guys more than the girls. They had been on their best behavior but the story loosened them up. Except Bonnie. Her mouth was sculpting some anxiety.

* * *

George himself was soon suffering. His buddy reported home.

"I told George to stay low when our LSM moved in with a hold full of Marines and five tanks, aimed right for the beach at Lingayen Bay. Mission was to land those jarheads on Luzon and point them straight for Manila. Everybody ready to get even with those bastards that marched our guys out of Bataan. George shouted down from topside that he couldn't see if he didn't stand up. The fucking sky was swarming with planes. Our big gunboats were laying down thunder on the beach—enough so's your ears burst. Smoke and cordite everywhere. Then they came from landside, like locusts. Those crazy kamikazes bastards—bandanas of death riding their suicide planes. One screeching in—with that horrible whine—on the cruiser Columbia*. Crashed right into her, right through the decks and into the ammo and gasoline and* Columbia *threw up a*

volcano of hot metal. It was like hell had exploded. Ripped right into George. Knocked him off the back deck and he falls in the hold.

Look at him, lying over there. Hallucinating. Said he had to hang around and live so he could play some baseball, and get up and steer his landing boat back into hell."

* * *

"What's with Bonnie?" Jim asked Mardi.

"She's got the curse."

Another miracle about girls.

Not that Jim felt blest. He was awkward, unable to control his hands when he wasn't smoking, at sea in a social situation where there were no games to distract him from the pitfalls of direct conversation and the irritability of the female reproductive system.

From the corner of his eye, Jim noticed that the tall and attractive private school guys were moving in on the loveliest of the ATA girls, many of whom looked startlingly beautiful this night. Laughter rose from those enclaves and knowing looks slid sideways from male to male behind the girls' bare shoulders.

Bonnie and Jim broke away from their circle and headed for the punch bowl. One of the heavy woolies approached them.

"May I introduce myself," he said, admiring Bonnie. "I'm Will Marlowe. My friends can't keep their eyes off you."

His simple message was that he was interested in Jim's date and believed he possessed sufficient male dominance to snatch her away. Bonnie, flattered by the attention, looked at Jim, who said nothing but his face showed that his defenses had shot up like a barricade. What bothered him the most was that Bonnie was cocking her head toward Marlowe as if she expected more.

"You're down from Andover, right?" she asked. "I heard you went there."

"Has my reputation preceded me? I'd like to think I was still remembered by my home town crowd."

"This crowd is pretty much locked up already. The gate might even be shut," she continued.

"A challenge. I'm used to that," Will boasted.

"Good to talk to you," Jim said, taking Bonnie's arm, leading her away. "Aggressive type," he added, not sure how he felt.

"I'm sure he's harmless like most preppies."

"I don't like these guys pushing their way in."

"Lighten up, Jimmy boy. You've got a cute girlfriend," she said, squeezing his arm and bringing her face close to his. He had survived round one.

But that wasn't the end of it. If they stood talking in a group, Marlowe would suddenly appear at her elbow. If they were seated on a couch, he would come over and sit on the edge. To avoid him, Jim steered Bonnie downstairs into the rec room that was decorated to match the upstairs. There was a tree, but smaller, another punch bowl but not made of cut glass and the ladle wasn't silver.

Will Marlowe must have been tapping into something stronger than the punch because when he found his prey downstairs, he became more aggressive. When he grabbed her and tried to lure Bonnie under the mistletoe, Jim hauled off and hit him in the face even though Marlowe had a couple inches on him and more weight. Swaying from the assault, Will staggered backwards, recuperated and came charging back. Jim took a fist to his forehead that hurt. Hurt badly. There were gasps of surprise from the other guests and the commotion started up the stairs. Jim stood up to the ragged onslaught, frightened but filled with protective juices that gave him strength. They flailed at each other while the alarm grew louder. Jim was never comfortable fighting, but once a brouhaha began, he tended to enjoy it. They were still scuffling in the center of a drawn-back crowd when Mrs. Applegate came screaming down the stairs.

"Stop that. Stop this instant," she shouted. "Ruining our party."

Both combatants were bleeding. Jim was a little woozy and feeling the pain as his face discolored. Shouts penetrated the circle and the combatants pulled back. The fight had been a standoff. Bonnie appeared shaken. She felt guilty that she had been the cause of the fight and now she could see that Jim was hurt. He had been rash and impulsive in attacking Marlowe, but she was not so appalled that she'd abandon him.

"I'll ask you both to leave," Mrs. Applegate said, visualizing an enterprising reporter's story in the society pages: "Brawl breaks out at holiday fest."

Bonnie loyally left the party with Jim after he stopped in the powder room to stem the bleeding. They walked out into the cold night, where Bonnie lowered her head into her mother's fur wrap, chin buried deep in a white scarf, her anxious eyes peeping out. During the long walk home, they hardly spoke, her words muffled.

Part way into their journey, a Lincoln pulled up beside them. Marlowe lowered the window and shouted, "Why don't you drop that creep. Come on with us. We're headed for SanSuSan."

She was tempted, but she bore up against the storm that Will had stirred. Jim told him to buzz off and the prepsters burned rubber as they hastened to their next event.

At Bonnie's front door, there was a quick kiss.

"I'll call you tomorrow."

"OK. I should be home."

"Hope you're not too upset."

"It'll pass. But we may miss some good parties."

"They're boring anyway."

"Not this one."

The unfriendly cold night, following the flare of passion, provided Jim a contrast as he made his way downhill. Below him spread the lights of the town center, stitched by a strip of lamps burning along Plandome Road. Further off, there was a radiating image. From two places in Manhasset—here on Mason hill and at Strathmore Village—the skyline of New York was visible. He could see the Bronx-Whitestone Bridge off to the right and his eyes followed a faint glow across the rolling hills. Eighteen miles away, he could make out a flickering light amid the city's taller buildings that were silhouetted against the crisp winter skyscape.

As he lay in bed, he thought of that flickering light that burned near the horizon. When he fell asleep, he dreamt he was walking through Times Square watching the illuminated billboards—Four Roses, the Camel guy blowing twenty-foot smoke rings near Bond Clothes—listening to the barker at Roseland, hearing the taxi horns and the crackly voices of the old ladies selling pencils and flowers and the exuberant crowds hurrying toward the theaters. Street music that was the lullaby of Broadway. The Paramount Theater came into view, home of swingtime's favorites, a place where Jim had seen Sinatra's SRO performance when it took hundreds of policemen and dozens of mounted horse police to maintain order among the swarm of excited teens. Then he looked up at the top of the Paramount Building and saw the flickering light, glittering inside a globe of the world that actually shone outside of his dream world. It was a beaçon he would someday follow, but now, stuck in the suburbs, the light was weak. He would first have to deal with his hometown and his own inadequacies before he could heed its light, encased in a symbolic image of the world. Startled, he awoke.

* * *

When the festivities surrounding Christmas began, the glow of the holidays, despite the war, flowed through the community. Wartime scarcity meant that favorite items like colored light bulbs and tinsel were scarce, but for worshipers of traditional yuletide charms—carols, crèches, and gooseberry stuffing—the season's energy wasn't to be diminished by material matters. There was a greater heart abroad. Military personnel flooded home on holiday furlough, brightening local nightlife. Each of the suburban communities had their rendezvous centers where young people could socialize, drink and oftentimes dance. Manhasset's contribution was the Plandome Gardens, a refurbished mansion on the main street at the top of the hill near Jim's house. The insides of the old homestead had been ripped out sometime in the Twenties to create a large dining room and a good-sized bar that now had to accommodate not only customers but also the longing of soldiers and sailors across the world who hoped to be home at this season. For the lucky ones, it was a poignant time because dozens of combat deaths had already been registered among the graduates of the early Forties' high school classes.

The Gardens and its cheery atmosphere were replicated in neighboring towns—the Polo Lounge of the Blue Spruce Inn above Roslyn where Hans made tasty Stingers, Wheatley Gardens Tavern to the south where the kids heard jazz, the Thatched Cottage out east, and SanSuSan on the way to Sea Cliff. These pleasure domes in the years ahead would become Jim's shrines that gave space to the rituals of his life, with their love and laughter, sadness and loss.

Now as 1943 closed, the year the war had turned in the Allies' favor, Jim remained an observer. Often passing the Gardens at night on his way home, he could hear the music and see the lively figures through the windows. He watched the senior girls, many torn between their longings involving their men away and their emotions at home: Ally with her face stolen from Botticelli, Bibs with her golden aura, Bev and her open-faced beauty, Slim with her perfect figure and wide eyes, the smart ones like Smithie and Patches and sensuous Marie, one of the Barbaras as sophisticated as New York itself, the other as compassionate as one's favorite nurse, alert Matsie—surely one of the premier classes of women ever to attend the high school. They literally jumped into the arms of the returning G.I.'s and sailors.

Male buddies shouted with whoops of glee when they encountered each other on the wide lawn in front of the white-painted mansion. Their spontaneous hilarity was almost complete except for the trembling memory of the mourned-for missing. All of them were caught in the wild feelings that went along with the frenzied tension of their lives. Baffled by war, these sexually frustrated women and young warriors, as everywhere, were in a state of perpetual anxiety. But here and now on these crisp December evenings when they could allow their emotions to spill out, there was a cascade of pure, unadulterated joy.

Inside in the crowded room with its bustling tables, patrons would spontaneously break into song. Mostly war tunes. Their repertoire was short but boisterous. Old chants like "When Johnny Comes Marching Home Again" and "Over There." were favorites. They complimented British versions of "Knees Up, Mother Brown" and "Tipperary."

A single voice would burst out and a vocal torrent would erupt in a rowdy chorus and Charlie on piano would pick up the melody :

Roll me over in the clover

Roll me over, lie me down
And do it again.

* * *

Jim and Bonnie went ice-skating on Copley Pond one night. The village had built a warming hut, so even on the coldest night, there was relief from the bitter cold starshine. He had long ago fallen in love with night and now there was the mystery of this girl to accompany him in the dark. They would embrace out on the ice, their bodies searching for warmth through layers of clothes. Everything around them, even though they were still, seemed to move. He remembered the aurora borealis from the year before—the night the northern skies danced.

* * *

On Christmas Eve, after Midnight Mass, Jim walked home past the low wall that contained the church graveyards fronting Plandome Road where he had once been struck by the thunder of faith and had become a self-confirmed Catholic. Once home, past 2:00a.m. he sat by the Christmas tree, whose lights created tiny rainbows around the room while the exhausted embers from the fireplace glowed a raw red. He flicked on the radio, kept the volume low and sat back. Though the world was in shambles, his own needs were being satisfied. Even if the war zones were saturated in blood, his narrow world was expanding with teenage euphoria.

Most stations went off air at sundown, and many others shut down at midnight. The late night dial carried only a few signals and from a great distance. Electricity, flowing through the dark ether, brought in a Chicago station, reminding Jim of his boyhood and the extended family he left behind, bringing to mind his deceased Uncle Jack. The catastrophe of his death finally reached him when he thought of his Gram, mourning tonight for her youngest son. The radio MC played "Away in the Manger," the children's hymn, and Jim was wrapped in the spirit of one son's birth and the depressing loss of another. He liked the line about "little Lord Jesus."

"An American hymn," said the announcer.

Jim was one with the radio, the instrument that had changed the country's perception of time and space—bringing the world closer. Now radio interconnected the night and his faith. He felt utter satisfaction, a gratification—a blessing of the mind—a song for the heart that left a sensation on the flesh. *Et in terra pax hominibus.* Except there was a global war under way.

He looked under the tree. It was his practice to open a present as he sat alone in the early hours of Christmas morning. There were the usual premiums from Pappy's advertising clients, giveaways like can openers and skillets. Presuming it to be a commercial gift, he chose a package, maybe ten inches long. Unwrapping the paper, he was amazed to find a kaleidoscope, the kind he treasured as a child. He lifted the device toward the lighted tree and a spectrum of color burst into his vision.

* * *

Manhasset and the adjoining town of Roslyn were half-surrounded by largely untended estates, some invested with six hundred or more acres. The most prominent of these on Manhasset's southern edge was the Whitney property, with its rolling hills where both dray and thoroughbred horses roamed. As a nod to the community and the problem of juvenile delinquency, the Whitneys promised free sleigh and hayrides through the estate if and when snow appeared. There was a storm between Christmas and New Year's, and a day afterward, word circulated that the estate workers were hauling out their sledges and farm wagons in order to treat the town's youngsters. Small kids would be offered rides in the afternoon and the teenagers' turn came that night.

When he was a kid, Jim thought of the estate as a park where he could ride his sled and skate in winter and plant Victory Gardens on the old polo field in summer. As kids, he and his friends would walk down the lanes behind St. Mary's and follow the fence bordering the Whitney grounds. Across a rolling meadow, a white picket fence ran alongside the field where thoroughbreds grazed. He and his buddies would sometimes watch a half-dozen handlers help a nervous red-coated stallion mount a wild-eyed mare. They had no idea what all the rutting meant.

Jim and Bonnie, blankets in hand, were near the head of the line. They missed the few seats available on the sleighs but they were soon cushioned down in a tractor-pulled farm wagon filled with hay where they snuggled into the soft bedding, their bodies stretched alongside each other. A caravan of eight vehicles, four of them horse drawn, left for a tour of the estate while a cold moon shone above.

The string of slow-moving vans refreshed memories concerning the simpler pleasures of the early century. That time was not so far removed and the war had stimulated a nostalgia for a safer America, so hoedowns and apple bobbing were popular ways to honor and recreate more settled times. As were these hayrides. The horses and tractors moved alongside fields that in peacetime had been occupied by famous racehorses like Twenty Grand. Now the crowd of teenagers began to sing almost forgotten tunes like the unseasonal "In the Good Old Summertime." The lyrics, captured by the cold, flowed alongside the caravan.

It was the first time Jim and Bonnie's bodies lay side by side. They embraced, their faces red and puffed, their bodies bristling under the blankets as their senses began to steam. They roiled there with fierce urgings struggling through their heavy clothing.

Bonnie suddenly sat straight up. "No more," she whispered. "It's too much to handle."

Jim tried to pin her back into the hay but she resisted.

"Hold off," she repeated, amazed at what her body was saying.

Frustrated, he lay silent. In time, they calmed down, lying on their backs amid the other snuggling couples, watching the bare limbs of the trees sway like dark bones against a moonlit sky.

"This is where I fell in love with night time," Jim said. "Before the war, the Whitneys used to hold a fair here in the meadows, set up with tents and all. One night I was here with Matt, and we got separated and all I wanted to do was disappear in the dark. Hoping the night would come and take away the pain of being a kid."

She held him tight again.

The winter train, sleighs slick with varnish and sporting inlaid wood, others simple rough-edged meadow wagons, slid over the snow. It was a parade out of time with a world at war, yet the resurrected memories of an older America were so strong, they helped eclipse the present. For Jim, it would be the last time he would do something "old-fashioned," hark back to the family farms of Iowa he didn't even know about. No more taffy pulls. No more cakewalks. There was about the night a faint, final echo from his nineteenth century ancestors, mixed with the frenzied pleasures and disasters of the twentieth.

* * *

After the holidays, Jim's pattern had become set. Moral guides and institutions spoke about building character, but instead he had the habit of constructing personal sand castles that could be wiped away by any and every tide. Ignoring the few, flimsy underpinnings offered by home and Church—while maintaining a vague belief in the fairness doctrine—he avoided most rules. He was becoming unstable and unaware of the pile of chaff to which he was secured.

Beer and pizza outings on Friday nights became routine after the Alpha meeting broke up. Most times the guys would ride in caravans to pick up their dates in whatever neighborhood the sororities met. The guys would then invade the big ten-room homes in a swarm of masculinity, re-perfuming the air and destabilizing the feminine serenity of the place with their hubris. Having changed the chemistry, they would linger over the refreshments. Most homes featured a piano in the large living rooms, usually a grand one that became a centerpiece on nights like this. There was always a group of kids two deep around the instrument, singing the latest hits until listeners made way for a solo performance by one of the better players, including Jim, who invariably played boogie-woogie, a sure crowd pleaser. Then it was up and out to the beer joints.

Saturday nights when there wasn't a party or dance to attend, foursomes would drive to the Great Neck movies and attend the jam-packed Playhouse or the new Squire where they would shout insults at the screen. Movies were much more interactive then; there was much bellowing out and even group singing. The cloud produced by smokers in the balcony was so thick that it dimmed the film's characters, the projectionist's magic lantern stubbornly piercing the haze. Film noir due partly to a fogbank of smoke.

It would be almost impossible to understand the Forties in America without acknowledging the impact of its music and the movies. Films offered a spectator the keys to understanding the way society dressed, spoke and acted. Many people dream walked in a blind romantic mist, their imaginations hitched to Hollywood's fairy tales. In 1943 there had been the release of Hemingway's *For Whom the Bell Tolls.* And a butchered version of Cole Porter's *DuBarry Was a Lady* as well as a Howard Hughes film that had turned a Ben Hecht vehicle into a sexual fantasy called *The Outlaw*. Tragic sex, funny sex, obvious sex—available with every stub.

Movies were both guides and cautionary stories that not only set moral standards and attitudes but were sure to exploit sex at the same time. Hollywood's moguls tried to navigate the shoals between sensual urges and heaven's call, yet retain the ability to channel emotions in a fixed Christian-oriented sort of way. But sitting in the dark viewing these subtle and not so subtle portrayals of sexual energy, the kids became saturated by their power and regularly baked in the lustful oven of a local movie house. There was much canoodling in the dark.

* * *

In February, Danny Devon was invited to attend and likewise asked to prod two other swains to join him at a Winter Holiday Dance at Dana Hall in Massachusetts, a woman's prep school for Wellesley. Danny, with his easy charm, and universal love of women and sporting his trademark elf ears, always showed an androgynous pixie's ability to discover exotic girl friends in remote climes. It was news to his friends that he had squirreled away some opportunities in austere New England. To accompany him as blind dates, Danny chose Hunter McKnight and also Jim, known for his reckless tendency to climb aboard any adventure. One Friday they skipped school and drove Dan's Model A Ford through a threatening snowstorm toward Boston. Because his relic of a car suffered a broken head gasket, the problem required some adjustments and forced Dan to drive the car at high speeds in order to produce steam rather than allow water into the combustion chamber. He hoped never to stop on the entire journey. But when the trio reached the tollbooths along the Merritt Parkway in Connecticut, another problem arose. Because they couldn't afford to slow down, they improvised and simply threw money out the window at the booth attendant, pleading for understanding: "We can't stop. We have to keep moving."

Once in Wellesley, they found the girl's dorm. Dressed in jeans and scruffy lumber jackets and smoking sotweeds that smelled liked cheroots, the trio entered and inquired after Danny's date, Helen, a girl from one of the Long Island estates. As they stood there puffing away, an enraged woman came flying out of her office.

"I smell smoke," she cried and when she spotted the interlopers, said, "You mustn't smoke. It will rise up through the stairwell and tempt the girls."

The guys looked at one another and searched for an ashtray but none was evident.

"Put them here," the woman said, indicating a potted plant.

Regaining her composure, the house lady, obviously irritated and certainly not assured by their appearance, judged them to be workmen and was surprised to discover that they were legitimate guests. She asked where they came from.

"Long Island."

"Which school? I know Saint Paul's in Garden City."

"Manhasset High."

"A public school?" She couldn't believe her ears. Her voice dripped with sarcasm.

"Yes."

"And you're visiting?"

"Helen Meadows."

"I see," she said, as if she were marking a bad grade against the girl's name.

Helen appeared, a chubby girl who was not amused by their unshaven looks. Huffily, she said, "Maybe you should have stopped off at the inn first." Then trying to smooth the matter, because girls here were not in the habit of being disagreeable, she turned on her charm and made herself as attractive as possible.

Plans were set for the evening, a get-together so that unacquainted couples could socialize. Outlining the next day's activities, Helen said there would be a trip to Boston followed by a dinner dance in the Oak Room at school. The three Alphas then left and signed in at a wooden firetrap of an inn located in downtown Wellesley. Their room was on the third floor, where bachelors parked for such occasions. The room that might have slept four was simple and priced to satisfy beaux seeking comity with the higher-type feminine spirits found in town. They showered down the hall, grabbed a quick bite and returned for the Friday night mixer.

They met in the commons room full of bridge tables, chintz sofas and leather chairs. The guys were in jackets and ties and the girls wore their party dresses. The room, swarming with genuine sub-debs, made Jim dizzy with the sight of all this fresh beauty. McKnight's date was Judy, a funny girl who graced the weekend with her wit. When Jim met the beautiful Audrey Keene, he was stunned, wishing he possessed better social skills. But she warmed to his looks and easy manner and led him through thirty-six hours of new ways at looking at his female peers. Perfection sometimes appears in a young woman like Audrey—fragile, spirited, energizing—and, above all, alive in a way not seen or felt by suburban romeos. He had never been in the presence of such a quiet force. He could barely control his emotions but her warm smile gave him hope that he might surrender without loss of honor to beauty's devastating victory over his poor defenses.

Helen spoke mostly of her horses harbored at the family's Sands Point estate, while Judy seemed to be chief compiler of stories involving awkward social blunders, annotating the peculiarities of the rich that she observed from her booth at Boston's Vanity Fair that spread between Brookline and the coast of Maine. Audrey mostly reminisced about her family, to whom she seemed dedicated. Compared to these well-bred ladies, the Manhasset trio's society credentials left them somewhere in the back of the pack and down at the other end of the bar. They mostly listened as the girls spread out their social wares as if they were only practicing until more enterprising game came along. But there was the hope that this mixture of unequals might produce a good time if they all smiled a great deal and remained pleasant.

"Shouldn't I be with him," horsewoman Helen said, "seeing that his name is Hunter and all?"

"You're not touching him," said Judy. "He's mine."

Telling stories was the way the girls sought to propel their personalities. There was a saying back then that social conversation was akin to keeping a feather airborne.

Helen began, "A friend of my brother came to visit one day and dad asked him if he wanted to go riding. This guy wanted to impress the family and said 'yes' even though he could barely sit on a horse. He had even gone out to buy riding clothes. He got on OK but when the horse started up, he held onto the mane for dear life. My father cursed him up one side, then down the other, told him he could ruin a horse riding like that, the horse of much greater value than the visitor. So father banished him still wearing his new jodhpurs."

Judy followed. "My mother, who is as patriotic as the flag, was having a dinner party one night. This guest started on about how Roosevelt was ruining the country and how he was all against the war. And even though my mother was a staunch Republican and had been known to abuse the President in peacetime, she felt that now that we were at war, no one should say anything negative about him or America. She told the man that if he wouldn't defend the country, he should move somewhere else. She added, 'As a matter of fact, you might as well leave now and be on your way.' And she handed him his hat."

Audrey added, "My parents could never turn anyone in need away. I have an uncle who was getting divorced, so he came to live with us—*for five years*. He was a painter so a bedroom wasn't enough; he had to have his own studio. Another uncle came too, but we were lucky, he only stayed three years. Family charity didn't end there. On Thanksgiving and Christmas, my dad would bundle me up in the car and we used to drive to Boston and stop the car and he would make me invite homeless people back to the house to eat.

One of them stayed on to be a handyman. He's still there and when all is said and done, I expect he'll be buried in the back garden."

Jim listened intently to the girls and took note of the way they conversed. He was feeling inadequate, but not totally paralyzed. His buoyant ego wouldn't allow him to slip too far into envy or timidity.

When they were alone, Audrey showed her interest in him and his intentions.

"What do you hope to do in life?" Audrey asked Jim. She was accustomed to young men with plans for college or careers with a relative in manufacturing, depending, of course, on the progress of the war.

"I have no idea," Jim said. He was barely able to look ahead to the next weekend's parties. He tended to be a day-by-day person.

"Haven't you made any plans with your parents?" she inquired further.

"No. But I'd like to get out of the East for a while. Check out the Midwest or West Coast. How about you?"

"I don't think I could survive outside New England."

"I don't know if I can stay in one place. I may need to wander."

"That's all right for a while, but someday, you'll have to settle down."

"Girls say that, but I don't know."

"Maybe you'll find the right girl and she'll change your mind."

"Maybe we're young enough not to worry about it just yet."

"You'll do well. Whatever road you take."

She had the knack for pleasing him, as if she believed in him.

Back at the inn, the guys flipped coins to see who was going to sleep in one of the two upper bunks. McKnight and Jim, cheating on the coin toss and taking advantage of his naiveté, colluded to give Dan that pleasure. Dan's belief in the natural goodness of people sometimes made him a victim of such deceptions and his peers would often trespass on his gullibility and lead him astray.

Searching around the room, McKnight spied a long coiled rope ladder to be used in case of fire and said, "I don't feel safe about sleeping in this tinderbox seeing it has no fire escape."

He nudged Jim and pointed at the primitive escape system.

"What if we smell smoke in the middle of the night?"

"That must be the only fire equipment they have," Danny said, pointing to the coiled hemp.

"I wonder how it works."

"Let's try it."

They opened the sash to the bitter cold night and tossed the rope ladder out.

"Do you think it's strong enough?"

"I don't know. Maybe we should test it."

"Danny, you're in good shape. Go out there and try it."

Danny crawled out the window backwards, took a grip on the ladder and found his footing on one of the rungs. Down he went.

"Seems OK," he called up to the pair in the window.

"Why don't you go down further and see if it holds."

"We'll just swing it back and forth a little to be sure it's safe."

"Hey! Cut it out," Danny yelled, as he glided sideways across the façade of the old wooden siding.

"If you're going to be *that* way about it."

McKnight closed the window, fastening it shut with a stopper stick. With that the pair prepared for bed and turned off the light.

Danny was hollering to let him in, pounding on the window. "I'm freezing."

When a certain change in tone indicated real difficulty, they opened the window.

"You guys!" Danny said as he got his shoes back in the room. He was still shivering. "I ought to smack you," and he open-handedly tried to cuff them, swatting air.

"You're going to make some fire chief happy climbing around like that."

"You could volunteer. Help the war effort."

"You can kiss my ass," Danny said and went to bed without another word.

They met the girls again late Saturday morning on a crisp but sunny day and took the cars into Boston. Danny and Helen chose to go to the museum where some horse paintings interested her. McKnight and Judy decided to go exploring on Beacon Hill. When

Audrey offered Jim a variety of options, she was surprised to hear that he wanted to attend a special Saturday afternoon concert of the BSO at Symphony Hall. There was to be a performance of American music. A Russian would conduct.

"You'd really like to go to Symphony?"

"Yes."

"You must enjoy music."

"Some. I play piano."

"And do you follow the season at Carnegie Hall?"

"No. But my piano teacher took me there once and Town Hall. Do you go often?"

"My folks take me. We have a subscription." Audrey continued, "Before the war, the orchestra used to go up into the Berkshires and play concerts. Sometimes in the rain and mud, and we trekked up there one year with them."

This was Jim's first trip to Boston, so unlike New York. As they paraded down Boylston, he noticed the low-rise architecture, the restored townhouses turned retail. They walked by the large square in the middle of town with its flanking library and churches and through the big park with its renowned sculpture and pond. They found a tearoom, clean but inexpensive where they frittered over a small luncheon salad.

The student tickets provided by the school gave them access to the balcony for the concert. Seated in the shoebox-shaped space, Jim absorbed the sense of the hall's history through a kind of musical intuition. He knew Symphony Hall was an important musical shrine and felt the pulse of its vibrations. The symphonic program began with all the recently composed fanfares: Thomson's *Fanfare for France,* Gould's *Fanfare for Freedom,* and Copland's *Fanfare for the Common Man*. Then Schuman's *A Free Song* after Whitman and Foss' *The Prairie* after Sandberg. The second half included Hanson's Fourth Symphony as well as the Harris Fifth.

Historically steeped in the knowledge that Glinka, the father of Russian music, had inspired a school of composers, the rotund conductor encouraged the playing of these native American works. Russian himself, he was inspired to believe that their acceptance would help recreate a national musical tradition here. Though Americans were increasingly exposed to original cultural works, an O'Neil drama here, an Ives symphony there—more solid on the literary side with Melville, Twain and James—the American arts were still trying to overcome the view that their efforts were pieces of statuary that had fallen away from the European temple. However, revolutionary mixtures of paint were already lurking on canvases in downtown Manhattan and brilliant tragedies lay amid the flourishing of dramatic quills that were being sharpened in Brooklyn and New Orleans. The country's art scene was about to burst open with works that pointed toward a homemade culture, not an imported one. An entire modernist movement was stirring. Along with the national bonding forged by the shared sacrifice during war, the path toward a single, unified nationhood was revealing itself, the continental dream realized, not just the New England way of life or the regional Southern and Western societies, but one United States. Not only the mixing bowl of Germans and Irish and Italians and Jews, but Swedes and Chinese and Slavs. Everyone together.

"I saw the look on your face during the concert," Audrey said. "Like you were mesmerized."

"It's just my one-track mind," he said. "I have to listen hard to get it all."

"I think you're underestimating yourself."

"And I think you're nice to say that."

As they walked away from the concert, she took his arm, something no girl had ever done before. The action felt spontaneous, a simple and generous way to say she liked him. On the way back to Wellesley, he reached for her hand, smoothed it in his, and smiled when she looked up. There was almost a connection, perhaps stimulated by the music. Jim had responded to the program and the emotions it stirred but its resonance had yet to engage him the way swing and his roaring ego did.

Later at dinner, the sextet monopolized a round-top table.

When the women came down in their evening gowns, they looked sensuous and sure of their powers over these helpless males. Jim's date, Audrey, was wearing a strapless green and Judy a red gown. The boys in their tuxedos had stopped for wrist corsages and after some color coordinating among the women, the flowers began to unfold their fragrance. After dinner, the band began to play.

Jim was surprised to see his pugilistic foe, Will Marlowe, at ease among these thoroughbred fillies. Aware that each other's temperaments had caused the Christmas fireworks at Vivien's house, they avoided one another, but Jim noticed some whispering in their plebian direction from the smart set's quarter.

Apparently Audrey knew him too because when he came over and asked her to dance, she beamed, excused herself with a pat on Jim's arm and headed toward the dance floor in her swishing gown. Jim, who had spied Will's date in a mutual cross-examination made by the fighting gamecocks, promptly rose and tapped his date's current dancing partner on the shoulder. They both looked at Jim quizzically, never having seen him before, then shrugged their eyebrows. As her former partner slipped away, Will's girl raised her arms to dance.

"To what do I owe this honor? And to whom?" she asked in her British accent.

She was regal looking, supremely confident of her powers. When she slowly turned her swan's neck so their faces were close, he said, "I didn't want the opportunity to pass by without dancing with the most exciting woman in the hall."

"Just here in the hall?" she asked. Her eyebrows rose to question his sincerity. "That discerning, are you? You must have had a lot of experience with women."

She appeared to be anesthetized, showing a haughty frozen face. Unblinking large eyes sat in a face with a mouth that he presumed couldn't utter an untruth, though there was something about her that seemed willing to deceive.

His boyishness felt her needles sting home, but he recovered.

"I'm always on the lookout for glamour."

"Such a society devil you are."

"We're the only ones that appreciate angels." His pursuit of women had given him the power to be slightly audacious.

She almost believed him, but turned her face away to judge his sincerity from the corner of her eye. He didn't blanch. It wasn't the first time he noticed that a princess of the realm would replace the arrows of her quiver if neutralized by flattery. And he knew that he must never show his fear of the opposite sex. He was learning the rudiments of social dueling.

With her icy bearing beginning to melt, Jim could feel some emotion rising in her.

"Why don't we go outside for a minute?" he suggested.

"Too cold. But follow me."

They found a niche in a side parlor. He closed the door with his heel and they embraced. They stayed long enough for their emotions to rise, then she abruptly lowered the heat. "This is impossible. You are impossible. But at least you had the imagination to find me out. You're a charming bastard."

They returned to the dance floor. When Marlowe cut back in, he thudded Jim on the shoulder. Jim flashed his best smile at his departing partner, then hooked Marlowe's shoulder, causing him to miss-step.

"Excuse me," Jim said innocently.

"Clumsy fool."

If Will was going to hit Jim, this was the time, but place and circumstance restrained him.

Jim returned to Audrey and found her telling more family stories. She spoke about her summers at Bar Harbor, prattling on that she had known most of her friends since childhood, that her life centered on her parents and siblings, her parents' friends, and their children. She spoke of her upper-class rituals: the annual buying trip to New York with her mother, the European tours before the war, the way her father introduced her to his professional colleagues, how the family always went places together, even on business trips to San Francisco and Chicago, and how the Keenes had a national network of friends, with whom they often stayed, where they enjoyed breakfasts in dining rooms filled with fresh-cut flowers, dinners where fire from either candlelight or the hearth complemented both the cutlery and the women's' complexions. And, the lessons: dancing, riding, tennis, golf, archery, sailing.

Jim interest in the rich was born from these conversations.

On Sunday morning, Jim found a Catholic church for early mass. Again in jeans and piles of sweaters—there was no heat in the car—the boys said their goodbye and set their course for home. Instead of paralleling the water, they headed for the mountains on Route 20. Looking for a place to stay that Sunday night, the lone suggestion came from Jim, who knew that somewhere to the west lay the home of his parents' friends, the Johanssens.

They started toward the Berkshires, Danny busy keeping the car constantly going even if he had to make u-turns or go around the block in order to maintain speed when they encountered a red light. It was a long trip and snow started as they ascended into the hills of western Massachusetts. They aimed for Queechy Lake across the border in New York State near Canaan. The afternoon began to close down on them and the cold with it. Misreading the map, they had difficulty finding a route toward their destination after they dropped south of Pittsfield. They finally found a narrow road bordered by tall snow-covered pines that led them down a long incline into the Hudson River Valley. There they encountered an ice-encrusted road surface, and halfway down the hill, Danny lost control of the Model A and they skidded sideways and slid off the pavement into a ditch. They were in an isolated area, miles from any town, and there was little chance there would be a passing car. To make matters worse, the weather was blasting through the hills. Luckily, there were no injuries, just some bumps and bruises, though the red scar on McKnight's face deepened with the remembered impact of his boyhood car/bike collision.

One of the advantages of a Model A was that it didn't weigh much. They were able to push the car, only partially banged up, out of the ditch and back on the road. However, the car was cranky and wouldn't start, so Jim and McKnight, slipping and sliding on the ice—the car likewise—tried to run and push the Model A into igniting. With all the pratfalls came laughter. Danny failed time and again to get a spark and he had trouble keeping the car centerline while his two passengers began to get giddy with all the flopping around on the ice. They started purposely pushing the car down hill sideways, with Danny screaming from the driver's seat.

The faithful Tin Lizzy, however, stirred by some angels' breath, finally caught, and they motored on to Queechy Lake and were welcomed by motherly Dottie Johanssen, who churned up the fires and fed the travelers.

Jim had his own room but McKnight and Danny shared two beds down the corridor. In surveying Danny's bed with its wiggly electric blanket, the other two began tapping into Danny's gullibility.

"You know, it's really good to sleep with a window open."

"Very healthy."

"I'll just crack it open a little."

McKnight got in bed under warm quilts and heavy blankets, while Danny slid under his thin, wire-stitched blanket.

"Goodnight, you guys," Jim said. After closing the light switch, he pulled the plug on the electric blanket from the wall socket. "See you all in the morning."

When dawn arrived, Danny was a shivering blob in fetal position under the snarley blanket.

After much grouching and with threats of leaving the offending pair in the hills, Danny followed the river south to their own island.

* * *

On one of those winter nights, following a Friday night Alpha meeting, a few of the brothers, at least those without dates, Jim included, headed for the Manhasset movie to take in the nine o'clock show. They were acting up as usual as they entered the theater, loud and obnoxious. Jim was surprised to see his parents exiting from the early show as he and his friends marauded through the lobby, noisily causing a scene.

The realization of Jim's questionable conduct had been leaking out into the community, and his parents were not happy with him. They were displeased that he was flunking two courses, questioning whether the older guys in the fraternity like Saylor were a bad influence, and wondered if he had begun drinking. Their suspicions that he was smoking had already been confirmed.

Bob Hill, whose temper and past authoritarian stance had calmed in recent years, could still become aroused at any flagrant behavior and he maintained the strength to enforce punishment.

Jim sat in the middle of the row with a dozen of his buddies spread on either side of him. As the lights dimmed and the movie began, there was a rumbling along the seating. Jim took a drag on his cigarette and heard his name being whispered. He turned and saw his old man standing in the aisle, beckoning him. Surprised to see Pappy, he rose and shuffled past his friends who were wondering what was going on.

"Follow me," Pappy said.

When they started down the mezzanine stairs, Pappy stopped and grabbed Jim by the hair violently and brought his face up to his. He smelled for liquor, but only inhaled cigarette breath.

"Have you been drinking?"

"No."

Satisfied that he was telling the truth, Pappy said, "Get home."

"What's the problem?"

"You were acting so goofy when you walked in the theater. I thought you'd been boozing. Anyway, get home."

* * *

In March, Jim's family said farewell to Matt after he received orders to report to the Army Air Corps. He was immediately sent south where he would spend the next two years being bounced from a base in Texas to one in Mississippi, then Florida. All across Dixie and westward along the Sunbelt, the entire southland bulged with military camps, airfields and naval sites. In those years the Old South began to disintegrate as the ancient order of moss and swamp was invaded by tens of thousands of northern kids who showed little or no respect for Southerners' mores or their daughters' virtue.

Jim, happy to have a room of his own at home, didn't even pretend to miss Matt. On the contrary, his brother's departure allowed him to act independently at school without having to consider Matt's censure. He and his brother had moved at different paces in recent years. Once, when they were very young and devoid of a father or sometimes a mother, Matt had been a buffer against severe bullying that had turned Jim into a frightened child. But the envelope of protection that Matt had provided at the boys' homes in which they had been deposited became unsealed after they moved East. The family's economic success protected Jim from the blows of orphaned fate and the Depression.

* * *

In Danny's living room window, a silk pennant honored three of his brothers in service; the McKnights displayed one star. While the younger boys had been teetering up and down the mountains, kids their brothers' age were slugging it out on the beleaguered Anzio beachhead in Italy. G.I.s, many of them veterans of Africa and Sicily, found, to their mortal peril, mass military confusion and timid leadership on the edge of the Tyrrhenian Sea. The past September when Jim was beginning high school, the Allies had invaded the Italian mainland at Salerno. Soon after, Naples fell, but the Germans took command away from the Italians and tightened their lines and it cost seven thousand American lives to break out of Anzio. A few days later the troops fought their first battle for bloody Monte Cassino. Thousands of American G.I.s would lay down their lives in Italy. France would cost many more.

* * *

Jim's grade school friend, Terri, had been a good influence on him in earlier years with her steady moral compass and her actual practice of Christian beliefs. They had drifted apart during their freshman year, but from time to time on his way home from Bonnie's, Jim would stop by and the pair would sit in her backyard that overlooked the overrun Japanese garden next door, where the Nodos lived before they were arrested and interned because if their ancestry. Terri and her family, though wary of Jim's lack of moral direction, nevertheless recommended him for babysitting jobs in the Flower Hill section when Terri found that she was overbooked. Oddly, Jim, against type, loved children and adapted his personality to match theirs. He became considerate, even caring and protecting in their presence. Innocence gave Jim a track back to a life of his own that was otherwise and elsewhere eroding.

So it wasn't altogether surprising when Terri called Jim one day in April to sit for the Bougher kids up the street from her house. When the parents, a pleasant couple, went out, Jim played with the children for a while and at eight put them down to sleep. He wandered around the house and came upon a startling sight in the rec room. There, the most elaborate train set he had ever seen, including the one F.A.O. Schwartz displayed at Christmas on Fifth Avenue, stretched over a multi-level, multi-track configuration that astounded him with its size and detail. There were bridges over rivers and tunnels through mountains as well as villages and mirrored lakes; and elaborate train yards and construction sites, all peopled in whatever costume the little kingdom condoned. Wishing to share his discovery, he called Frankie, who appeared within fifteen minutes.

They inspected the elaborate train console and wondered how to set the six or seven train lines in motion. They turned on the power but owing to their unfamiliarity, they quickly jammed the system and trains were flying around and smashing into one another, some falling off the train table. Finally the whole works were in a frenzy. They tried to cover the damage as best they could.

Frankie had departed by the time the parents came home. Jim was paid and left. Two days later, Terri's mother called Jim and skewered him with her wrath and insisted that he apologize to the Boughers and offer to pay for any damage. But he did neither. And burned another bridge back to his Catholic roots.

* * *

Jim had a habit of stopping by fellow student's homes unannounced as he wandered around town, and he discovered that many of the parents of these acquaintances were refugees from Europe. Because his friends spoke perfect English, it surprised him to hear the parents struggle verbally. One of his favorite drop-ins was Barbara Chuhuski's house. A sturdy, serious junior girl, she told exciting stories about the family's escape from Europe.

She was born in Danzig, a neutral zone between Germany and Poland until Hitler wanted it for himself. She was visiting just outside Warsaw when war broke out and the bombing began, jumping out of the way of bomb blasts as if they were dodgeballs. Then an extraordinary thing happened. Her mother and Barbara actually walked to southern France, half way across Europe. And when France fell after the Phony War, they crossed the Pyrenees into Spain and caught a boat, this time eluding submarines, to England, and finally to Canada.

Jim was introduced to Barbara's dumpy mother and wondered how she ever made it across the continent. But he remembered what she said, "Even Jesus couldn't forgive what the Nazis are doing."

Jim was fascinated by such stories, true adventures as opposed to his safe and sound journeys around his suburb. He longed for action, but this was merely wishful thinking. He could easily have passed for sixteen and joined the Navy but he chose to stay in his teenage roost and lounge in his nest of gossip, girls and parties.

* * *

On a whim one day, only because he was passing by, he made another stop in his wanderings around town. He rang the bell of the mother of a grade school girlfriend who had died. He somehow equated his unexamined loss of a father to the death of her child. In Mrs. Fast's case, it entailed unendurable pain. Not in Jim's.

She said, "I sit in front of the mirror looking for her, seeing something of Pat in myself. Trying to recreate her. Asking the mirror to cut me up and break me apart and restore her from my image. Waiting for a picture of her to help heal me."

He got out of there as soon as he could.

He had been led by the movies and the Church and the war to think that unselfishness was the most notable condition of man and that caring for the weak and the poor were man's greatest pursuits. Jim Mahoney would have none of it.

* * *

His maiden voyage into Manhattan's nightclub scene occurred when he was invited by family friends to escort a visiting teenage relative to the paper palm forest that concealed frisky May-December relationships at the well-known Copacabana club. The Brugnanis, artists and style conscious, did not look happy when they met Jim at the Manhasset station in his checked sports jacket and blue pants. But they quickly revived their natural enthusiasm for life and chatted amiably on their way to Manhattan. There, at the hotel where her parents were staying, they introduced him to his date, Julie Ann, a cute enough girl, who failed to ignite Jim's engine. Both the younger and older women wore long evening dresses. Untidy Jim looked out of place and soon felt so. Increasingly intimidated and switching to the defensive once inside the club's gaudy interior, Jim became moody as the evening progressed through dinner. He suddenly didn't want to be there and used that as an excuse to be difficult. His petulance was intractable.

"Why don't you and Julie Ann dance, Jim?" asked his host.

"I can't dance to this music," he said, listening to the businessman's bounce. His inflexibility was galling.

Sitting in one of the most famous nightclubs in the city, he listened with only mild attention to the café's headliner, Sinatra. Jim showed an uncomfortable disinterest in everything around him. The Brugnanis, only familiar with Jim at family outings, were appalled that he chose to take such a peevish role. The host inherited the pleasure of dancing with Julie Ann.

That was Jim's last invitation from that enclave.

* * *

Come spring, Frankie, Jim and Rocky found new ways to display their devilishness. Protected by the dark, they began parading around town after midnight looking for trouble. What they did was to wait until everyone at home was asleep and then sneak out and join one or both of their confederates and get on with their burglaries. Jim had just turned fifteen.

Once, earlier that winter, in tow with his buddies, Jim snuck in the back door of the Village Bath Club, where he worked as a busboy. Inside, squinting in the darkness, he waited until he could make out the outlines of the bar. Using his flashlight, he attempted to distinguish real booze from the awful-tasting Italian cordials served there. A huge mural depicting an era that was now as dead as the stone on the building's exterior occupied the wall surface behind the bar. The massive illustration was a celebration of the Roaring Twenties. The painting showed flappers in liquored pursuit of high times, depicting them as tempestuous, careening angels flinging themselves through the canvas on wild car rides with their beaus, or relaxing on a Hampton's beach, or caught among the dazzling nightlife and skyscrapers of Manhattan. The whole mural was spiced with pictures of jazz bands, movie cameras, floating cocktails, flying musical notes, Broadway shows, airplanes and luxury liners—the entire panoply representing the open, glistening oyster shell that was the 1920s.

While Jim rustled through the bottled whiskies and cordials that earlier night, he looked up at the large mural, surveyed its gayety, and said to himself, "That's the life for me. Save me a seat."

On this warmer night, knowing that there were no police in town except for sleepy Officer Barlow long in bed and that gas rationing kept cars off the street, the boys rambled through town unseen. Manhasset at 2:00a.m. was a town bereft of movement. It was overgrown with darkness punctuated by a few cats' eyes. Through that blackness, Jim would slip out and stealthily cross over into the Plandome section to Rocky's house where he would throw pebbles against a bedroom window until his sleepy-eyed friend appeared on the back lawn. His sister Ally hoarsely whispered down to them, "Where are you two going?" and Rocky would reply, "Go back to sleep, and don't snitch."

They headed up to North Strathmore where Frankie lived, the only humans weaving through the night. They roused their friend, and continued on their way to the Village Bath Club, where Jim's family held membership. The club was again the target of tonight's escapade. While on duty the previous evening, Jim had unlatched a narrow, horizontal window near the front door, and this was to be their portal of entrance tonight. On previous raids, aside from stealing liquor, they had helped themselves to pie and ice cream, but not this night.

They walked toward the club along Northern Boulevard, the town's most active highway. In twenty minutes' time, not one vehicle on the four-lane highway leading to America's largest city passed them. Reaching their objective, they came under the window cut five feet up into the rock exterior. Because Frankie was the lightest, the other two boosted him up until he found a purchase on the windowsill and was able to pull open the wide, narrow window. Then with another boost and a lunge forward Frankie disappeared through the opening, his legs slipping over the sill, followed by a gentle thud as he hit the floor inside. Jim and Rocky waited by the front door expecting Frankie to unlock it, when there was a sudden noise, more a snort than a snore, followed immediately by the sight of Frankie flying back through the window.

"Help me," Frankie whispered breathlessly. He was stuck, half his body out, half still in the club.

His friends pulled him the rest of the way out.

"It's Hans. He's sleeping on the couch by the door."

They could hear a small commotion inside and now a light went on, including the one over the front door. They ran, saved from time in the juvenile home by the slow response of the sleep-drenched Austrian manager.

* * *

Rocky and Jim soon had another experience that confirmed their audacity. The pair had gone to the movies and while walking home, they passed the Gardens, the town's favorite nightspot that evoked the ambience of the region's roadhouses where swing music began and adolescence ended. They decided to step inside even though they were three years under the legal drinking age. Because of wartime laxity, drinking among teenagers in pizza parlors and downscale bars was condoned, but absolution had not been granted for kids to enter the better places. Smaller bars allowed underage service because, aside from economic reasons, there was little fear that officials were available to enforce this or any other rule in society. In many ways, America had become locally self-governing during the war, as if the idea of self-reliance and observing categorical imperatives had become common law.

The urge for them to cross the threshold of childhood into the country's wartime cocktail party had a sentimental impetus. It wasn't that the Gardens appealed to them as the sophisticated center of the community. They were motivated by the wistful idea that this was the last good watering hole where the legion of young adults they had idolized for years would ever congregate and that they should savor its flavor. It involved the worship they felt about their older siblings, Matt and Ally, swept up in the confusion of emotions brought on by the displacement of war, repressed sex and a naïve way of life slipping away, the communion of friends that would soon never gather again. Not only did the Gardens symbolize the actual passing of youth—with the comings and goings between military transfers and shifts overseas—but its wondrous transition. Confounded by their raging emotions, the women wondered how and when they would ever be able to find marriage in the era's confusion and construct a home for their babies. Other females faced the lonely decision to escape into the New England hills and pursue scholarship, doubtful that any philosophy could defend a warped world now that word of the Holocaust began to leak out and the other horrors of war warned them that it might be fruitless to seed their minds with anything except moral outrage.

Another image that year that had stunned young people came from a report that German torpedoes had sunk two Allied troopships in a convoy carrying 800 soldiers to their cold deaths. An American vessel coming to their rescue the next day, pitching in the waters of the North Atlantic, sailed into a patch of surreal horror. They saw hundreds of soldiers floating in their life jackets on the wild sea, dead and caked in frost, others in rowboats frozen in position like ice sculptures.

In contrast, the Gardens, its gleaming windows shining from the warmth inside and brightened by Charlie's piano music floating through the air, was a place that could be said to radiate joy, elixired joy.

Jim and Rocky walked in and were met by a surprised look from Frank, the owner, who was appalled to see these changelings, one thin and tall, the other small and chubby, who dared defy the limitations placed on young fry by society and the New York State Beverage Commission. His eyes appealed for help. Frank looked in the dining room where a table of Matt and Ally's friends sat carousing. His instinct was to restrain the boys from sitting down in the dining room. Curvy Slim, the smart and spirited senior who had a reputation for befriending underclassmen at school, quickly decoded Frank's dilemma and walked into the vestibule.

"You guys," Slim said. "Couldn't wait to get in here, right?"

They were pleased to see her. Sensing the commotion they were causing, the boys had begun to reconsider their decision to make an early entrance into saloon society.

"C'mon," she said. "You probably shouldn't be in here. But as long as you are, I'll buy you a brew at the bar and then you can tell your friends you've had your first beer in the Gardens."

Slim, with her Hollywood body and her overwhelming confidence, wrapped her arms around them and led them into the taproom. She talked about school, how sad she would be to leave them after graduation, confiding how much she missed Matt and adored Ally. When it came time to pay the bill, Frank waived the charge and fifteen minutes after they had entered, the pair left, feeling smug that they had passed another barrier and laid down another marker on the detour they had chosen to travel.

* * *

Jim got a notion in his head that he wanted to visit his relatives in Chicago the next summer and sent a letter asking for his Gram's permission. Railroad tickets were almost impossible to obtain, but a bone-wearying twenty-four hour trip by bus could still be arranged with the proviso that civilians might be bumped off along the way in favor of military passengers with critical needs. He was aware as well that the lack of money and food on the West Side was worrisome. Jim had a reputation of drinking two quarts of milk a day, sometimes downing a quart in one gulp.

His Gram wrote back, "Why do you doubt that we could put you up? Of course, come. We have a nice strong hook we can hang you on. But Marge says you will have to buy a cow while you're here."

Through the shivering hand scroll, he felt his Gram's affection, emotional support that had sustained him since he was a child. She undoubtedly wanted to see him. In her eyes, he had the potential of resolving some of their pain, a princeling who might rescue them and relieve the grip of grim reality they faced. She had, however, unjustified faith in Jim's character and abilities, though she steadfastly sought solace by pursuing the notion that he might yet help salvage their broken Irish dreams.

* * *

Kids were daredevils, especially in cars. They were propelled toward danger by the movies and radio—war stories about some hero throwing his body on a live grenade to save his buddies, or guys jumping out of airplanes over enemy anti-aircraft batteries and having their chutes punctured on the way down, or battles involving a frontal attack on a machine-gun nest. With these stories ringing in their heads, what was so dangerous about an auto race? All it kicked up was a little roadhum.

When the country entered the war, the government had issued an East Coast warning banning all pleasure driving. As a result, roads were empty except for kids in jalopies who contrived to acquire gas by contractual or foul means. The only problem with the bureaucratic edict was that there was no one to enforce the warning. Cops had all been drafted into the military police.

"It's race night," Saylor told Jim. "Coming? We'll be up late."

"Where's the race?" Jim asked.

"On Northern Boulevard."

After lying to his parents about a sleepover, Jim and Saylor sat shaking in the upthrottled Ford along the starting line.

There was to be a drag race from Manhasset to Centerport, a distance of more than twenty miles, a contest that could only have happened mid-war. Around eleven at night, eight jalopies lined up, four abreast, near St. Mary's at the end of Plandome Road and prepared to roar east toward the Thatched Cottage, where mine host took care of young drinkers. The cars exploded off the line, revving up in second gear on the straightaway past the Whitney estate, hot-rodding along the wide smooth road. Heaven help the poor, unsuspecting driver coming over a hill in the opposite direction to find five or six cars speeding at him and occupying all four lanes. The first obstacle of the race was spinning down the hill into Roslyn Village, where the curving road narrowed treacherously from four to two lanes. Passing the center of town, and gunning uphill past the Blue Spruce Inn, the road widened and straightened out again and the fast cars burned hot through Brookville. But the most frightening test of all—and the maneuver that usually won the race—was of the ability of the lead car to roar past Rothmann's restaurant. Not only did the road narrow again to two lanes but there was a blind curve over the lip of a hill that had to be carefully steered. When two cars sped side by side into the intersection, the outside car functioned on faith alone.

Saylor was running fourth along the straightaway that ran through the estates area and caught up with the third car going into the Rothmann curve fearfully called Amen Corner. Recklessly, Saylor took the wrong-side track as the road narrowed and once under the tunnel of trees, was frightened to see oncoming headlights. Jim dropped to the floor in a crouch prepared for a crash, but Saylor managed to swerve without skidding and pull behind the competing car when he saw he couldn't beat his adversary up the hill in time to avoid a smash.

When they arrived at the Thatched Cottage, Saylor said he needed a drink and insisted on a concoction called a Boilermaker, a virulent drink that was currently making the rounds—a war-inspired mixture. First the bartender supplied a beer and a shot of rye whiskey. The pair took a sip of the draft, held the shot glass above the brim of the mug, then dropped glass and contents splashing into the beer, and simultaneously called out: "Depth Charge." It tasted awful to Jim and the floating shot glass rattled against his teeth. He had the sense to see to it that Saylor didn't have a second one.

"You almost killed us at the pass. Be nice to get home alive."

Jim had used up another of his nine lives. The first had been when he walked across the Great Neck train trestle as a kid and had tripped. He would have to wait a few years after tonight's close call to expend another when at work on a construction site as a *brushee* whose job was to burn the trees knocked down by a bulldozer. One day, recklessly, Jim tossed gasoline on a fire. The flame leapt back at him along a stream of gas, a river of fire, and exploded in what was now, luckily, an empty can. Had there been any propellant left in the container, the blunder would have sent him home in shreds.

* * *

Jim was floating sky high. It felt like this was the first spring of his life and he had unearthed his real self. He was somebody. His girlfriend Bonnie had just accepted his fraternity pin to wear. He was part of a lively crowd with ever-changing membership and diversions. Everything was coming up daffodils—bright, yellow, erect, good on the eyes, and cleansing. Salt air, entering his lungs, made him feel strong and alive. His eyes made out a world that was multicolored and beautiful. His ears were full of swing music and he could touch a beautiful girl's face with his own.

* * *

In late April, Bonnie and her family invited Jim to travel with them to Connecticut to open up their summer cottage on Highland Lake in the northern part of the state in the shadow of the Berkshire Mountains where the Cassidys had vacationed for twenty years. Mrs. Cassidy, though entangled in the texture of her Southern charm with its quaint, queer habits, admired the New England style. That is, once it was distanced from the Sound-side communities from Greenwich to Westport that to her mind were nothing but fresh-air versions of Manhattan's East Side, albeit with horses, golf courses and lawn parties. But up near the Massachusetts border, in the deepest part of the Nutmeg state, her lax Dixie code was stiffened by a bracing moral attitude, a sense of enlightenment that streamed from Harvard and the itchy ideas that leapt from the region's starchy Puritan pulpits.

The Cassidys traveled north on Friday and cruised into the lake district by afternoon. Once at the cottage, they peeled away the winter shutters and opened the sashes to allow the wooden smell of frosted lumber to air out. Mattresses were turned and rugs beaten on the wide front porch that overlooked the lake. Chimneys were tested against any invasion of over-winter furry guests.

Both in blue jeans, Bonnie and Jim sought the odd jobs that would keep them together such as loading up the fireplaces with neatly sawn logs. Mr. Cassidy greeted the handymen that came to connect up the electricity, water and gas services, and by nightfall they had prepared and eaten the first meal of the season.

At dinner, Mrs. Cassidy took the lead; her husband was a quieter, humorous man with an Irish sense of humor, a man whose joy was fulfilled by his two daughters.

"Bonnie and Jim. You two have been dating now, for what, about six months?"

"Uh oh!" said Bonnie. "I sense a lecture coming."

"You know, dear, I try not to interfere with your lives…"

"But you have something to say to us," Bonnie interrupted while Jim sat with a quizzical, amused look on his face.

"Go ahead, May."

"You two are cute as butter, of course, but you're so young. I just think when Bonnie's up here with all the young people from the lake club, that she shouldn't restrict herself from dating others. You should both be open to making different types of friends."

"I think your mother has a point," her dad added.

"If I wanted to date other people," Bonnie said, "I would. I'm just happy the way things are. It's not that we're going to elope."

"Jim, can you see it my way?"

"I thought it would be up to us."

Mrs. Cassidy tried to wrap herself in her wise woman's shawl.

"Your father and I have a good deal of experience on these matters. And we've come to the conclusion that it would be the best for both of you that you shouldn't get stuck in a 'going steady' rut."

"Ma, I think you're afraid we're having sex or something."

The forbidden word landed on the table.

"I'll be …"

"Young lady, mind your manners."

The authoritarian smoke kindled into fire.

"You are," Bonnie said. "For god's sake, Dad. Jim's Catholic."

Finally it came down as parental law. Bonnie and Jim should date others.

Later, alone, Bonnie said to Jim, "You didn't speak up."

"Fruitless. They knew what they wanted to say."

"Yeah. But some of it depends on us."

"Let it be," Jim said, never one for confrontation. He had learned early in life to dodge fights and the threat of hostility.

"No. I won't. I want you to stick up for us."

"You did and I'm proud of you."

"Jim, just kiss me."

Their necking had become intense. His body swelled up as the chemical rush urged him to engage. She was as vulnerable as he in her emotions.

"Jim, make something happen. I don't know how I can wait until we're twenty."

Frustrated and aroused, Jim held her tight to crush the demon out of both of them.

In the morning, when Bonnie came down in her pajamas, her breasts swayed with a rhythm that made her so desirable that he could barely control himself. She was vulnerable as well to the sexual longings that made her voluptuous body swell with desire.

* * *

When the month of May reached Long Island and the dogwoods began to bloom, summer plans blossomed as well. By mid-month the girls were already sunning themselves in order to lay in a base for a tan. The Alphas' Spring Fling at the Knickerbocker Yacht Club was coming up and Jim, on the dance committee, was negotiating with the popular Irwin Spivak band. Looking forward to summer, he had secured a lunch and dinner job working in the kitchen at the Village Bath Club. It also seemed certain that he was going to fail Algebra and Spanish so summer school loomed. Bonnie would be leaving for the lake by late June and Jim was already looking around for some warm weather dates. In addition, there would be bonfire parties at Jones Beach to round off the school year, leaving time to train into Manhattan to hear some big bands and maybe take a few trips to the Thatched Cottage for some carousing. There was even the possibility of a visit with his grandmother in Chicago late in the summer.

* * *

Schoolwork was becoming a problem. He had decided that learning was useless. The scrambled numbers of algebra, the dull workings of local and state governments. The worthlessness of knowing how to produce cold cream in a laboratory. What did the funny sounding words in Spanish matter? He had no motivation to understand the world around him. Besides, the teaching was so dull. He found no pleasure, discipline or need to contest life's fog of ignorance. His social life was where real life lay.

* * *

The boys would sometimes sleep over at each other's houses so that when the time came to venture out on their midnight excursions, the logistics of getting around were simpler. One night when Rocky stayed over at Jim's, a singular event occurred. Jim had his one homosexual experience in life.

The boys decided to sleep downstairs on a pullout couch so they could make a quick getaway on one of their foraging trips through town. Francy and Jim's folks were upstairs and the house grew quiet. Lying in the dark, with only stray shadows entering from the war-painted globe of the street lamp outside that had been dimmed so potential enemy aircraft would have a lesser target, Rocky began to express an inadequacy that was bothering him.

"I can't get my cock to grow," Rocky confided. "I see other guys at gym and they all seem bigger than me, but mine stays small even when I have a hard-on."

"You're smaller than most kids," Jim said.

"Yeah. But I'm not growing down here."

"Maybe you should stop smoking."

"Listen, do me a favor, will you? Show me how big you get when you have a hard-on. Here," he said, taking Jim's hand. "Look how small mine is even when it's standing at attention."

Rocky placed Jim's hand on his small dick, rigid but tiny.

"Get a hard-on. I got to know how big a guy should get."

Jim thought about breasts and asses. The sheet began to rise.

Rocky touched Jim's erection. "Like I thought, I'm puny."

They slept through the night without ever waking to take their midnight romp.

* * *

Even before Decoration Day when beaches and parks would officially open on Long Island, the sorority girls were busy working on their summer tans. One of the best places for water and sun exposure was the dock and lawn of the Plandome Yacht Club on Manhasset Bay. Where girls lolled in the sun, guys soon followed. Early one Saturday, Jim and two other Alphas arrived hoping to bask in the reflection of female flesh and found a new nymphet stretched out in a two-piece suit. June, an endowed girl from Texas, had arrived recently to live with her maiden aunt and had quickly developed a reputation for being fast, even though Jim had seen her praying devoutly at church. She was the only girl in sight.

"Hi, you guys. Spread your towels."

As they lay down beside her, lustful looks flashed her way.

They chatted briefly about the recent Alpha dance and the latest gossip. June, with her reputation as one of the town's hot girls, felt free to tease her victims, who were pleased by her show of flesh. She wiggled and squirmed and invited a close inspection of her mezzanine. She thrived in their company. She came alive, alert to every word and nuance. Hyper, she perked like a kettle at the slightest hint of steam. Self-assured, she lit fires under her prey, stood up and stretched her body for their admiration. Then all four walked to the end of the dock, plunged in and swam out.

They were about forty feet offshore when the boys started ducking one another, as if engaged in a close-scoring water polo game, splashes of spray flying. When the other two guys ganged up on Jim, he easily swam away from their grasp.

"What are you laughing at?" one of the guys asked June. "You're not getting away," and they began to duck her as well.

Perhaps they felt her reputation gave them license to be aggressive.

"What 'ya got down there? A mouse?

"Get away, you guys."

"I think you'd swim better with your bottoms off."

"Knock it off. Quit it!"

The three guys began tugging at her briefs, their hands wandering along her flesh. She couldn't yell because half the time her face was underwater. Try as she might, she couldn't protect her dignity. Her bottoms began to slide down and as the Alpha sharks churned up a commotion of water, they were like a school of thrashing fish. Underwater, Jim could see her dark part emerge.

"And you, Jim Mahoney, a Catholic boy. Stop it."

When her briefs were in danger of floating away, the boys backed off. Kicking and struggling, June swam back to shore.

"I'll never speak to you boys again."

They were all grinning and full of "Did you see it?"

"Think she'll tell?"

* * *

Even though the Allies had favorably turned the momentum of the war, parade grounds across the country this Decoration Day were steeped in mourning for local boys killed in action. The spectators knew nothing about plans already underweigh in Britain. Transports and landing barges at that moment were testing their engines and a hundred thousand G.I.s were moving toward the southern coast of England in preparation for the assault on Europe. Memorial Field in Manhasset reflected the mood of a saddened nation that had no knowledge of the awesome fortnight that was about to begin. As far as the home front was concerned, the war seemed to be grinding on and on. Never-ending pain and sacrifice was the price being paid. During the ceremony, the high school band played, as the old Legionnaires from WWI marched proudly, their medals never shinier. Flags flew everywhere. The war service organizations were much in evidence: the Red Cross, the junior nurses, the Scouts, the "Hands Across the Sea" contingent, the "Books for Britain" squad, the air raid wardens and the auxiliaries from the fire department. They listened to speeches encrusted with the destructive description of the horrors wrought by the war.

Jim attended the pageant but was barely listening. He seemed to be insensitive to the reading of the death roll of his friends' siblings: Bachor, Beckman, Gill, Gurney, Henderson, Rugato, Rybecky, Shakespeare and Vincent.

WWII didn't decimate our 7th and 8th generations the way the WWI generation in the U.K. had been riddled. Though not as drastic here, still every neighborhood in America suffered. In Manhasset, fifty died.

* * *

Summer had burst out early with soaring temperatures that holiday weekend. A caravan of Manhasset kids took advantage of the weather and headed for Jones Beach, the state park that stretched for ten miles along the Atlantic coast on the South Shore. Jones Beach for Long Islanders provided a physical reminder of their happiest memories. Before the war, tens of thousands of sun worshipers filled huge parking lots each summer day seeking a bromide against the Depression that had settled on the body politic. Jim was among the crowd of thirty or so that motored in search of the surf this pre-D-Day weekend.

The parking lot at Field Nine was deserted even though the sun was bright. The only ones who had extra gas in Nassau County were the kids and the military. The vast parking lot was empty and the guys insisted on having a softball game on the tarmac, while the girls were given the task of carrying the paraphernalia for the outing. They made their way like mules toward the sand that was light brown and wide and sealed off from the sea by the green and white edges of the waves. They could hear the intermittent whomps, and then silence, as the waves flopped ashore. Gulls wheeled at beach-umbrella level, squawking for food. On the sands, the only reminder of war was the sight of Coast Guardsmen patrolling along the beach on watch for German submarines, they and their dogs side-stepping the blankets of the bathers.

The females hashed over the latest stories. There was one tale circulating that June, the girl from Texas, had been caught stealing from the till at Young's Drugs and that Mr. Young was demanding repayment by Wednesday or he was going to inform her aunt. June was apparently begging for money all over town.

"How much did she steal?"

"I hear twenty-five dollars."

"Wow!"

It was an enormous amount. Kids in those years charged twenty-five cents an hour for babysitting.

"Yeah. She spent it on a trip to New York."

"Must have been *some* excursion."

By the time the guys reached the large circle established by the girls on the beach—the center of the circle was reserved for sand castles, portable radios, foodstuffs, ice chests for beer, room for slow sand dancing and gymnastic skills (the guys always built a pyramid)—the females had made a nesting place for their male birds, who were never more flamboyant than when they were near the ocean. In retrospect, a magic circle.

Lucy, thin as a broomstick, had already fallen asleep. Glober, one of the more mischievous Alphas, thought up a prank. With the holiday came a supply of patriotic streamers, red, white and blue beach towels, little Statues of Liberty for the front dashboard and toothpicks with little American flags attached that Glober brought along to top off a sand castle he contemplated building. Lucy, her bones dry of meat, had a reputation for wearing falsies that shifted around. The figure she constructed for her bathing suit always raised a few eyebrows. Glober, waving his toothpick flags, aimed them toward Lucy. Quietly and unobtrusively, he sidled up to the prone and sleeping girl and planted flags on Lucy's breastworks, the point sinking easily into the foam that covered her core bumps.

When Lucy awoke, flags flying, she didn't immediately notice her patriotism. Guys were falling down laughing in the sand as she walked around. When she discovered that her banners were flying, she only said, "You guys are mean."

"C'mon Lucy. Show us your milkers."

* * *

Evading everyone's control, like a good rumor should, further details about June's trouble reached Jim's ears through his male circuit. Frankie had an older brother who operated on a first-notified basis with the school's communication network.

Thinking about June's dilemma, Jim's mind took a devious turn. He wondered if he might uncover some of her erotic charms by offering to loan her some money. The next afternoon, he emptied his till and got up the courage to call her. She was staying with her aunt up the block from where he lived.

"June?"

"Yes."

"Jim. Jim Mahoney."

"Yes. What do you want?"

"Maybe it's what you want."

"What are you talking about?"

"I hear you need some money."

"Yes. How did. . . .? Can I see you?"

"Be up in ten minutes."

"Hurry. My aunt's due back."

Her voice was shaky and frightened. She was wearing jeans and a Sloppy Joe sweater when she opened the door.

"Quick. Come in. I have nosy neighbors," she said.

He stepped inside and reached out for her. In the confusion of arms, his hand slid along her breast. Excited as she was scared, he put his arms out to hold her.

"Did you bring the money?"

He moved in for the clinch, "And what do I get?"

Quick as a lit match, she flamed up and placed her arms over his shoulders. "You're going to hit the jackpot."

He leaned down to kiss her but only sideswiped her as she pulled away.

"Where is it?"

"I've got it."

"Let me have it."

"Show me you mean it," he replied.

"Come on. I'm in a lot of trouble. If my aunt catches you here, she'll send me packing." She was desperate and he played on her predicament.

His hand moved toward her breasts.

She exploded backward.

"Oh, god. Here she comes."

A prim-looking woman came to the door. June broke away toward her aunt.

"He just burst in here," June said to the scowling woman. "Forced his way in."

Her aunt gave Jim a withering look, and then turned to June, "I've just come from Young's Drug."

To Jim, "You may leave now, whistler boy."

He walked back home frustrated and angry, his seven dollars still in his pocket.

June never returned to town. Jim's corruption was nearly complete.

* * *

Summer playthings came out into the sun, including sailboats. Quite a few of the guys and many of the girls enjoyed sailing not only in nearby Manhasset Bay, but further east at Sea Cliff and Oyster Bay. In the other direction toward the city lay Little Neck Bay where Douglaston Yacht Club had its home. Quite a few of the high school population in Douglaston commuted to Manhasset High, and there was always traffic between the two communities to attend parties and other romps. The Rain family had provided three personable transfer students including Edgar, though no classmate ever used that name. He was known as Scooter. He and his sister Amelia were strong additions to Manhasset High life as were the Beakhubers, the Lorelieds and the Smith girls. Scooter was one of the most popular guys in school.

Boys tended to roam in car packs like wolves and one day near the end of the school year, a bunch of them landed next to the dock stretching out into the bay in front of the Rain home. Scooter was polishing the deck of the family boat, a Lightning, readying the S&S-designed day sailor for the coming Fourth of July races. Living close to the water, most of the guys were familiar with watercraft, but some of their knowledge was thinly coated bravado.

"What's its name?" one of the guys asked.

"Mud Bug."

"What kind of a name is that?"

"If you ever flipped and completely turtled and your mast got stuck on the bottom, you'd know why . . . Any of you guys want to go sailing? You'll have to take off your shoes," Scooter said.

There was a mild response. Danny stepped forward as well as Jim, who knew nothing of sailing but knew he needed a ride home with Danny.

Scooter buckled on the jib and raised it as the host of onlookers kidded gullible Danny and told him he would have to go up the boson's chair to untangle the halyards, but Scooter would have none of it. Sailing was serious. The young skipper then raised the main against a brisk west wind prowling across the bay in search of the lee shore. With the lines already unfastened and a couple guys holding the bouncing boat off the dock. Scooter said, "Anybody else up for a ride?"

With that, the herd mentality of teenage boys kicked in and a swarm of ten guys jumped on board.

"Hey! Hold it. Not so many. You'll sink us."

Bouncing around, they lowered their heads as the boom swung around wildly in the unsteady boat.

"I can't control it," Scooter shouted.

The boat heeled over in a puff, tipping precariously. The lines jammed and a large cracking noise followed. Down came sails, halyards, stays and all. The mast had split halfway up. The cockpit and deck were strewn with debris; the erstwhile pirates came out from under the entanglement and paddled back to the dock.

"My old man will kill me,"

Swiftly and sneakily, the wayward crew climbed up on the dock and drifted away, leaving Scooter to clean up.

Scooter's father insisted that the boys pay for the damage, and some contributed but not Jim. His lack of responsibility was ruining his reputation.

* * *

Pappy brought home an advanced copy of a new magazine distributed to his advertising agency that targeted teenage girls. It was coming out in the fall and called *Seventeen*. Jim was popular among the coeds when he brought in the dummy issue for sub-debs to inspect. There was something in its large colorful pages that appealed to a fancyman like Jim, pages indicating that modern youth's expression was reflecting something new, gaining power and assurance—the magazine a new kind of literate adhesive to hold the lives of his beauties together. America was paying attention to its young.

* * *

Bonnie's mother, Mrs. Cassidy, who was plagued with a bad back, asked Jim to help, for a fee, tend her garden, which was almost as dear to her as her peach cobbler recipe and pewter plates. She gave him detailed instructions one day before driving off to see her doctor.

Bonnie decided to tan herself on the lawn while Jim worked on the flowerbeds. She looked particularly attractive, alluring in her outfit, her flesh flowing out of her bathing suit. They were mutually aroused in each other's presence as the sun pressed upon them. Around them was the earthy smell of turned sod.

Lush, the beds had confederated into blooming splendor under Mrs. Cassidy's southern agrarian persuasiveness and trowel handling. Bonnie lazed on the lawn alongside the border while Jim worked on the soil. So sure of herself and in half a haze, she wondered who beside the bees was making the music she was hearing. It was one of those blowout June days when the air was so swollen with joy, everything was ready to burst. The scented air, licked by lilacs, stole into her feelings. She was quivering with the day's beauty. Literally making her own music. So tuned was she with the afternoon that she resonated with her own happiness. Jim, looking over and seeing something special on her face, acknowledged that he adored her.

He lay down beside her on the grass. They spread out on their backs watching the big cumulous clouds drift above like great galleons. They identified cloud forms—fish-shaped Long Island, Whitman's term, and sleek locomotives like the Zephyrs that raced across the West, and a paddle-wheeler, prompting them to recite the names of the great rivers—the Hudson, the Ohio, the Mississippi, the Colorado, the Missouri and the Columbia.

Bonnie felt close to him and was moved to tell him something important. "I've never told anyone this before. When I was a kid, I had scarlet fever and was paralyzed for a time and had to re-learn to walk. It happened before we moved here."

He wanted to share, so he told her about the ear operation he had as a kid, how he had endured tremendous pain, how he had been in the hospital for weeks, his whole head wrapped in bandages when he was only two.

Comfortable enough to describe their flaws, they felt closer to one another. They accepted each others' hurts. And they knew if they touched one another they'd burst so they just lay there under the wide blue tent. They were ripe for fruition.

"Can I touch your breasts?"

Her mouth was open with desire but she demurred.

Later she would say to Mardi, "Why didn't he just do it, instead of asking."

* * *

Frankie called Jim one day in June informing him that the grapevine was spreading the news of a midnight swim at the Strathmore-Vanderbilt Club that night. The club and the grounds were once part of a garden estate created by Louis Sherry, renowned for a series of high-quality restaurants in the city. On one of the highest hills in Manhasset, McKim, the builder of the original Madison Square Garden and Penn Station with its high-flying eagles on the façade, had designed the faux French chateau, intended to duplicate Marie Antoinette's "cottage." The club's interior included amenities reserved for the rich: a big reception hall, a paneled library imported intact from overseas, and a billiard room; outside, there was a landscaped pool area and a statue garden that ran down the lawn toward the tennis courts. The first owner's name was still preserved in Manhattan at the Sherry-Netherlands Hotel, itself topped by an elegant French pinnacle, located across from the Plaza. Frank Munsey, the intrepid publisher, who spawned the community that carried his name in Manhasset, next possessed the estate, followed by one of the Vanderbilts, and finally the homebuilder William Levitt, the man who developed the many Strathmore residential areas around town. Each homeowner in this section was bound by contract to contribute to the upkeep of this reborn Petit Trianon.

Jim stayed at Frank's house the night of the swim, and by midnight they had crept out of the Washington's home in North Strathmore and, crossing Northern Boulevard, climbed the crest of the hill to the club. About a dozen kids were paddling in the pool, attempting with difficulty to keep their voices low. The latecomers piled their clothes next to the other batches of trousers and skirts and jumped in the water wearing their skivvies. Most of the swimmers were upperclassmen, including a few like Vince Joseph who would be graduating in a few weeks. All in underwear. Some of the senior girls were there, Bev, Ally and Bibs along with the queen of the sophomore class, Pat St. Azure, who greeted them with a smile meant to melt their hearts.

Vince, irrepressible, was cutting up, exercising his freedom just weeks before reporting to the Navy. Against all precautions not to make noise, he executed a cannonball from the diving board. Suddenly, lights snapped on in the clubhouse mansion. The swimmers leapt out of the water. They reached for their clothes as the pool lights lit up the night. The illumination came up from underground, creating a shaft of light that cut out a patch of the dark. Awkward in their quick departure, guys were running, hopping along, trying to get one leg into their pants, while the girls tried to zip their skirts while juggling their shoes and tops. Vince, taking his time, laughed at the tugging and pulling. Loud voices emanated from the clubhouse and out came two burly figures probing with their flashlights. They could see dim figures running toward the various exits from the grounds. With a head start, most of the kids were halfway down the lawn when Vince finally decided he'd better move, and walked slowly toward the garden and tennis area.

Couples ran through the dark, pieces of clothes streaming behind them. Vince, seeing that he would be overtaken, jumped up on a birdbath—with a quickness of mind, he had grabbed a rake on the run and had taken the pose of Poseidon—and remained still to make himself indistinguishable from the other statues in the garden area. With kids hiding behind bushes and flashlights searching their whereabouts, Vince maintained his attitude until the chase was over and the pool lights were again damped down. He then climbed off his pedestal and joined his fellow swimmers at a nearby house where the parents were absent, always a good place to celebrate.

* * *

Bonnie had already left for the lake when summer school started after the Fourth holiday. Meanwhile, Jim started his kitchen job at the Bath Club. He would sometimes stand at the kitchen door smoking, with his food-stained apron, and wave to his friends in the pool area. Because he looked so scruffy, he didn't get much of a response. The idea of not working would never have entered his head, or more precisely, his parents' heads.

He had flunked both Algebra and Spanish but did fairly well in the accelerated summer school classes, as if the speed of instruction helped him learn. Algebraic formulae now began to click clearly in his head, thanks to the patient and jolly round man who taught math.

* * *

In mid-July, Jim switched his work schedule so he could take the weekend off. After classes on Friday, he and Frankie started hitchhiking toward Highland Lake in Connecticut to visit Bonnie. After long waits on low traffic roads and a few wrong turns, they arrived at about one o'clock the next morning. Very tired, they walked out the lake road and found the Cassidy summer place dark. Seeking a solution as to where to sleep, Jim remembered from his earlier trip that the cottage next door had been all but abandoned like many others in these war years.

They walked along the lakefront and found a side door to the untended cottage. The screen door was locked so they busted a hole in the wire mesh, released the lock and pushed the interior door open. Lighting matches, they discovered a sleeping room supplied with candles and two beds covered by old mattresses and pillows.

There they parked themselves for the night. At dawn, the commotion of the birds startled Jim and he lay in a dream state for a half hour waiting to see if Frankie would rise or if he himself was going to fall back asleep. A distant motorboat sounded, amplifying its sound across the water.

With the pair of them awake, they counted their blessings.

"It's been a good year, hasn't it?" Jim said. "Except for stinking school."

"Yeah. But I wish I had a girl like you."

They lit up cigarettes and the smoke curled up toward the wooden ceiling.

"Watch this," Frankie said, and, with his cigarette held vertically, he jerked his hand and an almost perfect smoke ring floated up.

"Groovy, let me try."

"See, it's easy. You'll get the hang of it."

They lay in the torpor of youth and the hot morning, unaffected by the fact that they had committed a felony.

There was about them the languid ease of adolescence, mixed with their irresponsible behavior. With no thought of the need to improve either themselves or society, they blew smoke rings instead. They were fraught with a frivolity meant to overrun caution, enabling them to express themselves wildly, as if that were the object of living.

* * *

Skinny had discovered a place called Irish Town in the Rockaways in Queens where beer was cheap and the girls were easy. Based on his description of this sin city, three cars of Manhasset boys made their way one night to the seaside village of wood-frame bars that littered the beachfront a few steps from the ocean. Rockaway was located on one of a progressive series of sandbars called barrier beaches that formed off Long Island's South Shore, each a renowned resort area. Jim rode with Saylor, McKnight and Danny in the red convertible across the island and on to the ocean road. There Skinny led them into the thickest congregation of hedonists that Jim had ever seen. Plein air drinking along with raucous dancing in the bars turned the raffish beer joints into a garish carnival. There were hundreds of young people on the streets, all looking for sexual release. It was understood that the object of the evening's trek was to get Skinny laid.

After parking the car, Saylor said, "It's such a zoo; we'll probably get separated, so let's agree to meet back here at midnight. If we're not all here by quarter after, I'll figure you got a ride with someone else or you got lucky."

McKnight and Danny entered the crowd together. Jim stuck with Saylor and the pair waded into the closest beer shack called Fitzgerald's. Before they reached the bar where kids were standing three deep trying to fill their mugs, along came trouble.

"Hey fella," a girl in short shorts and a midriff blouse approached Saylor and slung her arm around him.

Saylor, unsmiling, peeled away her arm. "Easy. You'll mash my smokes."

She merely turned to Jim and pulled him into her embrace. Jim could feel her flesh as he put his arm around her. Then she lifted her chin—a pretty Irish face showing signs of drinking—and said, "Haven't seen you here. You're cute."

"Never been." He felt overdressed amid all the beachwear. "You come often?"

"I'm here all summer. Then I take the winter off to recuperate."

Jim, who had a bad habit of looking over a crowd instead of paying attention to the person he was talking to, noticed that there were dozens of single girls floating by and decided that he would do the choosing, and not be one of the chosen.

"Maybe I'll see you later," he said.

"You're missing the "now" of it, baby. Good luck."

"She was a dog," Saylor said.

"Not really," Jim replied. "Just a little overanxious."

They spent the next half hour evaluating the girls, meanwhile denigrating all the males.

"Greaseballs. Look at how they dress and comb their hair."

"Yeah, loudmouths."

"Freaks."

"Most of the girls look hairy."

"Bush women."

"Look at the moustache on that one."

"A lot of those busty ones are fat."

Alphas liked their girls svelte.

They moved down the street into another bar. Skinny came in with a bright-eyed blonde from Brooklyn.

"What time we leaving?"

Skinny said, "I'm staying over."

"Mission accomplished," said Saylor.

Jim eventually found a soft-spoken, reserved girl who offered him what he was looking for. They talked for an hour and connected. Sweetly and directly, she asked him to sleep with her that night. She lived nearby with some other girls but had her own room. After hesitating for a long time, he said no. He had to get back. There was his job to go to. One more excuse that kept him from acting out his craving.

On the way home, Jim sat with Saylor in front while McKnight and Danny slept in the rumbleseat. The front seat pair spent the trip showering insults on the night's revelers. They thought they were better than everybody else, superior beings with a lot of privileges. Hubris emanated from their swollen egos. But it was all a delusion. They had no resources except their bad judgment and lack of character and courage. Yet they felt they held a special status—that they and their community stood above the flood of lower souls.

* * *

One night after Bonnie had come home in late August, she and Jim, Saylor and Boots, headed for the movies in Great Neck. The girls looked attractive in their printed cottons and chattered away relating their summer adventures, laughing at each other's exploits. Their larky entrance into the theater that night, a very attractive quartet from outward appearances, would soon dissipate and spin into a hurricane of emotions. A few moments later, they were stunned as they viewed the first newsreels of the liberation of the German death camps. Jim was dazed at the sight of the mounds of skeletal bodies. The pictures required him to psychologically construct a buffer between his eyes and the screen to distance him from the reality. Otherwise, he would have collapsed.

Stricken with the sight, he was lucky not to smell the stench of death. Slowly as the camera panned across the ditches filled with naked corpses, something in him withered at the sight. He watched two bulldozers pushing dozens of crooked dead angels wearing their bones through their skin into the final unforgiving hellhole of Western Civilization. It had been the greatest failure in history. The Church had failed. States had failed. Society failed. Culture failed. Mankind failed.

Bonnie, gagged, and then vomited on her new dress.

That evening, that newsreel killed the innocence of four teenagers. What the war had already done to the older members of their generation, the pictures of the camps did to the youngest members of the swing set. It enshrouded them in disgust. The doors of human redemption and the myth of human kindness clanged slowly shut.

History, culture and human consciousness ceased to enhance intelligence as the cameras turned toward the ovens. How could people do that to one another and why bother with the niceties of civility if this was the way men really acted?

Yet Jim was able to assume its filth into his blood as the natural business of messy times. Why was this not a transformative moment for him? He would later berate himself for the way his youthful self had responded with such an empty reaction. Where was evidence of his conscience when he was able to go out that night and drink beer and eat pizza after they took the girls home?

* * *

The summer was over now. What had he discovered in his freshman year? He had found out that he was an attractive kid. Among cute girls, he showed a natural tendency to strut in front of the timid and throw off some sparks. What he didn't know was that such effervescence was as impermanent as champagne. Importantly, he found a group of guys with like interests—chasing girls, making mischief, playing poker, dancing, drinking, carousing—a fellowship of ne'er-do-wells. Also he came to understand that he had no verbal skills and few social ones. He had no interest in knowledge—not in one pursuit save playing the piano. He seemed to have a slight flair in English class and a mild curiosity about History, but in comparison to what counted—his social life and especially his interaction with girls—scholarship meant little. He had become, by dint of no talent, one of the "popular" boys in his class. He was helping to lead the parade but didn't know which way to take it. Abstract interest in other forms of life only blossomed for him around his keyboard. And, of course, he usually feigned a sentimental, on occasion a heartfelt, relation with Christ.

Jim had begun to stray away from Church teachings and abjured the promise he made to his Maker when he was ten or eleven to be a soldier of Christ. He had become a cartoon Catholic, a blurred charcoal barely outlining a faith. He didn't know where else to look except to his friends. They were everything. More important than family or beliefs. Once, he had harbored a deep affection for Christ. Jim remembered the nuns' expression that said that each Christian in his heart knew what the right thing was to do and how to act. Then why didn't he?

Socialized to have fun and ignore the war dead, he existed in a bubble of ignorance, walled in by a palisade of wrong thinking. The war was all around him, but his interest was in finding gas for his friends' cars. No adult seemed to be interested in him. He had no real supervision, only a couple of monitors. Spiritually alone in many ways, Jim fumbled along with his scrambled morals and over-easy ethics.

Meanwhile, George was ordained to suffer. Again, his buddy

"They can't close him up. They don't know if he's dying or what. He just gets weaker. Why he doesn't give up, I don't know. I think it's because he'd never be able to drive again, feel his car purr, get in some souped-up jalopy and roar in style around his hometown. Lead the Memorial Day parade in a fancy convertible he'd polished up. In his delirium, what he's done is construct a windshield against death."

His parents continued to find Jim shallow, developing bad habits, keeping the wrong company and headed for scholastic disaster. So they decided to ship him away to military school where other authorities could stick a board up his backside.

Pappy said, “You strut around like you own the place. But you’re only on welfare here. All you have are your souvenirs and temporary housing. After that, you don’t have anything.”

There was, on the one hand, this jerky kid, and, on the other, a fecund imagination. The nexus between reality and illusion was unclear. Foggy and indistinct but close to each other. Hidden but near. An intersection that provided no crossing over.

What underlay his insensitivity? Certainly his lack of empathy, his self-absorption. He continued to think that what was important was finding a girl to pin, football games, dances, music in Manhattan and nights out drinking with his buddies—much like the Twenties booze scene in colleges fifteen years before. Now it was all happening in high school.

The attitude was blamed on the war. Everything was blamed on the war. At the same time, his high school set was in denial of the world catastrophe. It was almost as if they had to keep the war at arm’s length in order for them to grow.

Obviously, the right move was to touch as many girls as possible as often as possible, play a little sports or cards, drink some beer with the brothers, go to a lot of parties and stay popular.

Later a wise man would warn him to watch out for the narcosis of external delights without dealing with them internally. But for now Jim was too young and unaware to even know what that meant.

Chapter 2
(1944 - 1945)

Drifting around back there in the cigarette smoke....

Fork Union Military Academy, located somewhere on the great beyond of Virginia's plateau, was the scene of Jim Mahoney's second year in high school. He had been exiled from his cushy, albeit war-wrinkled, suburban community and banished to a remote southern hamlet. Jim, the convicted domestic wiseass, had been sentenced by his parents to a year's internment for bad behavior. He came to resent every day that he was away.

Years later he would agree that the academy helped him settle down, with its strict discipline along with the great quantities of saltpeter congealed in the mashed potatoes to slow up the libido. Dreary, its architecture was heavy and thick-walled, actually built to withstand military assault, a fort of sorts, made obsolete generations ago by modern warfare. Nevertheless, the grim pall of Mars clouded out civilized behavior. Life at FUMA was edgy with an under-stirring of simmering violence.

There was no need for Jim to describe boot camp life to friends back home; military schools were regularly defined in the literature of the times as brutal, undemocratic and disaffected prisons, crushing the sensitive, feelings that now eluded Jim who had become ever more hardened to life's whoop and warp. His was not a smooth transition to military life, although he finally adjusted to the early rising, eight o'clock classes, hours of close order drill and gunnery practice designed to simulate armed combat. On the positive side, he credited his tactical warfare classes with a life-long love of maps.

He was miserable in this juvenile shooting box. The barracks were strung around a parade ground that, when in full use, encompassed a battalion of social misfits and would-be southern gentlemen. The students were packed away into four large housing units comprising the same number of companies that formed the school's battalion. Jim was in Company A, and he was sequestered on a separate floor with twelve other members of his squad.

The routine at the academy was monotonous. The cadets from Company A would crowd in the barrack's doorway on rainy mornings, smoking up a storm before breakfast—the rough acidy smoke crawling through their darkened lungs—as they waited for the final bugle call that spurred them out the door. This early formation basically a headcount. *"All present and accounted for"* passed from squad leader to the first sergeant to the company's lieutenant and finally to the Battalion Commander, a thin, officious martinet named Snodgrass. A toady for the administration, he was despised by the entire corps, but he was smart and devious and dangerous.

Classes droned on until two. In September, at the beginning of the semester, there were long afternoon hours of close-order drill, followed by a sports break, and then dinner. At 7:00p.m. every cadet was anchored at his desk studying until nine. After that, like hymns in the night, their radios brought them the swing ballads that reconnected them with home. Or at least until taps sounded at ten.

The students had three sets of uniforms: one set of work clothes that were re-issued G.I. fatigues; by day, cadets wore heavy woolen trousers that went with a khaki shirt and tie, along with a black jacket for cooler days, and for Saturday morning parades, they appeared in a blue-gray West Point-type uniform with a black stripe down the front of a neck-high tunic and along the outside pants' legs. When cold weather set in, topped by their brass-crested garrison hats, cadets wore a military greatcoat with a scarlet cape that swept back flamboyantly.

Jim, appalled by the school's restrictions, was smart enough to play along with the rules. Misdeeds were swiftly and harshly dealt with here. He was in so much trouble at home that he knew he'd better conform, at least for a while. Suddenly, home became a warmer place in his imagination. He lived for letters postmarked Manhasset—reminders that he was still part of the gang, not some military robot.

Rifles were soon issued. The heavy reality of the instrument reminded cadets that there was a war on and that they would soon be part of it. In all their instructions—use of weapons, maneuvers in the woods, tactics—their teachers offered a simple maxim: Learn these lessons here or die in combat in a remote zone. Around the world, immense battles were underway. Under Ike, the First, Third, Seventh and Ninth armies slogged toward Germany while Pacific flotillas steamed, island by island, toward Tokyo, under the leadership of publicity-shy Admiral Nimitz. In the effort, American deaths reached the hundreds of thousands.

What Jim did acquire other than a hatred of authoritarianism; he gleaned from his relationship with other cadets. Hank Garnett offered him a way toward friendship; Bill Paton taught him about loyalty to both men and women; and Jack Favorsham, a way toward understanding society's layering. They all bunked on the same floor and collectively formed, along with eight other guys, one of the squads of Company A. Bill, who was like a big brother to his charges, was first sergeant. Hank and Jim, new recruits, became roommates. Jack was a corporal and their squad leader.

Hank was the first Southerner Jim ever knew. He was easygoing and friendly and admired by everyone. Soon, Hank had dozens of buddies and was more popular than the candy man at the canteen. A friendship between the roommates was forged through sports and the bonding that develops in any male military unit.

What amazed Jim about the place was the contrast it offered to the world he knew, as if Fork Union were an island with its own rules, military traditions and dysfunctional hierarchy, a desolate place like a remote foreign legion post. Fortunately, the real world leaked through the heavy walls by way of news from home. This was the one chink in Fork Union's battlements, a drip of sanity provided by the Postal Service that offered Jim word of Bonnie, the Alphas and his family.

On their first day of class, they had been so busy gathering books and uniforms that the new roommates hardly had a chance to talk. During the evening study hour, their noncoms, Bill and Jack, patrolled the corridors in order to maintain silence and see that their charges stayed awake and did their homework after a grueling day.

Before lights out, Jim and Hank finally had time to talk. The barracks were ringing with songs from Sinatra ("There Are Such Things") and the Glen Gray Orchestra ("My Heart Tells Me") beamed from a popular Richmond station as they lay in pajamas on their twin beds and smoked. Songs calmed them and awoke their feelings. Hank had a distinctively pinched appearance, a Southern look, a kind of pushed-up face, eyes close together, and a rural, vacant look. His total expression indicated confusion or lack of clarity, or a need for more information.

"Thinking about some gal?" Hank asked when he noticed Jim's faraway look as a swing band mooned over a sentimental tune.

"Yeah," Jim said, surprised. "Name's Bonnie."

"What's she like," Hank asked, hoping to survey his roommate's dreamscape.

"She's small and curvy. A lot of fun to be with. Very popular."

Hank absorbed Jim's words, and after waiting a decent interval for Jim to show some curiosity about him, Garnett offered, "My gal is sweet as a strawberry soda. Has big blue eyes and you wouldn't believe her temper. All I can do to keep her calm."

"Sounds like a handful."

"Keeps a step ahead of me all the time. I'm always puffing to keep up with her."

They swapped pictures of their home girls and were impressed by their beauty.

"You going to play ball while you're here?" Hank asked. "I'll probably wait until spring to try out for baseball."

"I may check out football, but baseball definitely."

"What do you play?"

"Shortstop."

"Me too. And I pitch some."

Even though they were potential competitors on the diamond, they managed to hit it off personally. Because this was their first experience knowing someone from the other side of the Mason-Dixon line, they became curious about each other's lives and families and friends, and before long they could both recognize the handwriting on each other's envelopes.

"Where you from?" Hank asked.

"Long Island. A suburb outside New York. How 'bout you?"

"Tappahannock on the Rappahannock," he said proudly. "How come you wound up way down here?"

"I think my folks wanted to send me as far away as possible. How about you?"

"My family always wanted me to go to one of the military academies—here or Staunton. It's a Virginia thing. But they couldn't afford it. But I pitched well enough last year that F.U. gave me a scholarship."

"What else you like to do?" Jim asked.

"I do a lot of hunting and fishing. You do some of that?"

"Not a lick. My old man fishes a little. But if you get caught with a gun around New York, you go to jail."

"You learn to shoot that Springfield straight and I'll take you out some night and we'll tree a coon."

"I'd rather go when it's light."

"Ah, no. If you plunk somebody at night, nobody'll know who's done it."

"You guys bullshitting?" came a voice from the door. It was Bill Paton, their first sergeant.

"Right, Sarge. Telling whoppers."

"Butts out and lights too," Paton said.

Hank snapped off the table lamp as the sergeant continued on his rounds.

"Nice to be tucked in at night. Seems like a good guy."

"Yeah. I heard he was a lieutenant last year, but he got busted."

"What for?"

"AWOL. His girl back home was stamping her feet and he jumped the fence."

After taps blew, Jim was still awake twenty minutes later when Jack Favorsham came by for a last look around. Jim could see him standing in the doorway, tall and thin. Even in the semi-dark, he looked like the confidant urbanite that he was, Manhattan version. There was something elegant about Jack's movements.

Next day, classes ended at two. Military drill followed between 2:30 and 5:00, a time that remained fixed while the weather was moderate. When the cold set in, and after the new cadets had learned to execute their drills well enough to cut practice down to an hour, they were allowed more time for sports before dinner.

Heavy rains interrupted the first week as a hurricane sideswiped the Virginia plateau. At home in Manhasset, an Atlantic hurricane wrought havoc and four hundred died in its wake. Jim's mother sent him the details of the storm's destruction; one ugly picture showed a body dangling in a tree. News photos depicted seashores covered in debris, littered with marine craft. Most pleasure boats had been cradled in a marina for the duration, but a number of weekend skippers had volunteered to operate their boats for the war effort. Unfortunately, many of these pleasure craft had washed up along the bay, landlocked now with their war-retired sisters. In order to maintain their boats, many sailors had joined the Coast Guard Auxiliary to patrol Long Island Sound, where from time to time, they would actually encounter a Nazi submarine.

Jim's first letter home complained about the food and a related outbreak of acne. He asked for additional spending money, plus his football cleats. He originally thought he might try out for the team but quickly saw that he was incapable of playing at varsity level. The team was dominated by twenty-year-olds who were able to escape induction into the regular army through the protection of the school's ROTC program. Many of these meat grinders had been deferred on the recommendation of the administration, able to dodge active service because they bulked up the prospects of a winning team. The football squad was more like a college team in terms of heft and experience. Jim took one look at the size of those bohunks and opted for Company A's 9-man intramural team. He quickly established himself as quarterback, while Garnett played in the backfield and Bill on the line. Jack was the team manager.

Because there was no outside school reputation to protect, there was a decided lack of discipline on the intramural field. Football remained fun—the kind of knock-‘em, sock-‘em rollicking wrestling match that Jim remembered from grade school. Free-for-all pile-on’s were standard. Much like bumper cars at a carnival, one could crash at will. A single coach had been appointed for all four teams because no other instructor wanted the job. But Captain Peavy liked kids and chided them in a non-painful insulting tone.

“Hey Paton. Get your ass down,” he would yell at the first sergeant “That thing’s big enough for artillery practice. You won’t get any traction with your butt hanging out like Maggie’s Drawers.”

“Yeah, Captain. But it gives me a target for those off-tackle plays,” chimed in halfback Hank.

“Garnett, when did you ever carry the ball past the line of scrimmage anyway?”

“When Mahoney here pushes me across.”

“That’s because Mahoney thinks blocking in front of the runner is beneath the role of quarterbacks. Mustn’t get his nails dirty. Favorsham, bring Mahoney some lemonade. He needs soothing.”

“Somebody’s gotta be in the backfield faking the plays, coach” Jim added.

“You’re about as deceitful as a nun, Mahoney. You couldn’t fool any of those gorillas from Company C.”

The banter continued all afternoon. This was the lightest part of their day because none of them was very serious until game time arrived later in the week. Then they took all that camaraderie and horseplay and turned it into teamwork.

Marching around for hours each afternoon gave the troops an additional opportunity to exercise in unified fashion. After a while, there was a casual swing in the rhythm of their mass drill. Marching in unison, especially when the school band played, offered them a chance to move en masse, made them feel part of the whole. This coalescence didn’t come with bonding instructions; it seemed to happen naturally. As isolated or as individualistic as a cadet might be, a certain kind of male harmony resulted from shared body movements, a new manifestation to Jim. These were no band of brothers, molded in a difficult crucible; it was more like joining forces as teammates. They began to honestly care about each other in a way Jim had never experienced before.

* * *

On the first Sunday morning of the school year, two dozen Northerners showed up for mass including Sergeant Bill and a pair of twins from New Jersey. They were joined by three local farmwomen, sisters perhaps. The service was held in the school chapel because the nearest Catholic Church was thirty miles away. The thin Irish priest asked for a volunteer to act as an altar boy and another to play the piano but no hand rose.

"One of you must have served," said the priest whose circuit included two other communities. "I don't have all day. Besides, the Baptists will descend on us at ten."

One boy rose, "I hope you have a mass card. I never memorized the Latin."

Jim volunteered at the piano.

The priest tried to be patient while the other boy stuttered the mispronounced words, often over-riding the acolyte with the next passage. It wasn't smooth but it was official.

Jim had also missed a few notes but the congregation did get a chance to sing.

"Good enough," said the priest at the end of the mass. Turning to Jim, "I'm appointing you part-time church warden. Just come in every once in a while and keep our desk in order."

That's how Jim obtained one of the keys to the chapel, which in turn gave him an opportunity to practice. A few heads would turn on odd afternoons when ragtime melodies sometime beat through the low-slung windows of the church.

* * *

The first letters he received from home were individual ones from his mother and another from Pappy. His mother recommended witch hazel and Fuller's Earth for his complexion ("Take a hot washrag. Try to loosen the pores before applying . . ."). She also said that Bonnie had called and that she had put in a subscription for him to receive the *Manhasset Mail* to keep up with news from home. The letter from Pappy was straightforward, tinged with good humor. He told Jim he was sending him a dollar a week to take care of his need for snacks and that emergency money could be applied for from a fund, a very small fund, he had established with the commandant's office. That left Jim with little cigarette money, so he began to cut back on his smoking. Luckily, cigarettes were cheap because Virginia was a tobacco state.

There was soon a letter from Jim's Aunt Marge, who had been tipped off by Gracie that he was under stress:

"So, they've got you tied down, have they? We think it's a break for you to go to a school like that although we realize you'd rather be home. We hear you're on some kind of football team. Do you like baseball better? Did you see where our poor Sox landed this year—seventh place? I thought the Browns were going to win.

We had a scare with Kate a month ago. She ran a high fever and she was in the hospital because there's been a polio scare.

We would like to see you next summer. If it wasn't for the trouble we had what with Johnny away and everything, you would have been welcome this past August. I received a letter from him that he landed, presumably in England, although he couldn't say exactly where. I sure hated to see him go across.

Your mom says it's like a morgue around your house with both you galoots away.

Write if you can. I'll send you some pictures if you want. Remember we love you, you big drip. You know, or do you, that you are Grandma's pet and she worries and frets about you."

He never did ask to see the snapshots.

* * *

There was one class that Jim really enjoyed, a survey course on World History. His teacher, as unmilitary as a waddling duck, was forced to wear a uniform and carry the title of captain. He had a round face and wore glasses topping his Humpty-Dumpty figure that required his bulging middle, a mass of moving jelly as he moved around the classroom, to be bypassed by suspenders. He pants top rode high above his belly. Captain Spode was a gentle, far-seeing person, who could look back into the civilizations that preceded our own and make them interesting subjects of study. Jim's later love of history stemmed from this classroom that fronted on the parade ground where a big American flag was daily run up and down in front of the whole school and serenaded by the bugler.

* * *

Then a letter arrived from Chicago with bad news. Marge's baby, Kate, had developed bone problems and was experiencing difficulty walking. X-rays showed some markings on her lungs. Because Kate had been born while Jack was still living at home, Marge feared her baby had been exposed to the TB that eventually killed her brother. Marge placed the child in a nearby hospital and awaited test results. They were inconclusive and the family doctor and the experts, confused by the findings, sent Kate home after a month even though she was still having trouble maneuvering. Both Marge and Jim's Gram, who took care of Kate while Marge went to work, were in distress. Gracie could do little except send Francy's old clothes west to ease her sister's expenditures. Jim hardly registered his cousin's problems, thinking so much about his own.

* * *

Cadets were able to walk off campus onto a dirt crossroads with a gas station, wood-framed retail shacks and a country store where they were able to buy purple grape drinks and peanut-crusted candy bars. It was the colored folks congregating next door that attracted Jim's attention the afternoon he wandered down. The men, lounging in front of the Negro barbershop, cautiously eyed the cadets, stirring something in Jim. It wasn't fear and it wasn't compassion. It was their difference, even though they too snacked on Grapette and Moon Pies.

In the barracks, Jim heard a lot of trash talk against Blacks, and though he was wary of any form of Southern hubris, he didn't raise a clamor against the explicit prejudice. He had never known any Negroes, never once thought about their plight and accepted their status as a normal positioning of society.

At the crossroads, a white man, a very fat man, sat in a huge, weather-beaten easy chair under the corrugated tin overhang of the general store as Jim stood eating a candy bar. The fat man, wearing suspenders over the country livery that included large-size boots, asked Jim, "You a Virginia boy?"

"No. New York. Just another damn Yankee."

"That ain't so bad, buddy. At least you try to treat the coloreds' right up there."

Jim had not expected him to say that. From his appearance and accent, Jim thought he'd hear the usual garbage.

"Them's my hands," the man said, pointing to the blacks sitting by the barber pole.

"You operate a farm?" Jim asked.

"Tobacco," the man said. "Forty—forty-five—years and don't have a damn male friend leastwise in the whole county.'

"You seem friendly enough."

"Too friendly is what they say. Too friendly to them."

"Why? They're not slaves."

"You'd hardly know the difference, son, if you looked at it hard. They're still slaves six days of the week. Even in the old days, they got Sunday off."

"You don't look much like a slave driver," Jim said, more flippant that usual.

"Boy, you have a fresh New York mouth. Bet you got yourself a lot of gals."

"Just one."

"Tell her to teach you how to speak to your elders."

"Only if she lets me get in a word sideways," Jim said, pushing along lightly.

"You rapscallion. You'd do well with these Southern girls.

"I haven't seen a girl in weeks. Do they still have tits?"

* * *

A letter from Bonnie said that she and Mardi and Maryjan had skipped school to take the train into Times Square to see Sinatra at the Paramount. That caused Jim to recall the dozens of occasions when he made the same pilgrimage. He tried to remember the sound of the bands rising from the depths of the theater on an iron lift. How the theme songs of the great orchestras began quietly from below and then rose, raising a wall of music that struck the audience with an explosive force.

* * *

By the end of October, Jim had made the honor roll and his football team was on the way to the battalion championship. As a result, letters from home became filled with praise and encouragement, and even that rarest of outpourings, closeness. His folks must have known he was suffering in his military confinement because he received mail not only from them but also from his Gram and Aunt Marge from Chicago, and even an once-in-a-lifetime occurrence, a missive from Matt, who was in pre-flight training in Georgia and commiserated with him about close-order drill.

It was the tone and the generosity of the letters from his folks that made Jim re-evaluate his relationship with his parents. Genuine affection from both his mother and step-father streamed through their messages. There was a new attitude toward him as he began to prosper academically. He absorbed their trust in him and felt closer to them both individually and as a couple. They told him that Frankie called to say that he was saving up enough money to visit Jim over Thanksgiving, but that plan never came off.

* * *

In France, World War II troops battled across the cemeteries of World War I.

* * *

The cadets at Fork Union were relatively free after noon on Saturdays, and that allowed them time for themselves. Many of those leisurely hours were spent in the service of sports. The troops had stayed up late the night before to scrub down the entire barracks. After inspection in the morning, the building resounded in radio song.

Jim decided to walk to the crossroads after lunch to fill up on sweets, and again found the fat man sitting on the porch of the general store.

"I remember you. You're that New York scoundrel," the old farmer said.

"And you're a slave-owner if I remember, or his opposite, I forget which."

"Boy, you have the smartest-ass tongue of any cadet I've ever knew."

"Maybe that's because I'm not so much a cadet as a temporary prisoner."

"Your folks must have really wanted to get you the hell outta their hair."

"Out of their life, more likely."

"Boy, I have to figure how you tick. You're coming home with me for dinner."

"Sorry. My first sergeant would miss me something terrible," Jim kidded him.

"Don't you worry about him. I'll get you home by taps."

"How do I know you can cook?"

"It'll be the best damn meal you've had all year."

"Do I have to bring my ration book?"

"Son, I have a whole farm full of animals and they don't even ask me to buy them war bonds."

Unorthodox as it was, Jim climbed into the Ford pick-up, surely one of Henry's first models, and drove a mile down the county road to a farmhouse where three women were working, one inside the house and two out in the barn. Black workers were helping out in the yard. Behind the barn, he spotted a bunkhouse. Mr. Tooker introduced Jim to his sisters, one of whom was setting a dinner table for fourteen.

"You having a party?" Jim asked.

"In your honor. Now come in here and tell me about yourself."

"I'm a kid. I have no history. I'd rather hear yours."

Mr. Tooker started in. Told Jim about growing up with his sisters on this very farm. Said how his mother always promised more boys and how his pappy hardly talked to her after the fifth girl. When his folks died, he took over the farm though by then he had proved his independence by not joining the Klan and paying his help more than the going rate. Besides, he owned the general store and if it closed, there'd be no place for locals to buy bread and milk.

"Them ole boys asked me where I got my queer ideas from, and I told them I read it in the Bible. They sent the preacher to straighten me out and that Bible-spinner had it so wrong that I upped and turned Catholic, and that's when the crosses started appearing on the front lawn regular. They probably would have strung me up long ago but they kept remembering that my pappy had been the Grand Dragon, whatever they call 'em, and that I was the best shot in the county. Now they just ignore me."

At 4:30 promptly, his sisters set a big plate for their brother at the head of the table. He motioned Jim to join him though no food was offered the guest.

"You'll have to wait. I get early service because I'm in charge of supper entertainment," the fat man explained.

At 5:30, a couple of black men walked into the kitchen and Mr. Tooker invited them and the half-dozen hands that followed to "set." Some were big-boned. All were in overalls. They seemed perfectly comfortable eating with the family and when the eight blacks were seated, they all bowed their heads and one of the sisters said grace. It was the first time that Jim had eaten with blacks and he was curious about them, but before he could begin a conversation, Mr. Tooker took charge of the proceedings. Having finished dinner himself, the old farmer opened the New Testament and began reading from St. Mark.

"And he came to Capernaum and being in the house he asked them, What was it ye disputed among yourselves by the way? But they held their peace: for by the way they had disputed among themselves, who should be the greatest. And he sat down and called the twelve, and saith unto them, If any man desire to be first, the same shall be last of all and servant to all. And he took a child and set him in the midst of them: and when he had taken him in his arms, he said unto them, Whomsoever shall receive one of such children in my name, receiveth not me, but him that sent me."

After dinner, Mr. Tooker aimed his rattle-trap Ford toward the academy and deposited Jim in front of his barracks. Once in his room, all hell broke out.

"Where have you been?" Hank asked. "Even Snodgrass is looking for you."

Within a minute, Bill Paton walked in. "You're in trouble, Mahoney. Get over to battalion and report up. Do you want me to come with you and run interference?"

"Thanks. I'll go alone. I've done nothing wrong."

When Jim arrived at Snodgrass's office, he was made to sit for a half hour before the thin, snake-like cadet commander ushered him in his office. His appearance seemed oily to Jim, and his hissing sustained itself at low volume.

"Where have you been this afternoon?" his voice soothing as Southern syrup.

"A local farmer, Mister Tooker, asked me for supper, sir."

"Yes, you were seen in his truck. What made you go with him?" The questions were posed in an almost seductively low voice.

"Seemed like a harmless old goat. We had talked at the store."

"Do you know that he is the most hated man in the county?"

Jim, fearing being tricked, took his time answering.

"Well, did you?" Snodgrass repeated.

"He mentioned that he had problems with his neighbors."

"I'd say. He's been shot at more than once."

"Seems to be a peaceful man to me, sir. A big Bible reader."

"I suppose you read the Bible together," Snodgrass sneered.

"Yes, sir."

"Yes sir? What do you mean, 'Yes, sir'? You read the Bible?"

"Yes, sir."

"Do you know it's an offense, what's your name...?"

"Mahoney, sir."

"Do you know it's an offense, Mahoney, to ride in a car?"

"No, I didn't know that, sir."

"Did you see any of his help there?"

"Yes, sir. We had dinner with them."

"What? At the same table?"

"Yes, sir."

"Get out of here," Snodgrass said in a low, threatening voice. "You're going to get a lot of exercise, Private. Never see that man again. He's hated. Send Paton here."

When Bill got back from his visit, he told Jim that his assignment would be to walk the yard for two weeks, four hours a day, a rather heavy penalty.

"OK," Jim answered. "But tell me what I did wrong."

"It's like pissing on their shoes with these Southerners. You can't cross the color line."

After two weeks of walking through rain and the increasing cold, Jim wrote home and said that he needed a new pair of shoes. "Mine got soaked in a Dixie storm."

* * *

The overwhelming presence of loud radios throughout the barracks kept the students tuned into their generation's music. Swing connected them to their own emotions. Sentimental ballads and bouncy numbers separated these songs from the waltz-filled, Charleston knee-banging, operetta-flavored pieces that had characterized their folks' youth. Feeding the needy broadcast behemoth required spicier novelties in the musical field every new season. One trend emerged that had the effect of ruining some of their future listening pleasure. Perhaps as a result of our alliance with the Soviet Union, the airwaves in these years were filled with melodies that had been pilfered from Eastern European classics. Entrepreneurs from Tin Pan Alley simply lifted the most beautiful portions of symphonic music, gave them lyrics and re-charted them for dance bands. World-renowned, heart-rending pieces that expressed the sorrow, yearning and depth of feeling found in the Slavic soul were ruthlessly copied and packaged for the ravenous American juke box, offering kids a Russian/Polish hit parade of songs that slurped across the country in slow time.

For Jim, as long as black-and-white sodas still fizzed, the first movement of Tchaikovsky's Sixth Symphony would always be known as "This Is the Story of a Starry Night." People who grew up with 78 records will automatically begin to hum "Full Moon and Empty Arms," and never know it was Rachmaninoff's 2nd. Classical harm was done by "Tonight We Love." Other heists were from Norwegian and French sources. These other stealth songs included:

"Moon Love" (Tchaikovsky's Fifth Symphony)
"Until the End of Time" (Chopin's *Polonaise*)
"If You Were But a Dream" (Rubinstein's *Romance*)
"Stranger in Paradise"/ "And This Is My Beloved" from the musical *Kismet* after *Prince Igor* (Borodin)
"I'm Always Chasing Rainbows" (Chopin's *Fantasy Impromptu*)
"Song of India" (Rimsky-Korsakov's *Scheherazade*)
"Summer Moon" (Stravinsky's *Firebird*)

* * *

One evening, when Hank and Jim were studying, the Duty Officer appeared.

"Which one of you is Mahoney? The one with the key to the chapel. Follow me."

Off Jim went with the cadet lieutenant. As they approached the chapel, Jim saw some local women, one of them Mr. Tooker's sister, standing beside a large casket. Six black farmhands stood in the background near a pick-up truck.

The sister said, "This Mister James in the box. I'm gonna hold service for him tomorrow. We gonna park him here overnight and I'll come by again in the morning."

"Mister Tooker died?"

"Yes, he did."

Jim, not familiar with local custom, followed her directions. He opened the double doors, and with some effort, the Black pallbearers labored up the steps. Once the casket was set on the floor near the altar, the woman instructed the bearers to open the lid so they could all say goodbye while Jim watched.

"He looks mighty peaceful," was all that was said. And the coffin was closed.

The next morning, Jim was excused from classes to assist at church. The farm lady arrived with her two sisters and friends. One of them set a jar of wildflowers on the casket and sat down. Outside, the six pallbearers stood in the bed of the pick-up so they could look in the church windows. They weren't allowed inside for the service.

The sisters waited a few minutes, but they knew no one else would appear. Each of the women read two psalms.

"And I hope Mister James gets some rewards in heaven, because they never allowed him any here."

* * *

Hank invited Jim home for Thanksgiving. A hundred miles away, Hank's home in Tappahannock lay on the banks of Virginia's Rappahannock River that rose in the Blue Ridge Mountains and flowed through numerous Civil War battlefields into the Chesapeake. On the way by bus, the pair stopped off to watch Richmond's scholastic archrivals—John Marshall and Thomas Jefferson—battle for football bragging rights. Jim had never seen a high school game like this: ten thousand people in the stands and seven bands on the field scurrying around to entertain the crowd. It was the premier game in the state and tension was high. As a 150 pound player, Jim noticed most lineman in the program weighed 185 pounds and many were over 200. He was glad he didn't have to contend with them.

Late Thanksgiving Day they reached Tappahannock where Jim was introduced to the Old South. His lifelong curiosity and his view of that region's outrageous character with its slow comfort were born this day. Nine family members—some resident and some not—circled around a heaped and steaming turkey dinner in the square clapboard house. Hank, adored by the younger children, let them crawl all over him. They were happy to have him home in their warm embrace. He was gentle and teasing with them and they responded with laughter. Jim was treated with hospitable ease by Hank's plain-looking parents, who didn't quite know what to make of their guest. Hank was the image of his pushed-up faced father. Following the conversation was difficult for Jim, not only because the subjects were new but also he didn't always catch the meaning of the slang that punctuated their Southern speech.

At dinner, Jim, requested the cranberries,

"The father said, "They ain't cranberries. Them's bog berries."

When Jim finally did get a chance to express himself, he asked, "Do you do much hunting for opossums?"

Everyone at the table stopped eating, looked at one another and started to laugh.

"Oooh-possums?"

They were all hooting. The father had a big grin and the mother was giggling with the girls.

Hank clued in the clueless, "Them's just plain possums."

When Jim tried to join the conversation a second time, one of the younger kids said, "He shur do talk purty."

After dinner, Sarah was waiting for Hank along with a blind date for Jim, a girl named Adie. Sarah leapt into Hank's arms, held there for a long time, as their breathing grew coarse. That provided Jim and Adie an awkward moment, but Jim ever resourceful when it came to women, said, "If they can do it, so can we," and audaciously took the full-bodied girl in his arms.

"No flies on him," Adie said, as he released her and she patted down her dress.

They went out to a drive-in movie and it was just warm enough so they didn't have to crank up the car's heater. Hank and Sarah maneuvered the other couple into the front seat after turning the speaker volume high enough to drown out the oh's and ah's coming from the back.

The next morning, Sarah called Hank and said, "Your buddy treated Adie like she was a piece of crystal. All Adie wanted to do was wrestle. Tell that good old boy to light up his furnace."

That was after Mr. Garnett and Hank took Jim fishing on the river. The overcast sky sheltered a wet shoreline and it was hard to distinguish the horizon in the gray soup. They stayed out for a couple of hours and caught enough fish to provide dinner. Hank's normally red cheeks glowed.

"That boy's never even been out fishing," Mr. Garnett told his wife. "What do they teach them up there?"

Sarah wore her war paint again on Saturday night and she and Hank managed to escape Jim and Adie after dancing and drinking at the local juke joint. That left the pair alone at Adie's house, where they began necking up a storm, squirming all over the couch. She might have shown him some flesh if he had pressed on, but something in him held him back. Adie's big-boned father upstairs might have had something to do with his reluctance.

On Sunday they traveled back to the Richmond bus station, crowded with servicemen, where they waited with the other cadets for the special coaches that were shuttling back and forth to and from the hinterlands. They were all chattering about the details of their escapades and a few were high on alcohol. Any sign of drinking was a major affront to school rules and delinquents were severely dealt with. It was the job of the sober to drown the offenders with coffee and cold water. And back they went to the strict round of drill and study.

Another breeze-by weekend to add to Jim's list.

* * *

A letter arrived from Chicago, this time from his grandmother:

"We are all worried sick about little Kate, who doesn't seem to be improving. I think of you every day and I get very lonesome. Marge and I are sending you our love. A whole world full.

From your Gram."

But he couldn't accept the affection and return her caring. He took her love for granted and moved on without reading between the lines and understand there was a disaster hovering.

* * *

Throughout December, the cadets waited patiently for Christmas furlough. But before the cadets headed home, they had to absorb the news that Glenn Miller's plane was reported missing over the Channel. Stung by the fact that their favorite bandleader was gone left an entire generation sad. He had been the one who held them together with his music. Jim didn't know if Miller was flying through a moonlit night on his way to entertain the troops in France or if the heavens had deceived him in darkness. The sky had been the music maker's dream district. With the help of celestial bodies, Glenn Miller had defined the starry sky for young lovers, veiling them in its light with his songs: "Moon Love," "The Man in the Moon," "Moonlight Becomes You," "Moonlight Cocktail," "Bluebirds in the Moonlight" and his signature, "Moonlight Serenade."

* * *

Jim received a letter from his mother:

"Be sure to bring your ration books home with you at Christmas. I'll need the red points and you'll need some shoes.

Keep your uncle Jack and your father in your prayers. Remember to pray for them on the anniversary of their deaths.

Bob and I are making plans for you to work as a lifeguard in Chicago next summer. That way you can help Marge and Gram through these difficult times. Remember how they helped when you were in the hospital and the long care after. Try and keep them cheered up and pray. Marge is so in need of moral support with Johnny overseas. He was recently in a rest home in Holland. I guess he was so tired from being constantly engaged during the Nazi breakthrough. He's now back at work in his railway battalion shuttling supplies from the coast to the main front."

Meanwhile, Marge wrote to Gracie:

"Johnny has been working 17 and 18 hours a day and living in a caboose and freezing his ears off. Stinky Mahoney from Virginia writes us about six lines now and then, but all he talks about is going home for Christmas. Poor thing. Gram looks forward so much to his letters, but that lug is worse than any serviceman. You'd think he was in the foxholes."

* * *

Jim had acquired some extra furlough hours thanks to his scholastic and sports pursuits and took advantage of this boon to head home for Christmas a day early. He couldn't wait to get away from the boring routine. Not that being away had cured his lack of compassion for others. His mother had asked him to say a prayer for her brother, Jack, but when the anniversary date arrived on the seventh, Jim had already forgotten. The only thought that motivated him was the pleasure of seeing his friends again. His negligence toward the fleeting spirit of genial Jack, who had attempted to steer the boy straight, was a sign of how undeveloped his emotional life had become. Jack had been the only adult male on the planet who cared enough about him to offer advice, remind him of where he came from—the good uncle who had tried to lighten the boy's confusion with trips to downtown Chicago and the city's broad faced Lake Michigan. Jack didn't deserve to be forgotten.

December days dragged and it seemed that the only news at school that interested Jim was the fact that Bill had been re-promoted to lieutenant and Jack Favorsham had moved up the noncom list to sergeant.

When the day of his holiday leave finally arrived, Jim was the first one at the garage for the early bus. Transportation had been arranged by the school to accommodate the logistics involved in moving five hundred students out of wayback Virginia. He was elated at the prospect of being with Bonnie before nightfall.

By late morning he entered Washington's majestic and immensely crowded Union Station to change trains. The terminus had become the bustling front gate of the bureaucratic war machine that functioned not only as a national government, but also as the worldwide military center for its partners in Russia and the U.K., whose combined mission was to crush Germany and Japan. Every day swarms of uniforms from all branches of the American services, plus those of the other Allied forces, filed through the station, a colorful hub of nations. For a railroad depot, it functioned as a cross-section of intrigue and a worldpool of intelligence, envoys arriving with small and intricate individual pieces of the puzzle that would be translated into larger victories. Intelligence officers and spies came from around the country and globe to scatter their secret information through thousands of filters located in hundreds of buildings that made up the capital city. Now that the war was progressing well, optimism could be seen in every step and bearing.

Jim stopped at the lunch counter spread across a portion of Union Station's entranceway. Because there were so many higher paying jobs available in the city, the quality of service in most retail operations was poor. Here, attempting to serve forty customers was a frazzled and distracted waitress in a frilly pink and white outfit, unable to keep up with the traffic. Jim waited and watched with the others as the poor soul stammered through the mechanics of taking and delivering fried-food orders. It was like observing a personal meltdown. Nobody could believe how inefficient the woman was at handling her job. Each arriving check brought another holdup, the wrong total, the wrong entrees, in some cases the wrong person's bill. When she was out of sight, Jim, in his most insensitive voice, said out loud what many were thinking, "A neurotic like her should quit working and get some help."

He was too ignorant to know that it wasn't that people could just take a pill and everything would go away. Or to know that the weak needed the comfort rather than the disdain of those stronger. His remark stunned people around him. A timid but intelligent-looking couple beside him confronted Jim for making such a public judgment. Unable to handle the criticism and feeling that he had revealed the worst of himself, he rose and left, his greatcoat and flapping scarlet cape outlining his embarrassed retreat.

Six hours later he was home. He was greeted by his mother who was genuinely happy to see him, and by his sister Francy, who was curious about his uniform.

'You look wonderful, son. So straight and trim. And feel your brother's muscles, honey. We're so proud of how you've done that we're busting our buttons. And so happy to see you," said Gracie, giving him another hug.

As soon as they sat down, each with a piece of hard-to-acquire chocolate cake that Gracie constructed from her meager rationing stamps, his mother pulled out the letters she had been receiving from her family in the Midwest. The Chicago relatives were in terrible straits and Jim absorbed the news without feeling because all he wanted to do was leave and visit his friends. His Gram and Aunt Marge were still grieving over the loss of his Uncle Jack to tuberculosis. At the same time there was the anxiety about Marge's husband overseas. To make matters worse, Marge's daughter had been ill for months and the doctors were confused about a diagnosis. Obsessed by his own interests, Jim showed no empathy for the suffering emanating from his old neighborhood on the West Side.

Brother Matt, from his Army Air Force base in Dixie, was more sympathetic at coping with the news coming from Chicago. He wrote funny and affectionate letters to Marge and Gram and sent toys along to his young cousin. He bought heavy wool socks in the PX and sent them to Marge's husband, freezing in the unheated cattle car in which he slept and worked. It was on one of those runs that Johnny's train stopped to help evacuate orphans from a raging fire after a bombing raid, when he had to carry a flesh-melting child to safety, the moment that became his hell on earth.

Jim raced up Flower Hill as soon as he could, still in uniform, to see Bonnie. She was slightly embarrassed by his appearance and the fact that her affections, though still strong, had been diminished by the attention she had been receiving from other boys since his departure. Many another lanky lad had come calling when Jim was out of the picture. But she quickly regained her poise when she saw past the uniform and beamed her message that she still wanted him to stick around.

They sat and made plans for the holiday season. There were events every night for the two plus weeks he was home. There would be Vivien's annual Christmas party, but maybe Bonnie would go to that one alone since he wasn't welcome after last year's boxing fracas. There was the Senior Prom at the high school on Friday; there were separate Gek and Sigma Chi dances at the Plandome Club, plus a host of parties. There would be nonstop dancing and drinking and that was all that they cared about. Jim couldn't wait to get his arms around her, so they slipped into the kitchen to avoid Mrs. Cassidy and enjoyed a long embrace.

Later, after their separate suppers, Jim returned to pick her up. Bonnie sailed into the kitchen where Jim was talking to her mother, wearing a button-down red dress. The buttons trailed down her bust line, over and down her geography all the way to her hem. He had changed into slacks and a sweater. Saylor picked them up and they made the usual rounds: the pizza place in Port Washington where they could buy beer in old cola glasses and an out-of-the-way bar in Manorhaven called the Harbor Inn that served the under-aged.

When they arrived back at Bonnie's house, they lingered in the chintz-drenched living room. Mrs. Cassidy called down from upstairs, specifying that twenty minutes was the allotted time Bonnie had before bed. The couple had already engaged in a heated tussle in the back of Saylor's car, and they were frazzled. They wanted to get out of her parent's hearing range so they opened the cellar door and sat on the steps down to the rec room.

"I'd forgotten how much I missed you," Bonnie said, laying her head on his shoulder.

"I needed you so many nights," he said, stroking her hair.

They kissed, wet and wild kisses, almost swallowing one another. Their throats pounded and he undid her top button.

"No!"

"Yes!"

Her hand moved slowly away.

Several more buttons sprung loose and her deep cleavage unveiled.

They were panting now, eyes swimming in their sockets. He reached inside and felt her breast and she threw her neck back. With one backward movement of her arms, she unclasped her bra and her fullness burst into his hand. Fantasy solidified into warm reality.

He stroked her and kissed her and tears started running down her cheeks.

"Sorry."

"It's OK."

"I'm just on fire."

"Two of us."

In time, she adjusted herself and he helped her button up.

"Do you hate me?"

"I love you."

That was all they needed to know.

* * *

Bonnie looked lovely as she descended the stairs to her living room wearing a long black gown. Seeing her in full bloom caused his emotions to swell at the sight of her. The heavy necking on his first night home had rekindled the certainty that there was something basically right about their romance. Saylor, driving his parents' car, arrived shortly thereafter with Boots, who was wearing a polka dot gown. Off they went to the MHS Senior Prom.

The gym had been transformed into a carnival setting by the parent/student decorating committee that included some high-powered Manhattan graphic designers. There were rides and booths and soothsayers to entice the couples. How they squeezed a functioning mini-merry-go-round into the building was a miracle that only the custodian, Mr. Sotz, could explain. But what came to Jim's mind as they strolled under the colored lights didn't involve the elaborate decorations or the lively orchestrations from the band. He wasn't thinking about what decorations were missing from this Senior Prom, but about the absence of those he revered.

Whenever Jim thought of high school seniors, he envisaged the previous year's class—his brother's '44 gang—that lived in his imagination. He felt they were the ones who should be dancing here—Ally and Bibs, Vince and Happy, Trudy and Babs, Harry and Artie, Connie, all of them. But he was without the power to revive their spirit. He was also having trouble connecting inwardly to the other stalwarts he had idolized—from shortstop Luke Appling to the dive-bombing squadrons on the old *Yorktown*, to Manhasset's Ernie Johanssen. He had no heroes left; at least he couldn't feel their presence, though he missed them. He had become bereft of role models and he mourned their loss. And he was confused. He wanted the war to be over and bring them all back, chronicle them in some special way, rewind their steps back to the time when he was their mascot, before he started staining his sheets, before his ability to care about others disappeared. He was caught in the lyrics of some sentimental ballad—one that offered false hope of renewal, with promises to remedy past mistakes, with offers that the unhealthy behavior that beset him could be alleviated. He was unable to escape the music and its romantic message that told him he could bend time and reconstruct the past out of air fluff. Still he persisted in embellishing his memories.

For the prom, instead of renting a tux, Jim wore his Class A uniform, looking for the entire world like a West Point plebe. He was not the only one in uniform. There were sailors home on leave, Merchant Marine cadets from King's Point, and a few G.I.s, some of whom were older brothers, dutifully escorting their sisters to the make-believe fair.

The Alphas were standoffish and leery of his vestments. Not gregarious Dumphy, of course, with his big open personality who was genuinely glad to see him. And not Ben, who was curious about his confinement in Virginia. Nor elfish Danny and McKnight of the Dana Hall caper. The girls, Mardi and Maryjan, were thrilled to see him, running their hands across his uniform, touching his shoulder.

At one stage of the dance, the stag line began cutting in on the girls. When Jim was tapped, he looked around and interrupted Ben and danced off with Maryjan.

"I've wanted to talk to you," she said. "I need some advice."

"What on?"

She hesitated and lowered her arm, "Let's find a quiet place."

They found a corner table and sat down.

"I'm embarrassed, so I don't know where to begin."

"Take your time."

"I trust you because I know how much you understand girls."

"Essentially they're better than we are."

"I don't know if it's because we're all turning sixteen next year or what. And you might as well know, Bonnie and I talk a lot, though I don't want her to know about this. She'd kill me. What she and I think is that it's getting harder and harder for us not to do it. There, I actually said it."

Jim was surprised that the two girls had confided in one another. It's something he would never talk about to anyone.

All the thickness of his emotional bloodstream—all the teachings of the Church, the admonition of parents, all the warnings about pregnancy—they raised their claws.

He didn't say anything and that lapse created anxiety in Maryjan that she had overstepped.

"I figured I could talk to you and you wouldn't blab. You mustn't tell Ben or anyone. My father would kill me if he knew I was even thinking about it."

"We'll all just have to wait," Jim said. "There's nothing else we can do. You don't want to ruin your life. You just have to know when to stop."

"I'm glad to hear you say so. I didn't know if I was turning into a prude or a prostitute."

This was the beginning of a new phase in Jim's life. The conversation with Maryjan later brought Mardi and Boots into his tent. They all swore secrecy and he became the confidante of the young women's' sex lives, or rather sexless lives. He encouraged them to wait, making his role one filled with an irony that bordered on sickness, as he himself was ill with frustration. He became the Captain of the Hymen Embattlements, and he kept their secret from the other guys. They would have lynched him if they had known he was encouraging abstinence.

Night after night during the Christmas vacation, they chased their revelries through the snow-laden air, attending multiple parties, rushing through the cold to the next warm welcoming and the next country club dance. The girls were lining up their corsages on their dressers; the guys were shining their shoes every night.

* * *

The blame for pranks pulled off around town in the early '40's was often assigned to George Hellas, the deli kid who was shot up in the Pacific. George would regularly be indicted for any hullabaloo whether he committed the offense or not. But the

Gardens caper on the weekend before Christmas was one that George missed; it was said he was still tending his wounds in some hospital. The trick, however, engaged both Jim and brother Matt, home on furlough.

Matt, standing with four other guys in front of the Gardens, spotted Jim trying to sneak into the bar.

"What are you doing here?"

"Same as you," Jim said. "Boozing."

"Then you might as well help us."

"What's up?"

"Soon as Vinny sits down at the table in there, we're going to re-park his car."

"Where about?"

"Up here. On the lawn."

The lawn in front of the Gardens entailed a two-level landscaped drop to the street.

"He sat down," came word from one of the conspirators.

"Let's do it."

With that, ten guys picked up Vinny's Chevy at the curb and carried it up and over the double rise and set it down in a position from which it would prove impossible for him to drive away.

It was the first time in years that the brothers had gotten into mischief since they were children. It felt good to Jim to re-connect with Matt who had protected him more than once when they were sprouts.

* * *

After the plainness of life at military school, Jim was stunned by the open gaiety in the homes and public places of Manhasset. It was like coming out of the desert of self-negation and stepping into an oasis of plenty. He was wide-eyed at the wealth that surrounded his community and a trip to Lord & Taylor confirmed his beliefs—the fashion outlet whose air was perfumed and whose styles were elegant. Having been stored away in Virginia listening to the gentleman cadets from the South talk about their rich traditions, Jim began to assess the wealthy society of his own community. He began to hope that he too might live the high life. Perhaps that's why he pretended to be a lady-killer and why he always took care to embellish his disguise as a social dragoon. Later, when he sought to secrete his charms among the cold beauties of Manhattan, they proved invulnerable, unlike the weak-willed aspirants to romance found here at home. But over the Christmas holiday, the night that Bonnie went alone to Vivien's party, Jim made plans to encounter some of these high-bred New York debutantes who feathered their nests among the classic preppies of ivied New England rather than among the scrub oak residue of military academies. Before Bonnie, he had dated some of the wealthy merchants' daughters in Manhasset, but he often found them deficient in the misty/dreamy department that his romantic soul required.

Now, at fifteen, he contemplated cutting a figure among the horsy and sailing set. He sought the role of young roué-about-town—an unrealistic hope for an ordinary, middle-class kid. He was lively enough and enthusiastic but not financially equipped to persuade New York girls to symbolically drop their knickers or forsake a secure life with men who were able to provide them with country homes and urban patios.

In those years, young guys could get an early boost up the social ladder from the moment their hormonal development sprang into action. Teenagers began drinking and smoking at thirteen and attending country club dances before they had body hair. All the eligible men were away fighting, and dancing partners were needed, no matter how small in mind or body a juvenile happened to be.

Jim's height and his easy way allowed women to find him non-threatening. He didn't really stir their imagination until he held them in his arms and then their blood heated just enough to tempt them without catapulting them into bed. He had been fairly well brought up and his manners were acceptable at most levels of society except the highest, or among the English, who intimidated him, or among the hard-edged poker players at the golf club where community elders practiced lying about their golf scores and gambling abilities.

Jim's aspirations for loftier social adventures had begun at Dana Hall's winter prom in his freshman year. That summer, while Bonnie was away at the lake, Dan's chubby friend Helen introduced

Jim and his pals into the Long Island estate crowd, and for a month or so, Jim swam in their pools and rode their sailboats and danced in their summerhouses. But the chubby girl set her eyes on him, which meant that her more sleek friends who held his interest began to backtrack. Soon Jim retreated as well. The dramatic moment arrived when the fat girl wanted to swim nude one hot July night in her tiny round pool. That's when he backed all the way down her long driveway, preferring the svelte locals to the stout horsewoman.

However, once introduced to tennis-and pool-house life, he sought higher social placement. Inspired by the successful examples of social climbing he had seen in the movies, Jim took heart. After all, didn't he look something like those studs on the stag line? The pursuit of his quest began in New York—the center of society's spinning whirligig—during Christmas furlough.

His school chum, Jack Favorsham, the charming young cadet from Manhattan's East Side, belonged to a well-established urban family that normally resided somewhere between its Park Avenue apartment and various ocean resorts. When the holidays arrived, the father was away fighting the war and the mother was in Palm Beach sunning herself, so the son was at loose ends and telephoned Jim about a night in town. In society terms, New York was partially subdued by wartime conditions, but still able to put on a merry face as one of the war's largest ports of call. For Jack, it was spot center.

Jack took one look at Jim's sports outfit when he arrived in the apartment and decided to lend him his father's tux. They left, sailing by the Irish doorman with his beefy red face and stepped out into the rain-painted night. They headed for Cheerio's, where they found other young Gothamites from private schools, carefully segregated from the military hordes on leave that were carousing in the hotels around Times Square. On the East Side, the women, wearing the cold Brenda Frazier look favored at the time, were decorated in flounced long gowns. Not one female's shoulder was covered, their long structures supported elegant necks that burst into delicate faces. The newcomers put down a few rye and gingers at the bar before Jack found his friends, who invited the pair to join them. At the large round table, they discovered a half-dozen roses from that year's crop of debutantes and enjoyed a few more drinks. The band played a bouncy two-step as Jim toured one of the cold angels around the tiny dance floor but quickly found they had little in common. Dancing school seemed to have braced up the girl's natural slouch but together they couldn't keep up with the beat. Still, he felt he was finally in the middle of things, twirling in the soft lights of high society. He sat down, drinking nervously, and was soon getting sloppy, so he excused himself.

In the bathroom, Jim felt dizzy and nauseated. One of the light-haired preppies from their table came in to comb his hair, ignoring Jim even though he had seen Jack sit down with this new kid. Jim and the blond guy hadn't introduced themselves in the swarm of hellos but the hair slicker was not the kind of guy who would introduce himself to someone in a men's room. Jim watched him comb his hair and carefully adjust his regalia. Then Jim got sick to his stomach. For the next two hours, Jim received periodic visits from Jack in his splotched stall in the gentlemen's restroom, where he had a most unglamorous time. His New York debut was a failure.

* * *

He was depressed about the thought of going back to school, especially after having enjoyed the holidays with Bonnie. He looked so forlorn that one of his neighbors, seeing his anxiety, came by and gave him a dollar before he headed back. He boarded a through train to Richmond with Jack and the two of them relayed tales of their furlough outings. The stories Jim told about partying every night were matched by Jack's tales of nightclubbing through Manhattan. Jim admired Jack's cosmopolitan swagger and nuanced arrogance and tried to imitate him.

When they detrained, they exited to the side of the station where the Fork Union buses were due to arrive and found a hundred or more cadets standing, smoking, and waiting for transportation back to the barracks. Jim noticed that there was a commotion among the greatcoats and flared red capes. The set of twins from New Jersey was causing a stir because one of them was drunk, stumbling around, leaning on his brother and another friend. The cadets were due back in three hours and the punishment for drunkenness was expulsion. The inebriated twin was a mess, cap askew, his face still dripping from when his brother shoved him under the faucet in the men's room in an effort to sober him up.

"We can't let him on the bus drunk," the brother said.

"He's gonna get thrown out."

"Better be AWOL than drunk," another cadet chimed in.

"He's already on probation. They'd can him anyway."

"Maybe he'll sleep it off."

"He won't sleep."

"Then somebody should coldcock him."

Eyebrows raised at the suggestion, like meat thrown to a pack of dogs.

" Knock him out. He'll be OK by the time he gets to school."

"OK. Somebody punch him."

Suddenly there was a backing away.

"Come on," said the brother. "Somebody come on and pop him." He could see from the reluctant faces around him that nobody wanted to get involved.

A moan came from the victim.

"Let's get out of the crowd and move around the corner."

They shuffled across the pavement. The kid's head was on his chest as his supporters dragged him along on either side.

"For god's sake, somebody hit him."

"I'll do it," Jim said.

"I wouldn't do that," Jack said.

"What the hell," Jim said.

"I'll hold his face up," his brother said as he yanked his sibling by the hair.

Jim reached back and hit the kid as hard as could. He could hear the sound. The punching bag fell back, shook his head and opened his eyes.

"Shit. You didn't even knock him out."

"His punch slipped. I could hear it."

A bus rolled up to the curb and cadets began clambering aboard. The twins struggled up the stairs.

"He's sick," the one twin explained to the bus driver who was not a school functionary and had no authority over the boys. Only someone from the administration could instill the necessary fear to produce alarm.

The two brothers went to the back of the bus and the one tried to get the other to lie down on the backbench and sleep it off. As the troops drove through the night, letting go of their last bit of exuberance before being clamped back into their military straitjackets, Jim would look back over the crowd of cadets and see the offending twin in a dazed state. At one stage, the kid got obstreperous and wanted to find the guy who had punched him.

They eventually pulled into the school's parking lot and the wasted twin seemed to be under his own power. Owing to the cold, the cadets quickly dispersed to their own barracks. Once inside, Jim discovered that Hank had returned and, while unpacking, they began swapping stories about their holiday adventures. Bill Paton came by, and displaying a long face, told them that he didn't think he could stay away from his girl until Easter. Jack also stopped by for a few minutes just before taps.

Instead, with a clarion call, the bugler sounded the call to assembly, requiring the pajama-clad corps to form up on the parade ground.

"What the hell is that all about?"

"Are they crazy?"

The whole building shook with activity as the irritable inhabitants reached for their clothes. Sweaters and jackets flew on as the second call rang through the school grounds. The troops bunched up at the barrack's doorway until the last minute, then a flood of cadets could be seen running to their company position, unhappy to return so soon to the school's discipline after a few weeks of leisure.

"Company up! 'Tenshon!" Bill commanded.

Instructions came to move the corps into the chapel where hundreds of youth filed into the pews. Up front on the altar stood the snarling battalion commander, Snodgrass, and the school's superintendent in his colonel's uniform. The cadets stood patiently until the full corps was inside. Their frosty breaths added a strange cloud to the unheated nave, which was dim and eerie-looking.

"Bring the prisoner forward," shouted the top cadet.

Jim could see two burly upperclassmen escorting the drunken twin down the aisle. Unlike the rest of the corps, he was wearing his full-dress uniform. Jim felt a sense of dread, thinking he might be implicated in the proceedings. The accused twin looked dazed, but he managed to walk on his own legs. Jim's stomach turned sour.

"Strip the prisoner!" came the command.

The twin's two attendants now reached into their jackets and each produced a pair of scissors. One roughly took the accused's garrison hat and ripped off the brass plate that displayed the school's heraldry. The other cut off the Fork Union shoulder patch, making a ragged hole in the sleeve. Then the first one yanked off the medals on the boy's chest. For some obscure reason, they also removed the boy's belt. All the dehumanization of the military was manifest in the ritual humiliation.

Shredded, the twin looked mournfully around for his brother.

Jim heard the commandant shout, "You are hereby expelled from Fork Union's corps of cadets."

The school population, still at attention, was ordered by the colonel to sit down. He railed for fifteen minutes about the hazards of drinking and the consequences of getting caught. There were five long school months ahead and the headmaster wanted to be sure that the troops knew that ceremonies like this could be easily convened to sting a fractious student. The disgraced boy had been led out and deposited on a slow-moving milk train that stopped at the nearest station twenty miles away.

* * *

Facing the long winter, his mother's letters in early January were supportive, sending her love, encouraging him that he could attain manhood if he could only sustain his strength without falling into his old habits. Pappy as well sent humorous letters that showed his bright and creative side. Jim discovered that people were able to express their unsaid feelings in letters, things they couldn't tell a person directly. Maybe that was the idea behind Dear John letters and suicide notes. Words on paper could be more expressive than chin-chat. Yet with all the effort on his parents' part, he pushed their advances away. His wasn't the family he would have chosen.

* * *

Later in the month, his mother sent Jim a copy of a long letter from Marge that read in part:

"My dear Grace:

I knew you would be very anxious to hear about Kate. It is pretty hard to talk about it. I think sometimes I'll lose my mind but God must make minds tough enough to take plenty. Kate definitely has tuberculosis of the hip and from what the doctor says, she will probably remain in the hospital for a year, maybe two. It's the idea that she will be in the hospital that gets me down and more so for mother. Mom has been holding up for my sake and the same for me for her, but we both feel it plenty. I can see Kate once a week. Her leg's in traction and she's as brave as any adult. When the nurses ask her how she is, she says 'I'm OK.' Tears will come to her eyes but she brushes them away and says, 'I won't cry.'

It takes about all I have in me to leave her there and not see her again for a whole week. That damned TB will haunt us for the rest of our lives. She must have gotten it from Jack.

Of course, I haven't told Johnny.

Thanks for your encouragement, but if you can find anybody that can put a broken heart together, refer him to me.

Pray hard."

And still, he did nothing.

* * *

In mid-February, there was a sense that something was amiss on the barrack's floor that housed Second Squad. Because Bill was the senior student officer, any prolonged agony he suffered was usually transmitted down the ranks. Bill now wore a downcast look, one sometimes visible on big men, as if the burdens of the world hung on their shoulders, causing them to display a kind of public depression. Nothing worse than a moody second lieutenant.

"Garnett, you might be some hot-shot pitcher down on the ball field, but up here, your job is to sift the cigarettes out of the sand bucket." This from Bill, the varsity catcher and captain.

Jack Favorsham, the squad's top non-com, filtered most of Bill's anger. Uncharacteristically, Jack began venting the pressure downward, "Mahoney, your job is to scrub down the walls of the shower. Get on it."

The cause of the problem soon emerged. The harassment stemmed from the fact that Bill had not received a valentine card from his girlfriend after they had a spat over the fact that she had attended her senior prom with another guy. Bill, who couldn't help displaying his emotions, had bullied himself into a fit.

"Talk some sense into him," Hank recommended to Jack, "before he starts kicking in the doors."

The tension built for three days and then abruptly ended with the actions of the main culprit. Bill snuck out of the barracks one night, hit the highway and headed home. It was his second AWOL offense in two years, both a result of his anxiety over his girlfriend.

Jim was impressed by Bill's daring. The deranged lover not only risked his officer's rank at FUMA but also jeopardized his matriculation in which case he would be immediately drafted into the regular army as a buck private rather than with an ROTC recommendation for Officer's Training School after graduating in May. He threw it all away for a girl. Jim couldn't fathom how someone could feel so strongly. It was nice having a girlfriend to hang around with and someone to take out necking, but why would a guy chuck away his prospects because of a greeting card?

Three days later prodigal Bill was escorted into courts martial, stripped of his rank, evicted from his one-person dorm room and put on probation. The next morning, Private Paton was marching in front of Hank and behind Jim.

* * *

In March, American troops crossed the Rhine into Germany at Remagan Bridge. A week later, the Manhasset Mail *reported that the big redhead from an early '40's class at MHS had been killed fighting there. Jim remembered Red riding around Manhasset in his car a few years back and standing in the center of the crowd at Pete's hot dog stand gesturing over some football story. He had been dynamically alive and now he was gone.*

* * *

The Fork Union baseball team, like the football team, was top-heavy with a roster of post-teenage semi-professionals. Different but interlocking causes heralded the thinly disguised fact that a half-dozen of the varsity players were showing signs of balding. First, attendance at school kept these "old boys" out of the regular military. It allowed them to enhance their playing ability and further their baseball careers by staying active on the diamond in case any major league scouts were roaming the South in hopes of filling the ranks of the depleted American and National League clubs that were struggling to keep the national game viable while the sluggers paraded off to well-publicized military service. Plus, of course, the administrators wanted a winning team.

There were three candidates for the shortstop position: a tall, rangy older guy who had played Double A ball, the likely starter; then there was Hank, who was eligible to play the infield if he wasn't pitching; and Jim, who made the team after thirty or more prospects were cut loose. Team membership allowed the ballplayers to be excused from drill so they could sharpen their batting and fielding skills. Given the balmy spring season in Dixie, the players had started limbering up in late February and were competing with other teams by the end of March. The wide field behind the school building offered Jim relief from the normal military drudgery.

Playing shortstop was the only time in his life when Jim experienced the sensation of dancing; his clumsiness seemed to disappear. There were wide slides and glides to the right to backhand a ball. There were times when a sizzling one-hopper cracked off a bat so hard, that after snagging it, he had to shuffle step waiting for the first baseman to get into position for his throw. There were little skips and even a brisé volé when he had to stretch for line drives. One of the challenges of playing the position was to stand rock solid when a shot off the bat hurtled like a missile toward his head. His instinct was to duck but it was a shortstop's credo to stand steady, a second or two like waiting for death. Then—wop—the ball was clawed by his glove.

That spring—the 1945 Spring of Western Civilization's victory—Jim felt like his body could do anything he wanted it to do. There had been six months of drill, calisthenics and inedible food that transformed his frame into athletic shape. He was stronger than he would ever be again and he had a zing in his muscles.

There was something else that transpired. He felt like he was a piece of the team even though he was a bench-warmer, and he relished the fact that he was part of an able and select group of strong young guys who were melding together in a common cause. Some of this cohesion was due to the competence of his friends: Hank's ability on the mound and team captain Bill Paton's power of orchestration behind the plate. Bill was the only one facing the entire team and through his arm movements, he conducted his grasslings. Such togetherness would have been a normal feeling for most sportsmen, but in Jim's frayed and shredded persona, the bonding created a special feeling of wholeness.

When the team began its season, only fifteen of the players dressed for an away game. Jim was excluded from this group, but Hank suited up for every trip in his dual capacity as pitcher and one of several utility infielders. Jim was disappointed not to make the traveling team but he was a realist in such matters and knew the limits of his own abilities. It was enough that he was on the squad, practiced and ate with members at separate mess tables, where they were served the best cuts of meat.

The coach ate with them as well, a large, red-faced cracker, with a taste for ultra-conservative political views. He was crude and surly and tended to spit a lot. Jim, as a potential Northern enemy, gave him no lip and tried his best to blend in with the other Dixiecrats. The two times that Jim best remembered the beet-shaped coach was the momentous afternoon of April 12th and the less than momentous day that Jim played his one and only varsity game.

On that April 12th day, the team was dragging itself off the field. Big raw-boned Southerners carried bags of equipment as they retreated toward the locker room after practice. Jim, carrying a load of bats, was walking near the coach when he saw a cadet running toward them.

"Coach! Coach!" the boy shouted.

"What, boy?"

The advancing messenger's news was garbled.

"What's he say? The President?"

"President Roosevelt's dead," the boy finally managed to say.

The coach appeared shaken by the news.

Jim had never known another president. A fixture tumbled off the wall.

"And now we'll have that milquetoast haberdasher for a president," said Coach.

Jim heard the name Harry Truman for the first time. Back in the barracks, the cadets, even if they didn't understand the implications of FDR's death, at least knew that something extraordinary had happened. As they did every afternoon in this pre-dinner hour, they turned on their radios expecting to hear Sinatra or Harry James.

"The president? That's the guy the rich people hate, right?"

"Yeah, the guy with the little black dog."

Instead of the smooth saxophone moan of Miller's brass section came strains of music they had never heard before. Jim's head snapped toward the radio, eyes squinting as if he could see the music, the most beautiful sounds he had ever heard floated into the room. There was pathos in the music. Something touched him.

"Shhh..." he said to Hank as he concentrated on the sound.

Even though Jim's piano repertoire was extensive, he hadn't paid attention to classical music. Could hardly play a note of it. Yet he was taken with this music.

Hank moved to change the station.

"Mind leaving that on?" The music had a sweet sorrow in it.

Jim sat down. As the music soared through the room, he was transformed. The music was asking him to reach for something.

There was a yearning in the strings. He sat quietly as Hank dressed for dinner. At the end of the piece, the announcer came on and said four words, "The President is dead." Then there was a short pause and music, the same music, began again. The solemnity was palpable. The music's lacerations cut deep.

At dinner, the head of the school confirmed that their commander-in-chief was gone, and the chaplain said a prayer. The gravity of the officers at the main table set the tone. The baseball coach, surrounded by the team, sat morosely. There was a respectful low tone among the cadets, taking their cue from the battalion staff.

Across America, the poor people cried. The nation had lost its great white father.

Back in their room, Jim switched on the radio. All evening long, Barber's *Adagio* poured out its sad refrain, over and over again. Each rendering seemed filled with a nation's tears. A great wail merged from America's factory floors that afternoon, workers who felt uneasy that their industrial powerhouse would fail to provide for them. Their welfare had been guaranteed by the crippled, generous man, and now he was gone.

For several days after, there would be the solemn sounds of the same piece coming between news bulletins and the funeral coverage, music matching the nation's grief.

* * *

A letter came from his mother:

"Jim, why do you come to the conclusion that you do not want to be a lifeguard this summer? All arrangements have already been made. Think how pleased Gram would be to have you there. It would certainly brighten her life considering Marge is worried about her so much. Gram feels that life is just too much for her with all the troubles they have, and she is so lonesome for Kate. You could do much to help. You would fill a place for Gram, give her something to do besides grieve for Jack and Kate, and worry about Johnny. They are badly in need of mental stimulus and you could fill a void in their lives. Besides you would be making $150 a month and I have told Marge you would pay them $50 a month. Do you realize what that would mean to them? You could provide a lot of happiness to them both and I want you to think of it as a small practical payment for all the love and care they have given you. You are getting too big not to assume responsibilities when it is possible for you to do so. They need you to give them a new slant on life."

But Jim refused to go. Didn't they realize he had Bonnie to think about?

* * *

One afternoon past the baseball team's mid-season, Jim was alternating at shortstop with Hank during practice. Just when the squad was supposed to be jelling, word came that the overage shortstop had been drafted into the service after all, despite all the precautions to extend his time on the ball field. The assistant coach conducted infield practice—the real coach was too fat to bother hitting fungos—who knocked grounders to a half-dozen players strung around the diamond.

Jim felt good that day and was whipping the ball across and around the infield, scooping up hard-to-reach grounders and making several good backhands.

"What are you doing? Showing me up?" Hank asked as they traded positions.

"Old "Aches and Pain" Appling would be proud of me," Jim answered, raising the nickname of his favorite White Sox player.

The coach came over and took the thin bat from his assistant.

"You other 'uns clear away except first base. I want to hit some to Mahoney."

It was the first time the coach had called out Jim's name.

Surprised, Hank and the others backed away and sat on the outfield grass. Jim stood there on the playing field by himself as coach removed his sunglasses and took his stance at home plate.

He smashed a hard grounder toward Jim, who scooped it out of the dirt and threw a rocket to first. Then came a ball to his left and then right, which the shortstop easily turned over. He pulled down another, a clothes-line drive that Jim leaped for. And then he snagged a ball by making a diving catch, and then threw to first base from his knees.

"OK," is all the coach said and handed the bat back to his assistant and the team resumed practice.

"Star," Hank needled Jim as they resumed practice.

"What was that all about?" Jim asked.

"Put you to the test, big fella."

When they returned to the locker room, they all showered. As they were leaving, Hank and Jim stopped in the hallway. The players assigned to the traveling team for the Massanutten game were announced on the bulletin board and Jim's name was on the list for the first time. He picked up his varsity uniform and fingered the thick woolen material emblazoned with the school colors and the team's name spread in an arc across the front of the loose-shouldered top. He ran his hand along the cloth and enjoyed a sense of accomplishment—as if all those hundreds of spring afternoons on the sandlot along Plandome Road were threaded through his uniform. That evening during study hour, Jim wrapped himself in the uniform top. Hank, who was a team regular, smiled across the desk at Jim's expression of pride.

The bus trip to the Shenandoah Valley took hours and when the team finally walked off the bus they were slightly stiff-legged and edgy. Already in playing uniform, they felt the hostility of the Massanutten cadets as they walked across the campus toward the diamond. They were as unwelcome as KP. It was Jim's first real evidence of the fact that Southerners took their baseball seriously. When the visiting team took the field to begin pre-game exercises, it appeared that the entire school had turned out for the event, the vocal crowd cat-calling after any Fork Union misplay during practice. It wasn't that the outcome was that important in terms of the schools' standings in the league. It was simply that the competition between the two institutions was high. Being sequestered in a quasi-military encampment had sharpened their hubris and stored up their energy.

When the coach read the starting line-up, Jim was surprised that he would play, not at his usual spot at shortstop, but third base.

Pleased to be in the game, he didn't question the coach's decision even though he had little experience with that position's chief task, guarding the left field line. He knew from experience that protecting third entailed a different style of play than at shortstop. Fielders on the "hot corner," expecting missiles to be hit so hard they sometimes barely saw the ball, anchored themselves near their base like guardians at the gate, while shortstops were usually free to wander laterally across their portion of the infield. There was not only the long throw to first from third, but also the necessity to stop any ball from skipping by into the "no man's land" of deep left field.

A pitcher's duel ensued. Hank was throwing well until the fifth inning, by which time Fork Union managed to score a run. Jim had yet to field a ball and his one time at bat proved ineffective when he rolled a grounder down the third base line and was thrown out at first. In the bottom of the inning, Hank allowed his first hit, a single, to the leadoff hitter and the stands came alive. Hank was upset and the second batter jumped on the first pitch and hit a slow grounder toward third, a dribbler that required Jim to charge the ball. Jim saw out of the corner of his eye that the man on first had begun steaming toward second, a hit-and-run play that signaled that the runner started early. Jim's peg should have been to second to cut down the lead runner, but looking up, and unsure of the distance, he could see that the opposing runner was less than ten steps away from second when he bare-handed the ball. From this new perspective Jim, who was off-balance, didn't think he could throw out the advancing runner and pegged the ball instead to first base. It was a mistake because an accurate throw would have nailed the advancing runner. The next batter hit a line drive to second that held the runner on. Then came disaster. A fast groundball spinning and whistling got past Jim and went trickling into the outfield. The left fielder had to come a long way to grab the ball and fired home but the runner from second slid into the plate in a cloud of dust and beat the throw, while the batter managed to get all the way around to third. Coach, big-voiced and red-faced, was hollering at Jim from the bench. The Massanutten cadets were screaming and jeering. After that, a hit to center drove in what would be the winning run and 2-1 was the final score. Jim almost redeemed himself in the late innings by hitting a long fly ball, but the left fielder made an over-the-shoulder catch on an upward slope near the fence. In effect, when the game was over, it was clear that Jim was responsible for the loss for muffing the throw and for his fielding error.

Hank and the whole team were cool toward him on the ride home. But larky Jim, who didn't comprehend the leaden impact that losing the game had on others, and so happy that he had actually played a varsity game, tried to laugh off the loss on the way back to their barracks. Even tried to get the others to sing the school song. He simply didn't get it. Bill had to tell him to shut up.

That night Hank exploded. "Why didn't you make the throw to the right base?"

Hank was clearly hurting. The game had tarnished his reputation and his roommate's apparent unconcern galled him. Jim had let Hank down and their bonding began to fray. Jim had trashed the sports dictum that one should perform well and that the cohesiveness among team members on and off the field relied on one's competence. To make mistakes was to forfeit friendships. It was the rule of games.

* * *

May of 1945 was one of the most bittersweet months that Europe and the world had ever known. The Russians hammered their way through the streets of Berlin, sifting through Hitler's ashes. It all seemed to be happening in slow motion. Clocks circled lugubriously during those first days of the month. Time's calendar hesitated and the enormity of the minute-by-minute cataclysmic headlines were like blood rushes that flooded through the veins of Western Civilization—arteries thumping, strings of veins throbbing in the neck as the Allied nations rumbled to victory.

May 2 – Berlin falls
May 4 – Holland is cleared of enemy
Denmark is freed
Patriots seize Prague

May 7 (2:00a.m. in Rheims) – German army surrenders
May 8 – Surrender ratified in Berlin

Europe was free once more. In America the VE Day story stumbled through the afternoon hours of May 8th in hitches and jumps until finally President Truman told a grateful nation that evening that the war on the ruined continent was over. At home, Gracie Mahoney could hear the bells of the churches ring. In Fork Union, the news sputtered through the barracks until the parade ground cannon exploded announcing to the cadets that they might live to fight another day—but not in Europe. Japan maybe.

Final exams followed in two weeks. Then came the dismantling of the battalion, farewell exchanges and the shipment of trunks home. His military year was over. On the train ride north, Jim made his decision. He would tell his parents that if they intended to send him back to Fork Union, he would leave home and join the Navy.

But first he scrambled up the hill to see Bonnie. It had been five months since they had been together and though she had been diligent in sending along cheerful notes that kept him abreast of hometown news, and in each letter expressed that she missed him, there was always the fright that one or the other had changed personality. She appeared glad to see him but showed the normal hesitancy of a young person forced to re-evaluate a relationship. Teenage friends changed so rapidly that only by reviewing their current disposition could they measure the emotional shifts that bound or broke friendships. There was tension between the two of them especially after she told Jim that she had been dating other guys, information that had been passed to him by Saylor. There didn't seem to be the heat of romance they previously shared.

* * *

With the sudden termination of so many war industry contracts, construction jobs that tended to be union based on Long Island proved more difficult to obtain this summer. Jim settled for a job as a soda jerk at the Munsey Park Drug Store, run as a concession by a somber, suspicious man by the name of Ray, who trusted no one and carried the conviction that all his employees were tipping the till. The extent of Ray's generosity required that his workers leave him 80% to 90% of the revenue. He was one of those oily-skinned diner managers that looked and smelled like they had boiled their shirts in grease. But Ray was wily and ambitious; he not only ran this soda fountain in Manhasset but he also managed the food and drink counter at Walgreen's in nearby Roslyn. Jim's work shift alternated between the two locations, depending on customer traffic. Dishing out sundaes and sandwiches, he worked seven days a week with a team of other teenagers. After a short period, Ray saw that Jim was capable so on Sunday he allowed him to run the Munsey Park operation alone. Employee hours normally began about ten each morning and ended eight hours later, offering Jim plenty of time to walk over to Flower Hill after work and pick up Bonnie for a movie date. Because Jim processed his orders at the soda fountain, he relied on tips and found that a good disposition and generous portions helped increase income.

Jim had been reprieved from returning to Fork Union, and presumably had learned his lesson. Nevertheless, he slipped back into his old habits. He was out every night. He quickly rejoined the Alpha guys even though some distance had grown among members after his year's absence from their ranks. Saylor and Boots soon resurfaced and the former foursome was shortly out drinking and partying together.

Manager Ray taught Jim how to be a corner-cutting employee. He taught him how to economize—using margarine mixed with butter, scooping air-filled balls of ice cream, trimming thinly sliced roast beef, preparing bread-filled tuna fish salads—necessary skills to ward off the suddenly rising prices now that the coming invasion of Japan prefigured an end to the war.

One weekend afternoon, Jim was working the lunch hour in Roslyn with the assistant manager, a gloomy-looking kid named Adam. They were so busy that Jim didn't notice that Ray was eyeing them from a crack in the storeroom door. He had apparently been there for some time watching Adam pocketing proceeds from the till. When Ray raged out of his hiding place and started after him, the kid could see he had been caught in the act. Digging into his pocket and fishing out the money, Adam bumped into Jim, thrust a bunch of bills into his hand and said, "Hold this for me." But Adam's ruse didn't work. Ray grabbed the kid and threw him out the door. By the time the manager returned to the fountain, Jim figured out what was going on and handed back the money.

"Thanks kid," said Ray. "Spend half my time keeping those little rats from the cheese. You get to step up as Assistant Manager."

* * *

Munsey Drug, tucked into an attractive shopping center with a half-dozen other shops, opened at 11a.m.on Sunday morning. Jim arrived after curing a hangover by inhaling his breakfast and multiple cups of coffee before attending mass. He found Doc Lyons ensconced among his prescription bottles behind a high counter in the back of the store. The old man waved to Jim as the young soda jerk stepped onto the raised wooden slats that ran between the fountain and the wall. There he donned his white service jacket, refusing to wear the white cap that went with the uniform.

The fountain separated the work area from the marble counter and fixed stools. From his position, Jim had access to the pull down seltzer handles and ice cream compartments. He saw that the stash of nuts and cherries was in good supply under their lift-up tin tops. Glass straw dispensers with metal caps stood on the glistening black counter. A wide mirror against the back wall reflected his image as he surveyed the rows of sundae glasses that stood in military ranks along a shelf next to the metal canisters that would frost up as the containers churned out malts and floats.

He opened the till and saw that Ray had left him twenty dollars in change. He would see how the day's receipts developed before he would decide if there was an opportunity to loot a few dollars for himself. He noted Doc Lyons eyeing him as he fished among the coins and counted out his starting purse.

Jim checked his inventory. There were four cans of ice cream in the frost-crusted cooling compartments that were capped by circular tops with rubber gaskets, holding the usual three flavors plus this month's special, peach. He started up the hot fudge and butterscotch warming machines and added some chocolate from a huge can of dark goodness from the back closet. There was plenty of milk and whipped cream. It was time to get the coffee going.

Jim took advantage of the slow start to prepare for the coming onslaught of kids that made stopping by Munsey Drug a Sunday morning ritual. A few stragglers came in after eleven o'clock high mass, and business was slow until his randy cohorts stopped by after the express mass at noon. The Alphas came in two waves—first Nick, Gib, Dumphy, Mitch and Skinny, the usual Irish and Italian Catholics. Then the Protestant contingent arrived: including Danny, McKnight, Saylor, Stu and Ben. Suddenly a dozen or more exuberant youths descended on Jim with orders. They boisterously filled all the seats along the small counter and began hollering.

"I'm starved."

"What's this month's flavor?"

"Peach."

"I hate peach."

"Pour some coffee, will 'ya?"

"Did you see Mardi last night at Janie's party? High as a kite."

"Ben got ambushed when he took Maryjan home late. Her old man cleared him off the property before he made it to first base."

"Yeah. Her old man winking the front porch lights like he's doing Morse Code."

Jim was scooping ice cream and fixing sodas and malts as he listened to the instructions and insults of his buddies.

"Throw some more chocolate in there, won't 'ya?

"You call that strawberry? Just count the strawberries in it."

A few of them sauntered behind the counter to help themselves to ice cream and globs of hot fudge.

"Thirty cents," Jim said, serving a soda to Dumphy. Collecting money during the half-hour melee often proved difficult.

"Nick's paying."

"Who says?"

"Skinny. You gonna get laid again this summer in Irish Town?"

"No. I'm thinking about pumping your girlfriend."

"Mahoney. When Doc isn't watching, why don't you steal some rubbers for us? We know he keeps 'em locked in a drawer back there."

Jim's apron was already splashed with malted milk and stained with strawberry.

"Come on, guys. Get up the money. Or Ray will be on my ass."

This was for the enlightenment of Doc who was observing the entire intrusion.

Soon, they were off to Danny Devon's cellar to play poker. Toward evening, there would be a softball game.

Families trudged into the store all afternoon. Closing time would come at five. In the middle of the afternoon, watching himself in the mirror, he stole five dollars from the register.

* * *

When the announcement came of the bombing at Hiroshima, Jim tried to imagine the view from the Enola Gay. Flying over the earth at 18,000 feet above the clouds, the pilots could see a shady blue carpet extend all the way to the horizon. Patches of it rose and bulged as the plane turned away from the hell it had brought to the surface of the earth. Suddenly whole rivers of red, as if from some inferno, lit up the ground and spread out through the gray. Fire burned through the clouds. On the ground rivulets of molten streaks, swelling through the dark mass—like stripes across the carpet—boiled up as if a floor had exploded. It was as if some god was watching the destruction of a world below. Did the airmen think of the firestorms of Tokyo and Dresden and Coventry as the skies became suffocated with human death and the smoke of their ashes? And carried civilized life with it?

After that, America, hemming and hawing, turned world leader.

* * *

On VJ night with the war finally ended, Jim was supposed to work, but he skipped out. He had no intention of missing this blowout. Saylor called and said he wanted to drive into Times Square, but by the time the foursome got together, the radio was reporting unholy amounts of traffic headed for midtown Manhattan.

So they opted for the Thatched Cottage, fifty miles from all the spontaneous kissing and skirt flying that appeared in the newsreels. Their suburban timidity kept them away from one of the greatest celebration in American history.

Bonnie always had her eye out for good times. Humor her and mercurial vibrations began to charge up through her personality. As on most nights, there was about her that devil-may-care attitude that illuminates the risk takers of the world and makes them special. Jim came to a new appreciation of her recklessness on this greatest night of the Twentieth Century. He watched her admiringly as she stood waving in the rumble seat of Saylor's Ford convertible steering a parade of cars east to Centerport.

Later, when they were drunk and cavorting along the extended beach at Bayville, Bonnie stripped to her underwear and jumped in the Sound. The others followed. Afterwards she and Jim lay on the beach and as the pair nestled together in a blanket, Jim's hands spread across Bonnie's lightly clad body. They lay there until Jim felt an overwhelming rush and eruption of feelings. Later he reached inside his briefs and discovered a mess of creamy sop. He had no idea what had happened to him.

* * *

The best two years of the Twentieth Century for New York were 1919 and the time between the summers of 1945 and 1946: the times after the great wars. There was such unbounded joy among those whose lives had been reprieved that the soul of the old republic was warmed by oceans of homecoming. The escape from death and the renewed prospect of love and the establishment of a family melted the fears and emotional rage of the long berserk war years. One could feel the dizziness that accompanied newly found peace; the actual realization of it softly rang in the mind like the sounds of faraway bells that pealed across the land. People radiated with heartfelt, uncontrollable happiness, punctuated by inexplicable torrents of weeping. There was such elation, imagining the creation of one's own children after life mates were reunited, unleashing suffocated emotions—except behind the dark windows where a gold star blazed on a square satin flag indicating death in action for a blown-apart son, the measure of sorrow deepened by the reality of eternal absence, causing racking pain during the awkward visits of returning friends.

The victory parades up Fifth Avenue sometimes included regiments just off transports wallowing along the river piers. Told to clean the mud of Europe off their boots and comb their hair, the troops trudged uptown, the heavy tread of thousands of men in rows, shoulder to shoulder—a show of massed manpower not witnessed along this same route since the spring of '19. This final parade was unlike the Paris celebration—the day after Hemingway "liberated the Ritz"—when G.I.s marched down the Champs Elysees in the morning, and some of those same troopers met death in the violet light of the late afternoon as they slogged north and east. But now it was over. All—irrevocably—over.

Some of the troops had been trucked in from their New Jersey debarkation depot, their division set to tramp alongside the skyscrapers of lower Broadway, entering Fifth Avenue at Madison Square, up through flag-drenched Midtown, brain center of America's new power, a power that rapidly discharged its men and machines into the local streets and small towns of the country, where the past could never be recaptured and the future was a misty amalgam of hopes and dreams and new beginnings. Optimism filled the air. People were talking about a new world. Everybody was going to take care of their sisters and brothers around the globe.

Jim's main concern continued to be his search for excitement. His personal creed was to enjoy the good times. A guy should keep going, fight off the bad eggs, and try not to be overwhelmed by authority. Have some laughs. He had turned into a pleasant though flawed guy, still ego-centered and if not compassionate and empathetic toward others, at least civil, despite his continuing arrogance that was based on a lack of achievements. He might have frozen at this level, settled out with this personality and matured in situ. He might have turned traditional, becoming a shopkeeper or a pharmacist. But as it turned out, his emotions and needs tore him away from the fabric of ordinary life.

Chapter 3
(1945 -1946)

When Jim Mahoney resumed attendance at Manhasset High School as a junior, he arrived on campus in Saylor's Ford. He was rejoining the collective pageant that included his former classmates. The '47 crop of students would prove to be a parade of high-steppers including Mardi who, this morning, was bunched between Saylor and Jim in the front seat, her tartan skirt at mid-thigh, her sweater filled with luscious orbs. When they pulled into the school's parking lot and walked under The Tree, his old gang was there—Frankie, Maryjan, Boots, Rocky, especially Bonnie, who ran into his arms out of sheer exuberance with the knowledge that her slim beau would be available for each and every play day.

Treats lay ahead for the pair. Bonnie and Jim along with Ben and Maryjan—the latter forming a new coupling—would lead one of the class cliques, the one associated with the senior class, the Alpha guys and ATA sorority princesses. Jim retained strong bonds with his old buddies, not only Saylor and Dumphy but also a half-dozen of the other brothers, especially Danny Devon and McKnight.

Jim would sub on the football team that fall and quarterback the Junior Varsity. Later, he and Bonnie would be nominated for the title of the junior class's regal couple but lose to the other clique—classmates with their own social club, one invested with a more casual style and a greater number of voters. In the spring, he would be a utility infielder. This was to be a liberating year.

They do come along. Those periods in everyone's life when entire seasons go well, when good fortune prevails and friends remain loyal and good times pop up in every direction. Such was Jim's junior year. It was a comfortable time. He would never again wish to be on top or bottom, but prefer engagement at a safe middle level. He would never lead but always manage to inform the leadership. His values and views would not be vital but usually essential to a consensus. He would filter most of the ideas, dreams and passions that flowed through his time but never construct solutions that sluiced the river of wind, nor bend it or force destiny to break his way. His life was assigned to the time between modernism and post-modernism—the latter a period of wars and existential atomic grief. He would remain historically friendly toward modernism and skeptical of post-modernism, setting his sails broadside to those latter disruptive winds and set some distance from the storm's leading edge. Some people like him are designed to be members of the cadre, one of the sloggers; he would come to realize his place in the next six to eight years. For now he couldn't care less. He was already on top of the world.

It was altogether Jim Mahoney's fault that his roller-coaster existence could plummet and ascend along steep gradients. He gauged that the time was coming when he would have to lay down a less stressful track, one more straight, level and true. Sixteen going on seventeen gave him the oxygenation to expand his best traits while his lesser ones, for a time, remained in the shadows, nevertheless breathing heavily. Aiding his rising spirits was the fact that the war was over and perhaps he would evade combat after all. During this winter of '45 and into '46 a period of halcyon brightness developed. Like 1919, these were times of pan-national joy.

What supported Jim's well-being was his social compact with Bonnie, even though they were sexually frustrated to the point of physical illness. Most Americans, except those still suffering the after-effects of war, were plum happy. Optimism spread through the nation and everyone was talking about a world of peace and harmony. Indeed, among the survivors of Western Civilization, it was a period of inescapable joy that ensued when the world's soldiers and sailors came home, some in the U.K. for the first time in five years, many to find the infants they left behind transformed into leggy school children. The future for almost everyone evoked a dream field where people could plant their hopes and aspirations without the dread of war's devastation hovering over them.

This was one of Jim's best years ever, squashed as it was between a boring year at military school and the coming disasters of his senior year.

At sixteen, his ego bloomed into full flower after his welcome back to school. His first task was to establish himself securely as quarterback on the junior varsity, an effort that he accomplished straightaway. His Alpha brothers, now seniors, set the social and sports pace for the school and he enjoyed the benefits of their influence. With a return to normalcy, and with gasoline once again easier to acquire, the school parking lot was filled with cars previously owned by his local war heroes. Other Chevy and Ford jalopies that had been put up in storage for the duration came down off their blocks.

Jim‘s closeness with Bonnie was renewed to the chagrin of her mother, who was, nevertheless, becoming less aggressive against her strong-willed daughter. The couple's personalities, their confidence, their assuredness ballooned into teenage euphoria. Saylor and Boots would be their constant weekend companions, and Ben and Maryjan joined the quartet in their drinking and dancing escapades. They regularly toured the North Shore roadhouses.

Bonnie's good looks had already been noted by one of the advertising and publicity people commuting to New York, who rewarded her beauty by introducing her to a modeling agency. She was soon appearing in teen magazines and catalogs and earning her own commissions that she promptly spent at Lord & Taylor. Those purchases made her all the more attractive when she paraded out with Jim in an assortment of cocktail dresses, some lace-topped, others in colorful satin.

At home, his old man got involved in Jim's football activities in much the same way that Pappy had followed Matt's exploits on the gridiron, though Jim wasn't half the ballplayer Matt was. Their mother, Gracie, at the same time, was turning her attention from bundling war stuffs for the troops to more peaceful community efforts. There was the North Shore Hospital to be built, a Community Chest Fund to be managed and the Plandome Women's' Club in need of programs favoring philanthropic action. Meanwhile Jim watched his grades and minded his books. At home, Francy was turning into a beautiful, frisky blond child. When the family favorite had her portrait painted by a well-known artist, the picture took a central place above the fireplace. Soon, Matt would be home from the Army Air Corps and getting married.

Though busy directing the junior varsity football team, quarterback Jim was pleased when he got to play some varsity minutes in front of the Saturday afternoon crowds, allowing him to command the play of his tough-skinned fraternity brothers—senior starters Nick, Stu, McKnight, Red, Dumphy, the Gremlin and Mitch. His JV team included a few third-string seniors, guys with an abundance of team spirit that plugged along, willing to play out of the spotlight on Wednesday afternoons and without accolades, cheerleaders or a band.

One of these less bulky seniors was Bob Gooden. What he wasn't able to achieve physically on the sports field, Gooden, with wit and brains, had learned to use to excel in a larger creative arena. His talent more than compensated for his lack of athletic agility. Early in the school year, he had written and directed a radio play performed at a school assembly about the uber-control of adults over the young, a fidgety topic not irrelevant to the fact that their mature overseers had sent a half-million young American warriors to their death. The young had begun to question blind obedience.

Gooden had hit a raw nerve with his radio play—a takeoff on a series of broadcasts during the war by Norman Corwin. With peace, the world's population sought solutions that would arrest wars of the future. Countries were taking pains to legitimize the United Nations. Ideas about one-worldliness were spreading over the globe as an antidote to the destructive force of nationalism. Plans were even under way to produce a single language for all mankind. The Bomb had shrunk an already wobbly world to a frightened blob. Gooden seized on these developments to question past priorities.

Ever since their days in the Boy Scouts, Gooden liked to needle Jim, who was an easy target for the bright young man. One day they were the last ones to leave the locker room. Perhaps because he remembered Gooden at the Scout bonfire rallies in the woods, Jim began singing a campfire song

I ain't a'gonna grieve my Lord no more

I ain't a'gonna grieve my Lord no more

Gooden joined in and they sang

Oh, you can't get to heaven on roller skates
You'll skate right by Saint Peter's gates
I ain't a'gonna grieve my Lord no more

"Song sounds like you, Mahoney. Skating right by all the important stuff in life."

"Stuff it, pal."

"You ought to quit loafing around," Gooden pursued. "High school goes by fast. It's not the classes that are important. But what you're supposed to be preparing for."

Jim didn't really want to hear a lecture. He wanted the pleasures of here and now.

"You think being popular is the cat's ass?" Gooden asked Jim.

"Better than the alternative," Jim said, meant as a stab. "Helps in the female department."

"Think the fast lane is hot stuff? Remember all that craziness in the Twenties? Flappers and gin slings and bearskin coats? All fads. Never involved more than ten percent of people anyway. Most just plod along from home to job to church."

"But who's having the fun? Not the church warden."

"Fun?" Gooden said, "You want to live your life in an amusement park, go ahead. Real life doesn't happen on the boardwalk. You'll be surprised to know there's life after high school."

"Why wait for the fun later? Enjoy some of it now."

"That's OK, but you better learn to vary your diet."

Jim had no intention of following Gooden's advice.

* * *

Gooden's name came up late in the year in a highly publicized way. He had attached himself to a couple who lived in Manhasset's media-saturated community, celebrities who were big personalities in Manhattan and important commentators on the American radio scene. Their program was aired daily nationally. Recognizing Bob's writing abilities, the couple had promoted him to cub reporter status after a lengthy internship. Gooden hatched a big news story on his own that fall, one involving the national coal strike that pitted the administration against a bull-headed labor leader, John L. Lewis.

Lewis had called thousands of coal miners out of the mines and the prospects for a cold winter sent shivers up politicians' backs, especially that of Harry S. Truman. But Lewis had barricaded himself at home and wouldn't talk to anyone. Gooden traveled to Lewis' hometown, obtained a job in the neighborhood as a grocery delivery boy, acquired access and confronted Lewis in his own kitchen. There and then he popped the question as to when the strike will end—and doesn't Lewis tell him

The next day, across the country, the headlines read: COAL STRIKE ENDS. BOY REPORTER SCOOPS NATION'S PRESS.

But Gooden's deeds didn't impress Jim. Just another story with no relation or meaning to his crowd. What good did it do for his football teammate? It wouldn't get him an ATA girl. They were the princesses of the realm and the real treasures. In a group photograph near Christmas, wearing their formal satins and silks, the sorority girls' faces gleamed. Their message: We're shiny ready for the social sacraments of college, courtship and marriage.

* * *

This year's holiday job, though different from the liquor dispersion job two years before, nevertheless entailed deliveries to Manhattan. In mid-December, crews from nearby high schools were recruited to work in Wantagh near the ocean at a huge floral operation, the company that dominated the metropolitan poinsettia market. Drudges were expected to work for fifteen or more hours a day for a week. It was good money and Jim jumped at the chance to participate. Workers were housed in wooden shacks knocked together for immigrant workers that harvested summer crops. A fat-bellied stove in the middle of his bunkhouse was surrounded by double-decker ledges without mattresses allowing sixteen guys to sleep together around a roaring fire. Workers were well-advised to bring extra blankets, though many guys slept in their clothes, too exhausted and too cold to undress, and as likely as not to be awakened in the middle of the night to process orders.

The glass city of greenhouses covered acres. These crystal palaces glowed a holiday red. Thousands of poinsettia plants were loaded into fleets of trucks that distributed the flaming red displays to flower shops around New York. Jim's job was to accompany the drivers who were responsible for negotiating the deliveries. Many of the stops were made in the dark of a December evening.

Jim, familiar with a darkened wartime New York, now had an opportunity to observe the city throw off its gloomy camouflage and come dancing into the postwar years. Broadway's lights were on again as well as the lanterns that pierced the night on top of the tall buildings. The Empire State Building sparkled with light again as did the Chrysler Building. What he didn't visualize was the opening round of events that brought on the New York Renaissance. He didn't know about the gallery openings for Pollock and de Kooning. He couldn't measure the effect of e. e. cummings, or Dr, Williams or the part-time American, Auden, and the other New York bards. He hadn't heard Barber's *First Essay* or Hanson's new symphony. Nor read Camus and Sartre. Chances were, he never would.

What he did notice was that the city seemed livelier. The pace had picked up. All the old places were being refurbished. Good food was available again in restaurants. One of New York's greatest parties was about to begin. And Jim Mahoney was totally unaware that he didn't have a seat at the table.

* * *

This year marked the last of Vivien's semi-formal Christmas parties; she was due to graduate and wander off to college in the fall. As the event neared, Jim was pleased to have been re-invited to the affair along with Bonnie. Given the fact that the invitation was a redemption of sorts, a reasonable person would have thought that the pugilistic freshman, who had caused such a ruckus two years before would not have so willingly agreed to the latest attempt to dent Mrs. Applegate's notion of propriety.

Jim always enjoyed the ritual of taking a shower and dressing up prior to a party, musing on the expectation of good times. As he showered, he wondered if this was how it felt to be really happy.

The night of the party, a bitterly cold winter wind was blowing. If Mr. Applegate had closely observed the arrival of the Alpha males, he might have noticed small square forms bulging from their jackets. As the party warmed up—a cocktail pianist played this year—the fraternity boys found their way to the upstairs bathroom off the bedroom where guests' coats overwhelmed the parents' bed. One by one, the boys deposited the contents of the containers stored in their pockets. Pounds of a red gelatinous material were dumped into the tub of the adjoining bathroom. The prank's manager, Dumphy, bent down and opened the faucet. He next opened the windows to allow the frozen air to congeal the contents of the bathtub into the world's largest batch of Jello. Before it solidified, he poured in a bottle of gin to create a punch. For the rest of the evening there was a commotion on the second story as the young bucks, some accompanied by their does, slurped jellied hooch.

Mrs. Applegate, ever on the lookout for couples ascending to the second floor, eventually investigated but neglected to inspect the bathroom. Feeling a draft however, she did raise the thermostat; the resulting heat caused the imbibers' faces to flush a rosy color that matched the punch.

* * *

This first winter and spring after the war were exuberant times. G.Is turned in their helmets for sporty fedoras and went out seeking work. Churches and dressmakers were busy with weddings; an entire generation seemed headed to the altar in '46, including Matt. The floral business was booming as was housing. Bill Levitt, from his office in Manhasset, where he had built the four Strathmore sections in town during the Thirties, announced the development of Levittown, the precursor and model for a suburban explosion that spread across the nation and totally changed the landscape of the country. The old city neighborhoods began to die. There was to be a new social establishment that didn't include ethnic separateness. The new America was to be churned-up and cross-pollinated.

Within ten years, the Irish had deserted the boroughs and moved out on the Island, to Jersey or Westchester. Italians and Jews would follow. Church and synagogue construction was as prevalent as the new malls and schools that sprang up everywhere on the old potato fields. The joke, as the land was gobbled up for development, was: *Too bad my father wasn't a dirt-poor Polish farmer from Hicksville. Now I'd be rich.*

As the economic boom materialized, high school kids began to lose the attention paid them during the war.

* * *

Jim was downtown one warm day during spring break when he bumped into Glober and Reagan, two of the Alpha guys with whom he seldom cavorted. Taking advantage of the fair weather, the pair announced that they were driving to Huntington and wondered if Jim wanted to tag along. Still naïve, Jim sensed that they were setting him up for some mischief.

"Maybe we can get in a little exercise," said Reagan.

"Yeah. Stretch our muscles," said Glober, laughing at his own insinuation.

The drive took them due east on Northern Boulevard through the estates where royal studs raised their aristocratic heads at the passing car and snuffled at the trio.

"Why don't we stop and see Gloria while we're here," Reagan said when they entered town.

"Good idea," said Glober. "Wonder if she's wearing shorts on a day like this?"

Indeed she was and barefoot. Slim and attractive, she greeted them saucily, "Who do we have here?" indicating Jim.

"Fresh meat."

"We might need reinforcements," she said.

"Not that much time," Glober said. "Gotta get back."

"Then we better get busy."

They all sat down in the living room, and Gloria distributed some cola. Shortly, she excused herself, and not long after, Reagan left too. Jim paid no attention and chatted with Glober, who seemed distracted. For a half hour, they waited for Reagan to re-appear. Soon thereafter, it was Glober who was gone.

Finally all three guys were back in the living room. Reagan said to Jim, "You up for a visit?"

"We're going somewhere else?"

That set the other guys laughing.

Gloria rejoined them, slightly flushed, and sat on the edge of an upholstered chair, her leggy posture draping through their imaginations.

The drive back was exuberant.

Jim was the butt of Alpha jokes all spring.

* * *

Late in the school year, Jim stood for election for one of the student leadership posts for his senior year, offering him an opportunity to show off the brio that he had been accumulating during the last two terms. Winning the honor set in place a capstone that anchored him as one of the leaders on campus. His popularity actually translated into achievement. One of the returning G.I. teachers would be his leadership advisor.

* * *

At the beach in May, fluffy female swimsuits disguised virginal breasts. To counter postwar drab, the Garment District scattered the colors of the tropics on women's fabrics, as if to lighten up the world after the dull uniforms prevalent during the war. The colors and patterns were the ugliest since Dada was in flower, but no amount of carnival collage could obscure the attractiveness of these seaside beauties—Alva, Pat, Melissa, Bonnie, Vivien, Mardi, Maryjan, imperious Boots.

The guys looked healthy following their recent lacrosse and baseball seasons. They featured springtime coloring—arms, necks, faces were tan—embroidered over white torsos that had been covered by their sports' outfits. It was the last roundup of the founding Alpha members at Jones Beach; Dumphy was spreading his special brand of quiet cheer, Stu who navigated life's balance buoyed by a keel of iron, Glober with the slyness of a fox, Saylor with his upwind view of the world.

They lounged beside the ocean, stretched out in a circle on the light brown sand as the white-capped waves thumped along the barrier beach. A dune-wide barrier beach separated them from their island-bound towns, which were themselves divided from the mainland. They were doubly distanced from care and responsibility—thirty or forty Alphas and ATA girls, beautiful to-look-at youths, on their last beach party together, reminiscing about the past, searching for the way forward. Not Jim, of course, immersed in today. The others had personally grown wiser owing to their relationships, rising to maturity on the spirit of their friends.

They would remember days like this for the rest of their lives, bright and warm, lazy and sexy and filled with laughter and good times. Remembering the trips back and forth to the cars, struggling in the deep sand over the dunes, unloading the food and beer and beach gear. Slapping into the waves, diving through the green water and coming up from under to witness a wide blue sky, and slip down again under the white force of the sea.

They stayed long past a shore dinner into the evening, on into the night to watch a moon rise before them out of the ocean. Coupled now all night, entangled for hours in each other's arms they watched the spreading majesty of the dawn seeping over the waves. Then the seniors all went their separate ways and never gathered again in such force, though there were a few reunions at weddings, and late in life when the decades ran fast, when they could hardly recognize each other, a few would come together and recall the moon and the days that their young bodies stretched on the sand. In the morning before they left, a few swam.

"Sunrise Serenade" was one of the hundreds of swing songs they had sung. Now, crashing into the surf and sun, they heard it for the last time.

* * *

In June, Ben told Jim that he was going to spend the summer on one of his grandfather's boats. The elderly seafarer owned a fleet of a half-dozen cargo ships that were seaworthy in a structurally novel way. Most cargo that arrived in New York was unloaded and then transferred to smaller boats for delivery up and down the coast, or transferred to ships going upriver, in some cases across the Erie Canal into the Great Lakes. Ben's grandfather had designed a flat-bottom ship that could pick up goods in Newport News, cruise up the Atlantic coast to New York, work its way up the Hudson, actually fit in the canal locks and go into the lakes beyond without ever shifting cargo. The design had protected the family's interest for generations.

Ben asked Jim to join him as a working crewmember for the summer on one of the boats and Jim agreed to go to sea with his buddy. After school let out, they applied for and were granted seaman's papers, eventually traveling to New York, duffle bags filled with necessities. For some odd, inexplicable reason, Jim also included a copy of *War and Peace* from his mother's library shelf.

The good ship *Alden* was only as long as one of the locks of the Erie Canal. That allowed the narrow and flat-bottomed boat to negotiate tight quarters. Captain Schallenberg, a Swiss perfectionist, who ran a tight ship, greeted them. He handed the pair off to the first mate, Jake, a gruff-looking conciliator who had learned to adjust to the style of the strict skipper. Ben and Jim deposited their belongings in a metal locker adjoining three double bunks below the waterline where they and some of the crewmembers would spend the summer in close and humid quarters.

Both Ben and Jim were assigned to the bowels of the ship as wipers. The chief of the engine room was an ebullient, pipe-smoking Norwegian, friendly and accommodating. He welcomed them, set their shifts—four hours on, eight hours off—and planned it so they would each work with a more experienced hand for tutelage. The new pair was briefed on the quality of different oils used to keep the big shaft rotating and shown the points of entry into the huge, noisy engine. Now that they were underway, the engine began to agitate the walls of the hull and make a noise so loud that voices could not travel more than a few feet down below. They slipped out of New York harbor past the lady with the light, out onto the sea and headed south toward Norfolk.

It took the new hands a couple days to adjust to their night watches, but they were soon feeling comfortable enough to interact with the other seamen and to enjoy their company and the offerings of the small, feisty cook. He had been allowed to bring along his wife on summer trips and her presence greatly improved the quality of their meals. They were a close and loving couple. Cook would confide to the boys, "We used to do it all night. Now it takes us all night to do it."

During the daytime when their shifts didn't collide, Ben and Jim sat on deck and gossiped about their new jobs.

"That Spanish guy is tough," Ben said, talking about one of the other wipers. "I don't think I'm going to mess with him."

"I saw him shooting craps with a guy down below."

"I wouldn't bet against him. He carries a knife."

"That Jake guy, the mate, he seems friendly."

"Yeah. Likes buddying up with the crew."

"We got the best boss, I think."

"Yeah, old Gus is OK. Knows that engine inside out."

After a short run down the coasts of Jersey, Delaware and Maryland, they turned into Virginia waters at the mouth of the Chesapeake and arrived at the Norfolk dockyards. During the day's layover as the hold was emptied of steel rods and replaced by lumber, the engine room was cleaned and polished and the crew took up the steel grating and swabbed the metal under-flooring where oil had been spilled by the new wipers.

Then Jake the mate, along with Gus, the engine room boss and the Spanish kid, Francis, went ashore, taking Jim with them to swirl down a few brews.

"Haven't been here for a while," said Gus, "but I spent a lot of time during the war, coming in and out of Newport News."

The mate added, "Me too. Lots of waterfront dives, filled to the rafters back then. Crawled into the Roads once on a wounded duck. Listing all the way from the Mediterranean. Came across the Atlantic standing on a short leg, scared shitless of Nazi subs."

"You guys crazy to fight in the war. I hid out in the Islands."

"That's why we're getting up a petition to deport you."

"You gonna have to catch me," said Francis, patting his knife.

Jim sat silent, innocent of worldly experience, naïve about real life, absorbing the dynamics of work life.

After a couple weeks at sea, Ben was promoted out of the engine room to the wheelhouse, perhaps with the understanding that, as one of the family, he might benefit from testing as many elements of seafaring as possible, so that he might utilize this knowledge in making a career decision to make sailing his life's work. Ben took to learning the charts and points of navigation.

Jim, coming up on deck after four hours with the noise of the throbbing engines in his head, would inhale the clean sea air. Looking up, he would see Ben standing straight as a rod behind the wheel, eyes concentrated on some distant point, cowlick waving over his wide brow. Jim would have an opportunity to see Ben in many guises, but the one he remembered best was the picture of the tall, big-boned seventeen-year-old steering the family vessel.

On one trip, the *Alden* was hauling bluestone from New Haven to Bayonne. As they pulled into New York Harbor at dawn and wended their way through the Jersey Channel, they were welcomed into port with two weeks pay. Jim fingered the folded sixty dollars housed in a small brown envelope that listed his name, his Social Security contribution, union dues and residual amount. The captain intended to hold a skeleton crew on board until later in the day, when, after off-loading, they would make the short trip to the West Side docks on the Hudson River to pick up new cargo. Berthing there would mean another day of loading when all hands would be eligible for shore leave. The older, more privileged, members of the crew quickly disappeared for the weekend. Even Ben got permission to leave early. The cook and his wife shut down their ovens and scampered away for ports unknown, carrying their laundry with them. That evening, after the ship traveled back across the harbor and circled into a dock near 14th Street, the captain passed around script to the remaining crew, the chits redeemable at local taverns and coffee shops.

Jim, Francis and Jake the mate disembarked for Moran's, a waterfront Irish pub that featured seafood and Celtic music. It was a sturdy brick-lined eatery; the kitchen still occupied a place near the entrance opposite the bar—a reminder of its free lunch and speakeasy past.

Francis was feeling exuberant, "Think I'll get uptown and find myself a queen. Maybe even catch a little action with my bones," he said, patting his hip pocket where he kept his dice.

Jake told him, "Just keep that other thing in your pants," referring to the knife Francis was always brandishing.

"No worry. Nobody's going to mess with me. I'm feeling too lucky," and proceeded to toss off a half-dozen glasses of Rhinebeck.

Content and filled with beer, they headed back to the ship where Gus, supervising the generator, awaited their return

"Let's shoot craps," Francis said, hoping to exploit the cash-flush crew.

"Sure," said Jake. "You in, Gus?"

"Why not?"

"Kid gonna play?"

Jim, one of the more stalwart of the gambling Alphas in Danny Devon's basement back home, knew the rudiments of play.

"Roll 'em," he replied.

They played outdoors on deck, using the bulkhead as a backboard. They rolled to see who would go first.

Jim won, took the dice in his hands, laid down three bucks like everybody else, and threw the cubes sharply against the steel plates in imitation of the others. Down tumbled a five and a two.

"Bingo."

"Beginner's luck."

Jim scooped up the money and shot again. He cast an eight, and after re-rolling a couple times, he hit his number.

On his third attempt, he bounced "snake eyes." And passed the dice to Gus.

"I've got a family so I can only lose too much," prefaced the Engine Room Chief, as good as predicting his outcome. Domestic felicities didn't prevent him from throwing "box cars."

When Francis' turn came, he whipped the dice around like he was a shark in blue jeans. But his luck was elsewhere tonight.

They played for twenty minutes and in that time, Jim's fortune held. He was up twenty dollars and they were all talking about the "lucky kid." Jim, never having been lucky at anything in his whole life, was as amazed as his fellow crapshooters.

Gus dropped out as Jim accumulated more winnings. Then Jake too abandoned the game. Francis became highly agitated and, because he had a nefarious reputation, Gus and Jake stayed to watch over the young wiper, who continued to win.

In the end, Francis lost his entire paycheck and Jim was up over a hundred dollars, a sum he had never before had to manage. There were consequences, of course, when the captain returned on Sunday. Some crewmembers would have to plug the hole in the schedule because Francis had disappeared the night he lost after rattling Jim's door, which the young wiper had been warned to lock.

Jim, coming off the morning watch the next day, stood at the rail of the *Alden*, his eyes ricocheting around, trying to capture the waterside bustle of a way-west Greenwich Village morning. He was totally unaware that he was viewing the fringes of America's creative center. Open eyes that did not see. He stretched, shaking off the night and the dark, smelly engine room. The docked ship would stay in port until Sunday, allowing the remainder of the crew an 18-hour break while the hold was refilled. First Mate Jake, who would supervise the loading, came up behind him.

"We're the only ones left aboard. You're looking pretty grungy. Want to take a shower in my cabin?"

Grateful, Jim agreed and went below to gather up a fresh outfit. Entering the mate's cabin for the first time, Jim was impressed by its size and furnishings.

"Right in here," Jake said.

Jim stripped and as he did, he had the feeling that Jake was watching him.

"Here, let me help you soap up."

Jim, flustered, didn't know what to say, as he turned on the water and felt the mate's hands move across his back. Jim, uncomfortable, quickly rinsed and turned off the shower.

"Let me help you towel off."

Jim knew that the words fag and homo meant effeminate, but had no idea what the terms implied. All he knew was that a guy with glittering eyes was toweling him off.

"Why don't you stay aboard this weekend instead of going home? We'd have the ship all to ourselves."

"No, I've got to see my girl," Jim said, the words tumbling out quickly, and he bolted off the ship as fast as he could.

"What a creep," Jim said as he stepped off toward the Eighth Avenue Subway.

An hour later, Jim was home. Bonnie, busy modeling for Christmas catalogs and in company with her mother, had chosen to skip July at the lake allowing the young couple to re-connect in Manhasset. When he arrived at her place in Flower Hill, she looked positively edible in shorts and a loose-fitting top.

"How's my sailor?"

"Missing you."

Bonnie opened a conversation that she knew would be divisive, "You might as well know. Mom is insisting that I date other guys. She's almost shopping me around."

Jim, who tended to go dark when confronted with bad news, waited for her to continue. Not her usual self, Bonnie was fidgety.

"Truth is, I've been out with a couple guys—one from Wesleyan and another from King's Point."

"Where does that leave us?" he asked, fumbling for clarity.

"Nothing changes," Bonnie said, a hesitation in her voice.

They agreed to meet later. As he was leaving, Mrs. Cassidy was cool. The door was barely closed when she said to Bonnie, "He smells like the inside of an oil drum."

"The old bat probably doesn't think I'm good enough for her," Jim thought, as he walked away.

They went bar-hopping with Ben and Maryjan in Port Washington and around nine, headed for a beach. With blankets slung over the guys' shoulders, each couple headed for a deserted place in the sand. Bonnie and Jim's passion was, as always, at fever pitch, and he remained confident that they belonged together.

The two novice sailors dropped off their dates and traveled back into the city on the milk train; the *Alden's* crew was due back on board by 2:00a.m. Loading was completed by dawn, and after stepping off to buy a newspaper, Jim and Ben sat on deck after breakfast reading as the engines came to life and the ship steered north en route to the boys' first trip through the Erie Canal. Manhattan's tall structures, many with lanterns on top that for generations had shone out to sea to guide seaman like them home, appeared formidable viewed from the river's waterline. The canyons between the buildings winked by in progression, sun shot by the morning beams, alleys of golden light. The Palisades that rose over the river on the Jersey side fell away as the northern suburbs arose onshore and later hills came into view along both sides of the river. They slipped past the narrow channel at West Point.

Ben's eyes wandered over the commercial ads in the paper until he came to an offering by the U.S Army. The next morning, the announcement read, there was to be an auction of wartime landing craft at one of the Manhattan armories.

"Look at this," he said. "They're selling off surplus LSTs. Probably for a song."

"Wouldn't it be great to have one of those babies to tool around Manhasset Bay?"

Confident in their seamanship based on their summer experience, they overestimated their ability to operate watercraft.

"What if we could get one, fix it up over the winter, and run tours next summer in the harbor? We could help pay for college."

"We could hold parties at night and putz around the Sound."

Their enthusiasm escalated on each other's bravado as the notion that they could engineer such a feat took hold. Their imaginations spread over the water like oil.

"Let's see if we can get one cheap."

"Only one problem. The auction's tomorrow morning and we're going to be on the Erie Canal."

"Maybe my dad and brother could go and bid for us," Ben said.

"Do you think they would?"

"Why not? But how do we tell them?"

Jim said, "What if I jump ship, swim to shore, and send them a telegram. Then I could hook up with you again in Troy—that's where we're docking tonight, right? But you'd have to stand my watch as well as your own."

"We're already short-handed."

"I'd be able to catch up with you by midnight."

"Do you have enough money?"

"Still have a twenty left." He had left his dice winnings home with his step-dad.

Once they agreed to the outlandish idea, the time came to execute. Jim, supremely confident in his swimming abilities, was wearing a pair of jeans and a tee shirt. He stuffed his oily loafers, one in each hip pocket.

Ben said, "The Captain's gonna be mad at me."

"I'll be back on board before he knows I'm gone."

With that, Jim jumped over the rail into the Hudson, a half-mile or more from the western shore. The dive was longer than he figured and was surprised by the pain when his head smacked into the water. He turned to watch the ship surging away and waved to Ben. Then he began swimming.

He underestimated the strength of the river. He was unaware that there were currents and that the most powerful force on earth was stirring beneath him. The water was carrying him and he was having trouble making progress.

Back on the *Alden*, there was commotion attending Jim's departure, as crewmembers watched the swimmer struggle in the strong flow. This soon reached the ears of the Captain. He was infuriated and hollered at Ben, not caring if he was owner's grandson. He picked up his binoculars to scan Jim's progress. Then the ship rounded a bend and the ship was out of sight. As a caution, the Captain called the Coast Guard and informed them of the problem. By the time the Coast Guard arrived on the scene, they found no swimmer, so guardsmen began dragging the river.

But Jim's swimming ability had carried him ashore; though he looked more aquatic than human by the time he touched land. He was physically exhausted from his efforts and staggered out of the river, collapsed and finally crawled up the rock and sand strand. He was breathing hard, and for twenty minutes he lay there testing the strength left in his body. He stood up and squished into his loafers and walked up to the road, still soaking wet, and began hitchhiking north. A farmer stopped and let him sit in the bed of his pick-up. In Kingston, Jim stopped and sent a telegram describing their wild-eyed scheme to Ben's family and then continued his journey north.

He arrived in Albany late in the afternoon and headed toward the river. He thought he might negotiate a ride with a local boater who could run him out on the river where he might be able to hail the ship. Ben, who had been apprised to watch out for him, might be able to throw him a line so he could be back on board before sunset. At one of the docks Jim found a kid with a boat and paid him to row out into the Hudson and wait for the *Alden* to come around the bend. They waited a half hour and here she comes. There was still enough light to execute a lariat toss, so Jim once more jumped into the river, almost upsetting the rowboat as he leapt out. He and the kid, who was infuriated by Jim's awkward dive, began yelling and waving their arms. Jim swam out into the channel, as the *Alden*, looking big as a castle, came steaming toward him. The fuss and hollering attracted Ben's attention on deck and he scooped up a long line and heaved it toward his flailing buddy. Jim thrashed through the water toward the rope but watched as it squiggled past him just out of reach. Perhaps it was for the best. Jim only later understood he was fortunate to have missed the snatch when he considered the alternative, being pulled into the maw of the engine he had been cleaning all summer, and being mashed up by the ship's propeller.

Back into the swamped rowboat Jim climbed; the kid cursed him all the way, as the pair saw the *Alden* chug north toward its berth in Troy. Sopping wet again, and without benefit of sunshine to dry him off, Jim, once ashore, got something to eat and experienced a cold and uncomfortable ride on an air-conditioned bus to Albany's twin city. He shivered his way across the river, watching night descend from his vantage in the rear seat, where he left his watermark on the upholstered cushion. Alighting near the dock area, he spent the next few hours searching for his vessel. He climbed up and over a dozen fences, trespassed onto innumerable shipyards without any success, waking a half-dozen watchdogs. He finally gave up around ten. Now out of money, he decided to take a train home, but first had to find a Western Union telegraph office, where he sat and waited for a reply, still moist from his swim and slightly randy. Already alerted to the possibility of a drowned step-son, Pappy sent along some cash, which allowed Jim to board the milk train to Manhattan. He arrived around dawn and made his way home on the LIRR.

"A tour boat! You guys are a couple whack-a-doodles," was his old man's comment later in the day.

* * *

Once home, Jim needed a job. He applied for and was hired to work in a lumberyard located in the Valley at the head of Manhasset Bay that served the Cullem Brothers, a construction company now concentrating their efforts in Plandome. New homes were sprouting up in the old sandpit where Jim and his grade school buddies fought war games and held BB gun fights when they were kids, near a natural phenomenon called the Big Rock, a glacial boulder that had rolled south during the Ice Age. The rock had been a gift of the play gods where youngsters could expand their imaginations by acting out intergalactic dramas on the craggy, thirty-foot-high outcropping.

The management people at the construction company took a shine to the ex-sailor, and in quick order, Jim was asked to keep the model home spruced up and to mow the lawn. Then the boss and general manager pulled him out of the mill and put him to work on the houses under construction where he became a carpenter's assistant. Finally, they invited him to dress up on the weekends and show prospective homebuyers around the property even though a wily English salesman kept absconding with Jim's best prospects. As the favored young apprentice, he was soon putting in long, profitable daily hours.

His workload bit into the time he spent with Bonnie, and one weekend night when he was free, she informed him that she had a date with some local college guy. Jim was furious and when he refused to call her, he became alarmed when she didn't try to reach him to patch things up. Maryjan managed to negotiate a truce between the pair and the foursome, now that the summer was ending and Ben was home again, resumed their bar-hopping. Something had been lost in the interchange, mainly because Bonnie's college admirers were more exotic than homeboy Jim. Based on her experiences modeling in New York, she had become convinced that raising her level of sophistication should be her new ambition. One night, when they turned toward the beaches for their normal midnight necking sessions, Bonnie rationed her expression of feelings and resisted surrendering to his advances. The light that burned between them was losing its radiance. Their romance, three-year-old, was guttering.

The final break came soon afterwards. The soon-to-be seniors had been to a movie downtown and stopped by the Greek's for a soda following the film. Talking about the forthcoming football season, Bonnie kidded Ben and Jim.

"I hear the other teams in the league are supposed to be good this year, especially Port. Maybe the two of you should save yourselves some embarrassment and go out for soccer instead."

With that, Jim, perhaps partly due to his vulnerability and motivated by her dating spree, tapped Bonnie on the cheek. The next day that tap had turned into a slap in public and Bonnie ended their entanglement, much to the delight of her mother and a raft of other girls that were happy to see Jim back on the open market, girls who had been hoping for a collapse in the couples' alliance.

Jim was crestfallen. She had helped prop up his confidence for years and now she was gone. He spent a couple of bad days as August retreated into the past. Out of sorts, he quickly dated some of his longtime admirers and tried snuggling with all of them without any of the excitement he had shared with Bonnie. Increasingly, he felt frustrated. He took on some meanness that corroded his "hale fellow" image.

He continued to work for Cullem Brothers and was soon confronted by one of those conundrums that require instantaneous decision-making. Wearing jeans and a sweatshirt, Jim, on an evening prior to the Labor Day weekend, after working all day installing windows in the eye-sockets of the houses under construction, returned to the model home after dinner and opened the garage door where the lawn mower was stored. Garden tools were housed there along with tons of bags of grass-growing nourishment. Some of the houses in the development were already occupied and the new residents were outdoors, spending an inordinate number of hours trying to encourage grass to grow on their thinly planted sand patches. One of the new residents came over to talk to Jim in the fading evening light after he had finished tending the lawn and was sweeping out the model home.

"I've come over to see of you could bring me one of those bags of Gro-Lawn you've got stored in the garage."

Presuming his boss had approved the action, Jim said, "OK. I'll bring it over when I've finished here."

Ten minutes later, Jim picked up one of the 50-pound sacks and carried it toward the new resident's house.

Out came the guy looking flushed. "I meant for you to bring it after dark," he said, glaring down the street where some of his neighbors were witnessing the interchange.

Jim didn't understand the negative tone in the man's voice. He shunted the bag into the man's arms. During the transaction, the guy handed him a five-dollar bill. Suddenly the deal became clear to Jim. He was being paid off for trading away company property. He hesitated but took the money. The negotiation was not unnoticed by the other new residents, who reported the incident to Jim's boss, who promptly told him there would be no more work for him. Jim never connected the bribe to the dismissal. He merely lugged on toward his senior year.

* * *

Sexually active girls suffered the branding inflicted on them by the coarse language of their peers, notably as hot numbers, perhaps as girls "who went the limit," and sometimes totally misidentified as "nymphomaniacs." There were some tarts around, wearing push-up bras and short shorts with flesh flowing midriffs under knotted man-tailored shirts that pocketed their breasts. Jim had tried to saddle onto a few of these sirens along the way but was always rebuffed as someone with big eyes and no technique. Males didn't suffer the same social ostracism as the women. Guys who screwed around a lot were celebrated as bounders

In Manhasset, there were a few girls who qualified as man-eaters; in Port Washington, there were several more, including a full-bodied wench named Doris. No guy would ever admit that he dated her, but rendezvous had often been arranged for assignations in the back seats of cars cleared of sports gear and rough edges. On warm nights, removable back seats often served a useful purpose. Doris was spared the hard looks that sometimes accompanied lusty girls. She was demure-eyed and cute, with a blooming body that was soft and ripe and inviting.

In between the time that Jim lost Bonnie and school started, he was dating a different girl every night. One afternoon he was walking around uptown. In his rage to conquer the whole of girlhood, he bumped into Doris just emerging from the railroad station for a sexual reconnaissance tour of her neighboring town. Jim promptly offered to be her guide.

They checked when the matinee would begin at the Manhasset movies and found that they had time to stop first for a soda. He kept away from the more popular Chocolate Shop as a way to minimize the social damage he would incur if he were seen with this hussy from Port. As they sat sipping their black-and-white floats, they found they had little to discuss—a few observations on the upcoming football season, a couple references to the new songs on the "Hit Parade," and some talk about the senior year they faced.

Entering the movies he was relieved to find that there were few customers. Jim ushered Doris into a dark corner at the back of the orchestra, and no sooner had the lights gone down and the newsreel began, he slipped his arm around the back of her seat and she responded by curling up on his shoulder. There were to be no preliminaries.

He kissed her and her tongue wiggled in at first touch. They softly mouthed one another into a rising fever and his hands were soon under her sweater and he was fondling her bra. With a quick motion, she unhooked the straps and his hands roamed across her breasts, stopping to feel her swollen nipples. As the movie began, they barely looked at the screen.

He had never before felt a girl's vagina. He slipped his hand under her skirt while she opened her legs. He felt her thighs and explored the passage under her loose panties. When he felt the warm, wet crevice, he soared into a place of ecstasy. She moaned and reached to undo his trousers and they sat there for twenty minutes massaging one another.

His fingers were wet and sticky and his nostrils were filled with her delicious smells. They didn't stay for the entire movie; he wanted to maneuver her into a more private place and asked if anyone was home at her place.

"Both parents work."

"Then let's get there first."

"I'm not sure."

"It'll be all right. I don't know where else to go."

But they lost the race.

* * *

As he finished this best of all years and he readied himself to accelerate into his graduation year, he had a feeling of invulnerability that was accompanied by a careless acceptance of his own physicality, knowing that his body might never be as strong and healthy as it was now.

Until the past year had gone sour at the end, Jim had learned that good times came naturally. He could enjoy his friends, share time with them, have fun and make some money. He experienced the fact that his body could spontaneously explode and that to be flesh-close to a girl of sixteen was one of the greatest ego lifts a boy could receive.

But there was distant thunder, announcing the storm ahead.

Chapter 4
(1946 - 1947)

When he stepped on the school grounds on the first day of his senior year, Jim accepted the perception that he was one of the school's hotshots. The yearly turnover of student regimes had brought him and his class to the forefront. With a cock's strut that had been modified over the years, his shoulder-weaving walk carried him through the crowd. He wore his signature vestment, his Alpha jacket, a red covering that identified him as reckless and aloof. A garment that signaled he was not to be toyed with.

Manhasset High's senior class enjoyed the normal, comfortable feeling that they had earned their way to the top of the pyramid after an eleven-year climb. They thought they deserved the right to celebrate their victories across their environment—plant banners on the homes that had raised them, on the churches that had confirmed their faith, on the schools that tested them, and the play yards that had fostered their grit. They, the seniors, would run the student government, proctor the halls, make up the roster of the varsity teams and begin to plan their escape from their families and town by evaluating and choosing colleges. They knew their university applications would be carefully scrutinized in the competitive scramble involving the need to accommodate the returning G.I.s who would attend college free of charge—their reward for saving Western Civilization, a subject they could now study at leisure and learn to appreciate what it was they had preserved.

Jim felt he belonged. Along with Ben, he had been elected as a school and fraternity officer. The greatest personal satisfaction that Jim had ever received was when he was elected as Secretary of the school's General Organization by a student body that had practically shown him the door a year and half before. Relying on his reputation as a social gadfly, he had been asked to organize the school dances and the fraternity's Christmas Ball. Confident, he stepped onto the football field knowing that the job of quarterbacking the team was his. He should have felt happy that he had succeeded in cracking into the top echelon but the fact was that he was disgruntled about almost everything except his ability to find dates. In that arena, Mardi and Maryjan tried to steer him toward some of the younger ATA sorority girls, secure in the knowledge that his intercoursal abstinence might make him a safer but still attractive bet for the more exploratory virgins, who were not ready yet for a conquistador.

One task he did take on with enthusiasm was preserving the ongoing success of the Alphas. June's graduation had taken away the cream and the bulk of the organization's membership and the ranks of this year's senior class were thin in terms of both numbers and winning types. As a result, the job of recruiting new and outstanding fraternity boys was the one commitment he wholeheartedly made. If he could re-establish the pre-eminence of the Alphas, he would not only have shown his loyalty to Danny, McKnight, Saylor, Dumphy and the rest, he would save his own reputation as a leading-edge male. This, even though the competing fraternity had overtaken his group's dominance.

The other fraternity, the Deltas, had circled around Barns after his beating at Saylor's hands on that Alpha initiation night years ago. Barns had convinced his friends to join together and ignore the restrictive membership practices of the older fraternity by starting an organization of their own. He pulled together the remaining leaders in the '47 class and they now dominated the school's scene, which itself was changing dramatically. Where Jim and the old Alphas were socially precocious and had been involved in the bar scene for years, dancing to the tune of their times, things in the postwar era were quickly turning conservative and were pointing more toward rec room games. The swirling bar scene of the war years was coming to an end, leaving the conflict's partygoers bereft of former playmates. Girls from AZP, the less-popular sorority, reflecting on the success of the Deltas, were also making a concerted effort to overcome their rival ATA's dominance. Glamour girls had been part of the war's frantic home front allure, so dutifully mimicked by the ATAs. However, the deb scene was melting away in favor of sock hops and pizza parties. Even skirt lengths had fallen far below the knee.

Jim was so focused on protecting the Alpha legend that he fantasized about what he would do when he got out into the work world and made some money. He would build an Alpha clubhouse that would outshine any sports club he had ever seen. He would construct an athletic pleasure palace with a swimming pool, tennis and basketball courts and even a big dancehall. He would leave an Alpha legacy to honor the bull-froth and male-woven hubris of his youthful companions in sin.

The first Friday of the school year—the night Greeklings convened—Jim accompanied newer members of the Alphas to one of the sorority meetings, partially as a way of connecting with the lower classmen that he had previously ignored, so involved was he with the class ahead of him. With the new reality and shift of power underway, social dynamics were changing patterns of behavior. Instead of protecting the interests of the Alphas among his former truehearts at ATA, he was scheduled to speak before the AZP group. Sensing that the gears were rotating differently, the AZPs had actually invited popular Jim to come by at the end of their first meeting and forecast happenings of the new school year. Mardi had called him and asked what he was thinking of, pandering to the opposition. She told him, that in retaliation, ATA had invited Barns of the Deltas to their meeting. Action and reaction.

Feeling somewhat disloyal for abandoning his former beauty queens, Jim entered a large living room where forty or so AZP girls occupied every inch of furniture and floor space. Squeezed together, they lit up when they saw him, the cool looking, handsome senior football player and renowned lady-killer—a reputation that few mature persons would be able to recognize. He stood in the middle of the room amid a garden of uplifted, shining faces. He enjoyed this image of himself, dozens of girls at his feet. He remembered back to the time he was a freshman and how he worshiped at the altar of the senior girls, Ally and the women of his brother's class. Now he was the object of similar adoration. The girls, young and vibrant, displayed their own attractiveness. These were the athletic girls of the school, the sailors, horseback riders and hockey players who looked more robust and healthy than the ATA swans.

Thin Lucy was president of the AZPs and knew that snaring Jim was a coup.

"Jim agreed to come by and give us some idea of how he thinks the new school year will shape up. Please give him your full attention."

She was precise and authoritative, displaying an ease that set her apart as a leader. There was no mistake that she was in charge. As she passed by, he noticed she had a dancer's way of walking, such that her legs churned but her upper body seemed not to move. She appeared to be upright and socially correct. A straight-up girl.

"And quit eyeing his belt," she said softly to a corner of the giggling crowd as she stepped out of the center.

"Just a couple words," Jim began, "to say that I hope we can hold on to some of the spirit and willingness to challenge ourselves, be a little reckless like we were around here during the war when there was a feeling that we were all in it together. It seems now that we're beginning to split apart. Everybody out for themselves."

He rumbled on about the past, trying to convince them and himself that they should look backwards for guidance at the exact time when nobody else in the room had anything like that in mind now that opportunities were opening in every direction, now that the prohibitions of war had lifted. Luckily his good looks were sufficiently distracting that his words didn't much matter.

There was the usual serving of cookies and apple juice in the dining room following the meeting. As an Alpha male, Jim enjoyed the acclamation he was receiving. He tried not to show his vulnerability, as if he was used to such adulation.

Lucy, after the droning had diminished, came up and thanked him for coming.

"Don't I get a speaker's fee or anything?" he joked.

"There might be a little reward if you're good," she teased him.

Lucy was normally as quiet and soulful as a Quaker meeting. Not as centered perhaps but nominally spiritual. She thanked her parents for helping her detect the hidden paths to maturity. They had also taught her to communicate with the divine—an entity as remote as the galaxies—which in turn gave her the courage to ask for the ability to shine. Hoping for greater acknowledgment from her peers, she tried to forgive herself for not liking popular boys and what they asked girls to do because when it came to sex, her kickstand was down, planted in a bed of future bridal roses. So she thought.

She had a quiet confidence in herself and an elfish streak that often resulted in giggles. She had a long face to go with her long body. Straight-backed and seemingly correct in her behavior, she tempered any generalization made about her with easy laughter and unpredictable mischievousness. Though shy and dry—actually something of a bluestocking—she had a wild slice in her that was ripe for consumption. Already girl smart, she was now endeavoring to understand her rival/friends from the other gender. There were many reasons to like her, her sense of independence being one, but it was her compulsive honesty that stood out.

He told her he was going to walk her home and she didn't even peep. They lingered through Munsey Park as if to make the journey last. As they did, she kept teasing him and pestering him about her desire to wear his Alpha jacket.

She prodded him.

She nettled him.

Finally, she convinced him.

He peeled off his sacred armor and she folded her thin body into its lining, looking ridiculous in the oversize garment. She laughed at herself and he responded by teasing her back, something he seldom did.

"I'm glad we're in the same Chemistry class," Lucy said.

"How's that?"

"Time to get to know you better."

"Yeah. Well, it's going to be hands on. Doc says he's going to teach us how to make cold cream."

"Maybe you'd be able to cover up some of your whiskers."

Jim didn't always shave every day.

Suddenly grabbing her, he pulled her face to his.

"All the better to scratch you with, my dear."

He swiped his face across her cheek, catching part of her underchin. She laughed and pulled away, but not until he felt her body shiver.

"Is this what they call necking?"

She was playful though he was sometimes slow to respond, stuck as he was in his own ego, wallowing in his sense of self-importance. She made him laugh, something else he didn't do often. When he discovered that his laugh was subtler now, more mature, it made him feel good.

Her thin body was different than Bonnie's. He liked the way she trembled in delight.

At her front door, still in his jacket, she fended off his arms that sought to enclose her, "Easy there. Mind the pelt."

When she slipped in the door, he gave her a quizzical look through the glass panel.

"My jacket, please."

"Maybe tomorrow," she said.

He had to laugh, appreciating her audacity.

She had caught his attention and smiled when he invited her out the next night.

* * *

Saturday football games wouldn't begin until later in September, so he was free to stop by to see Lucy the next day. They both had chores in the morning and agreed to meet after lunch. He walked up the hill to Munsey Park, and when he knocked on the door, Lucy's look-alike mother greeted him. Two sisters, one thin and one chunky, peered at him from the dining room. Jim had the feeling that he was the first swain to cross their doorstep.

Mrs. Gillette said, "I know your mother. We're working on the new hospital."

"I think I've seen your pictures together in the paper."

She was slim in the Thirties mode, boyishly handsome and very Philadelphia.

Lucy came down the stairs and replaced her in the doorway. He wondered if he was actually going to be invited in.

"Lose something?" she teased him.

"Looking for a donation. I'm stopping by on behalf of the new hospital fund."

"Suffering from recent wounds, are you?"

That was a zinger. All the town kids knew that Bonnie had dumped him.

"I'm looking for a nurse to change my bandage."

He had been amazed that he had suffered so little following the split-up, as if he didn't much care.

"Depends where the wound is."

Touching his belt, he said, "It might be hard to get at."

"You might need a specialist. 'Come into my parlor' said the spider to the fly."

They sat on the couch at the far end of a traditional suburban living room, complete with grand piano, while the other females of the family disappeared. The couple didn't break into conversation right away. They were surveying each other.

"We could do Chemistry homework," she finally teased.

"Or rake leaves."

"And then jump in them?"

They played with each other until her father walked in.

"Hi. I'm Ed Gillette," he said, stepping into the room with a perky gait and an outstretched hand.

Remembering his Fork Union manners, Jim rose, "A pleasure to meet you, sir."

"Playing quarterback, I hear. Brains of the team."

"If I stay healthy."

"Never played the game when I was young. Always needed to work and get ahead. Then I got lucky and was given a scholarship to textile school."

His was a familiar story among successful men of the period. Like his step-father and Mr. Gillette, working poor families often produced aggressive sparkplugs that ignited lives around them, often leaving a trail of burnt energy behind.

"Do you play chess?" asked Mr. Gillette.

"My brother taught me the rules."

"Lucy, why don't you help your mother? I'm going to test out this young fella."

"Daddy, he didn't come to play chess."

Wondering what the boy had come for, and knowing in his heart that the answer was his daughter, Mr. Gillette said, "OK. Forget it for now, but not for long."

When they did play later, the result came down to a stalemate. Jim held his own until the end of the game when he maneuvered his lonely king into a safe corner. His red-faced opponent came charging down the board at him, so Jim just moved diagonally over to the other safe corner square. Mr. Gillette was fuming that Jim wouldn't give up his refuge, so mad that he slammed the board, got up in a huff and stormed out of the room.

This larger-than-life patriarch, who had a tinge of the martinet, dominated the family. Existence meant combat to him. He had used chess as a way of checking Jim's abilities. He needed to engage the kid in a tournament and unhorse the intruder. If he dared to come anywhere near his oldest child, he'd skewer him.

* * *

That night they had their first date. She looked fresh and powdered. Lightly freckled, with patches of misapplied white, she was surrounded by golden brown hair.

As they were walking home from the movies, she said, "I never expected to go out with a Catholic boy. My father wonders if you're going to convert me. Basically, he thinks I'm doomed with you."

"Protestants," Jim said defensively, "get it all wrong. They should have stayed in the Church and reformed from within," mouthing platitudes.

"Episcopalians think we've paved a richer road to heaven. With better horses and carriages."

"What do you think of a church that's based on some king's itch to marry his whore," repeating his grade school propaganda.

"There must be more to it than that."

"No, there isn't," he said defiantly.

"Eating fish and going to confession won't make you a saint."

"Yeah, but I'm glad that I'm part of the true Church," he said, getting annoyed.

"It's all relative," Lucy replied, trying to lighten up. "Besides we're not supposed to talk about religion until our third date. That is, if there's going to be a third date."

"Don't let your father influence you so much that you've got blinders on."

"Don't worry, Alpha Boy. I know what's important and right now, that's you."

"Don't let anything get between us until we figure how we're doing." He was already angling for a relationship.

"No way."

"Let's forget it. We'll never agree anyway. Kiss me instead."

* * *

Jim's greatest ambition for six years, starting in the fifth grade, was to play on the Manhasset football team. His memory carried the image of the scrimmage plunges of his childhood heroes, Ernie Johanssen and Davy Lund, remembering the long pass from Ernie to Lonny, his Black end, that sealed a long-ago game. He sought to emulate their antic deeds. As he took the home field for the first game of the season against East Rockaway, he should have felt some sense of satisfaction and physical accomplishment. But he didn't. Instead, he experienced a uselessness of purpose; he was becoming aware of a certain rottenness seeping into his system.

Prospects for the team had been low, because last year's senior players, mostly his fellow Alphas, had graduated. Nevertheless Manhasset won their opener. He called plays on offense and played single safety on defense, standing back behind the team. His task was to stop any opponent that ran through the forward wall. After building up a big lead, the home team relaxed and almost lost the game in the final quarter,

At practice on Monday, the small, burly coach chewed them out, "You got overconfident and full of yourselves. You thought you were on a cakewalk and those tough little guys almost came back and whipped you. And you, Mahoney, standing out there at safety all by yourself with the whole world to see, with one foot crossed in front of the other"—he made a sissy gesture throwing one leg over the other—"looking like a chorus girl."

Jim hated the humiliation.

The next Saturday, the team traveled to Oyster Bay and Jim played the best game of his short career, throwing a couple of touchdown passes. On subsequent Saturdays, the team beat Farmingdale and tied the big South Side squad. That's when the sports writers at *Newsday* began to pay attention. However, the big games were still coming up—Port Washington, Garden City, closing with Roslyn.

Manhasset fans thought that the other upscale school in the league, Garden City, was their chief rival, but the supporters from Port Washington knew Manhasset was their biggest opponent People from Port, irritated by the put-on airs of their neighbors, hoped to best the crowd from the next community by demonstrating their football smarts and superior brawn.

* * *

At school, Jim and Lucy began spending time together—at lunch, in the library, and after his football workouts and her field hockey practice, walking the mile or more together in the late afternoon to her house. On weekends, they became enwrapped in each other's plans, going to the movies or attending impromptu parties. They walked everywhere. The irony was, that now that gas was more readily available, his car-owning buddies had other plans. He had deserted his former friends and they had returned the favor.

Jim and Lucy's relationship began as one of convenience. He needed a girlfriend after Bonnie and she needed a high-profile escort to match her sorority presidency. Her abilities were finally being admired, and now she needed some social power.

"How was practice?" Lucy asked one afternoon as they headed toward Munsey Park. Touching his shoulder and spoofing him, "Did they hurt you, darling?"

"Only my pride when they make me eat dirt."

* * *

After their third date, a walk to the movies, Jim and Lucy lay next to one another on the sofa in her living room and explored each other's bodies. There wasn't the madness of emotion that accompanied his fumbling with Bonnie. It was more serene as if this was a natural part of life. Even with their clothes on, there was no holding back. Their wet places flooded.

When they came up for air from the stale smell of the couch coverings, she laid her head in his lap.

"I never thought it would feel so good," she said.

"Did the bells ring?"

"Miraculous. Like a revelation. What did you do to me?" she touched his face. "Whatever it was, don't forget how to do it again."

"I'm glad you liked it."

"We'll practice."

"I think it's time you started wearing my pin."

Seventeen and ready.

* * *

Jim and Lucy began to notice a chubby Black freshman kid underfoot whenever they moved through the school corridors. He would be waiting outside their classroom doors at the end of a period or sitting next to them in the cafeteria.

During class breaks, thirty or forty kids would stand outside smoking, posing the question of whether their Tree, their symbol of youth, would be asphyxiated from nicotine poisoning. The truth was that The Tree wouldn't last much longer, but it was rooted in the consciousness of the Manhasset generation that traded saddle shoes for Army boots, the one that turned twenty sometime between the mid-Thirties and the mid-Fifties—the famous 8th Generation to reach their majority since the Revolution.

Under The Tree, during one of Jim's cigarette breaks, the same Black youngster who had been vying for their attention would approach Jim and Lucy, say a few words and move away, only to rejoin them so he could accompany them back inside. Flattered in a way, they began to look for him if he didn't show up. He was a lively kid from the Valley, named Donny. Totally unorthodox, Jim and Lucy began to respond to him and protect him from any insults that fellow students might be harboring because it was unheard of that whites should pal around with Blacks.

Every afternoon, Donny would hang about the sports fields watching his two senior friends practice. The couple thought it was just a case of hero worship and didn't discourage him. Donny, on his part, was a sassy, fearless kid who overflowed with good spirit, though the laughter seemed to have an edge to it as if cheerfulness might be an expression of something else below the surface.

* * *

Jim and Lucy were not shy about the preliminaries of sex; it was their development toward the endgame that would cause problems. When they returned from their Friday and Saturday night dates, they continued to sink into the recesses of the sofa in her living room once things were quiet on the second floor. Lucy was always careful about turning off the lights. A shadowy illumination from the outside street lamp allowed them to identify where their buttons were.

One night, her parents came home early from an event in Manhattan and flicked the switch inside the front door and caught the young couple lying on the couch.

"What's going on here?" asked the father, decked out in a tux. His wife stood behind him wearing a gown.

"Doing Chemistry," Jim lied.

It was such an obvious obfuscation that Lucy rolled her eyes.

After a talking-to by her father and a week's sabbatical from seeing one another, the couple resumed their dating and probing.

* * *

One afternoon after football practice, Jim exited the locker room and discovered Donny waiting for him.

"Where's Lucy?"

"She had a dentist appointment," Jim answered.

"Mind if I walk you downtown?"

Jim said, "C'mon."

Donny, short and chunky, came up to Jim's shoulders. Neatly dressed, he carried a book under his arm.

"What are you reading?"

"*Invisible Man.*"

"What's it about?"

"How Blacks are invisible to whites. Look right through us"

"I get it."

Jim and Donny entered the Chocolate Shop to find dozens of kids packed into the booths. There was a distinct hush as the unlikely pair entered but Mr. Polapolis didn't blink an eye. They ordered Broadways and sat down in a two-seater. The atmosphere chilled; none of these kids had ever seen one of the Valley Blacks in the soda shop. No one came over to their table or talked to them.

As they stepped back onto Plandome Road, Jim thought Donny would be heading home. Instead, the freshman walked along with his senior buddy. Because he continued to trail along, they arrived at the Hill-Mahoney's and Jim invited him in.

His mother looked like a spider had bitten her.

"What…?

"This is Donny I've been telling you about."

"How come he's here?"

"Just visiting... C'mon, I'll show you the rec room."

The two boys went downstairs and played a game of ping-pong. After the game ended, Jim provided a soft drink and they started a second game. His mother had disappeared to the upper reaches of the house. In due time, she called downstairs, "I think your friend better leave now. You have to set the table."

"Since when?"

After Donny departed, his mother tried to be tactful, "Jim, you know you can't cross the color line. You just can't do it."

"Who says?"

"Society says," she said smartly.

"Maybe there's something wrong with society."

"Let me just tell you then. Don't bring him around again. The neighbors must be in a knot."

"Let them be."

Jim was disappointed, but Donny never came around their door again. Jim was rebellious but he wasn't up to breaking glass. More tuned into bending the rules.

* * *

Mardi told him, "You've gone off the tracks, you know. I adore you but what the hell are you doing dating an AZP girl and running around town with a Black kid?"

* * *

Jim and Lucy argued about having sex. Every time they were wrestling together, Lucy would urge him to break into her, but he steadfastly refused, citing the pregnancy issue. The truth was that he was afraid of crossing over to any kind of mature binding. The Church did deter him; his distaste for condoms was another reason. He thought of himself as a natural man, not some hungry animal decked out in a rubber tire. Lucy complained and never failed to remind him that they should be indulging in healthy sex, not this groping game, even though they found pleasure one way or another.

* * *

Jim planned to arrive at the locker room an hour and a half before the start of the Port game. As he ambled through town, some kids honked and gave him the thumbs up sign; others stopped him on the sidewalk to say good luck. Even the jeweler, Mr. Sund, stepped out of his diamond hutch to wish him well. Jim had helped steer the team toward a successful season so far. Around town, all eyes were on him this morning. The real test would be today. Port had an outstanding running halfback named McDonough who was hard to bring down.

As he walked onto the school grounds, adults selling tickets at the gate greeted him. They waved and gave him the V for Victory sign. He walked up the drive with the football field on one side and, on the other, a wide lawn that fronted the brick school, its not so stately architectural tower dominating the institution's façade.

Like the years before, a half dozen grade school kids hung off the bleachers, hoping to avoid the ten-cent entrance fee. One of the kids, rising to the occasion, said, "You won't let those Port guys beat ya, will ya, Jim?"

"We'll do our best, Tommy."

The boy beamed and said to his friends, "He knows my name."

A lone band member sat in the bleachers, practicing his trombone. The melody, "Go in there, you Orange and Blue."

As Jim suited up in shoulder pads and a hip guard, a crowd of two thousand that would be the largest of the season began filing into the stands. Now that the war had been over for a year, people were more relaxed and had extra time for games and leisure. These spectators reflected the confidence and ambition that would bring unsurpassed prosperity during the next ten years. This year represented high times, the period before the developing Cold War and the Korean War, a period when the country could ease back and renew its acquaintance with the good things of life and try to reconfigure the heartstrings that made them who they were, even though, as everyone knew, there was no going back. Material acquisition was the rallying call of the general public. Everyone was angling to buy a new car, finally able to ditch the Thirties' models so carefully pampered during the years of scarcity. Many planned new homes that would bulge with new fangled washers and dryers—the old laundry machines with arm-mangling wringers would soon be scrapped along with backyard clotheslines. People were talking about television and home air-conditioning. Mr. Wright had already set up a TV in his hardware store window, and sometimes as many as fifty people came by and stood on the sidewalk to see the Friday night fights and wrestling matches.

But it was today's game that would provide North Shore bragging rights.

In the locker room, Ben asked Jim, "Ready to go?"

"Ready as I'll ever be."

"We'll try to stop McDonough at the line before he can break into the open."

"Good," said Jim. "Don't let him loose in my territory."

The team was engaged in their pregame calisthenics on the side field when the bus arrived carrying the Port players, who had been assigned the girls' side of the gym.

"Hey, you clamdiggers," Charlie Stowe yelled at the opponents.

"Boff off," came the reply. "Blow it out your ass."

"We all know Doris, your cheerleader. Girl really knows how to jump."

"We wouldn't want to lay any of the icecakes around here."

"We're going to freeze your dicks today," taunted Charlie.

"And we're going to wipe your faces in the mud."

The level of sports sophistication was already low, and now sank out of sight.

"Pipe down," said the assistant coach. "Treat them like guests."

"Or pests."

The two teams soon bounded onto the field. Both bands played at the same time. The MHS cheerleaders—Mardi, Betty, Maryjan, Buzz, mostly ATA girls—goaded the crowd into singing the fight song. Manhasset lost the toss and had to kick off. Ben was the team's kicker and Jim the placeholder. As Ben came up to adjust the angle of the football, he said, "Bonnie's in the stands."

Bonnie had broken off social contact with her old friends, much the same way Jim had. He heard stories about her. She was spending weekends on college campuses and trailing Merchant Marine cadets into New York, where she was spending a good deal of her time modeling. She was leaving the hometown behind.

Jim turned and spotted her immediately. Her beauty made her stand out. It was the last glance at their years together. Their focus was cold now.

Newsday predicted that Port Washington would win the game, but MHS scored first on an interception, raising the expectations of the underdogs and quelling the hubris of the likely winners, reminding them that winning the league championship might be in doubt. Port came back to score near the end of the first half.

Port's touchdown had made Jim look bad. The opposition sent two ends out, heading straight for Jim, who was playing lone safety.

The two players ran directly at him and then split in opposite directions. Jim didn't know which one to cover, so he fell back toward the goal line between them, and when the ball's trajectory spun to the left, Jim tried to get to the tall end before the ball arrived but the spheroid fell into the upraised arms of his opponent in the end zone.

The coach was still optimistic. "You can beat these guys," the chubby athletic director told them at halftime.

In the third quarter, Jim was unable to get any offensive movement going. His passes were falling too short or too long. The team's running game was stopped short by the husky Port players.

Then came the decisive moment of the game. McDonough, the excellent Port running back began wearing down the MHS front line. On an off-center play, McDonough found a hole and burst through the secondary. Now in the open field, only Jim stood between him and pay dirt. He came straight at Jim and Jim panicked. His courage failed him. He didn't have the guts to make an open field tackle. Diving at McDonough's feet, Jim made a weak feint to stop him but the runner's legs carried him to a touchdown. Jim had executed his fake tackle so well that his cowardice was not apparent, but he knew that he had chickened out. All the fears and timidity of his childhood had whelmed up and frozen his courage. He knew that he had personally failed and lost the game.

But in one sense, he didn't even care. He was sliding into a dark place.

* * *

In the Garden City game, so angry with himself because of his lack of courage in taking down the Port halfback, his instincts turned animal against their principal rival. He threw himself recklessly into any tackling situation that came his way. Garden City had a renowned fullback built like an ox with the appropriate sobriquet—Bull. Every time Bull, who would become a star in the Ivy League, came crashing into the line, Jim would charge up from his safety position and ram his slim body into the bulky ox. One time, he struck with such force that he rebounded with no feeling remaining in his right arm. Scared of the consequences, he nevertheless failed to remove himself from the game, but slogged on until feeling in his arm was restored.

In the last quarter with Manhasset behind, Bull carried the ball on nearly every play as a way of preserving a win. Sweeping the end on one play and with good blocking ahead, Bull headed for the sidelines near the Manhasset bench, with Jim and a couple of his teammates in hot pursuit. Enraged, Jim yelled, "Kill the bastard."

As they untangled after the punishing hit—Bull was slow to get up— Jim looked up to see a woman standing nearby with a shocked expression on her face. She had come out to attend a pleasant scholastic match and was instead forced to witness jungle warfare. Because the stands were so close to the sidelines, few spectators, who had traveled with the team to this away game, failed to hear Jim's screech.

The coach, as a rebuke to bad sportsmanship, immediately pulled Jim out of the game, the first time during the season that he had done so with the game's result still in question. Jim, hot with anger, actually needed the break. The coach waited to observe the effectiveness of his second string quarterback, and then quietly re-inserted Jim back into the game during a time-out period. The chubby coach actually didn't mind a little blood sport if it meant a win. Conventions had to be observed but for only so long.

But the team lost. Bull's efforts were rewarded with a victory.

Jim, before the night was over, threw a couple of objects around his rec room and punched the hell out of his pillow.

* * *

He woke on the morning after the Garden City game to the news that Bonnie had been in a serious automobile accident the night before. She had gone out on a double date with Bootsie and two wise asses from Great Neck. At a party on the South Shore, the driver, Bonnie's date, got blind drunk. Although the girls begged him to stop drinking, he ignored them and insisted that he was going to take them home. The two girls at first refused to get in the car and were asking around for alternative rides, but they were a bit high themselves and their judgment impaired, so they reluctantly climbed into the car, a brand new station wagon.

The driver, furious that the girls had questioned his driving skills, wanted to show off. He started down a straightaway at 65 miles an hour while the girls screeched at him to pull over. He lost control of the big heavy wagon on the first curve and it hurtled out of control and wound up on its side in a ditch. Bonnie in the passenger's seat was the most seriously injured.

The telephone rang continuously through the morning—Ben, Maryjan, even Saylor away at college, called. On his way back from church, he picked up a copy of the *Daily News* and turned to the center section. Five pictures of the accident covered the pictorial spread. In one, Bootsie looked to be in semi-shock in the back of a police car. In another, Bonnie lay unconscious, her white scarf stained with blood, with a deadly look on her face.

Jim's reaction to the accident once more proved his insensitivity. He blamed her and her mother for trying to start up with the rich set in the next town. "She should have stayed with me," he thought.

He didn't bother to visit her at the hospital. Never even sent a card. He had a new girl now. It took Bonnie a month to repair.

* * *

School was boring. Jim's government class was taught by a dull veteran with a monotone who rambled on endlessly about excise taxes and quorums. In English class, the literature teacher made them plow through a novel about a South Dakota farm family so overcast with dullness that the book left a fog in the literature chamber of his brain. His Chemistry class was full of "oses" and "ides" and fizzing test tubes. Regarding his pursuit of mathematical skill, he had bounded out of the Calculus class after the first day, lost in a host of undecipherable numbers. He had enough Spanish to fulfill his requirements, so he had opted for Home Economics as his fourth course. There had been a history of football players donning aprons and shoveling spinach with the Valley girls who hoped to become "nutritionists." The big bohunks got their pictures in the paper wearing chef's hats, Jim among them.

* * *

"Are you thinking about college?" Lucy asked him one night.

"Not a bit."

"You've got to get your applications in after Christmas."

"Maybe I'll join the Navy."

"The war's over. Haven't you heard?"

"If I stay in school, I'll get as far away from this place as I can." She knew about his ambivalence regarding Manhasset. "Probably some college in the Midwest."

"I'm thinking of a woman's college. So I won't be distracted by the likes of you."

"You better not starting dating those college pugs."

"Women's colleges are convents. They lock the gate at night."

"You'll be better off what with all that sexiness stored in you."

She laughed, "Unless I learn to climb the fence."

She was trying to keep him amused, but it was hard work.

"Maybe I can get into a Catholic women's college. That would kill two birds with one stone."

"You can take up permanent celibacy."

"Isn't that what I have now?"

"Only technically."

Sometimes she thought she was succeeding in getting him to lighten up.

* * *

The competition between the fraternities, plus the fact that a girl attempted suicide after being rejected by ATA last year, along with questions arising in the press about Greek activities on campus and parental concern over beer parties—all these doubts conflated to make these social clubs a volatile issue in town. Jim received a call from the principal asking him if he would assist in putting together a program on the subject. The schoolmaster was thinking of holding a debate. Jim, who had no background in public speaking and was deficient in verbal skills, discussed the situation with Ben. Jim finally told him he could handle the meeting, deciding that he and one of the sorority girls should appear in tandem. He made arrangements arbitrarily without consulting the Deltas. Barbara, one of the popular ATA girls, agreed to accompany him on the platform Halloween night.

Their opponents were the two smartest members in the class, the future valedictorian and salutatorian. The lack of publicity put no damper on the turnout; residents responded to the chattering of word-of-mouth and filled the auditorium. In the packed room, Jim made out his folks and friends and opposing Deltas, along with Lucy, who was there with her parents.

Barbara offered the opening remarks on the advantages of the Greek system, painting her sorority as pleasant as a garden club with social teas and proof of generous contributions to community projects through cupcake sales and car washes.

Then the opposition weighed in. The bright and witty Number One scholastic tried to shake the conceit that the fraternities were backslapping enclaves of mellow men. “They have a reputation of violence in their initiation ceremonies. They grope around together looking for trouble and getting drunk. One of them is going to drive into a tree late some night and get killed. Besides, who’d want to be in a club with them anyway?” which brought laughter.

Their opponents were making Barbara and Jim look silly.

“It’s just a lot of bull that we’re causing trouble,” Jim rambled on. “We’re just a bunch of friends. Last year, Danny Devon was head of his class. Stu Argyle was school president. We try to have some fun around this town which isn’t so easy.”

“Maybe you could learn to fish or work up some merit badges or, God forbid, study,” came the reply and more laughter.

The Greeks did not do well in this battle. Jim, mostly tongue-tied and illogical, had made a fool of himself.

* * *

On the day before Thanksgiving, Jim was sitting in the high school library. He sat there mulling over the bad grades he received following midterms. He felt uncomfortable about the progress of his senior year as if the pieces of his life weren’t coming together.

New forebodings were walking down the school hall. Through the door came Danny Devon, home from Hopkins to celebrate the holiday. He looked different, not in attire so much, though his clothes appeared to have made a stylish improvement somewhere along Madison Avenue. It was his looks, critical and hard, not his normal elfish self that was different. An unsmiling Danny Devon was not a sight anyone at Manhasset High comprehended. With a serious mien, he looked around the room but Jim spotted him first and flew to his feet. It wasn't until now that he realized that he had been sparkless this semester because he missed his older Alpha brothers. His self-confidence had been partially nurtured at the beginning of the football season and with his discovery of Lucy, but he had begun to lose direction and he suddenly understood why. In the soft light of the library windows, Jim had been thinking that his ill-constructed value system might be slipping away.

"Danny!" Jim raised his voice.

An odd thing happened. Danny succeeded in ignoring him.

"Hi," he finally said. It was a frosty greeting, un-nerving Jim, who always cultivated his friend's pixie image and was certain of a positive response. Danny walked right by him toward a table filled with sunny ATA girls who welcomed him. He finally smiled. Jim walked behind.

"Hey, Danny. How's college?" Maryjan asked. "Did you go out for any sports?"

Danny, remembered as the best athlete in school, replied, "No. I have more important things to do now."

"What kind of things?" asked Mardi.

"You have to make all these choices when you go away. School pressure is really intense. You have to start thinking for yourself and fast. Take on the big questions."

No one said anything.

"When you start realizing what's wrong with the world, you come away with a bunch of new thoughts."

Could this bookbag be Danny? Had Jim really ever known him? When you go away, do you change into somebody else, find a different self? How could a person accomplish that in two months? Even the girls held back. An aloof Danny was not a known entity.

"It's true," Mardi said later, "He was looking down on us."

Jim came away confused. What was he without last year's friends? How could he manage without them? Who else could buck him up? The Alpha founders had been his foundation.

* * *

Lucy continued to say, "We should be natural—follow our feelings— and do it."

But Jim would make excuses about pregnancy and how it would deter them, and how he hated the whole idea about wearing a rubber. Plus, there was the Church fiddling with his brain.

* * *

Jim had always lied about a lot of things. He had never been to California but insisted that he had spent time in San Diego watching Navy fliers spin through the balmy air. He had never seen Glenn Miller's Orchestra in the Café Rouge of the Pennsylvania Hotel, but blithely told everyone that hc had danced up a storm there. He boasted that he had seen the heel-kicking cowboys in the original Broadway production of *Oklahoma* that had changed the musical formula of the White Way—said this because he knew most of the tunes by heart. But his biggest lie was that he had a driver's license when in fact he had flunked the driving test twice.

This last prevarication got him into a bind when Ben asked him to transport a '32 Ford buggy that he purchased in Flushing back to Manhasset. Jim couldn't refuse without facing up to the truth that he didn't have permission to drive on public roads.

When the day arrived to retrieve the newly bought car, Ben was sidelined with a sports injury and his brother was designated to ride shotgun. He and Jim rode the LIRR into Flushing-Main Street and found the seller who turned over the keys and title. Jim tested the manual shift, a feature on all cars. Jim had learned to drive with Pappy in the family's '37 Plymouth, but he was finding this Ford shift tricky. Jim cranked the auto into first gear setting off a large grinding noise, starting the journey with a considerable racket.

"What 'ya doing?" asked Ben's brother. "Don't you know how to drive this thing?"

His answer came when the car began bucking down the street like an angry stallion. They lurched onto Northern Boulevard in fits and starts as the car creaked along, the mis-matched crunching of gears frightening other drivers.

The four-sided traffic signals on the main roads in New York City were handsome art-deco reminders of the days of the 1939 World's Fair, slim, brass poles showing small, but decorously attractive, yet hard to see, red and green lights. At diagonal intersections they were particularly difficult to read because the light's positioning and narrowness offered a sight of two sides of the traffic pole. Jim, unaccustomed to driving in the city limits, was confused by the lights and at one intersection, stopped on a green light in the middle of the busy road, thinking he was obeying the angled red light. Cars screeched to a halt behind him and one guy blared out invectives that saturated the air with oaths in a language unfamiliar to either of the teenagers.

"Don't ruin the car before we get it home," Ben's brother admonished Jim.

His lie remained secure because they managed to arrive safely. Two months later in Pappy's Plymouth, which Jim finally learned to control, he passed his road test.

* * *

Lucy's best friend was a girl named Kathy from one of the few artistic families in town. She was a fiery redhead who was sufficiently perceptive to see through Jim's façade of popularity and confident enough in her friendly ties to warn Lucy to be careful with this empty edition. "He's like a book with no pages."

Kathy was also a mouthy gossip, and whether for the protection of her friend or out of sheer belligerence, she began circulating her opinion that Jim was nothing but a cardboard Romeo. Her badmouthing was the beginning of a second look at Jim's position on the social pole around school. Negative evaluation set in behind.

Lucy confided to Kathy that Jim didn't want to penetrate her, though everything else in the sex manual was fair exercise.

"Alex and I do it all the time. Get him to wear a rubber. What's his problem?"

When Lucy suggested that they double date, Jim refused. Whether he was afraid to become friends with schoolmates further down the pecking order or younger than they, who could tell?

* * *

In opposition to the arrest of local Japanese families, who were taken forcefully from their homes and interned in war camps earlier in the Forties, the town had more recently received a number of incoming families either fleeing military coups or the revolutionary forces of Central and South America. That brought a number of elegant Hispanic families to Manhasset, widening, if ever so slightly, the nascent cosmopolitan nature of the upscale suburb. The infusion also had a sportive effect upon the junior members of the community, resulting in much better soccer teams

* * *

As Christmas approached, two social events loomed large. One was their Senior Prom on the 20th at school and the other was the Alpha dance in the Anchor Room at the Port Washington Yacht Club on the 26th. Jim, who had often managed the school dances, had recently been replaced by one of the Deltas, another indication that he and his fraternity were losing its social position. But the fraternity dance was still Jim's responsibility. In October, he negotiated the date with the club and shortly after visited the orchestra leader, and between the two of them, they figured out a fee, which then allowed Jim to set an entrance price and print the tickets. The foreman at the printer's shop laid out an attractive design for a brochure featuring a Christmas wreath surrounded by green and red holly margins. Jim was able to administer details like this with ease; controlling himself was harder. It was a foregone conclusion that he would escort Lucy to both holiday events. He asked her if yellow roses would match her prom gown and her less formal cocktail dress and the answer was positive.

For the school Christmas Ball, their classmates elected Maryjan as their queen. There had been a sympathy vote for Bonnie after the accident, but Maryjan's popularity won out. Jim and Ben were the remaining Alpha stalwarts in the class, but they were vastly outnumbered by the Deltas and one of these was selected to be Maryjan's royal consort. Ben had never had trouble remaining friends with the senior Delta guys because he had known most of them since kindergarten, but Jim never got along with any of them; he had entered the public system late and promptly joined the Alphas. The clamoring for social status had been settled during the course of the autumn and the Deltas had clearly won that battle. The scars of that fight had almost healed so the victors need not celebrate the fact that they were leading the parade and the losers were resigned to following. So it was with forgotten animosity on both sides that they could now finally, after years of skirmishing, sit comfortably with each other.

After the coronation ceremonies, Jim and Lucy sat with two of the Delta guys that he barely knew. One was Jake Freese, who turned out to be a big jazz fan and the other was Thad Smith, an already renowned sailor. They and their dates proved lively companions during the course of the evening.

Jake started out, "I've been going to hear PeeWee Russell and those guys at Nick's in the Village for years. I used to go alone, couldn't convince anybody to join me. I must have been fifteen or sixteen and just walked in the door. But the manager spotted me and said I had to leave. But he could see I was dying to hear the music, and I must have been wearing my woebegone face, because he sat me down at a tiny corner table and told the waiter to bring a Pepsi."

"I went in all the time by myself to hear the bands on Times Square," said Jim.

"Too bad we didn't get together," replied Jake.

Because of his dogged pride in his own set of friends, Jim had never seen the advantage of spreading out socially. It was only now, too late, that he was beginning to realize that he had lost out on potentially illuminating relationships.

Thad had been one of the more favored kids who owned his own sailboat by the time he was fourteen—one of the young skippers skimming across the water in newly constructed designs built in the boatyards along the North Shore, ship building sites that had manufactured landing crafts for the big invasions during the war. Thad and his friends raced in the junior regattas held in the Sound halfway between Greenwich and King's Point. Other races were held in Rye and Stamford and Sea Cliff where the youngsters were guests at big rambling suburban homes with wide porches built fifty years ago during the era of large families and big steam cars. These latter-day suburban kids had the advantage of meeting their peers long before attending private school or college. They were accomplished kids who knew night navigation and rules of the road. These skills came in handy when they would have to negotiate their way across the Sound at night in their tiny crafts from distant Westport after a day of races.

Thad described how his sailing season had progressed. He told a story of how he was beaming along one day and out of the depths of Long Island Sound, here comes a surfacing submarine right in front of him, causing him to lose air, jibe wildly and take in the wash stirred up by the ascending behemoth.

Jim had lost out on the whole sailing experience. He wondered how much else he had missed. He was learning that every sport had its mystique—tennis, horseback riding, flying. He had limited himself to team sports and missed the others.

* * *

The faculty advisor for the school Council was a returning G.I. who had taught at MHS before the war. His name was Mr. Tales and he was different from any other teacher Jim had ever known. He brought his dark, handsome looks to school each day attired in London fashions. He was quiet, well-spoken and wickedly smart with degrees from top schools here and abroad. A serious, war-weary demeanor, almost a sadness of expression that was attractive and a bit mysterious, burdened his handsomeness. No one in town could understand why such an outstanding person would want to be a high school teacher, a profession that was viewed as necessary but secondary in bully-boy America. Mr. Tales taught languages and knew full well why he wanted a simple life for himself and his family.

One afternoon, Jim had a question relating to the Council and knocked on the teacher's door after classes were dismissed.

"I'm wondering if you can help me find a typewriter to finish off a study of the Proctor system we're looking at."

"Sure. I'll work it out with the main office."

"Thanks," Jim said. "I'd appreciate that."

"Stay for awhile," Mr. Tales said quietly. "I've been watching you and I think I may have an idea for you."

Jim was astounded that anyone would volunteer to give him advice. No one had tried to do that since his Uncle Jack, years before his death, had tried to bolster his nephew's pride

"Some young people are more passionate than others," the teacher said, "and you seem to be frustrated about something and I was just going to pass along a suggestion."

Jim, who felt no passion for anything or body except for his urgent lunges at Lucy, was amazed that a teacher would have the confidence to talk about personal matters.

"You seem to be struggling with some demons, and you don't seem to be winning if I read you right. You happy here in town?"

"I think it's a phony place."

"Suburbs are a kind of compromise. Not a city with real culture. Not the country either—near nature. It's a kind of hybrid."

"I just know that I can't wait to get out of here."

"I know you're going steady with Lucy. She's from a good family that will send her along to college and the two of you might not be able to stay so close."

"We'll stick together."

"College changes people. You might not understand that yet, but it's true. You might be better off with a girl not going to college. Maybe one of the Valley girls. These up-town girls take a long time to find a mate and when they do, they need to lasso a good earner. But Valley girls just need a provider and a body to hold."

He was advising Jim to find a steady lay and stop frustrating himself. Jim, who had not thought about dating a Valley girl since grade school, was taken back by the idea, but the complexity of his and Lucy's future was an issue that was beginning to blur his vision.

* * *

Jim's folks decided to take a Caribbean cruise in January and arranged for the German teacher at MHS and his wife to supervise the household, especially watch over Francy who was going on ten. Mr. Rothschild was a large and gregarious man, raised in Europe before the war. His wife matched his outgoing personality.

On the second weekend that the Rothschilds were in residence at the Hill household, they asked Jim if he and Lucy would baby-sit Francy one night while they took in a double feature. After his sister was down for the night, Jim and Lucy found themselves for the first time with a house all to themselves for a couple hours.

"We can at least take off our clothes," Lucy said, hoping that would encourage him to have sex with her at last.

"Let me help."

They took off each other's garments, both feeling for the first time the full trembling body of a lover. It was a joyous moment for the two of them.

"Come on the couch," Jim said, "so we can hear if they come back early."

"I'd rather be in your bed upstairs."

"No sense in them catching us going at it."

They lay down and involuntarily began moving toward one another. It was the best feeling Jim ever had. Lucy's breath indicated that she was in fever.

They feasted for a half hour without connecting as one.

"It feels so good," he said.

"It's so right, I want to scream."

"I love you, Lucy."

"I love you too."

"We'll stick together and grow together."

"I think we're stuck already. But it will be better when you come into me."

"Soon I hope."

"Not soon," she said clearly. "There are four years of college and then time to find a career if you won't do it now."

"We can hold off."

"Optimist," she said, even though she had been noticing lately he was losing some of his self-confidence.

"This is the best thing that ever happened to me."

"To us," she corrected him.

Later, long into the night, lying in bed, hours after he walked her home, Jim felt that Lucy was still next to him. Could actually feel the afterglow of her flesh on his.

* * *

One afternoon in March as their senior year was beginning to evaporate, they sat in her living room. Jim was feeling uncomfortable about where the two of them were headed. In three months, they would be graduating. Then Lucy would spend the summer at the family's vacation house in Pennsylvania and college would follow in the fall. She had been accepted to a widely respected woman's college in Pittsburgh. There were only twelve weeks of high school left. The impending separation was making him anxious.

Her sisters were home, so they remained vertical.

He said, "I'm wondering about us. Trying to figure out how we can get through the next four years."

She threw her arms around him and kissed his neck, "You're not getting away from me, Mister."

"Yeah, but think about the differences."

"Why bother? Think of the warmth. Like when you touch me."

"No, I'm serious. What about the difference in religion?"

With that, he pulled out one of the stems moored in his matchbook and tossed it unlit into an ashtray.

"That's one," he said. "How about the argument over sex?" tossing a second match into the tile dish.

"What are you doing?" she said, concerned about his behavior.

"Just being realistic . . . How about the fact that I drink and smoke and you don't?" followed by another match.

"And how about the fact that you and I don't play the same sports. You ride and I don't. I play tennis but not you. You want to play golf and I can't stand the game." With that, he wrenched another match and added it to the mix.

By the time he finished with his exercise in self-destruction, he had accumulated a pile of match stems.

Lucy, who seldom got mad at him, was furious. She grabbed the matchbook, lit one, and tossed it into the pile, which set off the entire batch. Then marched off.

"I'm going upstairs to practice violin. You can put those matches to good use and smoke in the backyard. I'll see you later."

And with that, she left the room.

She came down a half hour later and he was still sitting there.

"What was that all about?"

"I'm afraid, I guess."

"What of?"

"That you'll dump me."

"Why don't you trust me?" she said with feeling. "You know I'm willing to give myself totally to you. What more can I do?"

"Just promise you'll be mine."

"I promise. For god's sake, I promise." She hesitated and said, "Come rest your head in my lap."

He said, "I don't want to lose you."

She stroked his head. "You never will."

* * *

A new baseball coach, a village old timer, appeared on the diamond on the first day of practice to guide the MHS nine. Jim thought, as he had presumed at the beginning of the football season, that he would be a designated starter on the team. He had warmed the bench last year when one of the best athletes in school, a senior, held the ground between second and third base. Jim expected to be this year's shortstop. In the first days of practice, the new coach tried him out at a couple locations including second base. Jim sensed that the coach favored a junior for shortstop and in the following week of practice, he got the distinct feeling that he was being eased out of position. In an intersquad game, he was assigned to play second base with the second team. The situation was turning tense as Jim began to foresee the outcome.

At batting practice one day, the coach was pitching.

"Let's see how you do, Mahoney."

Jim hit a couple solid line drives in answer to the fastballs that were being thrown.

"Let's see what you can do with a curve," and the coach threw a slow, roundhouse curve ball. Jim cocked his bat but the off-speed pitch surprised him with its movement. He shifted his feet around, but he belted the ball all the way to the tree line in deep center field.

"You moved your feet. You do that when you play the infield too." He hesitated, "Not everyone can hit a curve ball."

When the roster for the first game of the season was posted, Jim was not in the starting line-up. Frustrated, he turned in his uniform and never dressed for another team sport again.

* * *

Though Jim was finished with high school athletics, Ben, playing lacrosse, continued to hack away at opponents. It was a sport that would eventually honor him as an All-American. Before and after the season and on weekends, the two buddies along with one of the junior girls called Sabu, who had an immense crush on Ben, regularly motored east into the estate area and began trespassing on the once palatial domains that had flourished fifty years ago and were now in physical distress.

"C'mon, we're driving out to see how the rich live," Ben would suggest and off the three would go, piled tightly into the front seat of his car.

Long Island's heyday was long past but America's version of Mayfair was still able to light up the imagination of these youngsters. Country homes with sixty and seventy rooms dotted the landscape from Glen Cove to Huntington and south to Westbury. Wall Street financiers and railroad magnates discovered the coves along the North Shore in the 1880s. Sailors built near the water, while the horsy crowd settled inland near the Meadow Brook Club, where polo was the game of choice. Huge stables were constructed, on the estates some replicating versions of the mansions themselves. These stables often provided the horses that ran stake races at Belmont and Saratoga. In some gardens, statuary emerged in the shrubbery along tree-laden paths. Gazebos stood on great green lawns. Many of New York's socially endowed Four Hundred had luxuriated here during Long Island's salad days.

The Manhasset trio would wend their way down one of the country lanes off Northern Boulevard and meander along until they found the forlorn gates of a former estate. One contained an English Village upended and reconstructed on the grounds near the mansion. One rested on a high, man-made hill especially built to provide a better view. Owing to the Depression and the War and high taxes, many estates were in foreclosure or had been taken over by the local government to satisfy liens.

"This one looks abandoned" and they would ride along a tree-lined entranceway and view broken-down outbuildings and find the main house boarded up, its party days long over, shuttered against different times. They drove past gardens clogged with weeds, past tennis houses with broken windows, past golf courses, past leaf-filled swimming pools with the debris of seventeen autumns since the '29 crash.

Circling the mansions of the robber barons, running through their overgrown gardens, picnicking in their meadows and swimming at their secluded beaches, Jim was touched by the faded glory of the Gilded Age and began to romanticize about these broken castles. The ruins matched something in his own senses.

* * *

Jim attended an Alpha meeting one Friday in April and was voted down on a couple of his pet projects. Overnight, he quit the fraternity, abandoning his social life raft that had sustained him for four years. He was casting everything aside except Lucy. He didn't have a clue that he had established a pattern over which he had no control, his inability to be close to any male and to only one woman at a time. Things were slipping away. In the process, he had angered Ben, the fraternity president.

* * *

After he cut away from the Alphas, with no male friends left, he was driven into further isolation. He began to watch the junior boys who had filled out and had established true friendships among their team- and classmates. A year or two ago, they had all been terrified of girls. They had worn that blank frightened look of mid-teen age boys when encountering the opposite sex, their Adam's apple bobbing up and down, their voices warbling in nervous arias when confounded by any female. Now it was the girls' turn to look uneasy when talking to the boys, as if their own sexual perfumes were making them dizzy. Jim noticed that these guys no longer gave him the deference that had previously identified his position on the social pyramid. Now he was sinking in status. Only Lucy was at his side and his ATA girl-pals and a few of the younger coeds who had not yet come to understand that he was a fraud. When the younger guys were horsing around as Jim walked by, they no longer went silent. Now they ignored him as if he were invisible. He was beginning to dissolve like a ghost from a past class.

Another disappointment concerned the future. All his classmates were celebrating their college acceptances while he was turned down by all three of his Midwestern selections. He was failing at everything he did. His grades were so bad that he wasn't sure he was going to graduate. He was on a downward streak with no end in sight. He was becoming petulant and angry. Just as life had begun to open up for him socially when he was a younger teenager, it was now beginning to close up.

* * *

The whole thing about graduation night was that everyone was expected to stay awake until dawn. There were caravans to Jones Beach and all night dancing at the Thatched Cottage in Centerport and even a few forays into Manhattan, but most kids settled for local beaches. There would be a breakfast party in the morning at Boot's place overlooking the bay.

After the Frolics, Jim and Lucy headed for the end of Bay Driveway where reeds grew by the harbor, the marshy land where Jim as a boy held swordfights, where he had witnessed a gang bang without knowing what he was viewing, where he had seen George Hellas skid across the ice in his car years ago. As the bay widened, yacht clubs were sprinkled along the shore. The town of Port Washington dominated the harbor, and further on near its mouth where it joined Long Island Sound, the shores were studded with the palatial estates of Sands Point and King's Point, On the lee shore, Fitzgerald's green light blinked from the end of one of the docks, the navigational light that had come to express the naïve hopefulness of all America.

In the warm air, Jim and Lucy lay naked on the shore at the bottom of the bay. Exploring each other, they felt free. They looked for stars through the muggy haze but the night, instead of opening its wares, descended on them, enveloping them in moist and sensuous warmth. After squirming together, they lie quietly.

"When I think of us, I kinda think you helped tame me."

"How so?" Lucy asked.

"Because I never cared so much about anyone before. Never wanted to please anyone so much."

"I feel your need when you hold me. Though it's a little overwhelming sometimes."

"Having you like this," he said, holding her thin body tightly, "means everything."

"You've got me, or at least the part you want. Though you could have all of me"

"Let's not start."

"You're a little choosy on what parts of me you want."

"You make me sound selfish."

"It's hard with you sometimes, Jim. You get upset all the time. Angry. I sometimes feel like you're expressing some kind of rage."

"I'm just not getting anywhere," he admitted.

"At least you know you've helped me. What would I have been this year if it wasn't for you?"

"We've kind of soothed each other."

"Then smooth me some more." She rolled over on top of him.

The next afternoon, when she awoke from a long nap, Lucy finally wrote something in his yearbook. She wanted to be the last one to make an entry.

Day after Frolic
Jim darling:

I had the neatest time last night and this morning. It's been so much fun just being with you for such a long uninterrupted period of time

I am not gonna jilt you because I love you. It was fun having those kids tease us at Boots about ____. Thank you for all my eight months packed full of memories. Please give me the rest of my life packed with more of the same.

Don't worry about this summer because everything is very straight.

Remember, I love you.

Lucy

PS Thank you for helping me find the other half of me this year.

* * *

Two days later, Lucy left for her family summer home.

The future had finally arrived, and all he had to look forward to was a job on a construction gang for the summer. After that, nothing. He seemed incapable of planning ahead or taking control of his own destiny. That's when his mother stepped in and made an effort to help by searching for a college that would take him aboard. He didn't lift a finger to help her, hardly knew what she was doing.

* * *

In late July he made a weekend trip into the Pennsylvania hills to visit Lucy at Amish Lake. He was amazed at the change in her appearance. She had bleached her hair blonde and had a new and radiant demeanor. Looking ravishing to Jim, she was frothy and slightly aloof in her greetings, introducing him with a flourish to her friends sitting around the cottage. A half dozen young people lounged on the wide front porch overlooking the lake. A fashionable crowd in light bright cotton, they acted as if they had been summoned for an occasion.

"Here's the high school boyfriend now," a tall, good-looking guy, one of her friends, said in a friendly though cutting way.

"Don't think you're going to get much time alone with her."

"Give him a break, will you," one of the girls said. "He hasn't come all this way to dance with me."

"We'll see how he does at the club tonight. How he'll like it when everyone wants to dance with his girlfriend."

Lucy sat with a knowing smile, not saying a word, seemingly not caring if Jim joined in, not paying much attention to him, focusing on her summer crowd. Jim felt intimidated among these smoothies. He wondered if he had been drafted into somebody else's game. Was this drama or farce?

"I hear you're skipping college," a girl asked. "You're in construction work?"

"Somebody has to work for a living," Jim said defensively. "We're not all privileged."

"Touché, Alice. We're all just bounders from the leisure class."

"But, just think. After I graduate, I'll actually have important work to do. Whereas Jim here will still be lugging lumber."

Her friends doused him in ridicule, mocking him. It was an hour before Jim and Lucy were alone.

"What was that all about?"

"Aren't they a riot?" Lucy misdirected his question.

"It feels like they're protecting you from me."

"You and your imagination. You're always dreaming up stuff."

"Then why does this dream seem real?"

When her folks came in from their tennis match, they greeted him coolly and with condescension.

"Ah, The high school romeo graces our presence."

"Ed, he's our guest."

"But only until tomorrow, right?"

Jim didn't answer.

"Today then?" and laughed. "Come, let's shower and leave these couch crawlers to themselves. Maybe they can find some new furniture to wrestle on."

"Daddy, you're bad," Lucy taunted her father.

The dance that night at the lake club was a social disaster for Jim. Her friends swarmed around Lucy, isolating her from her high school beaux. Every dance with Lucy was interrupted. And none of the other girls showed any interest in him so he sat and glumly watched his senior year partner slide away.

Before he left the next day, she told him she was breaking up with him. They were going in different directions and they might as well make a clean break now.

After she told him it was over, he began to dissolve. If he was aimless before, he was now plainly lost.

* * *

When he arrived back home, he was greeted by the news that his mother had arranged for him to attend a southern university.

* * *

The disappointment, the failure and fragility of his relationships now brought him pain, and with it, a lack of confidence, self-belittlement and weird skids into the dark internal space of his own shadowbox.

He was filled with remorse. Wounded by Lucy's rejection, he wondered where he had gone wrong. He was not one to pity himself or blame others for his mistakes. Not self- pity because he had already overcome a blighted childhood before age ten by his own grit, and never dwelt long on the debris of the past. As for blaming others, that didn't happen. One of the residual benefits of being a Catholic was that one was always reminded, like boaters, that people were responsible for their own wake. But why hadn't he paid more attention to school and concentrated on his own betterment? Tough that classes were dull. And why so much partying? He was worn out by his own social schedule, driven by the constant urge to be out drinking with his buddies.

He was eighteen and he felt socially satiated. He had seen enough of country club dances and roadhouses. People saved matches, souvenirs, from the clubs they danced in and he had a drawerful. It hadn't bothered him during the school year that he avoided the college prep around him. Now he would pay the price.

He had gone, wearing a tux, into New York nightclubs at fifteen at a time when an acceleration of raw energy and nervous drive had propelled him into a whirling social fluster. It now finally struck him that it would be satisfying to be quiet, knowing he might re-emerge someday and be better for the effort. The war lasted four long years, and in that worldwide explosion everyone aged ten years in the process. He was no exception.

The waste. The utter waste. Four years of dull classes with only a few bright timeslots along the way—Humpty Dumpty who taught World History at FUMA, and the chunky Algebra teacher in summer school who had opened the door briefly to an understanding of math and the personal empathy of Mr. Tales.

He figured, "I don't belong in the suburbs. Maybe I did blow it early, but at least there was something big to lose."

The last day before he left for college, he borrowed the family car and went by himself to bid the ocean goodbye. He had gone through most of the stages of loss concerning Lucy and his psyche was for the moment moderately steady. Reaching the shore, he parked and walked through the sand. He felt like he was riding an outbound wave, leaving teen confusion behind. His choices were no longer confined to the dark selection between rampant physical urges and popular boyhood. Hovering at the edge of the sea, he looked out over the layered foam, abreast of the beach. It was then that he felt the first release, the initial hint that he would be able to guide himself into the deep and perhaps avoid the confusion of a worthless life stream. Perhaps there could be a new journey. As he turned into the offshore wind that unloaded the spray-topped waves, his old self collapsed at his feet. And left him empty.

He had nothing to fall back on—no real set of beliefs, no adult supervision and, sad to say, no real friend because he had been too busy overseeing his female exploits. He understood what it was to be alone. He also knew that his sense of self-esteem had really been self-delusion.

BOOK TWO

Chapter 5
(1947 - 1948)

"Are you helping someone move in?" she asked.

There was the light of social grace shining on her face. When she looked up at Jim, she flashed a wide and welcoming smile, presenting him with a flesh portrait of the type of beauty spawned by their movie generation. Long dark hair framed an angel's face, eyes sparkling brown. Her pertness shone bright and she signaled that she was ready to engage, almost daring him to acknowledge that she could please. Her perky air and perfectly fitting clothes gave her a confidence of manner that spoke through her diminutive stature. Aware that she was socially adept, he presumed that she knew how to provoke and stimulate. Chances are her family had prepared her well; no doubt her promenades included fetes and garden tours along a long coast from Newport's lawn tennis club to Manhattan's cafes. Petite, not five feet, she must have known from experience that men would want to protect and envelope her. Luckily for Jim, she saw something in his serious demeanor that would straightaway open a path to her emotions if he chose to bend her way, offering him an outlet for his newly established reticence. Would he be her first conquest here in the unruly jungles of Florida? Why not? After all, today was a new start for both of them, away from their families, independent and able to paste together their own personas. It was a day that she, but not he, had prepared for.

Jim was a foot taller, thin with a lot of dark hair and an unsmiling countenance. He recognized in her markings all the country-club-trained young women that he had grown up with on Long Island. Dressed perfectly in rich fabrics, she was obviously chiseled from affluent stock. He no longer offered the cheery façade that he once wore, before a set of discouragements sapped his early attempts at securing a nuanced personality. Nevertheless, she found his diffidence attractive.

"Yes. A girl named Boots," he said looking around for her. "We drove down together."

"Properly chaperoned, I'm sure."

She could see he was comfortable with girls who had the stage presence to provide sassy openings.

"By her sainted mother."

Boots and he had weathered a trip down the East Coast that included a hurricane and found themselves with five hundred other students at an abandoned Air Force base miles from anywhere instead of housed in the sleek modern buildings they had seen in the brochures depicting the University of Miami's main campus.

"Where do you call home?"

"Manhasset, outside New York."

"Surprise. I'm from Roslyn."

"You must be Kitty Warsaw. Your reputation preceded you. I'm Jim."

She gave him a fresh look, but quickly saw there was no criticism in the remark, "Is your friend as appalled as I am by what she's seen?"

"She's in shock," Jim answered.

Because of her tiny stature, she knew that people addressing her had the chance to peer down to inspect her entire visage from an elevated place, so she always made it a practice to appear finished looking, knowing that she would be inspected top down.

She said, almost as if she divined something about him and that he would understand, "To make matters worse, I'm rooming with this Southern girl. When I told her I was half-Jewish, the mint in her julep must have wilted because she ran away to cry to her mother."

They were forced to step aside while conversing, caught as they were in the commotion of moving-in day. New women students flowed past them, carrying suitcases of recently purchased clothes carefully protected by tissue paper. Parents hauled boxes, new typewriters, and pictures from home. It was their first day on the

South Campus in September of 1947, and they were all trying to hide their disappointment about their general surroundings.

A thin blonde, looking distressed, approached them. "What a dump!" she said to Jim and "Hi" to Kitty.

"This is Kitty from Roslyn that I told you about. Say hello to Boots."

"To make matters worse, I have a worm for a roommate," Boots said.

"You too?"

"We both got stuck?"

"I was saying that when I told my suitemate that I was Jewish, she almost fainted. She kept looking behind me to see if I had dragged a goat in for sacrifice."

"That must have unwrinkled her curls."

The two young women appeared comfortable with one another.

"You know Danny Devon? I dated him. A good kisser," said Kitty.

"I dated him too. He's one of Jim's best friends."

"A good guy," Jim said.

"I like your outfit.'

"Lord and Taylor."

"Why did I have to ask? Where else?"

Jim said, "Maybe the two of you should room together."

The girls looked at each other.

"Could we?"

"Great."

"Let's see what we can do."

That's how Jim found one of his best friends a new best friend.

For the next two hours, Jim wandered back and forth between administrators and the other assigners of destinies that determine college–directed lives. In the end, he succeeded in bringing the two girls together.

Boots was a long-time buddy. She and Jim had endured four years in hormone-high school to discover themselves shelved in the reconditioned Homestead Air Force Base instead of the ivy-covered walls—or at least Mediterranean villas—they imagined finding at alma mater. By mid-afternoon, the two Long Island girls were in better spirits and were boarded together in the former officer's barracks. The trio agreed to regroup after dinner and attend the mixer for new students.

Jim had settled in earlier that morning in one of the reopened barracks along the road bordered by scrub pines and tropical-looking bushes. The abundance of flowers in the South would always surprise him. He walked past several yellow wooden structures and a dining hall before entering his unorthodox two-story dorm. Estimating that the top floor would be less noisy, he climbed the barrack's stairs and noticed that while he was away, most of the compartments had been occupied. Ten by ten alcoves were sectioned off and bordered by high cabinets. He checked the lock on his clothes compartment, set his sunglasses down on the desk and walked over to the fire escape. A couple guys were lounging there.

"Here comes another recruit."

"Hi," he said. "I'm Jim Mahoney from Long Island."

"A duck out of water. Have a seat."

"Take in the view. If you look hard you can see the rifle range."

Two of the men were older. The war had been over for two years, and this was the second of the great surge of returning veterans taking advantage of a free education courtesy of the tax-supported G.I. Bill. Even though he was not a beneficiary of that largesse, Jim smarted at any criticism of the legislation, the view that not every army and navy shitkicker deserved or was ready for a college education. The attack dug at Jim's defenses because in his own heart, he knew he was not prepared for college.

The avalanche of ex-G.I.s was overwhelming institutions of higher learning across the country. Universities, flooded with applications, were doing their best to cope, adding staff and temporary housing in the form of Quonset huts or trailer parks to accommodate the vets and sometimes their brides and babies. University officials gave in to the college-bound pressure by leasing this old air base; a facility that lay twenty miles south of the main facility at Coral Gables. Though there was an active bus service, the new students would be housed, taught and isolated here—much closer to a bevy of swamp alligators than the main library. They would be going to classes in former storage buildings.

One said, "Like I'm back in the Army. Can't believe my eyes."

"A sailor arrived this morning after driving a thousand miles, took one look, and turned around and headed back."

The four of them stretched out on the wooden steps.

"Couldn't wait to get down here in the tropics," the other older guy said. "I was stationed in the Aleutians, and I figured my bones needed to be thawed out. Plus I heard it was a party school."

"Some party. Must be hiding the chorus girls in the swamp."

"I must be regressing. College is supposed to expand your mind. So far, I'm back in Camp Devon four years ago."

"Marty Lippman," the younger guy said. "From Westchester."

Jim and he shook hands.

"How did you manage to get down?" Jim asked.

"Motorcycle," Marty answered. "Or did you mean selection process. The answer there is that I goofed off in high school and didn't have too many choices."

"Two of us," Jim concurred.

"God! Barracks! Do you think they'll make us swab the decks? Or put us on KP?"

"Just pray they don't hire my old mess sergeant."

Jim showered and put on a fresh shirt and while he was getting dressed, a drenching thunderstorm developed and shook the wooden facilities with powerful gusts, introducing them to the real tropics.

The mess hall, which after dinner turned into their study hall, had been renovated to include a soda shop but still retained the grimness of its original purpose to feed troops quickly. The aroma of grease was soaked into its timbers. Jim sat there waiting for his friends who arrived in states of consternation.

"It rained so hard there were coral snakes in the puddles."

Kitty said, "I'm ready to leave. We're in the jungle."

The event with the coral snakes was not the end of their encounter with tropical wildlife. A couple of weeks later, the girls found an alligator on their front porch.

As the evening rainstorm thundered out to sea, the women calmed down and looked forward to the mixer. The university, not insensitive to the fact that they had plunked rambunctious youngsters down on a remote airstrip, tried to make up for their housing deficiencies by bringing in the Tex Benecke Orchestra to play that night in one of the immense airplane hangars that had once housed aircraft that prowled the ocean. Tex Benecke, a featured singer and saxophonist, had taken over the Glenn Miller Band after the famous leader's plane crashed in the English Channel. Anticipation among the students was high. They had all grown up enmeshed in the band's repertoire but had no forewarning that the swing era—and their teenage years—were about to come to a close.

"Get settled in OK?" Jim asked the girls as he and Boots finished a cigarette after their meal.

Kitty said, "Yes. So far, no cat fights."

Boots jumped in, "You should see the size of the shoes this one wears. I feel like an Amazon next to her."

They headed out to the dance in a light rain.

Kitty wore a yellow slicker. The rain trickled down the hood and her face glistened, butter-wet. Light surrounded her smile and the smell of oilcloth permeated the air. The salty, linoleum fragrance would recall for her this first night of their college adventure. Remind her wistfully of Jim for the rest of her life.

The hangar, once the dry dock for a huge amphibian that floated over the Florida coast searching for German submarines, bulged so large that the cavern overwhelmed the festivities. At one end, dwarfed by the space, the old Miller band sang out the melodies that were an emotional expression of all their young lives: the swinging, bouncing sax and clarinet-driven tunes that flowed in their bloodstream and reflected and almost explained their lives. The band, the most important cultural musical force of the war years and the signature sound of their emotional upbringing, was arrayed before them in white suits.

The upperclassmen, who had volunteered to help with decorations, found the work daunting. It was like stringing a necklace on a whale. The place was gargantuan. What they couldn't disguise was the charm and significance of the music. The band's thumping rhythm filled every square inch of space with familiar anthems that like a great current had floated under the war years, filling them again with longing and joy. Music that helped create who they were. The band couldn't fail with their selections, loud with a trumpery that re-wound the intimacy of memories of lost and torn emotions, the recollections of the romances that had spurred their lives.

The three sporty New Yorkers, who grew up fast during the war, had been early patrons of some of the best dance palaces in the country and had been listening to the big bands for years on Broadway and in the roadhouses that surrounded the metropolitan area. They had been regular customers in Manhattan's ballrooms so they were accustomed to the presence of hundreds of dancers.

Tex sang all his favorites—"Kalamazoo," "Chattanooga Choo Choo" and "Don't Sit under the Apple Tree"—songs embedded in the dancing muscles of an entire generation. Everyone here knew the words of all the tunes. But they were unaware of the new verses that awaited them. They would encounter the literature of all the ages but few of the revelers understood the depths of concentration needed to focus on civilization's march to educate its young.

Tonight was a snapshot of where life had led them and where they would go from here. They teetered on the fulcrum. Though he didn't know it, Jim Mahoney would make one of the greatest discoveries of his personal life here and secure one of his finest victories. And, more or less, retain it.

Because men outpopulated the women at a ten-to-one ratio, it didn't take Jim long to lose sight of his companions. Both girls, smooth dancers, were soon setting the standard among the handful of women on the base. They stood out because of their looks and their outpouring of gracelight. They dominated the scene that night. Before the week was out, Kitty was writing home asking her mom to ship down extra "date" dresses.

As the familiar music throbbed through the hangar, Jim bumped into Marty, the motorcyclist from Westchester. "I saw you parade in here with a girl on each arm. What happened? They ditch you for this crowd of vets?"

"Afraid so," Jim said. "I was saving one of them for you, but they both got snatched away."

"Odds are you won't see them again until Christmas."

"My loss."

"Before classes start, I think I'll take a ride around Miami to get the lay of the land. Want to go sightseeing with me?"

"Do I have to sit all day with my arms around you?"

"Don't worry. I won't let you fall in love with me."

They moved to the coke bar. They'd find no beer on campus.

"Just when I turn eighteen and am finally legal in New York State, I move to Florida where the law is twenty-one and I still can't buy a bottle of brew."

As they were standing there, other guys made a path for the approaching young beauty from Roslyn, small and bright and lovable.

"There you are," Kitty said to Jim. "Your turn to dance."

"The pleasure's mine," Jim replied as they walked through a gauntlet of randy G.I.s.

They were together for about five minutes before another guy cut in. During their time in each other's arms, Kitty's eyes never strayed from his. She focused on him as if they were alone in the mammoth hangar. So light on her feet.

"Aren't you intimidated by all this attention?" he asked.

"Did you forget I'm a drama major? I'm eating it up. I turn from pumpkin to princess with an audience. They're my oxygen."

"I feel like a couple hundred pairs of eyes are checking to see if my shoes know the right dance steps."

She responded to his awkward dancing with light steps and an easy swinging motion. Sashaying around the floor, she'd skidaway from his arms and twirl and be reeled back in. Weighing hardly a hundred pounds, her movements seemed airborne.

"Happy feet," she said.

"Happy arms."

"And I'm the one who gets to feel them."

He accepted it all. That she should be attracted to him. That he should naturally fill her expectations.

Later that night, after the dance, as they were putting up their hair, Kitty would say, "I really like Jim."

"I'd better tell you a couple things about him," Boots said. "He's on the rebound. He was going with this girl all senior year, this Lucy, and they were tight as ticks. But she dumped him this summer and he's been a mess since."

"Is that why he's so quiet?"

"He was one of those hammer from hell guys—drank a lot, got in trouble, flunked courses—but I think he has this basic need to straighten himself out. You might have caught him at a bad time."

"Maybe I could help him figure things out?" Kitty asked.

"Don't plan on it, honey. He's a tough case. Besides we need to find one of these older guys who has already settled down. Been through the growing-up stage."

* * *

The next day, a Sunday, Jim rose early and left the snoring row of vets in the barracks. Following instructions, he took the school's jitney to the Main Campus in Coral Gables, and then transferred to the municipal bus line after a long wait. He finally arrived at his destination—it entailed a forty mile round trip—St. Theresa's Catholic Church (Lisieux, not Avila). Jim walked through the warm, fragrant semi-tropical morning into the soft-looking church of the Little Flower, built in the Spanish style and surrounded by palm trees. It was Latin without the bleeding statues, yet eye-achingly golden. A small, thin girl was practicing on the organ.

Arriving early, he read the church bulletin that included a history of the parish. A mission church, outside the boundaries of any American diocese, St. Theresa's had some leeway concerning church rules. One of the priests was Father Bucko. ("Come here my little bucko," movie star W.C. Fields would say to unsuspecting children.). Jim smiled.

At mass, there was an announcement inviting college students to join the interscholastic Newman Club. He signed up on his way out of church while the slim girl played a high-blown recessional. When he returned to the barracks at noon, Marty was still asleep.

Jim sat down to write a letter home, but before he had finished his new friend from New Rochelle was mobile. After something to eat, the pair uncovered Marty's motorcycle and he laid his leg down hard on the starter and off they went on his gas-farting two-wheeler. They sped up U.S. #1 past flamingo farms and monkey zoos and soon arrived at the blue-green sea off a sandy beach called Matheson Hammock, a favorite student hangout. They motored around the Main Campus in Coral Gables, passing the grand Biltmore Hotel, one of the Spanish-inspired pink and orange Florida spas that reflected the flamboyance of the Twenties. Then they headed over the causeway and crossed Biscayne Bay to Miami Beach. They turned right on the beach road and chugged past the art deco-inspired small hotels that ran along the strand. Jim's appetite for slumming was rising with the heat of the day. Awash in pastels, the area claimed his attention. He wondered if America's dream, complete with palm trees, had already come true. Little old men and women on their way to the beachfront were dodging traffic on the wide highway, carrying umbrellas and wearing floppy hats. Jim inhaled the sensations of the warm and lazy ocean that surrounded him. Tropical siren calls were ringing in his head.

Turning north, they spotted gleaming white hotels stretched along the barrier beach. Near the Fontainebleau, Marty parked his bike on a side street, having no intention of leaving his precious metal with some parking jockey. Both young New Yorkers were familiar with Manhattan's dark-paneled hotels but had never seen this kind of open, bright, seaside architecture. In the lobby, both noticed a number of fellow students that they had encountered during sign-in, including a brood of sloe-eyed New York girls who knew their way around, escorted by cool-looking, Mediterranean-tinged males. Jim's sexual antenna immediately began to revolve.

They bumped into a pair of their classmates. The guy was tall and thin and very tan, with glistening, brilliantine hair, and his date was a dark, seductive-looking woman who appeared to be swathed in creams. They were both wearing out-of-control colors. Marty had vaguely known the guy, Daniel, from their Westchester social mix.

"Hi," said Marty. "We're checking up on the beautiful people."

"Look no further," said the young beauty named Marsha.

Daniel invited them for drinks. "Stay. You both need tans."

The lobby was light and airy, spreading away to an indoor courtyard with a splashing fountain. Through an opening in the floor to ceiling glass panels, they exited upon an outdoor terrace edged by a white marble balustrade. Wide stairs led them down to a huge pool area. Farther on, across the wide sands, lay the ocean. The sunshine bore down on the entire scene with harsh, startling light.

An immense deck surrounded the pool, lined with lounges. There were only a few people in the water and, oddly, no children. Lovers mostly, coupled under bright-colored umbrellas. Dominating the complex was a semi-circle of cabanas that opened onto the pool. The cabanas included dressing rooms, a small kitchen, a wet bar and heavily cushioned chaises, each enclosure a playhouse of pleasure. Above, on the outside terrace nearer the hotel, a Cuban band played.

Marsha excused herself and returned a few minutes later in her two-piece swimsuit covered with a light fabric wrap. A few cabanas away, four older guys, drinking and laughing loudly, played cards under the biggest deck umbrella Jim had ever seen.

"There are fresh trunks in the dressing room if you want to swim," Daniel suggested.

Marty said no, but Jim agreed to his offer. A waiter came by and Daniel ordered gin rickeys as they eased themselves into cushy lounges beneath flowery cloth shades, soon to be joined by water-dappled Jim. They provided a distinct portrait of New York's spoiled suburban children. They didn't seek luxury; they expected it. They had never been impressed with the trappings of wealth, only its absence.

Jim, however, was unfamiliar with the kind of cabana-casino life available here and momentarily fell under the spell of its seduction. A lazy, sensuous life could be enjoyed here. But in his current frame of mind, it struck him as shallow, though a year ago, the easy lassitude would have caught his fancy: soft girls in bathing suits strolling on a white beach in an alcoholic haze.

The lid on that kind of life was closing for him; he would reject the inviting semi-tropical existence that opened its pleasures here. He had begun to believe that he had a larger life at stake.

* * *

Jim went over to the women's dorm to check on Boots after they returned from their pastel-tinted bike tour. They sat outside as the western sky turned into a half circle of reds and golds and deep purples. Both Boots and Kitty had enjoyed coffee dates during the day and were already making their mark on the battalion of vets.

"Listen, I better tell you. Kitty's got a crush on you."

Jim, never surprised at the breadth of a female's emotional horizons, looked up at her and said, "I'd better straighten her out about that."

"Just thought I'd warn you."

"Notice taken."

They talked about class registration the next day. The girls had been worrying over the curriculum book most of the day. Jim had made his choices weeks ago. They compared notes and saw that all three of them would be in the History of Civilization class together.

"Are all your classes down here?" Boots asked.

"No. I have to go up to the Main Campus for Latin."

"Latin?"

"My dead soul is in need of a dead language. That way I can talk to myself."

The next day was spent registering and buying textbooks.

On Tuesday, they began classes. On this first day of college, Jim Mahoney was eighteen and, by his own estimates, a non-starter in life's futurity. He awakened in the dorm barracks and looked out the window toward the runways that were being reclaimed by Florida growth, the concrete along with the war years disappearing under the weeds. As he made his way to his first class, he acknowledged to himself that he was an empty shell. All that he knew was that he didn't know anything and that he somehow had to learn to clarify his confusion. He felt colorless and transparent and that his life was undistinguished. This morning he would struggle toward the starting line of a new life. He was empty of love, compassion and understanding. All he had was his Catholic faith, a belief system that told him he would probably need to renounce almost everything that had come before and rearrange everything anew. He walked up the ramp onto the loading docks surrounding the Air Force storage compartments that had been turned into classrooms, and he hoped for the best. Something deep inside him told him that only learning could save him.

Western Civ was the first class on his schedule. Kitty arrived in a clean, crisp dress that hung perfectly on her doll-sized body. Boots came in wearing a red jumper he recognized from their days at Manhasset High, taking him back for a moment to the messiness of his last year there. Their prof, recently removed from Harvard over some infraction, appeared to be smart and articulate and ruled like a benign dictator over his unformed students. His intention was to make them rethink their basic beliefs. Jim could hardly realize that within these wooden walls he would be exposed to ideas that would change him into a beneficiary of some of the knowledge embodied in Dr. Joseph King. The cumulative significance of Euro-Christian history would help release Jim from small town ignorance; he would serve as one of the recipients of the cultural treasures stored in this room. With his bow tie and black horn-rimmed glasses and beefy white face and floppy lips, Dr. King would be Jim's first teacher of note. That this academic would shortly take the most beautiful girl on campus as his lover would only increase Jim's respect for the ousted Harvard philosopher.

Dr. King began, "I want you to take yourselves seriously. Try to respect the emergence of a sense of responsibility within you. Don't imagine you don't know how to proceed and haven't got the means to absorb big ideas just because it's all new to you. You might be confused by an indifference to knowledge from wherever you came from or by your church or society. I know you don't want to be so different that you're objects of scorn but don't be afraid of not conforming. We don't live in a society where intelligence counts as much as money and prestige. But challenge yourselves. You don't have to automatically obey authority just because you're trying to please those who think they have a right to exercise power over you. Take control of your lives....We'll begin at the agora."

After class, a well-built ex-sailor squired Boots away, while Jim corralled Kitty.

"Do you have another class?"

"Not for an hour."

"I liked what he had to say," Jim said, motioning back to the class setting.

"I'm not used to such strong views, but I guess that's what I came to hear."

"Let's talk. Would you like some coffee?"

They strolled along to the soft-yellow wooden building that housed the soda shop. Seated, she looked at Jim carefully, knowing she was interested in him. And he could feel her curiosity and warmth. She waited for him to speak, deferred to him, as if she bowed to her own feelings that she was in his hands. She waited for him to shape the conversation. He chose to talk about Dr. King.

"Sounds like we'll be hearing some new messages."

"And tossing out old ones. But I'll never go against what my parents taught me."

"And I'll never go against the Church. But I like what he says. Maybe he can help clear some of the fog out of our heads. It seems forever, I've been running around with smoke in my brain."

"Just keep it out of your eyes so you can see what's in front of you."

"I need to clear up things. Maybe my whole life. What I need to do is buckle down. I just wasted four years in high school and know that the only path open to me is to get my head into the books. I've promised myself to do that."

"That won't leave you much time to play."

"Even worse. I need to find a job. Seeing I was such a lousy college prospect, I had to make a deal with my old man to pay half my college costs."

"Hello and Goodbye, Joe College."

"True," he said.

She accepted what he said. There was no room in his life this year for anyone but his own struggle with himself. But she wanted to be sure.

Kitty said, "We can't always control things. We think we need something and set our sights on getting it—but sometimes feelings come into play and trip us up."

He looked her in the eye. "I know I'll be missing a lot. But I'm not going to be any good for anyone until I fix myself."

"Maybe you're OK the way you are."

"I'm not," he said adamantly. "I'm a mess and I have to fix myself before I even think about reaching out to someone else. It's plain to me. I don't know where I am or where I'm going to land. All I know is that I won't be the same person a year from now. Nor two years or four years."

She watched him as he diminished himself and the attraction she felt for him began to ebb.

It was as if he had to sail off alone, waving to the crowd on the dock. Farewell to all the Vickys and their prospective future lives in the suburbs, their picnics, barbeques and soap operas. For now, he would have to do without their company.

They went their separate ways. A psychologically necessary journey on his part, a social, biological and economic necessity on hers. Women, without resources in a male world, depended on marriage. Finding a mate was one of the principal reasons for attending college. Whether by choice or chance, both Boots and Kitty found their husbands, ex-navy guys, during their school year on South Campus: tiny Kitty attracted a 6'5' sky-high suitor and Boots the well-built sailor she met on the first day of classes.

Jim would see them with their new beaus, happy and cheerful, and from time to time he would have lunch with one of them and they would catch up on campus gossip or news from home. Stories like the one about the pyromaniac in the women's residence who took a match to dresses hanging from dorm room doors. Alarmed, the girls decided to conduct their own fire drills by throwing their mattresses out of their second story windows to cushion any emergency jump. Sometimes tales filtered through Boots about

Saylor or one of the other Alphas. Jim had told Saylor that he would help protect Boots from other guys while they were away for college, but he quickly saw that was an impossible task The fish were jumping out of the tank to attract this pair of beauties.

He had other priorities. He intended to build a cocoon of solitude around himself. He would have to leave socializing behind.

That evening set the tone of his new life. He took his books across the road to the study area and sat for four hours until closing time at eleven. He read from the works of Plato and Aristotle, perhaps understanding half of what he read, so he would go back and struggle over the words three or four times, and on a fair average, the glimmer of an idea or two would gather in his head.

He realized how insignificant he was, how he would have to struggle to straighten himself out. In bed that night as the noise from the barracks began to settle down, he reviewed his first day. He had verbalized his intentions for the first time to Kitty about what he needed to do to save himself. He was humbled in Dr. King's class by his lack of knowledge. Realizing that he knew nothing, he also gleaned that such recognition was the beginning of knowledge.

Lastly he thought about Lucy and of her June promise of loyalty, and her August decision to part ways with him. He had been flattened by the experience, ground up and pan-fried. He had begun to lose weight and his sexual drive. He no longer inspected girls' bodies for signs of fantasy gratification. Emotional doors would be closing as intellectual ones opened. Duality was taking its hold on him. He had hit bottom, feeling defeated by his inability to secure relationships and to succeed in school. If only he had had this hunger in 1943 instead of wasting four years of indirection. He carried a sense of utter loss within him. He craved knowledge.

Meanwhile he needed a job. After settling into his new routine, Jim went searching for employment. He had almost run out of money after purchasing textbooks and paying for setup expenses and services, so the need was immediate. Because of the isolation of the South Campus, he took a series of bus rides to Coconut Grove and bought a local paper. In the jobs section he saw that the Walgreen's drug store in town needed a soda jerk, so he applied and was accepted. Organizing his class schedule and reserving study time, he signed on for a forty-hour week. Owing to the long commute, he chose to work long shifts, usually from 1:00 until 11:00 at night, leaving him three free days a week to hit the books. A defendant on trial before every court or forum of moral justice that existed in his youth, Jim was paying for his years of neglect.

Closing up the soda fountain one night, he had checked the cash against receipts and called over to the manager.

"The bank's right," Jim reported.

"Don't fall asleep on the bus and miss your connection."

But invariably on the way back to the barracks, the municipal bus driver would find Jim asleep over an open book when they arrived at the transfer point where he would ride the midnight jitney back to Homestead.

* * *

On his first day of class on the distant Main Campus, he wore his heavy white woolen sweater that had recently supported his orange M football letter. He wore it because he thought he looked good in it, and it didn't bother him on the air-conditioned bus ride up U.S #1. But when he exited onto university grounds, he began to sweat through his wool. A sympathetic upperclassman, obviously a G.I., approached him and suggested that Jim ought to reconsider wearing winter clothing in 85-degree heat. Jim dutifully followed the guy's suggestion, removed the offending garment and wrapped it around his waist. Nobody had ever mistaken him as sensible; he wasn't even smart enough to know what clime he was in.

* * *

Jim's first excursion into new thinking came from an offhand remark Dr. King made about a local Miami writer, Philip Wylie. Curious, Jim looked up Wylie in the library on one of his trips to the Main Campus for his Latin course. He signed out a copy of *A Generation of Vipers* and devoured it in a few days. The effect of reading the explosive book could be compared to a house being moved off its foundation. In quick order, Jim read three or four of Wylie's novels, along with *An Essay on Morals* and came to understand something about critical pessimism. It dawned on him that everything he had been taught wasn't true. Fire-eating Wylie pointed out a path toward a method to find one's own way of understanding things.

He had never read such an outrageous book as *Vipers,* a diatribe that attacked American schools, churches and businessmen and lambasted repressed sexual mores and, famously, motherhood. There was barely an unscathed institution—all this written in the middle of the patriotic Second War. Wylie rabble-roused through the American countryside, Jeremiah on a rampage. He used harsh and colorful language to taint and harass, raised perfervid ideas to insult and question national values. He scored America for having lost touch with Christ, leaving church members insensitive and unable to handle Twentieth Century horror. His rant included the view that science had murdered religion.

Wylie spewed venom on the poor unsuspecting "common man," as well as on doctors and other professionals. He lauded Christ. He introduced Jim to Carl Jung, providing the green and raw-edged student with an alternative view of his own worth. Wylie reflected on America's bastardization of the Cinderella tale—that we admired neither her integrity nor work ethic, just her ascent on the social register. But Jim questioned Wylie's thrust against women. Jim's conclusion: Leave the ladies alone. But the author's definition of the intellectual desert found in the suburbs nicked Jim's nerve center as the writer railed against materialism and phonyism. But toward the end of the book, Wylie moderated his voice to praise Jung. It was Philip Wylie who opened Jim's mind to controversy. And let some blue sky in.

Wylie led Jim to that other hell raiser, Mencken, and Mencken led him to a study of the Twenties, where he began to understand an era not his own for the first time.

He accepted Wylie's suggestion to be less stressed about sex, a modern view that had substance, but he knew his own conduct was still determined by the clean body mandate of Christ fortified by the Church.

Wylie taught him that it was all right to express anger—to hate the men and conditions that made people suffer in poverty, that made hordes of Africans enslaved, that allowed sadists to instill fear by establishing totalitarian and militaristic societies where women and children were abused. Wylie didn't advise him on what to do with the anger that he released in Jim or help him channel the sting that now began to sear his throat. Perhaps a lighter approach would help show Jim the way toward combating the dark side.

Wylie was only the first of several writers that popped open his head. He was so empty that he was susceptible to every idea that appeared on any page of any book he read.

Dr. King jumped ahead one day to the end of the Dark Ages and spoke of Saint Francis, minstrel of God. Francis was Jim's middle name and somewhere back in Chicago resided an uncle in whose honor he had been christened. Jim, for reasons he did not even bother to understand, launched into a study of the saint's life. His only previous awareness of the holy monk was the memory of a statue draped in a long brown outfit feeding birds out of plaster hands, hands that bore the stigmata of his Savior. On his own, Jim learned about the saint's warrior years, then his decision to live like Christ, humbly devoted to the poor and good works, his motives emanating from his feverish love of God. Jim marveled at the stories of how Francis wandered about the Italian countryside rehabilitating old churches and chapels, so struck by the thought that he couldn't dislodge it. He had an idea that the character of such a church builder would make an interesting hero in a play. The idea became the first of many projected written works that Jim would never set to paper. But his mind was beginning to churn.

It was Francis's view of humility that began to bore holes in Jim's arrogance and lead him quietly back to God. He had been an automatic Catholic for years, barely remembering the time when he was one of Christ's junior legionnaires. His visits to church after reading Francis became more meaningful, his prayers more thoughtful. He was shifting away from what he had become, back to what he once was—a long way back. His new attitudes were actually affecting him physically. His former cakewalk, his street strut, began to soften into a moderate stroll.

The years of drinking, dancing and driving jalopies to gin mills were fading behind him. He was becoming a social recluse at eighteen. Even his favorite music was dying out. Swing did not survive the year and all the big bands disbanded after the Christmas holidays. A new generation took over the jukeboxes and airwaves. Songs like "Mule Train." Awful stuff.

He was now thinking more about his actions and opinions and began to listen to others and respect them in ways he had not done before. Slowly, very slowly, he was learning to sympathize with others. And, he began to suffer the guilt for the pain he had inflicted on others in his life, especially his grandmother and aunt.

* * *

Marty Lippman wasn't the only freshman on campus to ride a motorcycle. There were about twenty bikes parked outside the numerous barracks.

"You want to learn how to drive my Indian?" Marty asked.

"Sure." Jim was never one to turn down a dare.

There were dozens of places on the former air base for test drives including the long weed-sprouting runways, but they chose to practice alongside the loading dock after classes let out. The biker patiently explained the shifting and control mechanisms and after a few trials and errors, with Marty literally running alongside his straddled bunkmate like a parent teaching a child on a two-wheeler, Jim began to take control of the Indian. He liked the feeling of power in his hands.

Sitting on the noisy, explosive machine, Jim felt a surge of excitement and, after a few lessons, he began to get the knack of operating it. In time, with Marty settled behind him as co-pilot, they took a ride down South Dixie Highway toward the Keys. Jim flew through the breeze and was exhilarated.

"You should get one of your own," Marty suggested. "A used one doesn't cost that much. Make your ride to work a lot easier."

Jim pondered the opportunity. He loved the freedom offered by the bike and the relationship between speed and the feeling of natural flight. Yet he knew riding a motorcycle was risky. There was a fair chance an enthusiast was going to get hurt one day and the consequences were severe at 60 MPH. Weighing the joy of it against the risks, Jim made an unnatural choice. He decided not to ride. It was a small compromise, opposing as it did, the thrust of his emotional instincts. He seemed to gain something and lose something in the transaction. He was settling down for a longer haul, as opposed to the immediacy of youthful derring-do. He had made a decision contrary to his natural recklessness.

* * *

But it was, after all, their college years and most students intended to stash away a few memories. The girls came and kidnapped Jim late one Friday afternoon when he wasn't working and took him to the Orange Bowl.

"We know you love football. So just put down those books and come with us."

"You have all weekend to do that stuff," said Kitty. Even though he didn't.

"Take a break, seeing as you never come to the beach with us."

"So where are the boyfriends?" Jim asked.

"They flew down to Havana together. They wanted to see the nightlife over there."

"As if Miami Beach wasn't enough."

It was true that the campus emptied on the weekend. That was fine with Jim. If he wasn't working, the lack of rumpus was conducive to his new pursuits. Rumor had it that many of the absent couples were nesting in one of the hotels along the ocean.

It was a warm October night, so different from the fall chill at home. The weather was more suitable for a donkey softball game in July. They rode the jitney with hundreds of others to the circus that was the Orange Bowl. Floridians love football and the spectacle that night reminded Jim of the gladiatorial battles he was studying in History. Bands were blaring under the special lighting, the crowd the noisiest he had heard since he listened to Giant fans scream during a Polo Grounds rally. The trio stomped up the stadium steps into the student section—freshmen sat far from the playing field. There they found three 10 x 10-inch colored cards on each seat

"What are these?"

"Flashcards for the halftime show."

"How do they work?"

"Where have you been? You never saw a card show before?"

As hundreds of students filed into the stands, the girls taught him how to display the cards. "We all hold them up in unison, see? And make a picture."

It was the custom at big universities to seat the students together. Then, on instruction from the cheerleaders, students would raise their colored cards at the appropriate moment and form a design composed of a thousand or more individual placards. The picture might spell out the name of the school, or show a portrait of their school symbol, an Illini Indian or a Southern Cal Trojan, or in the case here at Miami, display a big luscious orange or mimic the school's symbol (not an easy trick), a hurricane.

"Go Hurricanes," Kitty hollered when the team came on the field. She had been a cheerleader in high school and appreciated crowd participation, despite having no understanding of the game. When the spectators roared their approval on her side of the field, she would rise up and jump up and down. It turned out that she had cheered for Roslyn the year before, when the neighboring town beat Manhasset in a close game when Jim failed four times to march his team across the goal line from the three-yard marker.

Jim closely followed the game. His juices began to run, yet for the first time he was able to look at his own excitement from a distant place in his psyche. He didn't think he would ever be overwhelmed by the emotion of the game again. He was beginning to question his previous acceptance of violence. Blood sports like boxing and bull fighting now shook his moral position; he began to juxtapose his former calls for bloodshed with the new ideas percolating from his readings of St. Francis that promoted gentility.

"What's that brown thing on the field," Kitty asked Boots

"For god's sake, that's the football, Kitty," Boots said, rolling her eyes.

At halftime, out came the Miami band to exercise their formations on the gridiron, turning here and there in squad precision. The perky cheerleaders rose to coordinate the students who were all sitting with cards on their laps, ready to carry out their small part in the larger endeavor.

At the signal, a thousand students held up their cards and from across the field, a cheer went up as they viewed the results.

"What are we showing?"

"The orange and palm trees."

Next came the hurricane picture.

Massed "Oh's" and "Ah's" sounded from across the field.

"You're holding up the wrong card," Boots said to Jim. "You trying to mess up the picture?"

It was the next portrait the students presented that caused an uproar across the field, amid simultaneous, hilarious shouting. It was one of the better college pranks of the year. The student body blithely and without any knowledge of the overall content or consequences, composed a picture of a South American dictator taking a bribe from one of the American fruit companies. It was extraordinary criticism in a marketing area closely allied with South American trade. The insult required several State Department visits to quiet one of the many juntas operating in those years.

That was the end of flashcards for 1947.

* * *

Soon, Jim found a new inspiration, George Bernard Shaw, more Irish than he realized, uncompromisingly tweedy, still popping up in movie newsreels to celebrate his ninetieth birthday. He was a kind of aging thistle, standing in front of some castle, piping out a few humorous jibes at conventional living in his high, reedy voice. Reading through the old man's canon, Jim came to understand that GBS's dramatic works had something to do with preserving a lightly buttered political view aimed at maintaining a vibrant commonweal. He even came across Shaw's musical reviews and chuckled over the playwright's description that cellos sounded like bees flying around inside a stone jug. Jim studied Shaw's promotion of Fabian Socialism, the political action society that the playwright had created with Sidney and Beatrice Webb. His readings about them resulted in a seismic shift in Jim's political outlook. He became an advocate of the poor as well as for black and female equality. He came to believe that government control of transportation, medicine, utilities and fuel would protect the lower classes and ensure the social contract. From those readings, he became a life-long socialist. Shaw had given him a soft but significant shove on his way toward a personal philosophy.

Jim's observations about the phoniness of Manhasset and the attendant rat race in Manhattan provided mushy ground for the seeds of Marx. But Jim, following the Fabians, was suspicious of the way Stalin had twisted the basic socialist philosophy and vehemently repudiated any kind of communist-style violence. He became convinced, especially after reading Arthur Koestler's *Darkness at Noon* that the Russian system was badly flawed. But socialism was making headway in Europe. Shaw's and the Webb's efforts led to the creation of the British Labour Party and the London School of Economics, allowing Jim to learn how ideas turned into institutions. One old view made Jim chuckle: *If you look around at the world and you're not an idealistic Communist at nineteen, you're stupid. You're even more stupid if you're still a Marxist at thirty-nine*.

At the height of Jim's independent study of Shaw and the Fabians, Dr. King asked his students for a paper on any historical figure they admired. Jim promptly wrote up his findings on Shaw. When his teacher returned the grades for the assignment, he asked Jim to stay after class.

"I gave you a C-minus because this is an English lit paper. I hope you didn't cannibalize it from somebody's literature class."

Still naïve about academia, Jim was shocked.

"I researched it myself and think the Fabians made history."

"Nevertheless, a C-minus," Dr. King concluded.

But Doctor King, on second thought, had a more accepting view of the thin-looking young student and came to believe he may have misjudged the youth. Jim's final grade led the class.

* * *

Shaw's words stuck. Jim began to care about the poor, incensed that there should be hunger anywhere. Why couldn't America with all its surplus food feed the world? Midwest farmers were paid to store extra grain so that there wouldn't be a glut on the market and bring down prices, then after five years, they destroyed the crops. Why couldn't the U.S. just freight the surplus to the coasts and ship it oversees where it was needed? He was beginning to develop itchy convictions that would soon whip into a frenzy that was just below a controllable surface. He came to understand the importance of righteous anger.

* * *

In these sequestered months of study and work, Jim's social interaction with people revolved around St. Theresa's. There was Sunday mass, and sometimes a church party on Saturday at the Newman Club. One of the more notable visits to St. Theresa's occurred one Friday that fall when he stopped by church for confession on his way to his soda fountain job. He remembered the old joke about Friday confession. It was meant to keep sinners on lockdown over the weekend when their hormones howled. But busybodies at church on Sunday always checked to see if the confessant received communion; if not, it was presumed that he had faltered on the previous nights. Jim's offenses were so few and his behavior so correctly Christian that regular visits had become unnecessary, now that he was becoming more serene, not filled with a storm of infractions when it came time to face the once dreaded confessional. This particular occasion, after he entered the cramped closet, a hedonistic missionary priest confronted Jim.

"Bless me, father, for I have sinned. It's been a month since my last confession."

"Yes, son."

"I've had a few impure thoughts. Essentially, what's happening to me is that I'm trying to figure out all the new ideas I'm learning at school—dealing with science and Marxism."

The priest put aside the intellectual revelations and jumped on the sexual remark.

"You've only had thoughts about sex and didn't act out your temptations?"

"Yes, Father."

"You realize you could be selling your body over on the Beach, don't you? Haven't you heard about all the sexual commerce over there? You could go into any hotel any time you want and find some rich woman and make yourself a fortune giving her sex for money. Aren't you tempted to do that?"

Jim was amazed. What did this cleric want him to say?

"You could be wined and dined and dressed up in the latest fashions if you serviced their sexual needs. Have you ever thought of that?"

Even in the darkness, Jim sensed the priest was agitated. His voice wavered.

"You could be in some rich woman's bed right now overlooking the ocean."

Jim went silent. He had nothing more to say. He had done a lot of nasty things, but he had never entertained the idea of becoming a sexual service station. He received his blessing and left, wondering whose sins was echoing within the small wooden compartment.

* * *

One day in late October, Boots asked Jim to accompany her on an errand in Coral Gables; she was looking for a birthday gift for Kitty. He obliged. The side trip was on his way to work and only required a short detour before reporting to his job. After helping Boots select a present, he waited with her for a bus to take her back to the air base before going off to work. She looked attractive standing in the shade of a bright day in her cotton dress and shining blonde hair as they waited in the shelter out of the sun. A sparkling new Cadillac convertible motored past them. It was hard to avert their eyes as the open car hummed by. They were surprised when the car came to a screaming halt. The driver had slammed on his brakes and now threw the car in reverse, and the vehicle came lurching back toward them.

In the driver's seat was an almost familiar face.

"Aren't you Bootsie Harding?"

"Yes," she said, eyeing Jim for helpful signs of recognition.

"I'm George from Manhasset. George Hellas."

He had changed so dramatically that they didn't recognize him. He had been chubby and now he was thin. His face was drawn and he was barely able to smile.

"George! It's been a long time."

"A war in between. Where are you going? I'll give you a ride."

George had been one of the greatest hellions at Manhasset High. Always in trouble, fending off his parents, George learned how to express himself creatively by tinkering and rebuilding old cars. Jim remembered a long-ago afternoon when George played bumper tag on the Munsey Park hill with one of Jim's favorite cheerleaders, the one who taught him how to soul kiss.

Now he looked emaciated.

"We're living on South. You remember Jim Mahoney?"

"Matt's brother? I remember him. Good ball player. You shoulda told me you're here. I could have fixed you up on Main."

He parked and they entered a soda shop. They reminisced about Manhasset. They spoke of mutual friends and the hometown warriors and their waiting women who had endured the Second War. He had been in the Philippines and was still in recovery from wounds he received there.

"George, are you all right?" Bootsie asked after they sat. "You seem so different."

"Damned war, that's all. Truth is I'm not."

Jim felt empathy for the young naval veteran.

"We heard you were wounded."

"Seven times."

"My god."

"Still carrying around shrapnel. You could hang a magnet on me."

"We kids were so out of it. We never understood the suffering you guys were going through."

"Too busy having fun."

The pair of freshmen showed their embarrassment, knowing they had been insensitive during their school years. Now all the

G.I.s and sailors had come home, many with only part of their previous selves intact.

George said, "I'm back but everything seems changed."

Jim thought of the person he once knew, young, vibrant and alive, before George had to cope with injury. It seemed to the younger man that the light had gone out of the slightly older warrior's eyes. Jim wondered if George missed his war buddies. All that excitement and camaraderie. And how he must feel now that the war was won and it was every man for himself. Alone and mourning for the others and his younger self. He had paid dearly for his participation in the Pacific battles. Something had been burned out of him. He appeared to accept his own fragile mortality and the cruel whims of war. But it was sad. The war was over but the wounds still showed.

Finally, George rode off with Boots and they waved to Jim who was going in the other direction. Jim was humiliated by his lack of compassion for those of his generation who suffered during the war.

* * *

In spite of Jim's withdrawal into a quasi-reclusive state, intervals of physical passion arose within him. His desires had been rising for weeks and focused on the abundance of well-proportioned flesh that was pleasantly arranged on the bones of a girl named Rosemary from New Jersey. They took a couple of courses together and got to talking after class in that buzzy New York style of chatter that bound metropolitanites together.

"That last test was a bear," she said.

"All the better to stump you with, my dear."

"This little Goldilocks wasn't amused."

"Goldie's going to have to stay up later to study."

"You mean I have to cut my dates down to five a day?"

"Do you have any time to study between performances?"

She really looked at him for the first time, sizing him up. He had just been a nice kid in class. Now he turned challenger. Maybe he might have the right stuff after all.

"I'm not due in make-up for another hour."

All male-female relationships on the South Campus were regulated by the gender ratio, which greatly favored women. Because Rosemary was sensuous and sassy, she found she was more popular here in the South than goober pies.

"How are you getting along living away from home?"

"I'm majoring in ironing," Jim replied

"Do the older guys intimidate you?"

"No. I left my sense of competition way back there," indicating homeward. "Somewhere near shortstop."

"My friends over in your barracks say you've been hitting the books pretty hard."

"Yeah. I'll be wearing glasses before you know it."

"You better watch out," Rosemary said. "You'll end up looking like a palm tree. Everything on top and not much to show below."

They hit it off, but because Jim didn't have a car, his choices here in the swamps for dating destinations were limited. But he remembered there was to be a mixer that Friday night and asked her out. When she appeared for the night's events, she wore a dress a size too small for her that accentuated her ample body. But she had cared enough to fuss with her swept-up hairstyle in a way that made her look womanly and she had applied her prom night makeup. Her looks and easy manner rekindled all his youthful hubris.

But as they bade goodnight, she expressed no interest in snoogling. He was too thin and a little nervous. He was cute and all, but she was looking for something more substantial in terms of masculine fitness. They remained friendly classmates but discovered there was no fire in the basement. He returned that night to his cubicle and read until two in the morning. By the time he got to sleep, his lust for her had cooled. If a girl wasn't interested in him, there was no need for him to stay interested in her.

* * *

One Friday night in November, Jim arranged his work schedule so he could attend a Newman Club meeting, the school-affiliated youth group named after an intellectual English convert, who was one of the founders of the Oxford Movement, part of a worldwide surge in religious fever in the mid-nineteenth century. He was a gifted educator and preacher who inspired U.S. lay leaders to structure a Catholic organization in secular colleges. Their charge was to promote the idea that most of the new scientific views emerging from the laboratories were compatible with Catholicism. The club would provide skeptically trained undergraduates with a lecture series that would satisfy the sophistication of university-level fish eaters. Aside from Jim's docile interaction with his hometown beauties, he had made no effort to socialize with anyone except Rosemary until now. The Newman lecture, held in the church hall at St. Theresa's, was followed by a social hour. That entailed someone plugging in the Victrola so that couples would mingle. The dancing would be interrupted with conversation and sips of grape punch. But he had no interest in chatting with his fellow Samaritans. He focused on the slim girl that he had seen playing the organ at service, a day student from Coral Gables.

He simply went up to her—Mary Hall was her name—and asked her to dance. She was slight and perky and had a fey way about her that was appealing. She also had a slight limp. She wore a simple cotton dress; her attitude, homespun.

"I don't dance much," she said. "I have a gimpy leg. So, just sit here and tell me all your secrets."

"I'm afraid if I did, I'd scare you away."

"I notice you receive at mass," she said, spilling her own secret that she had been observing him as well, "so I know you can't be too dangerous."

"Fooled another one, did I?" he asked. "It's just that I'm on a long retreat."

"Praying for?"

He didn't know why he should hold back, "Merely a total change in my life."

"Like my dad says, you shouldn't just pray for winning horses"

"Come on, let's try to dance," he said, showing little empathy for her affliction. He wanted to hold her.

"You're taking your social life in your hands."

"I'll take the chance—seeing as I don't have one anyway."

He led her slowly. On occasion, she was forced to take a little hop to keep up.

"I'm so bad."

He pulled her toward her. "You mean so good."

He could feel her thin frame and small breasts where she crunched into him.

"I've heard you play a couple times," he said. "I guess musicians can't be all bad."

"How you northern boys treat us. Do you like music?"

"I play but I've hardly touched a keyboard since I got here."

They stepped off the dance floor while the other kids revved up for the Lindy.

"Is the organ as difficult as a piano?" he asked.

"Some," she said. "I can show you. Want to see?"

She took him by the hand and made a circuitous route through the buildings until she found a back door to the sacristy. Because she was the chief organist, she had unlimited access so that she could practice at times of her own choosing. The pair entered the church with its gold-bloated Baroque altar and climbed to the organ loft. In grade school, he had sung from a church loft and his piano teacher had been the choir organist, so he had some knowledge of the great instrument.

Mary chattered on as she ran her small hands across the multi-layered keyboards. She seemed less on fire than the women who usually attracted him. She had a quiet voice and seemed at peace with herself.

He said, "I get a kick out of you—such a petite thing—playing this big palooka."

"From little acorns, honey . . . Want to see what I can really do?" She proceeded to blast a few bars that rattled the glassware at the Newman meeting in the adjoining building. Then she settled into a quiet hymn.

"I like this one. Do you know it? Words from the other Theresa, the ecstatic one:

Christ has no body on earth but ours, no hands but ours, no feet but ours.

Ours are the eyes through which must look out Christ's compassion in the world

Ours are the feet with which he is to go about doing good."

"That's quite wonderful," Jim responded.

"I'm more interested in simpler songs, about the ways people act. I'm always amazed at how much people trust in one another."

Her quiet assurance appealed to him in his new state of consciousness. She was direct in a soft way. She appeared to be as simple and as complicated as a cloud.

When he left to take the bus, she said, "Don't be a stranger."

That Sunday Jim listened to the ringing of the bells as he approached St. Theresa's; the clear-sounding tolling that was a new experience for him, reminding him that he lived in a missionary culture where clanging bells called out to the faithful. He thought this mission church was a way station on a different kind of Camino Real that spread south and west across the Gulf into Mexico and into the lower Americas where Spanish flavored architecture and the simple faith of indigenous people made one's relationship with God seem natural. Not the same as the slog through the cold rain of the Northeast toward black stone remnants of immigrant faith.

As he walked through the church door, the sound of the bells became mixed with the welcoming sound from the organ loft. He looked forward to seeing Mary after mass, and when they found each other, she invited him home to meet her family. He stayed for the chicken and beans dinner. Sitting afterward on the sword grass, he accepted her expressions of friendship. Her single-minded faith and trustworthiness were beginning to emerge in their nascent relationship. His work schedule and study habits and his emotional fragility prevented him from pursuing her. But they would often chat following Sunday mass.

* * *

During Christmas vacation, through a fellow worker on the Main Campus, Jim found a higher-paying job at the Five & Dime in

Coral Gables, easing his transportation efforts and orienting him more toward the university's library. Because he didn't intend to go home for the holidays, he hoped to build a second semester nest egg by working long hours for two straight weeks over the break. In actuality, he couldn't face going home. He was still wounded from his rejection by Lucy, and Manhasset was an empty place that held too many bad memories. He was on to a new life and didn't want to interrupt the rhythm of it. On Christmas and New Year's Eve, he worked long shifts. Christmas Day he studied.

When the holiday revelers returned to campus, the monster of final exams came out of its cage to greet them. As was true at every institution of higher learning in America, millions of college G.I.s and their classmates buckled down to study, sometimes all night, in preparation for their end-of-semester tests. An over-the-counter substance called *No-Doz* was widely used to medicate tired minds and dispositions, the medicine's ingredients prevented students from falling asleep over crib notes. Jim experimented with the pill one night but felt so terrible the day of his test that he never bothered with the store-bought pick-me-up again. He did well on his finals and saw high-level grades posted next to his name, honors that he hadn't seen since grade school days.

At the same time, decisions had to be made regarding second semester living arrangements. Marty Lippman despised the barracks and spent several days searching for new quarters. Then he invited Jim and Kitty's boyfriend, Bob, to join him in renting a semi-detached bungalow just south of Coral Gables. Because the other guys had transportation and a handy bus line ran nearby, Jim agreed.

It was easy enough to move his meager goods into the three-bedroom wing that the New Yorkers shared. The furniture in his room could not have been sparer: a bed, a desk and lamp, a chair and the new Emerson radio he bought for $9.95. Not even a picture on the wall. The combined living-dining room was a small general-purpose space that included a couch, a coffee table and a table with four wobbly-legged chairs. The kitchen was the size of those found on two-engine passenger planes. A breezeway separated their apartment from the main house. Behind the house ran a ditch that filled with water and an occasional alligator.

Jim was often alone in the bungalow owing to the social activities of his two roommates, and the quiet suited him fine. It was there, in that tiny house, that he found another source of inspiration outside his regular schoolwork: he discovered the roisterous plots of Russian novels. Before the end of the school year he had come to the conclusion that the Russian Revolution was justified. It was just that the revolution got in the hands of the wrong people. That year he also followed the progress of the Chinese Revolution's long path, again agreeing with the need if not the solution. For the first time he began to consider American political issues, particularly the anti-Communist hysteria of Congress.

"Ever met a Communist?" he would ask those channeling conspiracy theories.

After a reply, "No? Well, you better watch out. There's one behind every bush."

* * *

A few weeks in his new digs and accompanied by his new radio, Jim began to listen to the Metropolitan Opera broadcasts on Saturday afternoons. He didn't particularly like the singing, so different from his pop favorites, but he continued to listen and dissect the bellowing that attended the quick-fix plots. He began to sense that there was something about higher culture that attracted his curiosity. It was the same as when he was eleven years old and he began to read the thick biographies on his mother's book shelf, not understanding much of what he was reading, but plowing ahead anyway under the self-guided impression that it was good for him, like mass on Sunday. It was the same with the Met broadcasts that stretched out into the dark afternoons of culture-less America. The journey toward higher art beckoned him. Radio had once before caused a major difference in his life when he began to listen to swing. Now, for a second time, the airwaves were wafting him to another level.

He was reading voraciously. He came upon Graham Greene and the Catholic world that Jim had just begun to restructure for himself. Greene posed questions in terms of fictional dilemmas that tested the freshman's religious outlook. Those questions led to deeper reflections. He was learning that answers didn't come easily.

He concluded that there were givers and takers and recognized that he had always been a taker. With his new sensibilities, he began consciously to change over to a more giving mode. He became more sensitive to others, less aggressive, more thoughtful, more understanding. More vulnerable. More how a sensitive human being should act. His primary nature until now had been essentially ego-driven and snarled in a protective coil of selfishness. He had had little compassion for his fellow beings; what had worked for him was self-assertion. Now a second nature was emerging, one centered on the suppression of ignorance. He began filing down the harshness that had made him coarse, attempting to replace shallowness with substance.

One Saturday afternoon, when Jim was home listening to the Met broadcast, his roommate Bob, the ex-gob, came in with his girlfriend Kitty.

"Hey, stranger," she said. "You've been forgetting your buddies in the swamp."

"How could I ever forget you in your yellow slicker?"

"I think you did. What's that? Tosca?"

"Yeah. About to take a leap."

"My folks used to take me to the Met. I mostly remember the ice cream we had afterwards at Louis Sherry's."

She looked different—she with the good fortune to have chosen wise parents and now a beau. She appeared more confident now that she was on her way to the wedding altar. Because she belonged to somebody else, Jim found her exceedingly attractive. He was beginning to understand there would be losses along the way.

* * *

One weeknight in April, there was an uproar in the women's dorm. One of the more aggressive motorcycle guys, feeling loose and half fried, ran his speedometer up past ninety on the long and narrow entrance road into the base. He thought he saw two motorcycle buddies coming at him and as a prank decided to scare the hell out of them and ride in between. Except that it was a car and he had to spin away at the last moment. He crashed and his broken body was picked up off the pavement and transferred to the building where Boots and Kitty lived. There was great consternation as the biker's body was brought in and set down in the front hallway.

Boots and Kitty reached the scene as calls went out for an ambulance and the police. Unconscious, the biker continued to breathe but he seemed to be struggling. The girls were all weeping; many had never seen a dying man. The guy's girlfriend lived in the same unit and came shrieking down the hall. She fell on his body and wiped the blood from his face and held him in her arms as he biked on to Valhalla.

The violent death cast a dark cloud over the campus. Living on the edge as the biker guy did and dying on a back road near the Everglades was not a college tale students chose to contemplate as they pursued their youthful agendas. The Long Island girls, shocked by the sight they witnessed, had to get out of the building. They walked over to the study hall and found Jim writing a paper following his class work. The girls cried as they told him the story. Marty, his cycling Westchester friend, was sitting nearby and when he heard the news, he turned white.

* * *

Though the women of the officer's barracks were appalled by the expiration of a life in their front room, they quickly resumed their main effort. That was to foster the possibility of early matrimony. Now that the school year was nearing completion, there was a need to solidify relationships. Sex flourished. Jim, one morning, visiting his old barracks, found Rosemary of New Jersey nestling in an upper bunk with a chunky-cheese guy from Wisconsin.

The accepted and often practiced routine among some of these college women was to shack up in a Miami Beach hotel on the weekends. Jim's two hometown beauties, well on their way to formal engagements with their Navy boyfriends, subscribed to an older tradition that required brides to be intact on their wedding nights. Yet they were sympathetic toward and supportive of the follies of their sister co-eds. They became nurses of a sort to these fallen angels, who often returned to the residence halls on Sunday nights with sand between their toes and elsewhere. Some girls came back from their weekend trysts in high states of anxiety and bounded into Kitty and Bootsie's dorm room.

"He came inside me" and "He didn't wear a rubber" were common complaints.

This called for a surgical room mentality. The afflicted girl would lie on one of the beds, legs akimbo. Taking an uncapped coke bottle and inserting it into the girl's vagina, either Kitty or Boots would administer a shaky procedure that was designed to drown any male remains in the cola, thus averting any adult responsibilities.

They were referred to as the pop bottle douche sisters, and their room as the dispensary.

* * *

In the warm sunshine of a Florida April, the dormant need in Jim Mahoney to find someone in whom to confide his emotions centered on the small frame of Mary Hall. One Sunday morning, she invited him to accompany her to the organ loft.

"Sit here," she said as the celebrant began the high mass.

She provided the musical background to the priest's incantations. During communion, Mary played a soft melody in keeping with the solemnity of the transubstantiation. When it came time for the recessional, Mary, agitated and nervous at the work before her, roared into a Bach toccata that seemed to lift the roof off the church. Her frail body exploded into action as she pounded the keys, rising off the bench, standing on the pedals. The air split in thunder as she thrust herself into the music. It was as if she was in a deadly match with the huge instrument. Jim watched her hurl her torso into the music, wildly attacking with her arms and legs. The crashing sounds produced a whirlwind—her tiny body moving against the beast with its broad encasement and angry pipes. Mesmerized, Jim saw this fiery girl consume herself ecstatically in the effort. When she finished, long after the last parishioner had left the nave, she was exhausted. She closed down the behemoth and its multi-layered keyboard, looked at Jim and fell into his arms. For the month that ended his freshman year, they were often together. Jim began to regain his confidence, to share his feelings and resumed living a more balanced life. He responded to this dynamo of a girl that now fought against his body with all the same passion she had wielded in battling the king of instruments. But the two young Catholic kids were forced by their faith to ignore their bodies' desires in favor of doctrine.

In the end, they knew their relationship wouldn't work out. He wouldn't be returning to school here. She needed a stability that she didn't think he could provide.

* * *

Jim had changed dramatically in just eight months. Thanks to a mendicant friar, a scowling commentator of the American scene, a successful West End playwright, a confused Catholic, and the sagacity of an exiled history teacher, he had emerged with a new way of understanding the confusion around him. The cock-sureness of his immature attitudes was abating as seven or more types of ambiguity confronted him.

As summer vacation neared, Jim read Thoreau, who put words to his recent development when the woodsman spoke of the necessity for a second birth and new religious experiences. For now, although some of the themes were clear to Jim, the more complicated conundrums would come later. That dark passage was still ahead.

Not much made sense to the young man as yet, but the sun had risen. He had learned that his position in the hierarchy was of a low rank and that he had little to offer to himself and nothing to the world. St. Francis had taught him to be gentle to others and one's self. Nevertheless, he had become confident that he could construct his way out of teenage mayhem.

He had run out of money, so he was forced to hitchhike home. Shipping his clothes C.O.D. in a steamer trunk, he made the trip from Miami to Long Island in twenty-eight hours. It was a routine journey until he reached Norfolk, where he hoped to catch the ferry to the Eastern Shore of Delmarva, then up north through Philadelphia to New York. It was well past midnight when he was let out near the naval shipyards. Some friendly sailors smuggled him on board a shuttle bus that deposited him near the ferry dock. But because he was so tired, he slept through the passage across the mouth of Chesapeake Bay. He didn't wake up until most of the cars were already on the road. He scrambled down to the exit ramp without minding his toilette, and because he looked so scruffy, no one dared offer him a ride. When the last car cleared the ramp, he shrugged his shoulders and began walking.

It was a brilliant, sun-filled dawn. The ground fog was on the tobacco crop whose odor soon filled the morning air as the rays began to penetrate the rows in the fields. It was the pungent smell of sotweed that he would remember from this dawn of his new life as he headed back to his old haunts. He was exhilarated as he walked along the road, filled with the knowledge that his scholarship had begun to set him free from some of the confusions of his hormone-stricken youth.

An old Black man offered Jim a ride, chugging to a stop in an ancient Model T. They spoke of the tobacco crop that he worked, and how once the Canadian geese were plentiful until the foul breath of tobacco made them change their migratory glide path, an early signal that the smoke everyone was inhaling might not be entirely salubrious.

* * *

When he arrived home, he amazed his parents with his thin appearance, his sense of seriousness and his ascetic look. He also knew he would soon have to face the challenge of re-configuring his past friendships. With his batteries now charged with political views about societal changes based on the formulas that newly defined his perception of himself and life around him, he would have to adjust this knowledge and re-examine his careless past as well as make some judgments about his former cast of co-conspirators. Would he be able merely to cut himself off from those pals who had shared his blind rush toward popularity? He remembered the overpowering smell of gardenia corsages mixed with whiskey, the inebriated and reckless nights. All that dancing in the dark. The half fog in which he had groped for happiness had turned into a maelstrom of self-recrimination, but it was now lifting to reveal a clearing sky. At a time when most young people were just beginning to stretch themselves out into a satisfying social life, Jim's feeling was that he had contributed his fecklessness to local society and it need not disturb his interest further. He had not yet figured out that one good friend was worth every fete and gala he ever attended. What he did know was that the dance of his teenage years was as finished as the big bands that had laid down their trumpets and trombones, proving that once the swing music of the '30s and '40s was silenced, his generation could get on with an unsentimental future. They could put behind them the deep purple nights and sloppy verses with their mooning about unrequited love.

What he did was compromise. Instead of discarding all his past, he flowed toward his true friends. Lucy and Bonnie were gone from his life, so it was to his pal Mardi that he turned. Instead of focusing on the suburbs, he began to edge toward Manhattan where he instinctively felt a richer life could be found.

But first, so as not to coldly dispatch his friendships with his boyhood buddies, he had to test his new persona among his old chums. With Mardi as an escort, he walked into the new town hangout, the Gay Dome, a narrow storefront bar near the movie house. He knew this night would not resemble a homecoming. What he didn't want to do was drink too much. After consuming bathtubs of gin, barrels of rye and lakes of beer in high school, he was now satisfied to nurse a Miller's.

Saylor was there and Ben and Rocky and Frankie, along with a dozen other of his high school buddies. The cool reception he received raised his awareness of change. He didn't know that he had already been blackballed by this fraternity.

It was like a slap in the face when Saylor opened with, "Thanks for looking out for Boots in Miami."

Jim was surprised by his response, too naïve about matters of the heart. The sneer and sarcasm once directed toward others was now aimed at him. Jim had no idea he would find Saylor so bruised and hurt.

Mardi, a true friend of Boots since she was seven, tried to fend Saylor off. “Loyalty doesn’t mean you have the right to put a lock on other people’s emotions.”

Saylor was dramatic. “Loyalty means you fight until the ship goes down.”

She answered, “You plainly can’t see that it had already sunk.”

They bypassed the booth in which Saylor was sitting and wiggled into another one with Ben and Maryjan, Rocky and Frankie. Jim quickly saw that Ben had taken Saylor’s side on the Boots question, but was less confrontational. He had just finished his freshman year at an Ivy League college. Maturing Maryjan was the crowd’s re-integrator. She and Mardi, fast friends, had attended a southern women’s seminary and were happy to be released from its Baptist theology. Neither would return to the Bible belt in the fall; they had already detoured to secular schools. Frankie and Rocky were trying to avoid being cornered by Saylor’s argument, which would have forced them to choose sides regarding Jim.

“Hey, *amigo*,” from Rocky, who had conquered the problems of his grade level at MHS by attending a PG course at a New England school. He was headed for Cornell.

“*Señor*!” Jim replied. “*Hasta* your life?”

“His blood is circulating again,” said Frank. “We’ve almost thawed him out from his sentence in New Hampshire.”

Frank’s parents, who enjoyed a thriving interior decorators’ business, had spotted their son’s good taste and appropriated his talents. He was currently adapting to the family trade, which offered him a promising career once he completed classes at a Manhattan design school.

Jim asked, sensing some disfavor, “Ben, how did it go for you this year?”

“A little math, a little engineering. A lot of lacrosse.”

Maryjan turned to Jim. “We missed you at Christmas. Not that you missed the blizzard sitting down there under your palm tree. So, we’re double-glad to finally see you and check out this change Boots said you’re going through.”

She could recognize shifts in natural forces.

He looked at his old friends, all of whom he had deceived at one stage or another.

"I guess I've changed. It might even be a surprise to hear the truth from me for once. You've got no obligation to believe any of it, but it's like I went away, and I don't know if I'll ever get home again. I'm on a path that will probably take a while, and I'll have to go it alone. A year ago, I was on plug empty. And I've got to replenish the jug or … well, never mind. You get the point." Die or go crazy is what he left out.

He may have thought that he could re-enfold himself somehow into the old life, but he had a feeling that his recitation of what had happened to him foretold a more ambiguous ending. As a result, only Mardi stood with him, would never let the present spoil the past, or vice versa. But the phone stopped ringing from the others. That night, in spirit, he left Manhasset and it left him, and he never did return.

* * *

He was able to find a construction job that paid a good wage and spent five days a week in splattered jeans and old work shirts. After work, though physically tired, he promptly turned his attention toward New York and to nightly reading. He continued to read through the translations of a half dozen classic Russian novels that gave him a view of nineteenth century dacha life that was to forever skew his vision regarding Slavic lifestyles. In effect, he figuratively raised his lantern toward the other shore of light that always beckoned the Russian intellectuals to express their sense that love is the highest aim of humanity. He learned to cherish all things Russian exactly when his own country was trying to diminish its former ally. America and the Soviets were chilling the world with mutual atomic threats. He could look out his back window and see his neighbors digging bomb shelters. Jim lost himself in last century's Russian backwaters, contemplating the outrageousness of Gogol, the horrific choices of Dostoyevsky and the wisdom of Tolstoy whose description of Natasha's sleigh ride would become Jim's most singular image of his new Russophile state.

At the same time that he searched for the complicated Russian soul, he became enamored with Broadway, specifically musical comedies. One of the questions for the next year was: How to reconcile this dual interest in Turgenev and Hammerstein?

It wasn't the first time that he turned to Broadway as a place to fulfill his musical needs. As a pre-teen, when he came under the influence of swing, he began trekking into wartime Broadway. On this, his second venture into the light show of 42nd Street, it was a combination of song and dance and glitter that invited him to loosen his uptight spirit. His passion for this happy genre had begun when he and Mardi saw *Annie Get Your Gun* and heard the full-throated Ethel Merman wail the songs of Irving Berlin. Jim went from appreciating the music of the now silenced big bands to the excitement of dollies tapping along a pony line. He loved the patter and larger-than-life personalities of grease-paint glamour.

By New Years, he would become a true believer in musical comedy. It was the season of Cole Porter's sex-tinged *Kiss Me Kate*, Ray Bolger—he of the long legs—in *Where's Charley?* Phil Silvers in *High Button Shoes*, the little people of *Finian's Rainbow* and the misty moors of *Brigadoon*. Shows that lit up like Christmas trees. He responded viscerally to the energy, the vivacity of a dancing chorus and the assured voice control of the leading ladies and men.

To partially understand what Jim was experiencing, one would have to remember the impact of the songs that formed the lyrical basis of his unexpressed and confused emotions—the popular poetry of "I'll Never Smile Again," "You Made Me Love You," "I'm Getting Sentimental Over You," the dozens—hundreds—of tunes that he had listened to on the radio and absorbed into his bloodstream, the rhythms he danced to during his jukebox years. Now Broadway melodies, sung by storybook characters, offered him glimpses of more mature feelings: "So In Love," "I Got Lost in His Arms," "Were Thine That Special Face," songs that didn't make the hit parade but habituated on the stands and staffs of supper club orchestras in svelte New York boites. Music that carried book and story line, surrounded by lights that freshened up the grimness of New York's street reality—the sight of seersucker jackets and straw boaters in *High Button Shoes*, the neverness of *Brigadoon*, the rainbow of *Finian*, and the harlequinade of *Kiss Me Kate.* He didn't realize it, but he was going through his third Golden Age of entertainment—first the movies, then radio, now musical comedies.

There in the magical amphitheaters of the West Forties' side streets—the Century, the 46th Street, the Imperial—he encountered a display of American brashness that pointed him toward an external personality—bunkum mixed with a touch of wiliness found in Phil Silvers, or the audacity of Ethel Merman, or the fickleness of "When I'm Not Near the Girl I Love."

He could reproduce those Broadways lullabies in his head because there was a sound from those years that Jim never forgot. The voices he heard had a resonance, an other-bodyness to them as if the singers brought the spirit of their passions into the room along with the song. The quavering tone came mostly from sweet-singing, second-lead tenors whose voices he never forgot: Robert Alda with "I'll Know," Harold Lang with "Bianca," William Tabbert with "Younger Than Springtime," David Brooks singing "From This Day On," and especially Jack McCauley trilling "I Still Get Jealous" and "Bye-Bye Baby."

Jim's piano was now covered with musical scores that went back before WWI. By the end of the summer, he knew what he wanted to do if he had a choice. He either wanted to write Broadway shows or Russian-like novels. He began to take on the copycat personality of those who decorated late 1940s musical comedy, portraying an external lightness of spirit, even as he developed the deeper sensitivities of a brooding Slavic, lost utopian.

He continued to make expensive forays into Manhattan nightlife. Jim asked Mardi to join him in finding a jazz nightclub he had heard about. They trained into Penn Station and Jim was so excited to be in the city, with its nervous under-bass of jittery noise, that he gave a cabdriver a five-dollar bill for a seventy-five cent ride and forgot to collect the change. They—she in her smartest summer dress and he in a tie and jacket—walked tentatively into the big barn that was Manhattan's answer to Storyville, the sprawling Dixieland jazz club on Sheridan Square, Nick's in the Village. They took their seats while the septet wailed away on "Bill Bailey."

The crowd was young and boisterous and reacted physically to the outrageous, thumping brass binge pouring from the floodlit stage. Fingers danced on the small tables, shoulders rolled, tapping feet could be seen all around the smoky, high-ceiling space with its smell of rye and bourbon. There was a wildness loose in the room. A veteran who played with Bix, Pee Wee Russell, wailed on clarinet; Peanuts Hucko on tenor sax; the fiery trumpeter "Wild Bill" Davison along with Jack Teagarden and the legendary Sidney Bechet tried to blow open the doors of paradise. It was this old-style, knock-your-socks-off jazz born downriver that also moved Jim. His and Mardi's blood flow rose to meet this late Jazz Age shout of exuberance. The young pair individually projected their feelings out into the room, rather than toward one another, each taking emotional solos. Like some inebriated patron dancing alone during intermission, they each moved to the music within the fiber of their own selves. The music wasn't quite barrelhouse or gut bucket, a little more nuanced, but it sounded like the roar of a lion and the rafters rang with their basin blues, strutting shuffles and stomps: Come and get it "jass."

"Oh, god! Was that exciting? It just lifts you. What a treat!"

"That got my juices going."

"Like sitting on an electric buzzer."

At intermission, once they had settled down from all the excitement, Jim asked Mardi, "How was it in your seminary?"

"Totally isolated. Enough to know I'm not going back."

"You're moving on?"

"Yeah," she said. "I got into Penn State in the fall."

She held many of her emotions in, but he could see she was pleased to be relocating at an upscale school.

"You're going to that place in the Midwest?" she asked

"Bradley. Nobody's ever heard of it. But I have to get out of the East. The South didn't do it for me. There's something I'm missing. Maybe I can find it out there."

"What? What's missing?"

"Less phoniness. Something more real. Where I don't get the feeling that everyone's hiding something."

"Maybe it's because you're hiding something yourself."

The music soon over-rode their talk of school transfers, though it was a major subject in those years as postwar collegians tried to steer toward career and marriage.

They had been captured by the vibrancy of Dixieland and the joyous expansion of feelings it generated.

"Jazz so infectious you want to open the window and let the whole world hear it."

Then they went next store to the Limelight and reveled in its Village ambiance.

* * *

Another night, Jim and Mardi rode the LIRR into Manhattan and made their way downtown on an open-air double-decker Fifth Avenue bus. The humid summer air wafting down Fifth pelted them. Walking across 18th Street to Third Avenue, their destination was the old German-American Club—Joe King's Rathskeller—once the social center of the expatriates from the 1848 Revolution who had settled in the area before trekking up to 86th Street to establish a new Germantown.

"I hear all the college kids come here," Mardi said.

Right she was. They found the Bavarian bierstube decorated in dark wood with stained glass windows and implanted with dozens of round tables where Ivy League casuals rested in comfortable association with their suds-drinking peers. Every night Oktoberfest. Jim and Mardi joined a half-empty table.

Not nearly as worldly as the other guests from the finest schools, Jim and Mardi stood out. They were a couple years behind the day's fashions. He was awkward in his movements; she wore last year's hairdo. The couple at the same table wore disapproving expressions as they sat down.

They tried to ignore each other while Jim ordered some beer.

"You ought to try the German draft," the other guy said, smoothing down his Harris Tweed jacket.

"Where you from?" asked the girl, coldly eyeing the arrivals.

"Long Island," Mardi answered pleasantly.

"Where all the city people are moving?"

"From Manhasset," Jim added, trusting the name had some social standing, hoping to differentiate their suburb from the influx of young couples looking for houses out east in the potato fields.

"I always thought Long Island people don't seem to get it."

"Get what?"

"You know. Not too swift on the uptake. Not too smooth when it comes to the social scene" said the other guy.

"Who are you to judge?" Mardi asked, showing some spirit.

"Just trying to be helpful. Maybe you should pay attention to experience. Listen to a little advice."

Instead of hunkering down against the abuse, Jim and Mardi rose and found a more compatible table.

"Snotty asses."

Trying to overcome the initial slights, they joined in the harmonizing that was the source of the Rathskeller's attraction—a "sit back with your beer and sausage and sing as loud as you can" atmosphere. The pair loosened up as the room boomed out the songs printed in Gothic type placed at each setting. The hall rang with German melodies. Joe King, the proprietor, had latched onto a primal need among students to bellow out their humor-spiked cynicism in public. This in turn fostered an ethnic/immigrant nostalgia that still lingered in a few corners of the country, corners that smelled of cabbage turned sauerkraut. It was as if these young people were trying to momentarily retreat into some earlier migrant America, a time before Miss Columbia led the country into world leadership. Just as the hot jazz at Nick's sought the carelessness of the Twenties, so the Rathskeller harked back toward a community singing experience loaded with Northern European kitsch and kugel.

The two evenings could not have been more different in terms of musical content. This was at a time when the country was evolving toward the music of cool jazz and the composure of the silent generation, toward a more laid back time that promoted lack of commitment, which meant checking all options and playing the odds. So different from the spontaneous and free-wheeling

Dixieland that stirred the blood and advocated direct action, whether to change one's attitude toward sex and society, or to celebrate Blacks, or to enjoy the feelings of fly-by emotions or to smoke funny cigarettes and drink quantities of gin.

"I've got to tell you, gorgeous, that I love going out with you. You're so easy to be with," Jim said

"That's sweet. You've always been my favorite male."

"It's good to have a woman for a friend. I don't have another. There's nobody like you."

"We've always been buddies," Mardi said, touching his arm.

Jim attempted to discover himself through all these experiences, but he doubted that any of the popular routes would bring him to a satisfactory end. He didn't want to be anyone but himself. He hoped to be without envy or greed. He need not be a doctor or a lawyer or a corporate executive, especially not the latter. Nor a political powerhouse. None of these held any fascination for him, nor propelled his ambitions. More inviting was something involving writing. Maybe newspapers.

What did not significantly matter to him yet was the construct of his character. He had not totally learned to apply ethics to his own behavior. He was still floating above the behavioral battlefield—like a barrage balloon looking for a landing field. He had been cut loose by rebellion but had not settled into a comfortable cultural meadow. He sensed the right attitude was to befriend the poor, doubt capitalism and its masters, and try to find a Catholic action plan that leaned toward Socialism. The thing for him to do was learn: literature, history and the rudiments of philosophy. Most important was to act independently by resolving his new beliefs into action. And seek a way out of the dark. It wasn't that he had forgotten about girls and the beach parties and the dances and the mellow, half-intoxicated lovemaking. It's just that he now had other imaginings. Figuratively, he was standing slightly left of understanding the big picture. But he was beginning to get it.

Chapter 6
(1948 - 1949)

Memories clarifying the shadows . . .

Back to Chicago and the Midwest he went. Back to the whistle-pierced Loop.

The August morning's rush hour had already begun when the Broadway Limited rolled up the lake into town. Jim, familiar with Chicago's city grid if not the details of its transportation system, moved sleepily through the crowds until he found a Madison Avenue streetcar. Born on the campus of the South Side's University of Chicago, his bereft, fatherless family in 1931 had consolidated their suitcases and moved into his Gram's apartment on the West Side when he was two. Then, when his mother remarried, the reconstituted family moved to the more affluent North Side. On whatever of the threes sides of the flattened city his family resided, each generation enjoyed the healing powers of Lake Michigan. Jim had been able to catch glimpses of water lazing under a summer haze, spread under an early morning sun. Even downtown, there was the fresh, cool smell of fish that he remembered as a boy. He had returned to his native region to attend his second year of college. But first he would visit his Gram.

Mary Agnes Cleveland was living alone now, after many years of embracing and housing her wayward progeny, even though her address would change fairly often owing to the fluctuating economics of renting in Saint Mel's parish. Jim's married Aunt Marge, to whom he was forever stitched by the loyalty she had shown him during the four years of his boyhood when they lived together, now resided a few blocks away and would come to visit Mother Mary Agnes as regularly as the postman, with the addition of twice on Sunday. Marge was there when Jim walked up the outside wooden back staircase, his college-bound luggage in hand.

"It's my darling boy."

Jim set down his bag and gave his Gram a big hug, and then another for Marge. He felt their pudgy waists under their cotton print dresses.

"Let me look at you, you big lug," Marge said.

"You've come to see your old Gram."

"Old, my eye. Don't let her kid you," Marge said. "She still arm-wrestles the priest in confession over penance."

"They're all so young, those pale-looking bookworms. What do they know?"

They asked about the train ride and his year in Miami and if his mother had been elected mayor of Manhasset yet.

"Bet you learned a lot under them palm trees," Marge teased him. "Or was it easier to study beneath a beach umbrella?"

Marge stayed for lunch. His aunt was happier now that her Johnny was home from his years overseas and now that daughter Kate had triumphed over TB after spending two years in the hospital. There was even a second healthy girl in the family.

"What the Lord put this poor woman through during the War was a hard test," said her mother.

"Might even get a free pass at the pearly gates," Marge added.

"You may not know it, Jim," said his grandmother, "but Bob Hill was real generous to Marge and me during those bad times."

This was news to Jim. Now that he was beginning to have a functioning conscience, he was twitted by guilt for having never helped them during their time of struggle when faced with Jack's death, Johnny's life-threatening exploits in northern Europe, Kate's illness and hospitalization, and a lack of income.

"Bob's even loaning Johnny and me money for a down payment on a house out in the western suburbs," Marge added.

It was time for Jim to re-evaluate his old man's sense of responsibility. And question his own.

Marge returned to her apartment to take care of her girls. They would all return for dinner and circle around the dining room table under which Jim had slept in winter as a child when times were tough and relatives had to double up in crowded flats. Back then, when summer came, he had been able to ditch the dusty carpet and sleep out on the back porch.

After the old woman and Jim had napped—he hadn't slept much in the coach section during his overnight train ride—they settled around the kitchen table, the true hub of Chicago lives. Gram poured her tea in a saucer and sipped from it, while Jim asked her questions about when she first came to America.

She told her immigrant story, "I came through New York from Cobh before they raised that big statue of Liberty and built Ellis Island in the harbor," she began. "It was 1879 and me with a sick husband. First we came to Chicago to find my relatives and I hired out as a maid with a big newspaper family on the North Shore. Then after going to a clinic and finding out that my Mister Lafferty had TB, I followed the doctor's advice and first went to Colorado where the air was clean and then to El Paso where it was dry. In the between times, I worked once as far west as the railroad tracks could carry me into Montana, where I saw John L. Sullivan fight bare-fisted.

"I probably told you that when Mister Lafferty lay sick down by Mexico, I needed to make money and went out on the Chisholm Trail riding with the cowboys and ran a chuck wagon. Sort of a mobile diner. It's where I learned to cook camp style. Gave me the skills to stir food for a living until I was seventy."

Jim never knew what to make of her stories about the cattle trail. Her bedroom dresser was lined with big/little books, all Westerns, and he remembered that she never missed a cowboy shoot-'em-up on the radio or at the movies.

"After Mister Lafferty died, I came back to Chicago and the newspaper people heard I was in town and hired me as cook. They were strange and wonderful people and very good to me. Prime Midwest. My favorite was the oldest daughter, tall and leggy, more boy than girl when she was young, until she blossomed into a princess and had all the college boys after her. Whenever I think of what an American girl should look like, I think of her—my Peggy. She could ride like an Indian, ran like one too. String of a thing but athletic as all get out. Played lots of tennis and golf even back then.

"She didn't know what to do with herself after she returned from school in Switzerland—I missed her those two long years. A perfect Gibson Girl by now. First she thought she'd help the German man who came and started an orchestra downtown—back when they had that big fair over by the lake. About that same time, she helped raise money for the new Art Institute. All the big boys in town were helping Chicago pull up its pants and boast about how Chicago was a thriving, up-to-date city before the fair opened. But she didn't cotton to all those cultural people. She'd become an heiress by now and she decides to back a young inventor in the telephone business. But she quickly finds out—especially in Chicago—that business is a dirty game and she didn't want to work with people she wouldn't say hello to on the street."

"North Shore debutante discovers reality."

"She sees that the arts are too soft and business too rough, so she finally settles on community service. Settlement houses were going up around Chicago about then. So she opens one for negra children and that's when her life started to come apart."

"I thought it was just getting going."

"So did she. But then along comes the big fair. This fancy African prince comes by Chicago to see the sights, and on his trip, he stops by Peggy's school, and to the amazement of the few people who knew about it, don't they fall in love, my beautiful Peggy and her dark prince.

"But they're doomed. They can't go out in public and she can't bring him home. It's hopeless and my girl spins out of control. But nothing can shake her until catastrophe hits.

"The settlement house—or it might have been some other building—catches fire while it's filled with women and children inside. The flames are everywhere and all of them screaming in pain. She rushes in to pull boys and girls out of there. And along comes the prince to visit and he sees her run back in again, headstrong as a firehouse dog. The African prince follows. Then the roof collapses, timbers falling and they never come out.

"First she thought she could find herself in the arts. And then business. But it was public service that mattered to her before it killed her. That was my Midwestern girl. If you ever find another like her, bring her around."

Jim absorbed his Gram's heritage and myths and let them float in the underground stream that would carry him past the many splendid and soiled shores of his individuated course. Though his grandmother had given him her Irish genes and Chicago had provided a dark sadness, he and his hormones needed to move away to flourish in the East. But he was not yet finished with the Midwest. It had called him back for a reason, and he would know why before 1949 was over.

One of the things he wanted to know from his Gram: Were there any other characters like him in their bloodline? He was disappointed to find there were no cultural questers in the family past, but plenty of risk takers who had crossed the ocean, made their way west, and had learned to overcome the gloom of the prairies. However there was one exception, his Aunt Mary, Gracie's other sister. She and her family lived in a huge Victorian mansion built about the time of the big fair when the city first flexed its national muscles at unsuspecting Eastern pantywaists who thought culture expired at the foot of the Appalachians. Mary had wanted to take ballet lessons when she was a girl and in her early photographs, she always wore her hair in braids. She possessed what could have been a dancer's body, thin and elegant, but she was not only frail looking but also often sick, thus thwarted in any career choices that strained her physical chassis. The afternoon of his visit to the Wicker Park area, he was greeted warmly. While Mary's unemployed husband secluded himself elsewhere in the overblown architecture, fighting the corporate monsters that he battled in court over his rights as a laboring man, the women of the house chose to improve Jim's social skills. Downstairs, the trio—aunt, cousin and nephew—danced, partnering each other slowly across the parquet floor.

"Hold your body straight," said his aunt.

They tried to teach him the Black Bottom and the Suzi Q, then the Turkey Trot and the Bunny Hug. They laughed so hard they finally had to sit down.

"Mary, how come you're so different from Marge and Gracie?"

"I had the best grades and was the only one that our folks could afford to send on to college. That gave me an incentive to study hard. The money ran out my second year but I had a good dowsing. An incomplete but satisfying liberal education. You know why they call it a liberal education, don't you? And why folks call themselves liberals? Because education opens the flytrap in your mind and lets some light in. They call that light rational thought—a missing ingredient in homes around here."

He couldn't see many books or musical instruments; truth was there was a dearth of furniture. But Mary was a cultural entity all to herself. And she would see to it that her so-inclined daughter would be educated and later take her turn developing her skills in the theater, allowing the generations to work out their own paths toward a family heritage

He had just enjoyed a high-octane summer involving the musical comedy stage and his introduction to the unorthodox wonders of Greenwich Village. Now he immersed himself in easy-going and taciturn Midwestern ways. He was becoming a two-region guy long before jet airplanes created bi-coastals.

* * *

The American higher education system was still bulging with students in the academic year of 1948-1949. The aim was to push an entire generation through reams of text and easy-to-forget theories toward adult fulfillment so that G.I.s could catch up with the American dream that had been interrupted by war. Universities graduated students en masse—preparing them to saddle up and ride the nation's sped-up postwar economic juggernaut. There was much transferring and academic jockeying for the best placements just as there was a shoveling of thousands through the intellectual process. Jim was part of the nationwide flux, moving from Miami to a college in the Midwest, where he hoped to find people more compatible with his plain beliefs and his renewed spiritualism—a place where he could continue on his path toward wholeness. The choice was Bradley in Peoria, a city where his mother grew up, a move that gave him the thin benediction of maternal blessing.

Peoria, with its one hundred thousand inhabitants, was the second largest city in the state, a hundred miles south of Chicago on the Illinois River. It was the home of Caterpillar and Schlitz beer, and the good thing about Caterpillar, aside from the fact that it employed half the town, was that it didn't exhale the smell of hops, which was the day-in, day-out beer smell of the city. A sour mash.

Bradley, speedily changing from an engineering college that specialized in clock making, was transforming itself into an instant university. Accommodating the overflow from the nearby University of Illinois, Bradley, like Jim, was looking for academic validation. Both he and the institution green as grass.

Students roomed in odd places and Jim's residence was no exception. This year, he rented a room in a Victorian mansion on the bluff overlooking downtown—below lay Peoria set on a floodplain of the river. The lower floors were occupied by a funeral home and one of the seniors from Bradley named Lance helped with the downstairs enterprise by acting as a dour-faced doorkeeper, hearse driver and mopey pallbearer. Lance, slim and wiry and maintaining his Navy toughness, did everything but dig graves. One of his responsibilities was to monitor police calls that might reveal the location of a prospective client for his boss, the funeral director. The morbid chattering of the radio disturbed Jim's study so he tried to keep the heavy wooden doors in the old mansion closed.

The twenty-room monolith, a vast showcase, complete with a rounded turret that extended up to the collegian's third floor, where an altogether mournful-looking guy with thick glasses lived, a misanthrope who found it hard to smile. Another, a fourth boarder, had arrived on a basketball scholarship; he was a burly, tall Indianan who spent his days trying out for Bradley's highly regarded team. He appeared to be a hotshot to Jim, full of blather, and must have liked hogging the ball, because the coach soon made it clear that he didn't need another primadonna on the team so the Hoosier soon wandered away looking for a more compatible gym.

When Jim met doleful Paul from New Haven, he tried to make a joke of the mortuary. "I didn't think I'd be living at death's door."

Paul answered, "Everyone's always knocking on death's door."

He was as grim as the haunted house they were living in.

"Maybe we could liven things up with a Halloween party."

With a shrug, Paul said, "It would probably cost too much."

This guy was a perfect candidate for the death and taxes party, Jim thought. Fishing for common interests, he asked, "You play any sports or have a hobby?"

"I collect stamps. And coins. Mostly I go to the movies."

That's a substitution for something, Jim thought. Maybe life.

The couple who ran the death parlor was a cheery pair, even though most nights they had to contend with the fact that there was a cadaver icing in the basement. Residential living in the wood-encrusted rooms with their high ceilings was satisfactory, except sometimes there was an odd smell from below.

Jim had done well academically in his freshman year. His folks now paid for his studies and gave him a small allowance that usually ran out by the middle of the month. He was always borrowing money, going hungry and overspending the little bit he had by attending a lot of movies with Paul from Connecticut.

His first real buddy was a former Navy guy named Jack, a day student, who was often in coffee-cup company with another ex-gob from New England, a Catholic by the name of Frank. Jack was tall and thin and a reader of note and quickly responded to Jim after he found out the youngster knew something about the war in the Pacific, where he had served as a chief petty officer. At a time when his principal interest was in books, Jim was soon depending on Jack to find titles in the library. Jack led him toward a new set of authors, namely Dreiser, Dos Passos and Steinbeck, earthy writers who didn't appeal to Jim as much as the Russians he was following. Aside from literature, many of their conversations dwelled on the upcoming election in which "Give'em Hell" Harry Truman was in a fierce battle with Dewey of New York. Currently the Show-Me president was on a cross-country whistle stop campaign seeking a full term that would be a confirmation of his policies.

Practical American political involvement—not theoretical Socialism—first attracted Jim's consciousness during this 1948 presidential campaign. In his Republican home town, he had listened to vituperative moaning against FDR including rants against the lame genius who had been elevated to near godhead status by the plain people. The ravings against the wartime president by otherwise worthy constituents of the upper middle class had previously confused Jim. When the same invective language was leveled at successor Harry Truman, Jim began to discern that the educated, conservative, upper class, choosing to protect the sources of its worth, felt entitled to rule the national agenda. With little, though sometimes charitably tax-protected empathy, the moneyed elite supported many good causes but stood against progressive political ideas involving the universal sufferings of the many. Jim already believed that the purpose of government was to take care of its less endowed, so his plebian views were clear. All fall, a stream of hatred aimed at drowning Harry Truman was pouring out of the conservative press which had an uncanny talent to demonize its opponents in such a way that middle-class citizens voted against their own best interests and cast their lot with the upper classes that otherwise ignored them. Meanwhile, Truman's opponent waited for what appeared to be a sure Republican win.

Jim, attempting to verify his belief that the Democratic Party was closer to the people and stood with the middle class, began reading a daily newspaper. In quick order, he chose not to ingest the vitriol stemming from the self-congratulating *Chicago Tribune* ("The World's Greatest Newspaper") and became familiar—a thousand miles from home—with the mildly plutocratic *New York Tines*. It was only then that he began to argue with his new conservative friends, Jack and Frank.

Jack, talking about Truman at a morning coffee break, said, "He's nothing but a small town shopkeeper. Way over his head. He looked like a pipsqueak in the pictures next to Churchill and Stalin."

Inarticulate Jim ventured boldly into his first political discussion. "He's been a senator for ten years, so he must have learned something. He actually commanded troops in combat in the First War which may be more than those other two ever did."

"But that doesn't make him a world leader."

Jim argued on, “And he didn’t blink when it came time to help Turkey and Greece. And no amount of belly-aching can say the Marshall Plan isn’t working.”

Jim continued, “I really hate it the way Republicans slander Truman. Same as they did to Roosevelt. Not that the Democrats don’t indulge too, but Republicans are better at it, because the hotshots that need public relations companies are the rich and the rich know about controlling the message. When politics gets dirty, and they trot out all their innuendoes, something sours in the country. Listening to character assassination is a spirit killer.”

Jim’s friend replied, “Nobody said it was going to be a clean fight. Does ‘em good to mix it up. Wasn’t it Truman himself who said something about—If you can’t stand the heat, you ought to get out of the kitchen.”

Jim continued, “But people are turned off by the garbage they have to listen to on radio. All that squabbling and name-calling depresses them. You know what it’s like? It’s like people who have to live someplace and know their government is corrupt. It takes people’s dignity away. It robs them of hope. Makes them feel dirty. Allows indecision to substitute for action. Nasty PR freezes people’s natural common sense.”

“No way he’s going to win with the Dixiecrats against him.”

“Stupid that Democrats cater to the South. Good riddance.”

Speaking up, Jim felt good about himself and in November reveled in Truman’s unpredicted return to the White House. With growing confidence in his political beliefs he remained alert to the country’s legislative and administrative intent.

He had been anxious to get back to his classes. He resumed his monkish mode once he left the summer distractions of New York behind. He had also loosened up a little, whether it was the result of Midwest naturalism or growing self-confidence, he was edging up on moderation and balance. Because he was still hurting from the pain endured in his senior year, his sexual thermometer remained on the cool side. When classes started up, he registered for a couple of business courses to keep his old man off his case, but found that his courses in Nineteenth Century Literature, one in Psychology and another in World History, stirred up his inquisitive juices.

He spent hours in the library searching for correlatives and that quickly brought him under the influence of the Romantic poets, as well as Jung and Europe's past. His mind became crowded with the beauty of nature, fairy tales and myths and the back regions of France and Italy. Vineyards lay in the landscape of his imagination and walled cities and cloisters. His outlook began to wander overseas and he began to imagine himself as a person of the larger world. His would be a circumscribed, not uninteresting literary journey this year; importantly one that was his own. One that had a Mediterranean feel with a touch of poetry and a broad embrace of the mystical and mysterious.

More mundane things also attracted his attention. Sports had played a part in his life since the 1933 All-Star baseball game, first held in Chicago in conjunction with that year's World's Fair—the Century of Progress— designed to provide cash and jobs for the Depression-poor city. Over the years he had rooted for only two teams: the White Sox and the MHS football team. His Catholic elementary school had not contained a gym and the nuns had no interest in indoor games, so he had never learned to play basketball. But now, here in the middle of the country, next to hoop-crazy Indiana, and surrounded geographically by future professional basketball teams and the old National Industrial League—Phillips 66, the Peoria Caterpillars and the Milwaukee Hamischfegers—he came to appreciate the hair-raising game endings that were almost guaranteed by round ball. Bradley had a championship team, and Jim's social life revolved largely around their doings on the court.

It was morose Paul who suggested a trip to a different kind of regional sports event, a match that would prove to be Jim's first experience as a Midwestern football fan. They planned to attend a Big Ten game in nearby Champaign-Urbana, home of the University of Illinois. Paul had been able to convince one of his engineering classmates to drive one glorious blue Saturday to watch the Illini match their football team and marching band against those of the Ohio State Buckeyes. Jim had never seen such a crowd anywhere except in Yankee Stadium; over fifty thousand fans came out to cheer. The air was colored with excitement as the game proceeded. The attractive and vibrant student body, the whooping sound of a vast crowd, the air swirling with music all contributed to new sensations. At half time, there was the spectacle of marching bands and barelegged cheerleaders. He enjoyed the festivities and gained an appreciation of the Big Ten with its mammoth campuses.

* * *

If being a sophomore meant being half-aware, Jim met the standard. The door to knowledge had opened for him, but the blackness inside still hid the light and left shadows on his mind. But he was determined to poke in the darkness. He studied the classics in translation. He became fascinated by the achievements and the bewilderment of the Enlightenment and the events that caused the revolutions and the convolutions that followed. On his own study time, he investigated first the Bolshevik upheaval, then the Irish, American, and French revolutions. There was a correspondence, of course, to what was transpiring within himself, less bloody, but nonetheless volcanic. His reading of Russian novels over the summer fostered the need to understand the consequences of the breakdown of feudalism in the eighteenth and nineteenth centuries. And eventually how Victorianism transitioned from its attempt to create social perfection to the confusion and the cynicism of WWI and the onslaught of Modernism.

New concepts were coming at him with fierce regularity, insisting that he use his powers to forge a new direction. The British idea about "the other" required his evaluation. How could a whole nation pretend to live with the idea that the other person was more important than one's self? Did one really live one's life to service others? Or was it celebrated more in the outer reaches than the fortified middle? The theory kept him busy with its implications. Certainly he understood the Catholic practice of charity, but what the Brits seemed to have in mind involved patterns of living where the individual always gave preference to the "other" human being. The strangeness of the concept and the generosity it insinuated astounded him.

He also ruminated over the idea that men were mainly inspired by their minds and women by their bodies. He was to hold this false concept for a long time until he came to recognize the illegitimacy of the notion that males had deserved the right to preside over the millennium's authoritarian patriarchy because of their superior intelligence He recognized finally that it boiled down to a power play of men over women. For years, he accepted the reasoning that male predominance in government, higher education and the arts was natural. He thought it was based on the notion that men were wired to listen to their higher spiritual needs and answer them while women, the progenitors of life, were more tied to the earth and the practical needs of civilized home life. But he was beginning to see women as the more intelligent gender and would eventually be disabused of his earlier ideas.

Another question that intrigued him was why it took such a long time for one's conscience to catch up with ambition.

He came to believe that life produced a certain kind of practical mediocrity, and that it was only the arts that were able to reveal important meanings that raised the quality of life and the higher aspirations in one's self or an entire democracy.

His mind was bubbling.

* * *

It was Miss Rose's class on the Romantic poets that raised the ladder that would get Jim across the wall into the land of creativity. There was no turning back for him now; it was straight up and over. The scrawny, bird-like Southern woman who gave him a toehold would wend her way through the rows of students, book open near her narrow nose, reciting the sonnets and other prayers to nature that opened up a stream in him that eventually flowed into a river of poetic appreciation. She was dusty looking as if she had spent her life as a bookmark. Studying Shelley opened Jim's eyes, Byron his sense of adventure, Keats his ears, Wordsworth his understanding, Coleridge his imagination. They splattered sunshine onto his mind, offering him a civilized way to deal with the mean streets of life. They gave him courage, if he so chose, either to be an intuitive, introspective person or be catapulted into the wide world of contemporary culture. Now he had reasons to push away from the commerce of mid-century and establish his own community of sensitive friends. There would be no money on the other side of the wall but the air smelled fragrant and ideas were in flower there, the fruit no doubt flavorful.

He began to direct the individual pieces of his reading toward some coherent whole. After reading *Moby Dick* and several novels by Henry James, he struggled up to the starting line of Modernism by ingesting Ford, Eliot, Fitzgerald, Stein, Hemingway, Cummings and the other wounded, who crawled blindly out of the chaotic slime of World War One. He came to understand and love the Parisian spirit that became the locus of that generation's saving grace. He saw Greenwich Village as the American repository of stateside skepticism and emotional havoc, which then brought him to O'Neil and soon to Millay and Wilson's *I Thought of Daisy.* Then he read through the overviews of Cowley and Kazin and began to have a bohemian's view of his native ground and literary landscape, and found it to be more fertile than he imagined.

There was a slice of contemporary thinking that suggested that the current postwar generation of Americans interested in the arts should attempt to mimic the burst of creativity that followed the First War. A Euro-centric idea, young artists again began to flock toward Paris. Jim fell into this trap. He hoped the glamorous Parisian past could be recreated. Aside from the fact that eras can never be repeated, Jim forgot that the modernism he was attracted to stemmed from a crawl through the wasteland. But the idea of resuscitating the Twenties was seductive. After all, French study was so much more interesting than life in Kansas. He would have been better off to see that the American arts were about to explode. But perhaps a dream past was a required precedent for sophomores.

* * *

Some European movies that he saw encouraged Jim to think that the life he strove to create for himself had long been identified and attained by others. It came as a surprise that there were creative forces so strong that they could cause an eruption of emotions in his ever more thin and nervous body. The first movie to stun him was

Olivier's *Henry V*, filmed during the war, sets made out of whole cloth, the production created out of brilliant imagination. It was as if Shakespeare had come alive, portrayed by his knowing countrymen who had shaved every word down to its essential meaning. Mesmerizing from the opening scene set at the Bard's Globe Theatre, the film proceeded to portray, in fiery and elevated language, a reformer's pursuit of responsible action and personal growth. It encouraged Jim to think that he might do the same. The movie prodded him to continue to change and reflect on every action he took. His mouth might run on uncensored, but his head was advised to re-evaluate everything.

Now entertain conjuncture of a time
When creeping murmur and the poring dark
Fills the wide vessel of the universe ...
A little touch of Harry in the night

* * *

Ms. Rose, the dainty teacher with sonnets hidden like dried flowers in her memory book, could refresh them and hold forth:

"The Romantic poetry we're studying now was revolutionary in its day. It opened poetry to a second Enlightenment, an enlightenment of feelings, a dawning of the acknowledgment that personal emotions provide the oil that can help us glide into an expressive life. As opposed to the classical allusions heaped up in a jumble of tightly corseted forms.

"This poetry—Keats, Shelley—comes from the heart not the brain. It's not God-based or church-based or royal-based. It expresses the love within us and asks us to join in its revelry or sorrow. It looks to nature, but it's really looking at our emotions in the everyday language of lovers."

Jim had listened to his heart, and felt confirmed in his ways.

* * *

Dickering with the radio dial one night, Jim tuned into a station from Chicago playing Samuel Barber. The host came on, sounding like a Midwestern version of Jim's favorite New York radio raconteur, Henry Morgan. In later years, in the still of the night, would come Jean Shepherd, a South Sider and White Sox fan.

Jim heard a rambling voice, "Al here. I tell you, I can't get to New York often enough. Something big's happening there right now and you should buy a ticket on the *Twentieth Century* and see for yourself. They have all those wild painters, slashing away at their work——De Kooning, Pollack, Kline and that bunch. Kline, I really like. I can see him swashing those black streaks across his canvas. Must put those colors on with a mop... And poets like Berryman and Merrill… and the best plays since O'Neil from that Tennessee fella and now Arthur Miller with *Death of a Salesman.* I tell you there's more talent running around Manhattan than chickens in old John-Arthur's barnyard. Music, of course, is what I care most about, but most new concertos are stuck in classrooms afraid to come out in public. Luckily, a couple of melodies are creeping out of Copland. Even in opera, that Menotti man, he's not waiting for an invitation from the Met. He's putting his work right on Broadway. He's mostly Italian but his best friend Barber is as American as Knoxville and way ahead of most. Then there's so many writers, you can hardly walk down Fifth without stumbling over one.

"I tell you, New York is chucking off its bad accents and has thrown down the gauntlet to Paris to see who's the biggest grizzly in the culture wars. I'm thinking about settling in the Village myself."

Funny old coot, Jim thought. Who are all these people he's talking about? I'd better start finding out for myself, he thought. And I'd better get back to playing more piano. Have to reserve more time in the music room.

* * *

Jim arrived home for Christmas with so many new sensibilities that he encountered a confusion of choices. He wanted to demonstrate his new persona, what he assumed to be that of the airy young aesthete, but he was still partially enmeshed in the machinations of his youthful suburban subculture. Mainly he wanted to spend time in Manhattan. Meanwhile, his folks were hoping he would go out and make a little Christmas money, but he was having none of it. It was in these straits that he decided to forget the money and continue his quest to find himself. He did eventually put in some hours at Wright's Hardware, where he had previously dealt out screws and nuts and saw blades from the myriad stacks of little drawers that surrounded the main selling floor.

The night he arrived home, he asked after Lucy, even though he knew there were barricades to that inquiry. He contacted Mardi and Ben and they all met at the Gardens. Soon Bootsie with her Navy beau, and Maryjan, and the entire tribe of old friends had gathered—a few of his high school fraternity brothers and the now married sports stars and older bobbysoxers who had been his boyhood heroes and goddesses. The Gardens was so packed and the activity so frenzied that the building seemed to be rocking on its foundation. Charlie's piano music soared over the noise. Most customers were in college now, some in married quarters on campus. A few peacetime servicemen were home on furlough. The fruit of Manhasset High's last ten harvest years reveled there.

It was to be the last war-influenced holiday reunion. A year later, a strip mall would replace the Gardens. They would be older then, many searching for employment. The Pied Pipers of their youth had been silenced; the big bands, out of touch with postwar economics, were going out of business. The great wartime unity was beginning to unravel. Former G.I.s now became rival job seekers. The diaspora into the many theaters of war had ended and the warriors had all been called home, still bonded together this winter of '48, then hardly again, helping Jim to make his exit from his past with few regrets. He would no longer require nurturing from his kid-worshipped Olympians.

The next day he traveled to Penn Station and took the Seventh Avenue IRT to Sheridan Square, avoiding the Christmas shoppers, moving against the tide on a downtown subway. After the inspirations conjured up by writers living and acting out their lives in Greenwich Village and the tenuous co-relationship that his imagination had made with Paris in the Twenties, Jim wanted more than anything to hang out on Bleecker Street.

Now, in his visits to Manhattan, Jim began seeking out architectural monuments. He had already visited St. Patrick's Cathedral a few times after the saint's parade and also the Metropolitan Museum of Art with friends of his mother. These grand settings had lifted his spirits, as if the voluminous space, imposing arches and classical pillars gave him reasons to celebrate man's work in God's world. He embraced the intentions of grandeur. Large ideas and works of art required cathedral-sized sanctuaries. Now in full Romantic bloom on his downtown roamings, he sought out the literary landmarks that he had been cataloging in his imagination. He stopped to consider Stanford White's arch at the bottom of Fifth Avenue and contemplated the symmetry and order of the redbrick row houses alongside Washington Square made famous by Henry James. He subwayed down to City Hall and studied the gargoyles in the Woolworth Building lobby. He bribed the elevator operator to take him up to the Observation Platform, once the highest man-built point on earth. He sat in a worn pew in Trinity Church, then went and walked beside the river and watched the light play off the Brooklyn Bridge. Finally, he talked his way into the Counting Room of the Custom's Building. In all of these grandiose locations, his imagination soared, as if he somehow prospered in their shadow. He was deeply moved, but without the understanding that he was personally alone, without referencing his own lack of shared humanity. In his propulsion from aesthetic wilderness to the creative bower he was planting, he forgot to people his garden.

Returning to the Village, he walked for hours toward the Hudson in the labyrinth of streets off Washington Square. He wandered west to Millay's narrow house and stopped at Chumley's to have a beer. He peered down Patchin Place, where poets lived. He sought out the address of *The Masses*, then roved eastward through the elegance of 11th Street. He enjoyed the profane and the sacred. He stopped by the Church of the Ascension, buoyed by the reminder that the vicar had kept the doors of the church open all night to accommodate the homeless during the Depression. There he sat quietly in a back pew admiring the LaFarge mural and the St.

Gaudens angels. He then headed for MacDougal Street, the home of the Provincetown Players that had fostered the rise of American drama, wondering if the radical Polly's Restaurant still existed. When he found that it did not, he settled into the Caffe Reggio.

He sat through the late afternoon with a pad and a pencil thinking he might write some poetry. He had arrived at the new starting point in his life. And he was elated.

There was much he didn't know. He didn't know that the Beats were already in full bloom in the East Village. And he had not yet figured out the relationship between the New York School of Painting and the New York School of Poetry. Didn't understand that two strains of poetry were battling on the streets around him. And he didn't yet understand the significance of the *Partisan Review*. The truth was he had not had the background or insight to comprehend poetry and the emotions rising from today's young minstrels. Writers from early in the century and those writing current drama he cherished, but he wasn't yet engaged with the latest work of the poets and artists.

He thought about what the Village meant to America's artistic and intellectual life—about Wharton and Cather and the Ashcan school. He didn't yet know about Herbert Crowley and Randolph Bourne, but he knew about Max Eastman and Walter Lippmann, the latter still appearing in the *Herald Tribune*. And Van Wyck Brooks. And about Mabel Dodge and John Reed. But he had little or no idea what was current. He was sure that the Village was where his real, second-stage life's journey would begin. He knew he was making his way alone along the first furlong through the fog of intellectual neglect that he was attempting to disperse. He made five trips to town that holiday, one to see a show with Mardi and another solo visit to Nick's to hear some Dixieland. He also went to Carnegie Hall, then covered with the soot of sixty years of coal smoke.

A Carnegie program of American music was planned one wintry Friday afternoon, and he wondered if the off-hour and subsequently small audience had been designed to correlate with the public's lack of esteem for these works. He was seated high in the balcony where only six other concertgoers were visible, all sitting in the front row leaning over the railing to view the Philharmonic. The orchestra, conducted by a round little man with a walrus mustache, opened with Copland's *Billy the Kid* and *Music for the Theater.* After a pause, the orchestra launched into David Diamond's war symphony. It started with a funeral march—for the millions already dead—then erupted into battle music. Through the volatile music of the second movement, Jim's mind turned to the tank battles he had been watching just two years ago in the newsreels. The war was over but the wounds were still raw and sensitive. There was more hope in the last movement of the symphony. Out of the horror came a will to live, prophesying that the battles would finally end. Then the trumpets blew. Victory.

As much as he responded favorably to the music, Jim was suddenly angry. Here he was sitting in a real concert hall, but why had it taken him so long to get here? Why hadn't his parents introduced him to good music? Resentment, a new emotion, pulsed through him, making him wonder about all the other performances and opportunities he had missed.

* * *

Now in high Romantic fettle, Jim wanted to recreate his sense of developing self-aestheticism on film. He asked the local photographer, a Mister Tarzan, if he would oblige him by taking a picture of him in the woods in one of the few patches of nature remaining amid the suburban sprawl. The short and stocky photographer, whose profession often gave him an opportunity to be obsequious and hyper-sensitive about his customer's needs and their unreasonable views of their own portrayal, agreed.

One sunny, cool December day, the pair drove up to the Flower Hill woods. Mr. Tarzan loaded with tripod, camera and film bag stumbled through the limb-littered lot, careening between the trees. Jim offered to help him but Mr. Tarzan, a true professional, insisted on hauling his own gear, even though his tripod encountered numerous hazards that caused him to buckle at the knees and spin into the undergrowth. Jim, with Mr. Tarzan tottering behind him, went deep in the woods and found a downed tree to perch on.

Wearing his woodsy wear, a lumber jacket and jeans, the young Romantic smiled his most benevolent smile into the camera.

Jim liked the proofs that Mr. Tarzan sent afterwards, but couldn't afford to purchase them, so he never was able to enjoy the finished product. Nor pay for his mischief.

* * *

When he finally got up the courage at the end of the vacation to call Lucy, all the storm and stress of his senior year crashed back on him. His voice wavered after her mother reluctantly gave up the phone to her eldest daughter, who might be ready to execute a final coup de grace. He had been emotionally stuck. He couldn't forget her and he couldn't open another relationship until some finality was brought to this one. Eighteen months had not been sufficient time to disperse the strong feelings and pain that he had left behind in Munsey Park

"Hi, Jim."

Her voice was even and secure, even more assured than he remembered. She was able to convey the weight of her strong personality over the wire. He could see her standing there in the living room where they had tested the limits of their incomplete lovemaking.

"I didn't want to leave without calling," he said.

"I heard you were home."

"And I heard you were off skiing over Christmas."

"Yes. Daddy's idea."

They had been enemies, her father and Jim, during ten months of wrangling over parental or romantic control of the first-born.

"I'm calling to be sure you're OK."

"You mean," she said, "that you wanted to know if I thought you were OK."

"Maybe something like that," absorbing the finality that sounded in her voice.

"You're OK. How's that?" she stung.

"On odd Thursdays, I sometimes believe it myself."

Jim's voice sounded different to her. More mature. She had heard that he was doing well at school and that he was undergoing a personality change for the better.

"You're enjoying school?" thinking she had satisfied the reason he called.

"Yes, for a change. And you're going to major in science?"

"Yes. Have you figured out yours?"

"Probably English Lit. I don't think there's any gold along that path, but that seems to be my route to El Dorado."

"You remember from Spanish?"

"I hear you were in France last summer."

"Yes, we bicycled through the Loire."

"Lucky you."

"Jim, did you think I was going to change my mind about us?"

Her voice suddenly sounded more caring. Perhaps there were more good times than she remembered. He had given her the courage to overcome teenage anonymity.

" I just wondered if our paths had found the same highway."

Perhaps he had changed. She had heard that his confidence had been shattered.

"Jim, I'm going to give you my address at school. Write me if you get a chance."

* * *

Back in the upper reaches of the Victorian mansion that housed the funeral home in Peoria, Jim studied and enjoyed his breaks by watching Bradley's basketball team march toward conference and national invitational tournaments.

In February, his friend Jack off-handedly informed Jim that another student, a big, friendly guy from Chicago named Bill, was driving to Dennison College for the weekend to visit his girlfriend. Jim wondered how close the Ohio school was to Pittsburgh and checked a map. Not that far. He called Bill and asked if he could share a ride. After a favorable reply, he phoned Lucy, with whom he had begun to correspond, and asked her if she was free Saturday night. She was reluctant but finally agreed to see him, perhaps for a final friendly farewell to their relationship. Off he went on Friday morning for an 800- mile round trip date. A zany college ploy.

Bill was easy-going and they shared the driving and gas expenses to eastern Ohio. At Dennison, Bill introduced his lively and big-boned Chicago girlfriend to Jim and she immediately tried to tempt him to stay for the weekend and brought on stage her luscious looking roommate. Jim, startled by the sexiness of the girl, momentarily hesitated, but stuck to his plans and within an hour started hitchhiking across Route # 40 to Pittsburgh.

Somewhat bedraggled after an all night trip, spent partially napping in a booth at a truck stop, he arrived Saturday morning in the steel city's downtown. He located the lodging that Lucy had arranged for him, and slept past lunch. Then he called. She had reserved a room on Pennsylvania College for Women's campus and he should come by at three o'clock. Because they hadn't met in such a long time, they were both pleased and surprised at the change in each other's appearance. She never took off her glasses and hardly smiled; he was thinner than thin.

As they sat on a huge green sofa in the parlor of a converted mansion, one with immense windows, they wondered if they would find common ground sufficient to carry them through a long afternoon and evening. By unsaid mutual consent, every subject they touched was new. There was no going back and reminiscing about what had been; that part of their lives was behind them. In the ensuing hours, they tried to re-connect, their high-strung feelings not far below the surface.

"In freshman year, I got to like science and that quickly steered the rest of my schedule," Lucy said.

"Me? I needed a general overhaul in my thinking," he replied.

"And you'll never believe it, but I've converted to Catholicism."

"There's a switch. Your father must have had a cow."

Many of their perceptions during their year of high school turmoil were colored by their parents' religious stands.

Discussions on how they both succeeded in overcoming the doldrums of high school and latched on to their academic choices brought them almost to dinner. In that period, Jim began to see her in a different light, not as a former romantic object but as a woman struggling to find her way in a mature job-dominating world.

Like college students, they spoke about their hopes and ideals.

"What I'd like to do," Lucy said, "is spend time in Africa and work with children. Maybe in a clinic." They had all come to know and admire Doctor Schweitzer.

"Good project. I hear Freese,"—one of their high school friends—"wants to teach in the sub-Sahara. Maybe the two of you could set up an MHS outpost."

"And teach them how to play jazz."

"And drink beer while lying down."

"How about you? How do you want to save the world?"

"Write a book that people could use to ease the pain of love." It just popped out.

The past stabbed back. He shielded them from its attack. "One way of overcoming the hurt and remembering the good part."

She was quiet. Then they began again. She would like to do medical research. Inspired by *Gatsby*, he wanted to write a social history of Long Island's North Shore in the Twenties. Then an extraordinary thing began to happen. They realized they had turned into two serious kids and the old sting began to lessen. Their larger thoughts and goals, their natural idealism began to raise them above the pain of their teenage confusion. He came to understand the healing that a higher order of living offered. It was liberating.

As he hitchhiked back along Route #40, after he and Lucy attended mass on Sunday morning, Jim felt a lightening inside him as if a great burden had been lifted. He was actively decompressing the bittersweet past, as if he were drifting away from her. Lucy would no longer be the shadow on his spirit. His unrequited loyalty was evaporating as he made his way back; the oppressive East left behind, and with it, the remains of his teenage love.

He had been broken before as a child—fatherless, sometimes homeless in the sense that he had been warehoused in three different Catholic institutions—but he had overcome his bad breaks thanks to the hormones that set his body free and the soporific suburbs and boyhood friends that had quieted his anxiety. And now he was confidant that he could mend a second time.

Back on the Dennison campus, Bill and his Chicago amazons welcomed Jim into small college life by going out and drinking. Jim remembered late that night that he had been rolling around the floor with the aggressive North Shore girl but fell asleep before he fell into mortal sin. On Monday, the Bradleyites paid for their bacchanal by driving with heavy heads across 300 miles of Midwest cornfields. When Jim arrived in Peoria at the funeral home, he looked like one of the temporary occupants of the chemical-smelling basement.

* * *

Peoria and Bradley were in an uproar and Jim responded to the sports madness. A delirious basketball fever hovered over the beer-flavored air of the city and caught him up and bounced him up and down in fan frenzy, reviving a form of school loyalty that had been dormant in him for years. In a cheer-on-the-team way, he was re-entering the main stream, while at the same time escaping to another level. He was feeling like himself again for the first time in three years, only better and more confident now that he had found his scholastic footing and an emotional balance as a result of his Pittsburgh trip. One could feel normal and maintain an independent streak after all.

By mid-March, the campus was in full euphoric flight—the Bradley basketball team had been invited to the National Invitational Tournament in New York's Madison Square Garden. The NIT and the competing NCAA tournaments would determine the best in the country. The eventually devastated basketball squad—Paul Unruh, Billy Mann, Gene Melchiorre—though seemingly outgunned, became a Cinderella team. That they were from a backwater, wooden-basket league only enhanced their reputation; they rose up and beat off the early tournament contenders and advanced for a shot at the title. They won their first two games but lost in the semifinals to another Illinois team. For such a small school, the pride of reaching these collegiate heights stirred the community into fits of joy and, with the loss, disappointment.

* * *

April arrived and his Romantic Poetry studies led Jim into fresh pastures of the mind. He had always loved the springtime, his own Aries time. He particularly loved the fresh smell of the earth, the pungent, fecund mother lode that germinated all of life. Miss Rose was in her glory, matching rhymes with the flowering that exploded around the countryside allowing nature, great artist that she is, to paint the world a young green.

Curiously he had fallen in love with nature in his mind before he discovered actual trees and meadows and flowers. All the disappointments and self-abrasive attitudes that plagued his childhood and teen years began to fall away, replacing his once churlish demeanor. He became through romantic poetry a lighter-hearted person who had experienced a dark side.

He was no longer alienated but his greenness showed. Others might say he had simply not entered the modern world yet, that his naiveté was out harvesting dreamy fields. He himself now felt knightly bound to truth and contemplation, though he was not actually accomplishing manly good works, just thinking about them. He was not the melancholic romantic; he had transformed into a sunny one. Nor did he worry at this stage of development that he lacked the depth of feelings and intellect expected from an authentic academic personage. Still, his rebellious streak remained and pointed him toward certain dissatisfactions that would make him later re-think Romanticism. It wasn't that he was content with society or his country—he was particularly aghast at the practices in the South as they related to the region's treatment of Blacks—or the money-laundering suburbs. For now, he remained jovial, even though he couldn't deny the corrosive impact of love gone awry.

Jim's spiritual reconfiguring was also visible from the outside. His nervous system and body weight suffered as he grasped the new ideas and the emotional turmoil they created. He would sometimes feel shaky and he knew that part of his problem was the sexual repression that affected him daily. He presumed he could balance his life better if he could find a sleeping partner and if he had a creative outlet. As it was, frustration had stored such unfulfilled chaff in his system that he had a sense of wasting away.

* * *

As the week long Easter break approached, Jim made plans to visit Chicago and arranged as well to journey into Wisconsin to stay with family friends at a resort town called Lake Delavan, just over the Illinois border. He stopped by his Gram's West Side apartment for the holiday itself, attending lily-scented mass. He and his Gram sat quietly through the gospels that recalled that glorious long ago Christian morning. Mid-day, the extended family congregated around Gram's savory kitchen smells and samples, giving the old woman a sense of re-nesting with her munchkins, allowing her to spread her bountiful largesse around the table filled with those she loved and who loved her in return.

On Monday morning Jim ventured into the Loop and caught a northbound bus to Wisconsin, changing coaches at the sly-sounding town of Brass Ball Corners. His hosts in Delavan were the Woodwords. Harry and Maryon, old Chicago friends of his mother and step-father, who had moved at the beginning of the war to this small town where Harry took up a management position at the local clock-manufacturing company. They had first lived in a home on the nearby lake, a renowned playground, ringed with cottages. However, after a few isolating winters and too many stalled cars in the snow, the Woodwords had bought a place in town.

Maryon, alerted by his mother Grace, invited Jim the month before and mentioned that there was a girl she wanted him to meet. Meanwhile, Maryon went about setting her bait with one of the local beauties. She was so successful in her campaign that Jim and the girl had heard a great deal about each other prior to his arrival. Patiently the pair anticipated meeting. Before he arrived, they had already made a space in each other's schedule and booked a welcome tent in one another's camp.

The Woodwords—including their cheery son David—greeted Jim with wide-open Midwestern hospitality. They wanted to know everything that was going on in his life, more genuinely interested in him than were his own family. They were also curious about Gracie and Bob and about brother Matt, who had stayed with the Woodwords in previous summers while working on a local farm. Was Matt settling into his marriage?

"Now that you're here, you're in for a treat. You know the girl I wrote to you about," Maryon alerted Jim. "She's beyond beautiful and" she said with local pride, "she's just been named Miss Dairy Queen of Walworth County."

"Does she come with her own cowbell?"

"Maybe she'll ring yours. She's competing in a big speaking contest. She's the pick of the crop around here, I tell you. College boys are falling all over themselves trying to get up her sidewalk."

Jim, whose fancies mainly turned to urban and suburban minxes, wondered about these smaller town varieties. He was in for a surprise. He would soon learn they were foxier than their urban sisters. Her name was Barbara Hanover.

"I've told her all about you. Big New York guy and all."

"That will surely scare her away."

"She kind of intrigued, I think," Maryon, a born matchmaker, continued. "She's sophisticated for around here. I've even figured out a way for you to meet her—accidentally, if you get my drift."

Later in the afternoon, he walked to the library on the edge of the town proper, down the street from the excruciatingly brown Catholic church with its Norman look and tall spire—its finger pointing to God. The library, a Carnegie gift, seemed contentedly planted, the foundation set comfortably in the black earth, centered on a small plot—cozy with books. Welcoming.

He pushed the door open to a dusky interior lit by shafts of light streaming through long windows, a sunburst glistening with thousands of dust particles. On the other side of the ray of light, sitting at the circulation desk was a girl with one of the most beautiful faces he had ever seen. Olive skin and dark hair, Boticelli beautiful Barbara Hanover. As he walked toward her, he sensed she was waiting for him.

She appeared to be well placed among the rows of books. He would soon learn that a burning curiosity for life's answers guided her. Her reading interests would prove to be rapacious. He was about to discover a new kind of heat. A controlled fire appeared to be waiting to erupt in her, with slivers of anger sometimes flaming up to remind her which new injustice had just scratched her match.

"Hi. You must be Barbara. I'm Jim. Staying with the Woodwords."

"I heard you were in town." Her voice was rich and musical. A born actress. "Welcome to our local center of culture."

"Should I have worn my poet's shirt?"

"The one with ruffles around the neck?"

"Yeah, and the blue tailcoat and yellow vest."

"You didn't forget the high boots?"

She was mischievous and tart. An attractive smile played around her mouth and her nose crinkled when she laughed. He could easily see a seriousness of purpose in her composed centeredness that could not hide an anticipation of untried passions.

"So, how does a guy ask a girl out around here?"

"In a couple months when the season opens, they'll be plenty to do. As for now, there's the movies across the street. And did I mention the movies? Or a soda when I'm finished."

"That would be at ..."

"Five."

"Meanwhile, can I shake some dust off a volume or two?"

"I don't know," she teased him. "Without a card?"

"I'll enroll. I promise."

"You'll have to stay all summer. Then you can check out the best sellers."

"I hear librarians are introverted and don't go out much. Where are your glasses?"

"I must have left them back in the stacks, along with my inhibitions."

"Yeah. Ditch those. Let yourself go. Just think of something devilish. Like attending a book fair. Something dangerous like that."

At five, they walked across the street to the soda shop that sat next to the movie house, one that featured a twinkling marquee. The retail placement of the two businesses confirmed a successful

American commercial juxtaposition that combined the Thirties' union of film fantasy and gooey, nonsexual pleasure for lovers with few coins in their pockets. There was a smell of chocolate malt.

"What's this I hear about a speaking contest?" he asked after they sat in a booth. "You recreating the Lincoln-Douglas debates?"

She answered, "The local teacher's college offers scholarship money to the winners, and I need all the school aid I can get."

"What will you recite?"

"Saint Vincent Millay's 'Renascence.'"

"Excellent. I went looking for her house in the Village over Christmas."

"Take me there some time."

"Gladly. Happily... What college are you thinking about?"

"Lawrence, up north in Appleton."

"Can't take the winter heat down here?"

"North or south, Wisconsin kids never see green grass between November and April."

Returning to his hostess, Maryon asked, "How did the two of you get along?"

"Fabulously. You were sure right about her."

"Just goes to show ya."

Barbara and Jim planned a date. When he called to confirm, she said, "My folks gulped when I told them you were Catholic."

"I can't wear my hair shirt with the rosary around my neck?"

When she opened her front door, he said, "I hear there's a movie house in town."

"Yes. You can even smoke in the mezzanine."

"Anything more dangerous than that going on in the dark?"

"Well, if you want to hold a girl's hand, who's to complain?"

Her father and mother were sitting in the living room, one reading the paper, the other sewing. Mr. Hanover scowled, stern as a bear. Her mother looked like a muffin with extensions. They did not appear happy. Papists were bad enough. But a New Yorker to boot?

They walked along Walworth Avenue past the town's Victorian mansions. The old Allyn house, where a turn-of-the-century fountain splashed in the wide front yard, would remain in Jim's memory for years. Its many porches and wooden decorations impressed him. A three-level wedding cake, the antique wood frame was painted a dark green that gave the mansion a sinister look. He visualized it with springtime's lighter green—or maybe yellow with brown trim—an immense family home where he could imagine a half-dozen laughing children. The porte cochère was a reminder of a horse-oriented culture that reflected the area's farm life.

Tall, rough-barked elms, whose high canopy arched over the street and lawns, framed the street's architecture. This allowed a patterned leaf-filtered midday light to dapple the homes and green enclosures with sunbursts that on some surfaces coalesced into rainbows. Just now as they walked along, the evening light was diffused and shadowy.

The trees had been planted when the town was young at the same time that the red brick roadway had been cobbled together with horses and carriages in mind. The flowering trees and flowers, the fountain and the mansions blended into a spring harmony—the season that Midwesterners dream of during their snowbound winters. Walworth Avenue invited visitors to enjoy a sense of comfort and simplicity and settled nature. Christian beliefs and societal conformity ruled.

Alternate clouds and patches of blue sky appeared above—both at once, light and dark. In the clearing blue, the trees were alive with sunshine. Briefly they glistened until the clouds scudded by overhead. For that moment, the trees held the light and they shone brightly in the darkening sky. The frightened clouds would tumble in confusion but the trees would remain light, a signal that a time of transition was at hand.

So strong an impression did the Allyn mansion have on his imagination that it became engraved on his creative channels. Within a year he would be writing a novel, involving a setting that featured the old house as an independent-studies college. Barbara the heroine.

That night he learned that Barbara's work in the library came naturally; she was an avid reader, much more advanced than he, owing to the fact that she had been devouring books since she was six and reading the "hundred best books" since puberty. He sprang Philip Wylie on her and she thrust back with de Beauvoir. Their conversation was non-stop; their interests matched in numerous ways though she was the more creative, already skilled on the local stage. Projecting a bundle of skills, she even played he clarinet. Plus, she was incredibly beautiful, mischievously smart and funny

They actually did hold hands in the movies—wet clasping hands that had never known real sex. Afterward, they stopped at the malt shop and spooned up a hot fudge sundae. Back at her house, they sat on her stoop and talked into the night.

"Do you know the plays of Christopher Fry?" she asked.

He didn't. She began to quote the dramatist's verse, words with a light-hearted foolery whose humor she now passed along to Jim, touching a chord within him that previewed his love of *The Little Prince* in the following year.

"You have to hand it to playwrights. They're so creative," Jim said. "I don't know how they do it. They present a set of actions in the first act and you think you're going along on one level. Then they take all the ingredients and they're able to transform the first set of ideas into something so different it's mind-boggling. Slips right by you. They've got you concentrating on one thing and bingo, here comes a whole other understanding. Without you even realizing it, they've transformed the story and surprised you with a much richer meaning."

"Magicians among us."

He was surprised that he found a girl so compatible. How easy it was to talk to her! He hadn't expected to locate a like soul so close in time to his own stretching awareness. It was almost too soon to find her. In many ways, he wasn't ready for the onslaught of emotions that would soon engulf him. He was about to learn that life didn't telegraph its intentions.

The next day after she finished helping at the library, she worked a shift at the soda shop, where he waited for her while she polished the syrup pumps. Because Delavan High was also on vacation, her evenings were free and they met after dinner and sat on a swing in her backyard—the spring evening exhaling newly burst buds.

Because they were both so influenced by their reading, their conversation tended toward the literary, though they often dwelt in its lower echelons.

"Miss Jane, the head librarian, is the town censor. She keeps a locked cabinet filled with books she disapproves of—like poor, harmless *Mister Roberts.*"

"I don't know. Those Navy guys know how to swear. Might wrinkle a spinster's prayer shawl."

"There's even an 'adult' section back in the corner where she stores all the 'breast and bedclothes' books."

"Does she wrap them in brown paper to hide them?"

"No. But you'll like this. I'm reading my friend Peg's copy of *Forever Amber.* It's hiding in the jacket of Sikorsky's *Victory through Airpower*."

"Zoom! Zoom!"

They glided into book conversations with ease.

People usually tagged Jim as a non-verbal specimen. This was his first potential relationship since his conversion to cultural growth and he was in new territory. Previously, it had not been easy for him to participate in a conversation, especially small talk. Personal self-confidence had carried him over the breezy threshold of teenage relationships but he had never experienced a deep involvement, except for his hormone-drenched attraction to Bonnie and Lucy. Now with his head full of soaring couplets, mind-clearing novels and world-weary dramas, he was beginning to express himself. He was more comfortable with pen and paper in the study hall but Barbara was helping him open up his vocal chords.

The next day she drove them out to the lake and they walked along the shoreline.

When he looked across the lake, the blue reflection spread into his brain as if he had internally absorbed the color. He felt the placidness of the Midwestern lake system spread into his consciousness as he had once let in Long Island's ocean. His eyes roamed the sky and music seemed to be playing in his head. That or some kind of harmony.

"What I'm reading now," she said, "are Fitzgerald and the Brontes."

As she expounded on their virtues, he felt assured in his conviction that she was helping him reach some quiet place in his heart. He noticed that his anger was subsiding. His anxiety was retreating too. His hatred of blind injustice and cruelty to others was diminishing into balanced caring, a caring where he began to seek mature solutions. Where the scars of his childhood ran red, a white pulpiness was visible. Something in him was being healed over, replaced by a mellowness that might last a day or two until some stupidity of Senator McCarthy or any one of several Southern senators again ruffled his conscience. Then he would rail against those who re-jiggered the status quo for their own gains or to satisfy their prejudices.

On the last day before he left, they walked in the cemetery, a pleasant hillside covered with tall trees sloping down to a marshy area where they sat on the fallen trunk of a willow that still sprouted a few shoots.

He asked her to recite "Renascence" and he would remember the musicality of her expression all his life. As Millay's personal resurrection in verse ascended to light and sight, Barbara's voice rose in ecstasy. When she came to the passage where the heroine rises from the earth, he knew Barbara must have already experienced some transcendence in her own life. And she was carrying him with her. She had lifted them to an emotionally high place where they joined in passionate kissing when she finished the poem. His desires melted into love. He wondered if he had found his other self; if she had found her urban knight.

Jim projected Barbara onto the screen of his romantic visions. All those love notes he gleaned from Keats and Shelley, compounded with his own yearning, flashed in the soft light of his fuzzy desires. All his imprisoned emotions, that storehouse of anxiety, strove to surrender to her. He began to lust after her, confirming her parent's doubts about him. His deep sexual longing overwhelmed him. He had been a relatively chaste puppet in recent years, still under the control of the Church. But his desires now caused him to act like a high-hatted mannequin on his first dizzy appearance in the theater of sexual imagination. With bravado, he set his own puppet strings dancing. Himself now both the puppeteer and the doppelganger.

* * *

Back at school, their twice-weekly letters during April and May were filled with the optimism of romance, encouraging both to express their feelings and insight. They mutually supported an awareness of each other's longing that would flare up in extravagant sentences, offering the comforting illusion of intimate budding love. His letters opened with "Barbara darling" and hers, "Dearest Jim." It was a sweet, young time for both of them—that spring of '49. He would always remember that it was the best springtime of his life. He had certainly never been happier.

He wrote, *Nothing has ever touched me as you have. I've never known or felt the strength and purity of such emotions.*

She responded, *That's because you're sure of your feelings. I'm confused and conflicted.*

Answer back, *What I feel is so clean.*

He had found love because he was ready. His problem with Lucy was that he had not been ready. His high school senior fling wasn't about love. It was more of a crazy blood sport.

* * *

He was floating in a daze of love and literature. In his Nineteenth Century Lit class, he began to understand what it was like to fly. Emerson led him to believe that the American experience could be validated against other cultures if the individual sought a quality of life that followed the precepts of Transcendentalism. Jim felt that Emerson's views, conjoined with the Romantics, amplified the view that nature stands as "an apparition of God"—an equivalency. Learning that "every generation should carve out its own destiny." Emerson and Thoreau braced Jim up. Gave him some stays for his loose britches. Gave him the incentive to be himself.

* * *

One night, alone in his room in the Victorian turret at midnight, Jim's radio was tuned into the oddball classical music station from Chicago. The homespun announcer was playing a great deal of American music, and Jim hummed along, half listening and half reading Wordsworth.

The commentator was saying, "You know what turning fifty is like? That's what I'll be next year. It's like being up in the clock tower of a big city building and the bells start bonging— two-three-four. Your ears are busting and your hands are shaking and the noise seems to be getting louder as the bells swing. And they don't stop at twelve. Or twenty. It keeps crashing and banging until you've about had enough and wonder if you should grab a parachute and jump off. Those clapperknockers keep booming. When they ring fifty, you're basically pudding. That's what it's like to turn fifty. It means you better wake up and change your shook-up life.

"I've made a decision. Next year, I'm moving to New York. Don't call me a traitor. I have it nice and cushy right here in Chi-Town because I have the Midwest in my heart, but when you're fifty, you check your meters that got you this far, and you're allowed to say to yourself: the end is nigh. Do what you always wanted to do.

"Besides they have all these nice reminders of Columbia around Manhattan, even a university. And a big reminder out in the harbor, so I expect she won't let me down, And when I turn a hundred, I'm moving back to Chicago, because by then they'll be some good restaurants in town."

* * *

He decided to spend the summer in Delavan to be with Barbara. He knew he was taking a chance and that his efforts to win her might elude him. She had already warned him that her folks would only allow them to be together once a week; they were that adamantly opposed to her dating a Catholic. So anti-Papist, she said, they flinched whenever the nearby bells of St. Andrews rang.

On her part Barbara stoutly defended her decision to maintain a relationship with the New York boy. She not only had to fend off her parents' disfavor but the complaints of her best friend, Peg, who preferred burly college football heroes and fraternity rats. It took the young pair considerable skill to combine their pursuit of each other's affection. They each could see in the other that there was a strong bond. Always keep a little bit of Wisconsin in your heart, she had written him. And a Broadway light in your own, he had replied.

With the help of one of her bridge partners, Maryon helped Jim find a job at Lake Lawn, a comfortable inn and vacation destination that was Lake Delavan's principal resort. Its amenities included a golf course, small airfield as well as a large lakeside ballroom where an assortment of high flyers could maneuver and spread whatever wings they chose to unfurl.

Jim arrived in town just prior to Barbara's high school graduation. It was a newsworthy time for her, accepting, as she did, a variety of honors. She offered classmates baccalaureate advice and welcomed her many relatives from surrounding farm towns who came laden with flowers, recently butchered chickens and greeting cards. The pair did manage to share embraces in the back stacks of the library and behind the sweet shop as Barbara sped between senior class chorale performances, the senior prom, graduation rehearsals and work. They even slipped away into the cemetery one evening and found the fallen willow tree where they embraced at Easter. He attended her graduation with Maryon who wore a new hat for the occasion, and the pair joined the crowd bubbling around Barbara in her scholastic gown. Surrounded by a dozen admirers, she surreptitiously offered Jim the look of affection that he relished whenever they were together.

As a present, he gave her a collection of Romantic poetry.

On the weekend, Jim pulled out his recording of *South Pacific* from the bottom of his suitcase and brought it over to Barbara's. On the Stromberg-Carlson player in the living room, they sat and listened to the Rogers-Hammerstein sounds of the best musical Jim would ever know. They laughed at the sailor scenes and warmed at the singing of Mary Martin and Ezio Pinza. When the lyrics of "Younger than Springtime" poured out, Jim reached over and took her hand and she didn't resist until she heard her father rumbling toward them from the back of the house. Mr. Hanover would look in with a scowl and remark that they should be outside taking a walk. On his next tour fifteen minutes later, he recommended a bike ride.

"He must have a predilection for fresh air," Jim commented.

"He's not used to the idea that Broadway music could make somebody happy. Very Calvinistic about things like that."

Musicals helped bring them together. In quick order, Jim brought along the original cast album of *Where's Charlie*, a college farce, complete with Ray Bolger, the old-line Broadway hoofer, dressed up in widow's weeds

On their next date, they walked down Walworth to the movies. On the way home, they began to sing Bolger's showstopper, "Once in Love with Amy." He took her in his arms and they danced past the old Allyn mansion.

"Always in love with Barbara," Jim sang, substituting the line. She smiled up at him, that quiet, deeply felt look of affection.

He had hoped that every summer night would be a festival, until her father had slammed down the gavel. Neither of the young people liked the verdict.

* * *

Jim was manager of the snack bar set on the grounds of Lake Lawn, leaving him time in the evening to pursue Barbara when his lottery number came up on her calendar. The food shack on the resort's grounds was located between the pool and the golf course and enjoyed a good lunch business, with kids shivering in wet bathing suits and lady golfers in their pastels and tam-o'-shanters. The pay was not that good and gratuities were minimal because customers in swim suits and golf get-ups normally carried little tip money. It was only because the Woodwords allowed him to live board free that he was able to save money for tuition. As to where he was going to spend that money, he now knew. After negotiations and pressure from alumni on his behalf he was accepted as an upperclassman at the University of Michigan.

Jim had little appetite for running a short-order food operation but he duly performed his one-man show as cook and soda dispenser. Things went along satisfactorily until the day he almost burned down the shack. His grill was loaded with grease one lunch hour when the whole range exploded in fire. Jim automatically reached for a water bucket when one of the golfers yelled at him.

"Don't throw water on that grease fire. Smother it."

Jim dropped the water and threw off his long apron and covered the fire, beating down the flames with some wet towels lying about. When the fire was contained, he was frazzled by what had happened. The hotel manager came out and after some clean-up chores, Jim was soon mixing malts again. Because his hands were shaking, he probably contributed extra sweetness to his offerings.

* * *

When Lake Lawn Ballroom opened in the middle of June, Jim and Barbara joined some of her friends to make up a table of six. Her pal Peg brought along an All-American football player from Notre Dame, whose name was nationally recognized by sports fans. The other college couple hailed from Chicago's North Shore; they were summer residents whose families had built cottages on the lake a generation ago. An eighteen-piece orchestra spread across the bandstand, one of largest stages Jim ever saw, easily as big at those found on Broadway. The orchestra sounded too much like Guy Lombardo for his taste, more oom-pah than Jim could tolerate. It sounded like a band that had once played a lot of polkas in Milwaukee or was familiar with the fast tempos of the late Twenties. They even played "Hindustan" and "Stars Fell on Alabama."

The orchestra and the swing sound offered them a last listen to the sound track of the Second War. The conflict had now been over for four years and the country was moving ahead toward the baby boom and the affluent Fifties when the economic dreams of the country's middle class would finally be realized. What had supported the spirits of his generation during the dark times were the movies, the lively liquor-filled bars and the music that was being played tonight. They were all of a piece: The intention was that people should keep faith with each other and the country. When the War was over, the guys came home, started earning some money and let their high-haired, long-curled, lipsticked women lead them to bed. The fear, frenzy and pall of war's memory were dissipating except when, in the depths of the night, horror might return in a G.I. nightmare. But here and now, at the end of the Forties, these musical memories were diminishing—the music that had kept the country's faith alive long enough for America to dance with destiny. But the need for swing, America's adhesive to cover stress, was quieting into the past. The Lake Lawn band, dressed in white suits, played the standard swing charts but the new era was warming up off-stage. It would be the very last summer of swing. Elvis and the "shoo-be-do's" were loosening up in the wings.

Peg, blonde and cheerleader chunky, possessed a soft face and a fast mind that adapted well to the badinage around her. She was a quick responder, curiously tart, sometimes spicy, another time sweet—a relish of Midwestern emotions. Her date, hoofing toward the goal of football All-Americanism, was too big for his chair and smoked a cigarette so daintily from lack of practice that it seemed like a twig in his paws. He overwhelmed the proceedings.

Peg, her social awareness illuminating the round table, observed, "This old barn of a place seemed so immense the first summer I danced here."

"Could play a game of touch in here. Could even punt," said Ted, the thickest brick of Notre Dame's center line.

Jim loved the foursquare, high-ceilinged dance pavilion with its long windows that were flared on top by a fan-shaped blossom of glass that scattered the evening glow. Spinning over the heads of the dancers, there was a glistening, revolving chandelier that spun shards of colored light across the polished dance floor.

Barbara, whose excitement at such times increased her color as well as the light in her eyes, seemed conflicted by her wish, on the one hand, to reflect her quiet literary pursuits with Jim, and at the same time appeal to the others with their understanding of corporate America, the type of men that would have to provide for her.

Said Ted, "We could play Michigan right here."

His friend, another escapee from football training camp and summer business school, said, "General Motors is holding its regional sales meeting here next April. One of my profs will talk about obsolescence and how they can make money by building cars that last only so long, guaranteeing that customers have to buy a new one every other year."

Jim turned to Barbara, "Like to dance?"

She rose quickly, eager to ditch her dilemma.

"So, poet man," she asked over her shoulder as they strolled between tables, attempting to regain their subject matter, "Have you read Proust yet?"

"No."

"Me neither."

"And I'm not going to start until two things happen."

"Which are?"

"Someone treats me to a Madeleine and I get to hold you in these aching arms."

"Ache no more, Lancelot."

"I hate to mix myth with fairy tales, but how come I get to dance with Cinderella?"

"Because she hates to talk business on Friday night."

"A girl after my own heart."

"Only if you've decided to engage mine."

"Decision made."

"Then, dance on."

For a guy who wasn't a high stepper, he certainly danced enough. He wasn't smooth enough to win prizes, he at least he had moved to the timesteps of his own era.

Back at the table as the others became enmeshed in their early quest for jobs, income, settled bank accounts and insurance policies, Jim wondered what kind of pineapples these people really were and how was he going to deal with them.

* * *

Though rationed to one date a week, the pair found ways to see each other daily. If she worked in the evening, he would visit her at work and they would share her breaks. If she went out dancing with someone else, he would appear and monopolize her time. One night, in company with some guys from work—Jerry, Smittie and Kornflower—Jim, on instructions from Barbara, followed her and her date to the nearby Lake Geneva Casino that overlooked the waters of that famous resort. The band's music harmonized with the young couple's exploding desires.

His buddies, classmates of Barbara, helped Jim spend time with her. Her date would escort Barbara onto the floor and before he executed a dozen heel-lifters, along would come Jerry to cut in, followed moments later by Jim. Then at the end of the dance set, Smittie would come by and walk her back to her table, so that her date had no way to suspect that the New York guy was enjoying the fruits of his bill-paying. For the rest of the night, Jim and his friends alternated roles in the charade.

Barbara, who felt an obligation to be fair to her date, was nevertheless amused at the antics of her admiring book buddy. She reprimanded him mildly for his part in the ploy, but wasn't really angry, more chagrined than anything.

"Accept it," Jim said. "We're having our summer fling."

"And comes the reality of September?"

"We'll only be a Great Lake apart."

"That counts as a long swim."

"No, it'll freeze over and I'll skate over in no time."

"Not so easy. You'd be bow-legged by the time you got to Sheboygan."

"I'll rent an ice boat. Cut off some time."

"Which may or not work so well in that we have this thing called snow. It does snow out on the lake."

"You never heard of snowshoes? Tennis rackets for the feet?"

"Why don't you practice dancing in them."

"You're not aware that I'm wearing them now?" he said, humming the Amy song.

Kornflower would then interrupt their playfulness. "Time's up."

* * *

A few days later, Barbara and Jim were standing alone in the hallway of her home. He was holding her and their bodies were throbbing with desire.

"I want you more than you know," he said.

"We can't. We mustn't."

"We've got to do something. Just come lie with me on the couch. I'm busting out of my skin."

She looked away. "No. It's hopeless."

"Give it up."

"I love you. What more do you want from me?"

"Everything."

"I can't give you everything. I'm still part of a family and I rely on them and they rely on me. The pieces of me that I control, meaning most of me, are yours. Take what's yours."

He reached under her sweater and touched her breast.

But she pulled away. "But you can't have me that way."

He was flattened by her response.

"The hell with it," Jim said, and moved toward the door. "You figure it out."

With that, he bolted outside. He was sick from all the frustration.

He stalked up the street, not needing at this moment to face the tall brown spire of St. Andrew's in front of him.

He heard her steps behind him. She caught up and stopped him.

"OK. You have me. Do you hear? I'll give you all I can. But I don't know where or how."

He couldn't hold her on a public street. They turned back and returned indoors.

She had surrendered, and he touched her face and her breasts and they overcame their frustration by closing their eyes and making their promises in spoken words in order to deny the ravaging strength of their grunting desire.

* * *

"You know that I'm getting more out of this relationship than you are," she said.

"It's not possible," he responded. "You're the one who's transformed me. And transformation, 'tis said, counts more than mere change."

"Is mere change something like small change?"

"We have here gen-u-wine life-enhancing, soul-comforting love."

Their language finally began to capture their feelings.

She looked up him with expectant eyes.

"Because I do love you," he said. "Obsessed with you."

He took her in his arms. She rose on her toes so that her mons could reach his crotch and they swayed with sexual energy.

"You're perfect for me," Barbara sighed.

"For each other. A matched pair."

"Does that go with my pear-shaped body?"

"Such delicious fruit."

* * *

The summer flew by. There were keg parties beside the lake with friends whose parents owned cottages, relaxed afternoons and evenings under the large trees that lined the shoreline. There was a shopping trip to Milwaukee for college clothes, and a day trip to Chicago to see the matinee of a traveling Broadway production of *Finian's Rainbow*. With any activity, they found that they naturally blended into one another's psyche. There was a kind of compatibility that he had never known before because he had become a new person.

When it was time to depart for Ann Arbor, they made no promises. In a way they didn't have to do so. They had both found one of the treasures of their lives.

Whether it was because he was back in the Middle West, he had trusted himself to enjoy and expand his second self. He needn't add any airs or try to impress anyone with his social confabulations. He just allowed things to be and rode with the consequences. That he had found Barbara was paramount. It changed him by deepening him. He grew up into love. In Delavan he closed the circle on the first loop of the discovery of a holistic life.

As they parted they knew that the relationship had to change. They would be hundreds of miles from each other with a very great lake in between. There was no way they could have eloped; it was never even discussed. They were both on an emotional and intellectual journey and the way toward self-definition and self-fulfillment needed to come first. Their hearts were entwined but their minds still as impressionable as nuns in a grotto.

What he had come to believe was that love was all. That he soared to a higher level when he learned he could lock on to another.

On the last night before leaving, he dreamt he possessed a magic pen. In his dream, when his pen touched paper, there was an explosion of images that produced an intricately laced picture. The images were black and white—bucolic in nature, snow scenes, orchards, an older America. The black contours of the picture had been scissored out and silhouetted on a white background. Repeatedly in his dream, he touched a new blank paper with his magic pen and a landscape began spreading across the page, rolling out its treasure. He believed that dreams were created by some power other than himself—some universal creative artist. Jung called it the collective unconscious and came closest to an answer.

Jung or God, one or the other.

Chapter 7
(1949 - 1950)

Upon leaving Union Station in Chicago bound for his junior year at Michigan, twenty-year-old Jim Mahoney had a feeling that his past studies were only a precursor to finding his way to contemporary thought and personal creativity. It was as if he had enjoyed his slow ride on the Victorian local—Romanticism, the Renaissance, back to the classics—prior to the whiplash he was about to receive when he ventured toward Modernism, a bullet train that awaited him after he decided to change tracks for the Ann Arbor Express.

He stepped off the train, two suitcases in hand, and made his way to the main campus. There he was impressed by the wide, tree-lined Diagonal surrounded with the solemnity and stolidity of last century's building that mixed in with a few modern ones. The ponderous-looking old block-stone structures made him feel that he had come to a place of reckoning, as if hard-to-reach knowledge resided here, and that well-guarded intellectual treasures lay hidden and might be shared if a serious person were willing to dig. The look of determination on the faces of the students re-enforced the notion and led him to feel that mediocrity wasn't welcome here.

His housing had been arranged beforehand; he had sent a trunk ahead, heavy with a pile of books. After securing a packet of information for new arrivals at the Student Union and acquiring a student ID at Admissions, he walked a few blocks to a side street where he found a row of bulging, porch-enclosed homes built in the 1890s, all surrounded by large elms. One of these overblown architectural monstrosities with its cut-up warrens would be his residence for the autumn months. The university population had soared; sleeping and reading space was at a premium. Places in the regular men's dorms had long been assigned. With so many servicemen matriculating, half the homes in town had been converted into study bins.

At the appointed address, a tall, sexy woman opened the door and with sloe eyes estimated Jim's body type. She had a hungry and mistrustful look and was not impressed with Jim's gregariousness. Behind the woman stood another older woman, perhaps her mother. Oddly, both were wearing kimonos late in the day.

"Hi. I'm Jim Mahoney. Are you Mrs. Acer?"

"We didn't expect you today," she said. "Sheets and towels won't be available until tomorrow."

"No problem," he said, and with that the two women led him up an ornate stairwell and deposited him in a bedroom with two double-decker bunk beds. Contents also included a card table, four fold-up chairs, a pair of two-sided desks and some lamps.

"Your roommates are a couple brothers from Muskegon and one of their friends. But before you make yourself comfortable, I got your rent for September and October but didn't get the damage deposit. So before you unpack, you'll have to come up with another twenty-five dollars."

Jim produced his wallet and felt her eyes surveying the contents as he extracted the amount from his billfold.

Taking the money and washing it around in her hands, she said "OK. The rules are: No girls. No drinking. No smoking in bed. No wet laundry. And no wet food."

Jim didn't quite understand the full meaning of the last prohibition, but nodded. Later in the day, the three guys from Muskegon arrived, filling the ordinary room to the wooden trim. They choose lots for the bunks. Cramped, there would be little space for gymnastics or tea service. They would be lucky to maintain a regimen of civility over the use of the adjoining bathroom.

They were pleasant enough guys. The two older vets were in grad school, one in dentistry, the other in engineering. The younger brother, Chuck, was a freshman in LS&A. That was Jim's school as well, Literature, Science and the Arts. The three Michiganders were solid, no-nonsense students who showed little interest in Jim's pursuits of the bookend subjects of LS&A—the lit and arts part. Science, squashed in the middle of the designation, would provide a surprise for Jim.

While the others got settled, Jim took a walk around campus. He was amazed at the size of the school but it failed to daunt him. Familiar enough with large enclaves like Manhattan, he knew that a city as well as a mammoth university was segmented into neighborhoods, each with its own traditions and special sausage. No one could be privy to the whole. He intuited that Big 10 social structures might be separated by housing classification—by dorms, coops, rooming houses and Greek enclaves. One fraternity, for instance, was reserved for jocks while one of the leading sororities was designed for Detroit suburban girls. One coop was populated with Asian students and another with Africans. He would have to find his own cupboard within the community but felt confident that he would locate his niche. He was not overwhelmed by the presence of twenty thousand other students. He presumed he could find a few friends among the many.

He noticed the pinched look of some of the women walking on the quad. Other coeds were reflective of a more Eastern appearance and style, smooth-skinned with alert eyes. Almost all were attired in skirts and sweaters, mostly shod in saddle shoes, with, hair uniformly short. Skirts had lowered to mid-calf, way below the length girls had worn them during the war when thighs received a great deal of airing. Later, attending prom events, he noticed that the hems of informal dance dresses bobbed just above the ankle. The Fifties with its conservatism encouraged the downdraught.

Campus town, adjoining the Diagonal, differed from downtown Ann Arbor in that it was strictly suited to students' needs. Two bookstores, several coffee shops, a candy shop, and two movie houses, plus clothing and other retail operations, were designed to serve the university community—for a new string for one's banjo, a cookbook, a tripod, an argyle sweater; they were all available here along State Street. Jim entered one of the coffee shops and surveyed a nest of twenty-eight booths packed with students, all jabbering about the new school year and the summer just ending. He would have liked to join the gabfest, but instead sat alone at the counter. He would find friends soon enough.

He moved on to Follett's bookstore. It was an immense location that not only supplied texts for class work, but also carried a wide array of titles, a treasury for readers. Jim wandered into the fiction and poetry section where he discovered stacks and tables piled with books with a flood of exotic titles—obscure histories of women novelists, poetry books handcrafted by North Carolina and Tennessee mountain dwellers, a section carrying first editions—the store was a cornucopia of literature. There were streams of books by the world's great authors, many not familiar to Jim, but names that frequented book reviews, minds that he looked forward to knowing. An hour went by as he moved among the crowded tables. He was reading from the latest Eliot collection when a fellow browser asked him a question.

"Reading much Eliot? Lots of fans here."

"Just started last year. 'Prufrock' and the basics."

"Have you gotten to the *Four Quartets* yet?"

"On the list. Did you like them?"

"Immensely. How about Pound?"

"On the same list."

"Sounds like you're an English major."

"Of course. Where else could you experience such chills and thrills? . . . You?"

"In grad school. Modern Lit."

"Lucky devil. How long before your degree?"

"If I play my cards right and Uncle Sam keeps sending checks, I may be here forever."

"Nirvana."

"Lot of buzz about Eliot's idea of the 'objective correlative.' Be prepared in class."

"About symbolism mimicking physical reality?"

"Approximately. Profs are also talking about I. A. Richards and Existentialism."

"No surprise. Sartre's probably a big seller here."

"They're performing one of his plays in a month or so."

"Sounds like a must-see."

"Lots of chatter about his ideas. About being responsible for your own actions."

"That and the part about being emotionally authentic sound right. Any buzz about Kierkegaard? I'm trapped between his take on the individual against Hegel's worldview—the all men are brothers business? I'm hung up trying to figure out about either maintaining a solitary life, keeping it private, or taking my act public."

"Yeah. Hide or seek."

Jim said, "Me? I believe in personal rights but I'm a leftie, so I have to accept Hegel's idea that history's steers us in its flow."

"Go ahead. Have it both ways."

Jim realized that this was the kind of language he had been searching for, easy conversation about ideas he cared about. They talked for a long time, sometimes merging in their views, sometimes not. Greg was a good-looking guy, very sure of himself, with a deep voice. Jim was excited that his first conversation at Michigan had been stimulated by someone who loved literature more than he did.

Jim memories of Ann Arbor always began with this conversation that opened his eyes to the experiences that lay ahead and the feeling that he had arrived at a new level on his academic journey, where he could interact with like-minded people. He began to feel that he might be able to bring together the random ideas that had captured him so far, and by degree, meld his beliefs into a contained whole. Indeed most of the great writers and thinkers often came to the same conclusions that honesty, authenticity, sharing and caring were the foundations of the good life.

Greg suggested that they have a bite together, and they found an empty booth in the coffee shop.

"Are you doing any writing?" Greg asked.

"I've been thinking about starting a novel," Jim replied. It was the first time he verbalized a notion that had been running through his head. "How about you?"

"Fooling around with some essay possibilities...Is the place where you're living quiet enough to get some work done?"

"No, I'm cooped up with a bunch of other guys."

"Too bad we didn't meet a week ago. We had an opening in our apartment. I'm in with a couple guys who spend most of their lives in the lab."

"It might have been too pricey for me. I'm on a tight budget. Praying I don't have to find a job this semester. Must be nice to have an apartment."

"Yeah. It's lively. It's by the hospital, so we have a lot of nurses in the building."

"Simplifies the dating game."

Greg said, "But they get itchy. My roommate had one of them hanging around his neck and couldn't get rid of her, so he tried thinking of a way to ditch her so we decided to play a trick on her. He took her to bed a couple nights ago and we made sure that the room was pitch black. After they're screwing around for a while, my buddy says that he has to get up for a rubber in the next room and bounces out of bed. Then, we pull a fast one. Another roommate is about the same size as the boyfriend, and we send the new guy into the dark. Pretty soon, they're going at it hot and heavy until she realizes this guy isn't her boyfriend. Mortified, she screams bloody murder and hightails out of there. The next morning, she had packed up all her gear and left campus for good."

Jim was appalled by the story, disillusioned. What kind of trick was that? That Greg was part of the ruse and wasn't even ashamed struck Jim with horror. How could he have done such a thing?

They finished eating and Jim headed back to his digs in a conflicted state. He had been enjoying an interesting talk about new ideas, and along comes this story of rancid misbehavior that smacks down his belief system. He was furious.

* * *

During his first week at Michigan, Jim was swept into an orbit that included one of the most inspirational teachers he would ever have. The lecturer's ingenuity was such that he not only had the ability to clarify his subject, but portray himself as a worldly specimen in such a way that people eagerly responded to his sophistication. Jim, captured by the art history teacher's personal grace, absorbed the nuances of the good doctor's gentle spirit, then tried to emulate him. Jim came to understand that civility, humility, caring and deference to others were essential ingredients in completing one's own valid personality. In a youthful burst of adulation, Jim opened himself to the art of the world and the art of personal presentation.

Dr. Eisenstein's survey course on the history of art covered two semesters. The slight, elegant instructor introduced his class to Greek and Roman art, then on through the medieval darkness, before advancing into the rose-tinted light of Florence. Jim's response to the beauty of classical art encouraged him to read both the Latin historians and Attic playwrights, coordinating the small bit of "dead language" that he had remembered and merging it with this new stimulation to survey the classics. He made lists of the Olympian gods and their progeny, wondering how much farther along he might have been if he had only paid attention or attended the right schools where he might have been forced to deposit these classical references in his early-teen memory bank. He was now sorry that he hadn't taken Greek as well as Latin and was always certain that learning both languages was a sure sign of an educated person. He tried to stuff years of learning into a few months.

In an amphitheater filled with several hundred students, the popular Dr. Eisenstein, with his gift for reaching young minds, clicked through dozens of examples of classical work.

He explained, "Think of it this way. Art is the tangible record of experience transformed by the imagination of the artist." He then stepped back and let that sink in, never for a moment presuming he had all the answers, searching his audience, waiting for commentary from the bright faces he saw before him, respecting them, eager to help them learn. Hearing no response, he proceeded in a cultured voice, "The grout and mortar of a painter and sculptor's life plus his ability to spontaneously create are paramount." He hesitated again, looking up at the Praxiteles slide. He was captured for a moment by its beauty, then turning again to his students, embracing them with his warm eyes and selfless demeanor, he added, "These were craftsmen. Artists in the Christian era were anonymous until the early Thirteenth Century, when painters belonged to the Druggist Guild and sculptors to the Mason's Guild."

The marble perfection of the images that Eisenstein illuminated inspired Jim to continue to chase after the beautiful. He began to understand that his search for lovely women coincided with his attempt to discover a more ideal kind of beauty. He finally figured out that it wasn't truth and beauty he sought but love and beauty.

"The seeds of the Renaissance are in Dante's writing and Giotto's painting," Eisenstein went on, "and the fact that strong towns made strong men."

Jim liked that part. New York was tough enough, but he was afraid the suburbs that spawned him were a little wimpy.

His other classes were designed to fill out requirements for graduation, courses he had avoided in his first two years of college. Except for a year of Geology, he had taken no science, so he signed up for Botany, avoiding anything to do with Physics or Chemistry. Luckily the Logic class at Bradley and a pass by the Michigan registrar had satisfied his math credentials—frail as they were. The Shakespeare class was mandatory for English majors. The motivation for taking a class on Constitutional Law devolved from a vague notion that he might study to become a lawyer.

* * *

The Botany Department offered a long and lean scientist to Jim and his mostly freshman classmates, a professor who lectured the large class with the help of a couple of assistants. They helped fumble-fingered students like Jim adjust their microscopes and slides in the lab to watch a hidden world came alive. The moving ingredients in plant life squirming around under magnification fascinated Jim. During lab, a girl named Beatrice, an open, happy young woman who wore colorful cotton dresses, shared a table with Jim. They became instant friends and were soon flirting in each other's direction.

On good weather days, the Botany class retreated to the large and leafy Arboretum on the edge of campus on a tract embracing the Huron River that flowed in a depression between the eroded hills. Hundreds of donated trees from around the world joined with the native growth, many marked with descriptive brass plates. Stands of local specimens rambled naturally over the countryside and gleamed with foliage, colors that gladdened the professor's heart. He tramped through the woods, booted in his element, pointing out species along the way, an expert comfortable in his elm realm. He strode across the leaf-scattered floor of hardwoods, admonishing students to choose crisp samples, stopping sometimes to admire and bend down: "Ah! Trembling aspens. Where could they be?" he asked, looking around.

The students gathered around him. The elegant shape of the leaf would provide him an opportunity to wax on about its properties.

Beatrice said, "See, Jim. The perfect ribbing."

Jim, less visually acute than Beatrice, smiled as much at her as for the natural design.

"Why trembling?" he asked aloud.

"See the row of them down by the river?" the botanist pointed. "Watch them."

Along the riverbank, a string of tall, thin trees grew, studded with leaves that quaked frenetically along their narrow trunks. The trees appeared to be shivering in the wind. The tree's shallow roots made it vulnerable and prompted it to waver, accentuating its fragile energy. The aspen shook in the slightest wind, flashing two sides of its leaves, one almost silver, the other green. In motion, the trees simulated an outdoor dance recital.

The sight opened Jim's imagination to a natural metaphor—that the tall fragile women whom he found attractive often quivered in the breezes that stirred their emotions. Not Beatrice whose tall robust body was oak-steady, nor Barbara's, whose low center was rooted to the soil.

"I've never noticed them before," Jim said, looking again at the shining display of leaves waving in anxiety.

With all his love of Romanticism and its emphasis on the outdoors, Jim had never been a nature-oriented citizen of the earth. True, as a boy he often played in a stream near his house and in the nearby woods. He had liked to climb limbs, especially the big apple tree up on an abandoned farm where generations of town kids had etched their initials. And as well he loved the ocean. But he had been a listless Boy Scout. Aside from mountain walks on a family friend's farm on the edge of the Berkshires, he had not tramped through hills or camped in the wilderness or trekked across pastures, one eye out for a rambunctious bull. He was an oceanside kid and his medium was wet.

"I don't think I wore the right shoes," Beatrice said, holding him with her bright brown eyes. Her colorful green skirt and pink blouse were crisp and immaculately clean. She refreshed Jim's images of the girls he grew up with in Manhasset, and she proved comfortable to engage.

"It's fun to be out here with you," she said in her generous way, making him feel as if he were contributing to the quality of her day.

"Right. Just holler if you need any help distinguishing the apples from the oranges."

"How about separating the fake from the real."

"OK. I'm fake. You're real."

"No, you can't fake a smile like that."

"I think we better become friends."

She brightened up again. "Done."

* * *

Jim's step-father had been a fraternity man at Northwestern, a member of a chapter that eventually merged with the national Alpha Chi organization. Jim considered pledging the Michigan chapter as a way of bridging the gap between Bob Hill and himself. Soon after the start of the semester, the Greeks held a rush weekend. The initiation process entailed thousands of new students trudging from one fraternity house to the next seeking acceptance and comradeship. Applicants sought a community of friends or perhaps a good party location. Or maybe, considering the closets most of them lived in, better lodging.

Jim had doubts about the entire fraternity system, afraid that it would be crowded with suburban guys like the tradition-bound types he had abandoned, and in turn been abandoned by, in Manhasset. But his instinct to bond with his old man prevailed and he paraded into the Greek enclosure of Alpha Chi. He didn't approach any other house. If he were accepted in this one, fine; if not, that would be all right, too.

The Alpha Chi house, designed by Frank Lloyd Wright, was a low-profile prairie home with an enormous living room and a variety of nooks and crannies on the first floor. The guys looked preppy and the smells of shaving lotion and lemon oil used to clean the wooden walls were everywhere. The main room was filled with members preparing to be polite to a gaggle of uncomfortable freshmen. At the door, Jim filled out a quick form providing a few details about himself. There was a brief flurry of interest when he verified that he was an Alpha legatee. He quickly received extra attention. A short, blond, attractive young man was brought forward to engage Jim and escort him around the facilities.

"Hi. I'm Buster Scott. Welcome to Alpha Chi. I'm one of the vice-presidents."

"A pleasure," Jim said. "Nice digs."

"Yeah," Buster said. "Some big architect built it . . . So your dad's an Alpha?"

"Yes. He encouraged me to come by."

"You didn't pledge elsewhere in your first two years?" His blue eyes were quizzical.

"No. Too busy trying to get my grades up."

Looking at the card Jim had filled out, Buster said, "I've heard of Manhasset. Outside New York, right?"

"Yes. About twenty miles out. A commuter town. How about yourself? Are you a Michigander?"

"Grosse Point."

Jim's mind played with the "gross" word.

"We have a diverse group here," Buster said, and with a motion to the corner where a giant student stood, continued, "We have an all-American football player living in the house. That's Ricky Rafensburger over there."

Jim watched the big man move through the crowd.

"Let me introduce you to some of the brothers. One of them is from Garden City, out your way, I think."

Jim liked the guy from Long Island, Bill Turner, and his buddy, Ribs Robinson from the North Shore of Chicago.

They were both vets, Navy guys. Adults, they were plainly bored by this passel of greenbeans that was disturbing their afternoon. Jim, at least, was a few years older and seemed to understand about major metropolitan centers and especially about the war, how it dragged on forever, how guys were suffocated by its authoritarianism. He stayed and talked for a half hour and left, satisfied that he had distributed his personality traits around the prairie home as well as could be expected.

He was invited back for a "smoker" where the hardy members measured out their testosterone and labored, sometimes with difficulty, to talk dirty.

"How's your old clitoris?" was an expression that floated around that night and again at a house meal a few days later. Jim had no idea what a clitoris was.

At a mixer, where the Alpha girlfriends were invited, the coeds were encouraged to inspect the new prospects, looking for any sign of effeminacy or political irregularity that might compromise their swains. The women seemed like a cold lot to Jim. His lack of interest in them probably increased their interest in him.

Walking up to Buster Scott and his date, Jim smiled dumbly and said, "Hey, Buster. How's your old clitoris?"

The look of horror on both their faces was enough to penetrate Jim's social consciousness. Gaffes were not uncommon occurrences in Jim's past. The next day, cool Buster took Jim aside and said, "There are some things we say to one another when just guys are around. But you have to be more careful in front of the women."

Apparently his ungracious boner did not impede his path toward membership, though he later discovered that there had been some question about his naiveté.

"Turner, isn't this guy from New York? Not too hip."

A few nights later, several members came knocking on his door to tell him he had been accepted as a pledge.

Meanwhile, his new friend Beatrice had taken a parallel journey. She had participated in the sorority rush exercises and decided to join forces with a bevy of sharp and politically astute women housed behind the Phi Pi shield that nestled in the capital of their chapter house's front porch. Beatrice, who was as skeptical as Jim about Greek life, found herself pleasantly surprised by the intelligent streak in her would-be sisters.

For the next few months, Jim and Beatrice exchanged invitations to each other's house parties. One Saturday night, they were duly reverential toward the all-American who had scored a touchdown before a hundred thousand spectators the same afternoon, and who remained faithful to his training schedule while, all around him, others had difficulty staying sober. Though in his mind, Jim was bound to Barbara and their every-other-day letters were filled with affection, he began to snuggle Beatrice in a quiet corner of the fraternity house or under the dim lights in front of the women's dorm.

* * *

"Dearest Jim," Barbara's letters began. "There was a big all-campus dance last night after our Homecoming game, and I am sad to say I got slightly smashed. OK, really smashed. My girlfriends said I didn't do anything too rash."

She was getting around, too.

* * *

Ribs Robinson took over the job of steering quirky Jim through the fraternity admission process. A colorful and happy-go-lucky vet, Ribs represented all that was attractive about Chicago's North Shore. His milieu was the suburban society that Jim's family never attained in their pre-war years in Chicago when Bob Hill took over the thankless job of regulating the lives of Jim and his brother Matt, both of whom rebelled against their step-father's authority.

Ribs and Jim sat in an upstairs bedroom in the Alpha Chi house that the carefree senior shared with his buddy from Garden City.

"This is the thing, Jim," Ribs advised. "You have to go along with the rules and this initiation shit. It's like in business. You give them lip service, saying the things they want to hear, then you just go your own way and do what you like. It's a game."

Jim was doubtful that he could play that kind of charade.

Ribs continued, "Look, what's it gonna cost you? You just spout out a couple platitudes. Nobody's gonna get hurt."

"Except its phony,"

"It's the same anywhere you start out. Here on campus or when you go for a job. You have to learn to fit in. After a while, when you have some power of your own . . . gain some standing . . . then you can call the tune and everybody will have to dance to your tune. But in the beginning, you have to keep your head low."

Jim never bought the theory. Doubting its efficacy, and bolstered by his egotistical stubbornness, he chose not to be snookered by phoniness.

Ribs tried to help Jim in other ways. One was to secure him a job waiting tables at the Phi Sigma house next door so he could save some of his allowance. As Jim began to work and know the brothers there, he thought of them as typical American collegians—ambitious, job-oriented, sports crazed males who appeared to be most comfortable when they were playing golf. Not all filled the mold, but enough of them retained a conventional masculine flavor to convince Jim that he would never again be a regular guy. He wasn't going to "go along." with the "normal" crowd. His way was bound to wander in a different direction. He thought life should provide more excitement, encourage cross-cultural mixing, and generate deeper feelings and empathy for those trampled by the bad guys of the world. He loved his buddies' funny stories and how they melded together when they weren't threatened, and he tried not to be a snob, but he wasn't going to play their game. His had begun to think that his ambition might lie in the direction of broadcasting his views through writing, while, at the same time, not losing himself to any conforming system.

It was a simplistic observation. There were dozens of variations on the masculine theme, and a lot of these guys would become doctors and lawyers and scientists, and do good work. Most of them had a kind of moral courage, as well as organized smarts, and were responsible to causes greater than themselves, but in general, Jim resisted conforming to the crowd for fear of not being able to travel his own path. He was rather selfish in a way. In arriving at these conclusions, he revised his "good guy" persona to one more likely to be viewed as an outsider and non-believer. He was tilting back into rebellion, but this time he had reasons to resist the crowd.

* * *

Aside from Eisenstein's art class, Jim was also studying Shakespeare though he didn't respect the Prof who was a stuck-in-the-mud Aristotelian at a time when Jim was flying high with Plato. On his own, he concentrated on reading Emerson and Jung, as if to confirm that he was more interested in following the adventures of the Oversoul paddling in the stream of the Collective Unconscious.

Through his outside reading, he finally became acquainted with Edmund Wilson. He was forced to do so, because everyone in the English Department was talking about *Axel's Castle*. He also read Kazin's *On Native Ground* and Van Brook's *Flowering of New England* to widen his views on American Lit. He added Malcolm Cowley's *Exile's Return* as a way of pursuing his fascination with the Parisian influence on American writers in the Twenties. Then he found Fitzgerald, whose canon he now devoured, associating himself totally, almost unnervingly, with the Delegate from Great Neck. He loved the grace of Fitzgerald's style and thought he understood Fitz's ambivalent reaction toward the rich. From a southern direction, there was much discussion about Faulkner's Nobel speech—cautioning folks to be unafraid and endure—from the year before. On that same wind blew the Southern Agrarians. He was again sailing in native American waters.

The question was: Where was he going with all this? Where did all this reading fall on the timeline of his life's progress? Was he seeking knowledge for its own purity and sake? He certainly admired those who did. But self-inculcation didn't seem to be his motivation. The conundrums of existence didn't make him stay up all night and brood, even when he could understand the arguments. The truth was that he never acquired existential angst. Other doubts and worries, yes.

What he was principally doing was building up an anger against the injustices he saw playing out on the world stage—the suppression of blacks in the South; the meddling of the CIA in South America; the undeserving undernourishment of children in Africa and Asia; the Mafia's intrusion on labor unions, a move that would eventually cut the heart out of the middle class, leaving only its pocketbook, not its ability to fight for equality and collective harmony; plus all the stupid politicians like the guy from California who spewed Americanism against the left where Jim now stood politically. People didn't deserve the kind of treatment they were receiving from the rich and the dictatorial powerful. He thought: Why didn't those rich bastards just look in the mirror and get wise to themselves that they were not really part of the race's struggle? And he was frustrated because he had no way to combat these forces, he wasn't smart enough to know what do about the problems presented by poverty so he convinced himself that he should just keep studying and perhaps some directional lights would turn on. In a few years he would be out in that world himself, where he might be able to do some good while he was learning to make a living.

His piecing together of knowledge wasn't aimed at receiving a paycheck. He presumed that a career as a teacher, standing in front of a class year after year, was daunting. What felt right was the need to be surrounded by literature. He discovered there was a growing urge in him to do something with the literary patterns and feelings that he was now beginning to fit together. How could he best be responsive to all these stimuli? Maybe he could write something about the emotions that were bursting through him. Maybe he would try to write that novel he had been thinking about or a play. He didn't just want to sample literature; he wanted to feast on it.

All in all, he was encouraged by his development, more optimistic about his own powers to pierce the fog of complexity that hung over the world. He was beginning to put it all together: The history, the literature, the art, the philosophy were all merging to form an understanding of life and his place in it. It was now his task to form a personal belief system.

* * *

One warm Saturday in early fall, when the football team was away battling other cornhuskers, Jim and Beatrice planned a trip to the Arboretum—a walk in the woods and perhaps the discovery of a specimen or two. The fact that Jim was carrying a blanket under his arm indicated the stroll was not exactly a field trip.

"How are classes going?" Jim asked.

"So exciting," Beatrice said. "It's everything I ever hoped it would be. I'm learning so much from all these really neat teachers as well as from you that my brain is popping. Ann Arbor is helping me come alive—just the way I've always wanted."

"We all need to get some of that buttermilk out of us," Jim said. "We have to mentally leave those dinky towns we grew up in. If you stay in one long enough, you get sautéed in vanilla syrup."

"Maybe you'll be my guide out."

"Or you, me."

"Or us, us."

"Speaking of guides, let's go find a river."

Listening to the water flow through the small valley, they walked down to the Huron, overhung with willow trees and root-exposed saplings. The river, thirty yards across, cut through the woods on its way out of town. Its smell was pleasantly fishy.

"I've got an idea," he said. "Let's have a race."

They constructed small wooden barks and raised a couple of masts with sails of leaves. He slid down the embankment and launched the vessels. Walking along the bank, they watched their entries capsize or crash into rocks and sink. Then they found remnants of cartons that were sturdier and fashioned them into watercraft. Their ships were plainly marked: Beatrice was Golden Cereal and Jim was Milwaukee Manure.

After splashing along the river, they spread out the blanket.

"It's so beautiful here. I wish I could contain it, store it up, save it by painting it," said Beatrice.

Jim said, "Me? I'd rather paint with my imagination. Want my pen to float over the paper and convey a vision of what it's like to live now, right now, mid-century."

Beatrice said, "It's so good to talk about things without being embarrassed."

"So, talk, as they say in the Bronx."

"I have this yearning, this passion, for finding color in life."

"It's out there waiting for you. Open yourself to it."

"You make me feel I can actually find it. But how do I do it?"

"Listen and read."

"How do other people manage?"

"I've always been impressed by how Europeans seem to be closer to nature than we are. They seem to revere it, equate it to beauty. I often wondered why it is we don't have the same feeling."

"I'm going to have to get back to you on that."

"Don't wait too long. Time's a-beating."

"Thanks for helping me chart the way."

"You did it yourself. Just don't let those flowers in you wilt."

They lay down on the blanket and inched their bodies toward one another. Excited, they began to naturally move and explore.

* * *

In early October, he attended a performance by pianist Artur Rubinstein in an all-Chopin program. The concert was held in Hill, the big hall on campus whose stage mimicked Sullivan's half-circle proscenium in his Chicago Auditorium. Here a much larger arc spanned the stage. Jim had previously dropped into the concert hall for student recitals but nothing matched the excitement of the sounds he heard the night the suave genius played, a veritable patriarch of the piano.

When Rubinstein came on stage, Jim felt an eminent grace had come to bestow his blessing on a cultural wayfair. He had never seen such elegance in a man: white hair and austere, formally dressed, sadly solemn—a Polish prince bearing the bitter knowledge that the Holocaust had devoured his family. The pianist and the instrument erupted, then modulated, then lyrically brought Eastern European musical genius to southern Michigan. A cortege of Polish dances, a touring polonaise.

Who knew that the august Rubinstein was one of the many grand bon vivants ousted by anti-Semitism from the jaws of hell to decorate American shores— Schoenberg, Stravinsky, Bartok—who tried to transfer old Europe to sunburned California or brash New York? Failing, they had to be content with the knowledge that they were teaching others how to live well. Unable to ingest new revelations without taking some action, Jim booked the music room in the student Union for the next few weeks to practice his mazurkas. Later in the school year he heard Munch and the Boston Symphony, Szell with the Cleveland, Reiner and the Chicago. He heard Risë Stevens singing *Carmen*, and, on another occasion, he listened to the scourge of the desert, Nelson Eddy, a sheik of the sands, figuratively waving his *djellaba*.

* * *

Beatrice had become friends in her dorm with a sweet, perky and intellectually gifted girl named Mary Cambridge, and the Botany pair arranged a double date with his roommate, Chuck. The foursome attended a few of the spectacular Michigan football games that fall—the team was usually in pursuit of the national championship in those years—in the immense university stadium that seated a hundred thousand. Turned companions, the quartet began to explore the countryside. Chuck's brother owned a car that gave them a chance to drive to Detroit where Mary introduced them to the art museum and symphony hall. One day, they even managed to go to the horse races at Northville where they all made silly bets. They drove to Marshall to eat at a famous German restaurant. These lighter moments, when they put aside their books for more relaxed recreational and cultural activities, rounded out their growing appreciation of one another as friends.

* * *

A giant cowbell was the centerpiece of the university's social melting pot—a speakeasy of a place called the Pretzel Bell where all were equal if they were but twenty-one. Centered above the long drinking boards was a big clanger that had been rung for generations of UM students signaling their passage into adulthood, tolled by a waiter pulling on a jerry-rigged line to announce the arrival of junior and senior students into their majorities. Underage undergraduates were discouraged from participating in these rowdy beerfests but were allowed in the door under a strict code that their lips never touch hooch. Jim joined a party for the fraternity's blond vice president, Buster Scott, whose Hollywood looks tended to collapse slightly during the night's bacchanal.

The tin ceiling, the dark wood enclosing the service bar, the smell of beer escaping from the kegs in the cellar, the sepia pictures on the wall depicting the exploits of heroes long in their rocking chairs were all familiar saloon markers to Jim, whose downtown bierstubes in Manhattan were tailored to the same look. Here, around a large, carved table, the birthday boy took the head-of-household chair and accepted dozens of toasts and received wacky presents in the nature of buzz-bottom whoopee cushions. The vets, Ribs Robinson and Bill Turner, had drunk through dozens of such occasions; their own manhood already established as nineteen-year-old swabs standing watch on warships in the far Pacific.

"Here's to you, Scottie," Ribs yelled over the noisy crowd. Then sotto voce, "Now that the ceremonies are over, let's do some serious drinking."

"But not this whelp," Bill said.

"I get my turn in April," Jim replied.

* * *

One of the signs of change that marked Jim's latest alienation from the structured, middle way was that he wasn't getting along with his roommates. The two older ones were so boring that they effectively drove him out. When he asked the landlady if she had any other rooms available, she escorted him to a redecorated former coal bin in the cellar next to the furnace. She was wearing her kimono, which she allowed to slip open so that her pendulous breasts were on view. She looked needy.

"You'll be better off down here. And I'll see you won't be lonely. I'll come check on you once in a while and see you're taken care of."

He really did want to lie her down; he knew she would be willing, but the idea of sex alone, without the trimmings of affection, was not enough for him, even though he was overpowered by the smell of the juices seeping from her.

So he quietly rejected both offers, the coal bin and the landlady. He preferred to make love to Barbara or Beatrice. Or both.

* * *

He moved out toward the cemetery and the Arb into a single room, where he was much more content. Then he acquired a new radio. He was able to pull in a few Detroit stations, one that still played swing instead of the Mitch Miller garbage that followed the demise of the big bands. At night, there were a few Chicago stations and one from Ohio that played hick music. Only a few classical programs aired, the Met Opera and the once-a-month broadcast of the NBC Symphony with Toscanini.

One night, a familiar voice came rattling through the ether. It was the radioman who liked American classical music.

"You know I'm trying to get things moving on the music front. You got to believe that the big creative burst after the First War is due to explode again any minute now. Right? The theater is coming back and artists are shaking up the colorfield. But don't hold your breath that music is going to come singing back right away. That chorus got lost in the Mathematics Department of some university. What's happening in music right now is scary. These guys are in the process of burying melody; they're going in the wrong direction. Maybe we can help refresh some ears by playing music you can actually hum. I get mad as hell with those composers sometimes.

"It's OK to feel angry. Be angry as hell for all I care. It would do some of you some good to get mad. You young people seem to need a blood transfusion anyway. You need a shot of Copland or Barber to wake you up. A little Ives would probably kill you."

"The G.I.s came home from the war, full of vinegar, and now five years later they're settling so far down into their conformity couch that it's going to take a revolution to get them back up on their feet. Peace is good and all. But some of you better start reacting to domestic weirdoes like that senator from Wisconsin. Wisconsin of all places. Home of La Follette.

"Do you think all that angst you're always bellyaching about is new? Even in our Erie Canal days—back when Columbia was sitting pretty—even then, Thoreau, relaxing in his fishing shack, told us that most men live lives of quiet desperation."

I thought that was Eliot, Jim said to himself.

"Have to play some music now. I suppose you think American composers don't know much about the radio? Later, I'll play Roy Harris and his *Time Suite* and Copland's *Music for Radio*. Bet you never heard of *The Enchanted Pear Tree*—a radio opera by Overton. I'll play a little Gottschalk now to get your courage back."

And out of the speaker came a piece about the Union, with its "Hail Columbia" tune embedded in the midst of the rattle.

* * *

When Jim entered Rackham Hall one late autumn evening, Ann Arbor was edging toward winter; freezing weather was hovering on the northern border. The cold that would numb the outside environment allowed the town's students—stunned by the university's challenge to excellence—an opportunity to stoke their interior fires. Rackham itself, dedicated to graduate students, was perilously close to being as austere as a philosophical syllogism.

Jim's own development matched the student population's need to stay cool. Bombarded every day as he was by new ideas, his internal embers were smoldering into a burning organic change. Thoughts about New Criticism were instructing him to "close read" literature line by line. He had just finished Joyce's *Portrait of the Artist as a Young Man* and was staggering from its shivering religious underpinnings. He was steaming from his encounters with Hardy and Brahms and the pre-Renaissance. The influence of Eliot and the American doctor and the American lawyer—Williams and Stevens—had seeped through every class window in the English Department and into those bull sessions attended by LS&A students who cared, were actually passionate about modern literature.

Now was the turn of Dylan Thomas. He would read tonight in Rackham. Word of the poet's noisy habits had preceded him and stories were circulating in the hall that the mischievous Welsh elf had lost his way from New York, had misplaced his luggage again and was currently holed up in a professor's home while borrowed pants and jacket were being ironed.

Jim was hot with expectation, waiting to hear his first great poet. He had read some of the Welsh bard's works during the week and was floating on its high-octane language. Nervous and excited, Jim was like a dry sponge sopping up creative juices.

Thomas came on stage to thunderous applause. The age had created a literary gem—a distracted cherub, who was fattening on the world's vine; he was round with pouty lips. When he began to recite other poet's works, he read with a passion that Jim had never heard—a ringing, reedy voice, piercing like a sharp ocean wind, with a slight howl in it, filled with the laments of old sailors. Jim knew that he was experiencing a great performance.

A wall of human sound flooded over the stage after Thomas read his own poetry. It was as if Jim heard a voice from the center of the earth. Dylan's words rumbled through him, the most sensitive voice he ever heard, cascading along in fluting s's—sand, soul, shack, stars and scars—sounds wandering into the sea garden of Jim's oceanic youth, blowing petals from the dune roses of his imagination. Stunned, elated, burning, Jim went back to his digs and started writing the first chapter of the novel that the poet by his passions had encouraged him to begin.

Jim would never need another example of what an artist should look like or how he should sound. Listening to Dylan express himself—sharing the droll, brotherly laughter of life, the aching pull of the heart, the sharpness of mind, the attention to craft, the assurance of time's dominion—all helped Jim realize how to behave and how to engage. He knew an artist was about substance, not appearance; about giving not receiving; a spirit lit from within, not directed from without. And his hair need not always be combed.

* * *

Jim ventured into a creative jungle when he chose a plot for his novel. He decided to write about a non-traditional college based in the Victorian mansions of Delavan, with Barbara as the ingénue.

He had discovered that if some mind-popping act of newly discovered creation sufficiently stunned him with its force, he wasn't content simply to bury himself in its significance. He had to do something with the knowledge he accumulated. A response was required as a consequence of his learning. He couldn't keep it in. He had to let it out. That's why he wrote the novel about Barbara.

Jim was doing so much peripheral reading and writing that he was slipping academically. He began to miss reading assignments in favor of his personal studies. As a result, his test scores began to reflect his decisions. Rewarded by the impact of his favorite writers, he was failing to pay attention to the subjects that demanded his attention, the elements of his paid-for search for accreditation. The novel would be his undoing.

* * *

When they met one day, Beatrice said, "I've been thinking about what we were talking about by the river. Remember?"

"You mean the softness of your breasts."

"Stop. . .I mean about nature."

"What's more natural than. . .?"

"You're not listening."

She continued, "I'll try to make sense of it. Never tried describing this before. I just want to say that I can hold a scene like the one in the Arb in my mind three dimensionally. I can even relocate and adjust what I look at and arrange things into different shapes—all in my head."

"That's amazing," Jim said.

"I can look at something and correct its symmetry."

Jim said, "Hey, that's a special talent. For me landscape is almost two-dimensional. I must be missing the depth part. I know I'm not as visual as most. But I know how I react to a beautiful scene. It can generate sparks but it's not the landscape itself that gets my juices going. It's how I respond. It's probably just self-reflection, mirror of the mind stuff, but what happens to me happens internally. Not what's sitting out there in the pasture, but what it stimulates inside here. Obviously there's beauty in the scene or I wouldn't fall for it. But I only feel good about it when somebody close is involved, when I can translate what I feel to another person, share some physical presence, but it's not the bushes and trees."

He may not have realized, but he was beginning to abandon his sense of the Romantic that had sustained him for the past year. After reading parts of Darwin, he saw that there was nothing garden-fresh in the fact that nature had a ferocious and bloody appetite for killing its prey. He now seemed to be drifting into Modernism, which had mentally to deal with the wasted blood of millions in the First and Second Wars. Caught between the love of nature that seemed like one of the entranceways into beauty and the moving train of contemporary life and thought, he began to shift the weight of his personal ideals and holdings. His love of lyricism and its reliance on expressed emotions had been important in showing him how passions could result in personal change, but now the contemporary world called.

* * *

The first time Jim began reading *Ulysses* he was filled with amazement at the audacity of the writer. Joyce's river-running imagination encapsulated a city and a country in one volume by dressing up and taking the Irish-English language out for a walk in the neighborhood. Eight more times in his life Jim read halfway through the novel, with the same result as when he tried the first time. Though he wanted to skip ahead and read the Molly section like Hemingway did, he could never sin against fictional continuity. Near death, as a tribute to English literature that had buttressed his life, he, yes, finished—finished yes—finished—it.

* * *

When Jim compared Beatrice to Barbara, his reaction was that Beatrice was looking for beauty and that Barbara already possessed it. In his confusion, it was Barbara who supplied the strongest conviction that they were indeed a matched pair.

* * *

In early December, the Ballets Russes came through town and danced at one of the movie houses, the one with a vertical maize and blue sign out front. Cary Grant and Bette Davis remained off-screen long enough to allow young dancers to parade across the stage to the sound of worn records. Jim enjoyed the performance, the first time he had witnessed such controlled emotion in motion. He was once more surprised that there were so many ways to express oneself, other forms of art to explore, not realizing that this first encounter would plant a throbbing seed. For the moment, seeing ballet was another path into a cultural life in which he was beginning to feel comfortable.

* * *

Barbara and Jim agreed to spend the day together in Chicago the Wednesday before Christmas, coinciding with the beginning of their holiday vacations. Jim took a bus from Ann Arbor into the Loop the night before and boarded a streetcar to the West Side to visit his aunt and grandmother. The enflamed grief of their war years was subsiding. There would soon be a move to a home in the suburbs. His Gram would get to be a mall trotter.

Early the next morning, he rode back downtown and waited in Union Station for what he was beginning to recognize as his first, true, shared love. Throughout Barbara's college years, the rail station came to represent Jim's unification with the Midwest, stitched together by his Delavan beauty. The country's crossroad became his own intersection as the young couple enjoyed, suffered and were fulfilled by a love that was never physically actualized and at the same time never languished. Uncharacteristically, she ran into his arms and they embraced a long time, many moments past the era's intolerant code regarding public displays of affection. Her radiant face made him realize that he was lucky to have her love.

She was excited, "You're mine for the whole day."

"You've got me every day."

"Then tell me why we live so far apart?" she asked.

"Because we haven't learned how to beat the system."

"I feel sometimes we're living on somebody else's timetable."

"Exactly. Like I'm not in charge of my own calendar," he said.

"I don't want to live a determined life. I want it to be mine."

"We can at least control it today."

"I'd like never to be separate," she said, touching him.

"I wish we could live as one."

They blended together naturally and became one with the city.

Chicago and New York in 1949 were places of immense joy. Both had come alive as the country relearned how to enjoy its holidays at a time when the nation's prosperity was soaring. There had been many eras of good feeling: The early America in the years when canals expressed national expansion, TR's Naughty Oughties, the Twenties. Now America the mighty, with its Bomb and bustling economy, was expanding again. The glow from the excited, crowded downtown streets, the Christmas elegance of State Street and Fifth Avenue made these cities sparkle.

A cultural spree had begun in America complementing and reflecting these feelings. Though America's music was caught in a web of its own making, the other arts were flourishing, enhancing an urban trend toward worldly sophistication. Painting and drama flourished. Popular music everywhere. A piano played in Marshall Fields, an organ in Wanamaker's in Philadelphia, violins in New York's Plaza, jazz at the College Inn. American cities bristled with intensity, marking the end of the difficult sky high and bloody low markers that made up the first half of the century, and before the nonsense of the second half started up. Into this high point of the American Century's life walked the reunited pair.

Jim, who had begun to look at architecture in a more critical way, was determined to take Barbara to see three downtown sites: Sullivan's Carson, Pirie, Scott and the same designer's Auditorium plus Wright's Rookery, three outstanding examples that helped make Chicago the country's architectural leader. At the Auditorium Building, they had to persuade the janitor to allow them into the hall. Sullivan's half circle that arched over the stage was a case of mathematically pleasing engineering that transformed itself into art.

When they emerged onto Congress Street, Jim said, "There's a ballet school somewhere in the studio building. Let's see if we can watch a class."

"Will we disturb them?" Barbara asked, more practical than he.

"They're lucky to have us observe."

They entered and looked for the name of Ruth Page. They ascended the rickety elevator to an upper floor, where they peered in a window to discover a dozen or more dancers on point.

"We can't just burst in."

"Watch us," Jim said, opening the door.

When they shuffled in, the surprised teacher didn't know what to make of them. They would certainly have to improve their physiques if they were ever going to meet her standards. Everyone stopped, including the piano player. The dancers heaped them with unspoken scorn.

"May I help you?" asked the teacher.

"We were hoping to watch a class," Jim offered.

The teacher looked around. "It's a little unusual." Eyeing some chairs, she said, "OK. Sit over there. But no more interruptions."

The purveyors of art in the Midwestern capital were normally more enthusiastic about enlightening the young than in other major metropolitan areas because mid-America's masters knew there were cornfields for hundreds of miles in every direction and that the arts needed every recruit they could muster.

Embarrassed, Barbara hoped she could dissolve into thin air, but Jim sat unaware that he had broken a basic rule: Never halt an artist at work. They sat there quietly for fifteen minutes until Barbara, feeling uncomfortable, tugged on Jim's sleeve, asking to leave. Jim wanted another five minutes. At a natural break in the music, they nodded to the ballet mistress, and walked out backwards like palace servants.

"That was not pleasant," Barbara said.

"I simply wanted you to see them," said Jim, unaware that his intensity sometimes brimmed over into other people's spaces.

They had lunch in a dark German restaurant near the theater where they arranged to see a traveling Broadway show. *High Button Shoes* was a throwback to the Twenties, a slapstick musical that parodied another time replete with a pre-WWI mindset. It was the show that gave Jerome Robbins the opportunity to create one of the most entertaining romps ever danced on any stage, his "Bathing Beauty Ballet"—a take-off on a Mack Sennett movie chase complete with Keystone Kops. The "ballet" was set in a beach house on the sands of Atlantic City with swimmers flying in and out of a dozen or more bathhouse doors—kewpie-doll bathing beauties, con men, Kops. All of them were performing madcap turns, skidding stops and swirled-around gyrations. The dancers created near-mayhem without ever colliding and crashing into one another though the near misses were hilarious as thirty or more hoofers chased or fled through the opening and closing doors at breakneck speed and fast-footed acrobatics.

"Such fun," Barbara said as they left the theater. Jim was pleased that she liked the popular fare.

They had planned an early dinner before each boarded their respective trains, hers north, his east.

"Are you having fun at school?" he asked when they sat down to have a small meal in another German restaurant. Painted dark panels surrounded them. The merry monks pictured there were cavorting in their beergarden and smiling down on the handsome pair.

"The Phi Pi house is filled with all these fantastic women. And I've dated a couple of seniors, mostly G.I.s."

Jim knew that she had chosen the same sorority as Beatrice, but the dating was new information.

"How about you?" she asked, watching his eyes.

"Mostly batched it. Had a couple dates for the Alpha parties. Sisters of some of the brothers who needed a night out," he lied.

"Any tugs on the heartstring?"

"I'm saving my vibrations for you," he said and on they went to other matters.

He knew she was his top girl, but he had a funny way of showing his loyalty.

"Your favorite class?" he asked.

"No doubt. Western Civ. Taught by the president of the college. A remarkable man who makes his material sing. And you? Anybody special?"

He provided some details about Dr. Eisenstein.

"I can't wait to get into advanced classes," she said.

"All in good time, my fair lady."

"Is that before or after the mid-Fifties?" The mention of time passing made her add, "Jim, 'All in good time' isn't working for us.

"Only choice unless we buy a car and head for the coast."

"On lonely nights, that seems like a pretty good alternative."

She hesitated for a moment and added, "And I'm a little worried about you. You look really thin. And you seem jumpy. I hope all these great books passing through your system aren't leaving some nasty bugs inside you."

"I feel OK," he said. "I don't seem to have as much strength as I once did. But thanks to Chi Sigma, I get at least one good meal a day. My head burns sometime and I do get antsy. I guess I can chalk it up to late night reading and too many cigarettes and too much coffee. I'm always a little tired."

"Take care of yourself, mister. We have a long road to travel."

At Union Station, they embraced. They resisted fleeing to California, but it wouldn't have been that hard to find an auto lot.

* * *

Back home at Christmas, he was supposed to be writing three papers, and ended up doing none of them, owing to his hectic social calendar. He and Mardi did manage to visit Broadway and see *Brigadoon,* but her new boyfriend at Penn State took up most of her time. The show Jim had to see was *South Pacific,* the Rogers and Hammerstein musical, whose original cast album had so entertained Barbara the summer before. Having worn the grooves of his LP down to a scratchy squawk, he longed to see a live performance. So, he got up one morning in the dark, took the first train to New York and waited patiently in a cold line for three hours to purchase a standing-room-only spot in the rear of the mezzanine for that day's matinee. Securely ticketed, he walked to the library on Fifth Avenue to keep warm and get some sleep. Luckily, a kindly attendant woke him in time to make the curtain.

Now that the war was over, Broadway producers, who were good at popularizing any hint of dramatic tension between change artists and traditionalists, asked song writers to unplug the prohibition against producing a musical comedy about military life. The term musical comedy itself would soon be changed to musical drama, after Rogers and Hammerstein created their masterpiece out of the fungus-covered lives of Seabees toiling in the Pacific islands. Some asked what legitimate right these song-and-dance men possessed to disturb and exploit the wounds of jungle warfare. Contrarily, why not celebrate the spirit of those that survived. Wise in the ways of wars that had ended successfully, *South Pacific* became the best musical ever to reach Times Square unless, of course, one preferred *Showboat* or *Oklahoma*.

Jim reveled in the original *SP* production celebrating both the bristling and tender moments that erupted on Espíritu Santo, an isolated island that caged the exuberant fantasies of tens of hundreds of American kids. Overly familiar with the cast recording, Jim's emotions were lifted by the first sounds emanating from the orchestra pit. He would hum Robert Russell Bennett's orchestration for years—TUM, dum, dum, dum. . . *Bloody Mary*.

Already highly charged by the impact of the recording he shared with Barbara, Jim's reaction spiked to a satisfying intensity that physically made him feel whole and right with his generation—his war, his guys, his kind of melodies, his kind of brash, wholly American, *cockeyed optimists*. All from the vantage of a kid's outlook on the deeds of his generation's big brothers. They were his war lords. And now here they were all on stage, prancing around with their chests stuck out, smoking cigars.

He reached Barbara by phone the next evening, "If I live to be seventy, I'll still get goose bumps listening to the orchestra. It burst out of the pit like a wave. Great songs just kept pouring out. I could feel Pinza's voice in my vertebrae. When he hit that last note, you know which one, the audience melted. The sailors on stage were as raucous as skirt-chasers in a waterside dive. And you know how Martin's voice wobbles along a note? Like a bird, I swear. And when they sang our song, I thought you were sitting next to me. Your love was in the room."

* * *

Saylor had mellowed his anger somewhat after the Bootsie episode at Miami two years earlier, and he had taken up with a variety of women at the small school he attended in West Virginia, so, after a peace-making lunch, the high school Alpha pals had a few beer nights out with some of their other old friends, but, even in reconciliation, it felt to Jim that their once-snug attachment lines had loosened.

One night Saylor and Jim got fairly drunk.

"You know wad I'm gonna do when I die. Going to Lagerland," Jim said.

"Whad we doing pissing away our parents' money going to college? Whad a ya gonna get out of it?" Saylor asked.

"A draft deferment. Don't bother me with that do-it-for-the parents crap. Things bad enuf. Can't you see I'm in the middle of an intellectual upheaval," Jim replied and laughed at his own words.

"You know it's gonna be 1950 in a couple days. Whad a' you doing to celebrate half a century?" Saylor asked.

"Gonna try to forget most of it. It was OK. Couple years here, couple years there. Think of the poor schlumps born around 1896 and had to spend their whole lives fightn' two wars, a depression, a couple stock market crashes, and all they got out of it was a little time off when they were kids and a few years during the Twenties."

"We're the lucky ones. Got it easy. Born at the right time"

"Damn straight. Missed it all," Jim said and burped.

* * *

Back in Ann Arbor, Jim continued his writing and spent his social time with Beatrice. His class work was suffering and he received bad grades for his first semester, so bad that he was put in probation.

* * *

In late January, stopping by a paper store to buy a pack of Chesterfields after one of those final exams, Jim's eyes popped open at the sight of a new magazine sitting on the counter called *Flair*. Jim picked up the oversize magazine and riffled through its colorful, stylized photo layouts and ran his fingers along the thick paper inserts meant to be savored as detached literary treasures. The rough/smooth textures and startling pictures and drawings amazed him. He dug into his trousers to pay for the publication, went next door to a coffee shop and spent the afternoon reading the contents when he should have been back in his room studying. Instead he turned and re-turned each page of the magazine. Here it finally was—an expression of the creative explosion in the arts that he had been waiting for. If he had known where to look, for instance, in the doorway of New York's Cedar Bar or in one of the summer sheds at Tanglewood in the Berkshires, he would have discovered the new American wave of postwar art and music earlier. He hoped that America's homegrown talent would flower so that it could be favorably compared with the likes of Dylan Thomas and Picasso.

The search for cultural monuments that heightened his vision of a future filled with quality artistic expression created a path for his budding motivation. Jim's discovery of *Flair* was an important marker. The choice for a career in publishing had already begun to figure in his plans. The new publication encouraged him to pursue a vocation in the field and he began looking for past examples of elegant periodicals. In his reading, he had often come across references to *Vanity Fair*, published before the War. He began searching for copies and for months he pestered the Periodicals Department of the university library with his newfound interest. Having caught up with the Dorothy Parker-flavored reflections of New York in the Twenties and Thirties found in *Vanity Fair,* he realized that magazines provided the kind of pictorial and literate view of the immediate times that appealed to him. A frequent reader of the *New Yorker*, Jim related to its non-pictorial format on the literate grounds that its witty commentary was sufficient. But the use of graphics raised other publications to another dimension. *Vanity Fair* led Jim back to the *Smart Set*, which showcased the aesthetics of Mencken and Nathan—the wit of the one and the drama analysis of the other. Mencken's hot-Baltimore view of life offered Jim an appreciation of urban-oriented magazines like Boston's *Atlantic Monthly*, which in turn drilled down to earlier publications like the *Century*. Magazines during those winter months of 1950 provided Jim with a fresh incentive to enmesh himself in the creative reflections of his own times. He hoped to participate in its abundance. He now knew what he wanted to do with his life. He wanted to be a magazine man. He didn't want to research the past; he wanted to express the present.

Confirming his intentions, he pored through the magazine archives and began to recognize the contributors and their characteristics. He became familiar with the names of the great editors—Frank Crowninshield of *Vanity Fair*, Harold Ross of the *New Yorker*, Herbert Swope of the *Sun*, and Max Perkins of *Scribner's*. Shooting high, he knew he had a career direction and notable guides to show the way.

* * *

Before Ann Arbor's slow-to-unfold springtime arrived, he felt the larger world outside the academic walls was calling him. Jim wanted to create his own work. Wasn't that what an artist was supposed to do? And wasn't he striving to become an artist of sorts? He was writing a novel, after all. He could even point out that he had shown an early ambition toward that goal, writing a manuscript about the Pacific War when he was thirteen.

Even further back in time, when he was a kid in Chicago during the Depression, Jim had begun his love affair with magazines. He remembered the powerful acrid smell of the newly printed periodicals that he peddled door-to-door, up and down the back wooden staircases of his Rogers Park neighborhood. His greatest childhood treasure, with the exception of his red wagon and his Jack Armstrong Hike-O-Meter, was the cloth bag the distributor gave him in which to carry his magazines. He would carefully pack the colorful editions—the *Saturday Evening Post* and the *Women's Home Companion* in a sack with a long shoulder strap and trudge up the rickety steps accessible through Chicago's alleys lined with high fences and garbage bins. Magazines expressed the American material dream in those years and Jim was part of the sales force. Some days he made as much as thirty-two cents.

* * *

For his twenty-first birthday, Jim sent out an ambiguous set of invitations to join him at the Pretzel Bell for a celebration, ambiguous because he didn't wish to generate a crowd that might think he was going to pay for the privilege. The invitation specified seven o'clock, past the dinner hour, which obviated food orders. Only a half-dozen or so people turned up. They were the ones who had been informed of the real identity of the birthday boy, each carrying inspired gifts, one of which was a bathroom plunger displaying a bold red rubber color.

Beatrice and Mary were there along with former roommate Chuck, plus Ribs and few other Alpha Chi brothers. Jim was quaffing down beers at a fast rate, including the large stein that arrived with compliments of the house. The other tables in the saloon filled with fellow students, who cheered when the waiter rang the big cowbell to herald the entrance of another mature adult into the Age of Anxiety.

"Drink 'em up," Jim encouraged them, secure in the knowledge that the bill wouldn't be too exorbitant. There is no frugality like a student's frugality, a defined cheapskate who must show off a hot social life on a subzero budget.

Jim's crowd was getting rowdy, and a German man of girth came over to quiet them down, but who could smother a raucous coming-of-age party? Jim inspected his gifts—a used toaster that didn't toast, plus a red-checked bandana that looked familiarly like a napkin from the Italian restaurant that the others tied around his neck, and, of course, the plunger.

When nine o'clock rolled around, guests began to disappear into their responsibilities. By then, Jim, drunk, was soon alone. Staggering to the men's room, he no longer was able to feel any censor or prohibition on his behavior. Returning to the now empty table crowded with beer-stained glasses and overflowing ashtrays, Jim looked at a neighboring crowd, who sat quietly socializing, probably married vets, a couple of the women pregnant. Some of the guys looked familiar.

Jim, juggling his presents, picked up the plunger and walked toward the adjoining table. Able to discern a very pregnant woman, Jim waved his plunger.

"Hey, lady. Let me help you deliver the baby."

With that, her husband rose and slammed his fist into Jim's face, sending him sprawling on the floor. Waiters and the large German man came and literally hoisted him out of the building.

On the street, he had no comprehension of what he was doing or where he was. His only salvation that night was that he didn't encounter a patrol car. He lurched along the streets for hours, unconscious of his surroundings. When the rain began, it helped revive his memory and set him in the general direction of his room. He must have stopped to sleep somewhere, because when he looked at his watch, it was after three. By the time he found the house he lived in, there was a light haze in the east. The next couple of hours he spent in the bathroom, either asleep on the floor or hanging over the john. Finally, splashed with his excesses, he fell into bed.

He woke about eleven feeling ravaged and made his way to the mirror where he viewed his living corpse, wondering where the bruise on his cheek came from. He had already missed a few classes, so he tried to wade through his daze and come up with some answers, Oh, yes, he was due at the Sigma house to wait on tables at noon. Ribs was already in his white apron when Jim walked into the big kitchen.

"It's all over fraternity row what you did."

"What did I do?"

"You tried to deliver Jack High's wife's baby with a toilet plunger."

"Oh, god."

"It's worse than that. He's an old Sigma and he's sitting out there for lunch."

"I didn't really do that?"

"Yes, you did."

"I got to get out of here."

"You're going out there and tell him you're sorry."

"I can't."

"No excuses. You've got to do it."

Jim, still white and not so sure of his footwork, entered the dining room to face the coldest crowd of fifty people he would ever know. They stopped eating and went silent. Ribs had pointed out where the offended vet sat.

Jim approached him. "I'm deeply sorry. I just found out what I did last night. I want to apologize to you and your friends."

"My wife, godamnit."

"Yes. Your wife."

"OK," the guy said, and turned away from Jim.

Jim stood for a moment waiting for further words or action, any form of communication, He retreated to the kitchen, took off his apron, and never stepped into the Chi Sigma house again.

And he never again in his life got dead drunk, so mortified was he by his behavior that night. His remorse needed some soothing.

* * *

Ann Arbor welcomed the Philadelphia Orchestra to the annual 57th May Festival, a cornucopia of classical sound. Ormandy conducted three of the six concerts that were to be played on four consecutive days. The festival had featured the Chicago Orchestra until 1936 when Stokowski brought his band boxes west. Each year thereafter it was Ormandy's turn to tune his instruments in the great corn bowl that was the Midwest. Holst, Hanson, Grainger and Enesco had guest conducted. Scheduled to join the performances this year were Jan Peerce, William Kapell, Nathan Milstein, Ljuba Welitch and a favorite American singer in the closing concert.

Jim went to the first in the series and was so inspired by the sounds elicited by the impeccably dressed musical director—Jim would remember that Ormandy had a habit of tugging on the studded cuffs of his formal attire—that he scrimped and saved in an effort to attend as many of the concerts as he could afford. The music was a revelation to him, especially the smooth violin section and the extraordinary flute playing of William Kincaid.

Too broke to invite Beatrice, Jim attended alone. He opened his pores to the music in a way that he had never done before, so much so that his insides were churned up by the bombardment of sound. The music poured into him like some elixir that satisfied his great need for meaning, He was actually wet by the time Welitch sang the final scene from *Salome*. Hearing her artistically cascading into madness, he did some additional sweating.

Ormandy's violins were sonorous, rich and deep tuned. Over the years, Jim would sometimes hear a program when the same silky sound crept into the string section of another orchestra. Luckily, he could always enjoy the Philadelphia sound in absentia. He could spin his 33s any time he needed to refresh his memory of the original harmonies, even though he was now able to carry the sound in his mind.

During the second concert, Kincaid was a soloist and his flute sounded as silvery and sweet as dawn in the forest. Like an amazing bird in full morning glory. Later in the year, when he first heard the Philadelphia play the Brahms First, Jim was stunned by the sound. When Kincaid's flute rose out of the depths of the orchestra for the clock theme, Jim literally shivered in response. When the finale of the fourth movement burst through, Jim thought that he was listening to the voice of God.

To complete the last night's program, Marion Anderson sang. She was already an iconic figure. Jim was nearly brought to tears by her rendition of the spirituals that she sang with the whole heart of her Black experience. She revealed to him the Negro plight that he had not fully appreciated. And so he grew.

After the concert, he was so excited that he couldn't sleep. He had to work off the enthusiasm that burned in him like electricity. It was too late to see Beatrice so he walked toward the Arboretum. The park was quiet, but he could hear the sound of the river flowing in the distance. What had just happened to him, he wondered?

Music, as well as reading, was giving him an alternative way to savor the quality of life. The same intensity would never jolt him when he viewed artwork, even though Eisenstein taught him to appreciate the Renaissance. He had to wait for ballet to make him soar anew before he added a third beam to his creative platform.

* * *

Jim left campus toward the end of May, and he knew he was not only in scholastic trouble but personal difficulty as well. He had disappointed just about everyone, his folks, his friends, and he was coasting precariously on the goodwill of two beautiful coeds whom he was misleading with his forked tongue. He was more embarrassed than remorseful at his poor behavior, and didn't fully understand the seriousness of his actions. After having shored up his integrity during his first two years of college, he had slipped back into a sloppy disregard for others, leaving a bad scent behind him. His grades contributed to the Alpha Chi's being placed on probation. Shortly Jim received notice that the university no longer required his presence.

After seeing Beatrice off, Jim made a quick trip to Delevan to keep that end of his romantic seesaw in play. Barbara wondered why he wasn't spending the summer with her and confronted him regarding his dating in Ann Arbor. but he lied and left her convinced that he still cared, which he did in his immature way.

To make matters worse, another war had started. The country had hardly loosened its defenses and eased into civilian mode when a major new conflict began. Aimed at repulsing China's client state, North Korea, America went back to fighting in the Pacific. President Truman hardly hesitated before sending an armed force to the Korean peninsula that was aimed like a dagger at Japan. Jim, now without a deferment, faced time in the service.

* * *

When he reached home, his wounded ambition, dented and frayed, continued to warn him to avoid the pitfalls that had previously trapped him. He was determined to maintain his reading and writing schedule. That meant keeping clear of his old buddies and their drinking parlors as well as their women, as warm and charming as they were. Promising himself not to slip back into his unruly suburban ways, he focused on the future that would require deeper involvement with New York, where he might finally center himself. He promised not to let the commute hinder him in his desire to broaden his city life. As to university studies, the hell with them, he said to himself. I'll take real life.

He contemplated a return to Delavan to finish the first draft of his novel, but he discarded that notion in favor of immersing himself in New York's delights. Currently without funds, he resumed his part-time job, mostly on weekends, in Wright's hardware store and proceeded to scan the *Herald Tribune's* employment notices, setting his sights on the publishing business.

Essentially, he was exhausted by all the mental battles he had waged during the school year. He had depleted himself trying to juggle two love affairs. There were consequences. His bent toward aestheticism had actually begun to change his looks. He was quite thin now and fraught with a nervousness that sometimes made him shake. He had paid little attention to what he ate and drank and had no physical regimen that kept his system well oiled. His head burned most of the time. The feeling was so bad that, one day, sitting on the subway, he was so tense that he thought people were watching him tremble. This made him remember the word in nineteenth century literature that explained such phenomenon—neurasthenia. And in psychology he dreaded the knowledge of the time frame that captured schizoids at age twenty. He was reacting intensely to things now. He bore through these problems, sharing them with no one.

* * *

He had never seen an opera before. So one of the first things he did when he went "into town," an expression for any excursion to Manhattan, he bought a ticket to a performance of a new production. Though he had been an infrequent listener to the Saturday afternoon Met broadcasts, he was perplexed as to why the country's most prestigious company rarely mounted new operas, only old warhorses. Those high art decisions appalled Jim who sought contemporary work, not museum pieces. When Gian-Carlo Menotti, thumbing his nose at the establishment, brought his opera, *The Consul* to a regular Broadway theater, Jim jumped at the chance to see it. Though attending the performance felt like an ordinary theater outing, listening to the musical tone quickly convinced him that he was experiencing a more serious piece.

* * *

He came across an ad from an obscure publishing house seeking a salesman. He figured he would answer the listing even though his heart was set on editing. He might learn a few things while he looked for the right job. He made an appointment for the next day. Dressed in slacks and sports jacket—he didn't currently own a suit—and after calling to confirm, Jim boarded the LIRR and made his way to Varick Street. He viewed going into the downtown chaos an adventure. There were so many neighborhoods to know and he wanted to experience them all. Taking a freight elevator up to the top of the building that included a few print shops, Jim came across a nest of offices. Paris Publishing appeared on one of the doors. He knocked.

"Wait up," came a voice with an accent. "This door, it sticks." After some heaving and hauling, "There it is."

When the French publisher opened the door and spied a thin, nervous looking young man who looked as green as lettuce, he said to himself, "Perfect."

"I'm Jim Mahoney. I called about the job."

"Yes. Come in. LaSalle's my name. My staff's on vacation."

There was a reception room of sorts that appeared also to function as the mailing room. In the room beyond, Jim could see rows of book and dozens of stored cartons.

"Sit down and fill out this application while I finish a project."

Jim accepted the form and watched as Mr. LaSalle went into the back room. From the sounds within, Jim realized the owner was filling up a box full of books and taping it closed.

"We publish Jules Verne books in translation," LaSalle said during the interview. "So let me see here, what do we have?" He scanned the application and put it down.

"Nice town, Manhasset. Wealthy community, right? Maybe your folks would like to invest in an up-and-coming business."

Was LaSalle more interested in his parents than Jim?

"What we have here is a publishing house that specializes in one author, Jules Verne. We have all fifty-four of his novels for sale in America. You know him?"

"My brother was a big fan," Jim said, wondering how one man could write so many books.

"These books are easy to sell. The job is to go around to all the distributors and book stores and you make a nice sales commission."

"How much is the pay?"

"As much as you can make, young man. Two percent commission on every book you sell."

Pappy had tried to warn him. "And salary?"

"No, there's no salary. It's a sales job. You sell. I pay."

"I'm just out of school and need a paycheck."

"I'll make you a deal. I'll give you fifteen dollars a week to get you started, and then we can deduct that from the sales you're going to make. You want the job?"

"I'll try it."

"You have to have a lot of enthusiasm. You'll be selling the biggest selling author the world has ever known. Almost as big as the Bible."

"When do I start?"

"Today is gone. Start tomorrow. Nine a.m. Take some copies to read tonight," Mr. LaSalle said, handing Jim four copies of the famous science fiction writer's work, including *Thirty Leagues under the Sea*, a boy's favorite for over fifty years. Before Jim arrived home Mr. LaSalle had already called his mother to tell her what a nice son she had.

"He's such an elegant Frenchman. He'll even provide you with subway money. Sounds like a good experience."

"Why did he call you?"

"He's just friendly, I guess. Misses his wife back in France. And his children."

"So when's his birthday?"

"What?"

"Sounds like he gave you his complete bio."

The next morning, Jim was up early and on his way to town. Mr. LaSalle sat him down and gave him an itinerary.

"Here's a list of distributors that I've been working with. You go around and get them to restock. But first you have to collect on their old bills. No new orders until they've cleaned up the old one. You have to be tough with these guys. They're slithery as snakes."

Along with the past due bills, Jim carried along sample copies and order sheets in a briefcase supplied by Mr. LaSalle and off he went into the jungles of lower Manhattan.

He went to the farthest stop first, by subway, and walked up an old ironclad building south of Houston Street. He climbed up a flight of wide, worn, curled-up stairs that always reminded Jim of

Charlie Chaplin's shoes, and knocked on the door. Three burly guys were sitting around a desk schmoozing.

"How can we help you, young fella? You want some copies of *Broadway Babe*?"

"I represent the Paris Publishing Company and have come to show you our latest list of Jules Verne novels."

They all laughed.

"Lookee here. LaSalle's got a new one."

"Nobody wants those books, kid. You're wasting your time. They were happy to be out-of-print. Let'em lie."

"He's the best selling author in the history of publishing. My brother used to stay up nights in the bathroom reading them."

"Are you sure he wasn't doing something else in there?"

Ignoring that, Jim said, "And I've come to collect on the past due bill."

They all smiled at him in amusement.

"C'mon. You owe the guy money. He's got a small outfit. Packs his own shipping, for god's sake. Give him a break."

They stopped smiling and bristled.

"That phony got us involved in his messy problems. We don't have to do nothing."

"What if we just take the books back?" Jim asked.

"They're all out in the stores."

Seeing that he was getting nowhere, Jim left, feeling unsure of his mission.

He made three other stops and received the same reaction. He called in at noon and reported on his lack of progress.

"Be tougher and get the money," was LaSalle's response.

He stopped for a quick lunch at a downtown deli where he ordered one of his favorite concoctions: turkey and cheese with Russian dressing and cole slaw. He would have preferred the pastrami but he didn't want to smell like a garlic bin all afternoon. Surrounded by dozens of workers from the sweatshops along lower Broadway, Jim felt he was part of the working mix. He wouldn't have felt very compatible with any of the people there but at least he was among the kinds of people his socialism was committed to help.

His afternoon calls resulted in the same treatment he received in the morning. One bookseller did pay thirty dollars on his outstanding bill. Back at the office, he was received with a chill.

"You didn't do so well."

"You didn't tell me about the lawsuits."

"Everybody's got lawsuits. Doesn't stop people from doing business."

When he got home that night, his mother was waiting for him. "That nice Mister LaSalle called and said that you didn't have such a good day, and that he wasn't happy with your work."

"Did he tell you he's unlawfully trespassing on French copyright laws?"

"No, he didn't. He just said that he was disappointed and you might not be cut out for the publishing business."

"Why is he calling you? What 'not cut out'? After one day in grungy firetraps? I dealt with so many printing houses today, I probably smell like an ink pot."

The next day, facing his downcast supervisor, he received his morning sermon, "You're not being hard enough on them. You got to threaten them. Lean on them. Show some muscle."

Jim went out again with his due bills and came back late in the afternoon with the same results. Not even thirty dollars this time.

"You're just not right for the job."

His mother told him that she had received another call. "He sounded blue and asked if I could help? But what can I do?"

The third day brought the same results and when he got home that night, his mother told him that he had been fired, thus ending Jim's first experience in New York's publishing field. He never did receive the fifteen dollars.

The next week, when he was in midtown seeking another job, he stopped by Scribner's bookshop across from Rockefeller Center and wandered through the aisles, talking to the attendants about new titles. He knew that the firm's publishing offices were upstairs.

Rashly and with unbridled naïveté, he walked up the steps to Scribner's Publishing and asked to see Maxwell Perkins, the editor of Fitzgerald, Hemingway and Thomas Wolfe. A pleasant man came out into the waiting room, with its large circular window overlooking Fifth Avenue. Middle-aged, the sporty-looking man, smiling and gracious, greeted Jim with a friendly quizzical look.

"I'm afraid Mr. Perkins is tied up now, but is there some way I can help you?"

"My name's Jim Mahoney and I was hoping to see Mister Perkins about a novel I'm writing and also to inquire if there might be any editorial jobs open."

"OK," he said, spreading out the sounds with skepticism, turning the letters into a question. "Excellent," he said, recovering his polish. "A novel. Good for you. Yes, Scribner's is the place for good novels." He hesitated and continued, "Probably the best thing to do is send Mister Perkins the first chapter so he would have something to talk to you about. Then, let's see if I can find an application for the editorial staff. You've graduated I presume?"

"Not yet."

"And your draft status?"

"A 1."

"Hmmm… Let's leave it there. Send in your material and we'll have a look at it."

"Is there an editorial opening available now?"

"There was one but it's been filled. Can you believe we had thirty-four applicants from Ivy League schools alone? But that doesn't mean there won't be another opportunity next week, though its true people tend to stay on staff for a long time."

* * *

After another week of reconnoitering, Jim took a job at Doubleday Book Shops, and was assigned to the branch located on the ground floor of Lord & Taylor. Because he also received word from the local draft board that he would undoubtedly be called up in a few months, he stopped looking for an editing job.

Doubleday, one of the principal names in book publishing, maintained its own chain of stores across the country. The L&T location wasn't the book purveyor's prime outlet in New York, but was certainly its most stylish. Models, matrons and refugees from the Seven Sisters paraded through the store regularly. The passageway through the franchised book department had an easier access to Fifth Avenue than the main entrance. Delightful-looking women and the men who attended them streamed past Jim daily as he waited on customers or straightened out bookshelves of popular books. One didn't shop at Doubleday's for learned tomes; that was the purview of libraries and dusty places in the Village. Hemingway and Agatha Christie were favorites here. And *Red Channels*, a blacklist of media people who were presumed guilty of treason because they had given donations to anti-censoring causes or to suspect children's funds in Ethiopia.

His schedule varied, and that worked out well because the LIRR provided hourly service from Manhasset. His work associates were all bright and alert people, some of whom were attractive enough to raise his attention, but for the most part, Jim's romantic inclinations that fall were quiet. He was writing regularly to Barbara and Beatrice, who kept up their end of the correspondence.

* * *

Almost every night after work, he would walk over to Broadway by himself or with one of his new friends from the bookshop to see a play or musical or attend a concert at Carnegie Hall. Sometimes he would invite along one of the Manhasset girls riding on their regular commuting trains.

Still totally enamored of Broadway musicals, he invited Maryjan to attend the latest arrival. Maryjan had developed into the lovely woman that her personality always predicted she would become. Warm and vivacious, she had been his friend since he was a freshman at MHS. They had been confidantes and supporters of each other since then, with never a cross word between them. He had always known, come hellions or saints, that he had at least one other good female friend besides Mardi and Boots. They traveled to Broadway to attend Irving Berlin's *Miss Liberty*, a musical that portrayed the construction of the Statue of Liberty. The show's sentiments instilled in Jim a greater appreciation for the lady in the harbor. Others may have thought the lyrics soppy but Jim's response to the sung version of the Lazarus poem on the base of Miss Columbia's statue warmed his third-generation immigrant heart:

Give me your tired and your poor
Your huddled masses yearning to breathe free
The wretched refuse of your teeming shore.
Send these, the homeless tempest-tost to me.
I lift my lamp above the golden door.

The sung poem reaffirmed and sharpened his belief that those ideals represented what America was all about, no matter what the views of its forgetful voting public, the mendacity of its politicians or the machinations of the rich, who all wrapped themselves in silk flags, hoisted to belay the rights of the unswerving seekers of individual freedom and dignity.

"Wasn't she cute?" Maryjan asked.

"Allyn McLerie? Like being stunned by a honey bee."

"See how we get you guys to bow down and adore us."

"I'm bowing. I'm bowing. I've always bowed. I'll continue to bow no matter how much trouble it'll get me into."

Another night, he and Hunter McKnight, commuted into town to see *Death of a Salesman.* They both considered themselves young men about town by now. Impressed that McKnight, who was waiting for his call into the Navy, had matured in such a natural way, Jim responded favorably to his scar-bearing friend. They stopped for cocktails at Sardi's, standing at the bar with a hundred other playgoers. They hadn't been able to afford dinner.

"Do you hear from Danny Devon?" Jim asked. The pair had remained friends.

"He's off to law school," was the reply.

"Remember that time at Dana Hall when we got him out on the rope ladder?"

"Yeah. Weren't we the bunch of hellions?"

"Too much helling around, probably."

"I think so."

Jim's remorse about their high school antics was clearly shared.

The play, with its startling set, a see-through house, captured Jim's imagination as no other drama had ever done. Maybe Miller's

Salesman was the best thing since O'Neil, its message clear, and for the most part, unheeded.

Another night, he invited one of the young women from the book shop to attend a new revue, a light and frothy Broadway parfait, layered together with various song and dance numbers, a throwback to vaudeville and the music halls, a format that television would kill by overuse.

Adrienne was a thoughtful young woman, appealing in her intelligent way. Jim had been slightly awed by her grave demeanor and was hoping to discover the source of her hauteur. As they got to know one another better, shuffling around the store selling and stacking best sellers, he asked her out to see a show.

When they were seated in the theater, Adrienne asked him, "Do you still get excited before the curtain rises?"

"I guess I do. Especially this year. It's been a bumper crop. How about you?"

"No. Not for a long time. My family started taking me to the theater when I was six. I think I've seen too many flops. It's hard to get worked up."

"I hope this one won't disappoint you."

"The truth is that I don't like musicals. Mostly fluff. And revues are worse, so don't be surprised if I'm not impressed."

"What do you like?"

"Opera mostly. Ballet. European movies."

"The woman has taste."

"'Refuse to be bored' would be more like it."

As they were leaving the theater, he put his arm around her waist, an invitation to prolong the evening. Perhaps at her place. Maybe her folks were away. She bristled and shook his arm away.

"Just find me a cab."

* * *

Beatrice wrote in July and told Jim that she had been invited to join a friend and her family for a visit to Manhattan. Jim immediately set about making plans for the trip, writing funny letters, planning their upcoming urban adventures. When she arrived, he was impressed how much he missed her warmth and good spirits.

Her friend Janice was a delight and her parents were welcoming and generous to Jim. The visitors stayed at the Roosevelt Hotel and began rummaging through Manhattan as if they were on a treasure hunt. The parents treated the young people to dinner at the old German stube on once-fabled 14th Street, Luchow's, where they enjoyed the oom-pah band and sauerbraten. An important social center in the early century, the restaurant, lit by soft lights that were once gas jets, was a Manhattan gem. Its enormous dining rooms and hundred-foot long bar offered a sense of life in the days of Edith Wharton, "Bet-a-Million" Gates, the Whitneys and Astors, Lily Langtry and "Diamond Jim" Brady, names that rolled around the tongues of old New Yorkers like butter off a waffle. In the cultural soup that made up Manhattan, it was wise to be mindful of the importance of the contribution made by the ethnic minorities, the Germans, Irish, Italians Jews and Chinese that made up the spine of the rock that ran down the center of Manhattan, With ethnicity in mind, the visitors also made trips to P.J. Clarke's, Little Italy, Ratner's Deli and tasted Peking duck in Chinatown.

In four nights, they saw four musicals: *South Pacific*, *Gentlemen Prefer Blondes*, *Kiss Me Kate* and *Where's Charley,* enough melodies to hum for a year.

Jim and Beatrice slipped into their comfortable relationship with ease. They were both open with each other and consequently got along well. There were never any tantrums; they were always laughing and hugging. He was her urban cavalier and she was his reminder of the softness, good cheer, natural manners and social sensitivity of many of the women of their age.

Janice and her parents planned to continue south leaving Beatrice's homebound travel arrangements to the whims of the New York Central Railroad. Jim arranged his work schedule so he could treat his college chum to some souvenir procurement the morning of her departure. The parents and Janice transferred their responsibility for Beatrice over to Jim in the hotel lobby after their rooms were securely back in the hands of management. Any whiff of sex or sight of bachelors cruising on the upper floors in the Roosevelt attracted the attention of a couple of heavies, called hotel dicks, who were prepared to take their last vows if there were any lapses in unmarried behavior or illegal bundling in their jurisdiction.

The Stork Club opened for lunch at 11:30 and Beatrice's train was at 1:00pm, so the pair arrived at the well-known club with suitcase in hand. The visit was predicated on the idea of stealing one of the club's black and white triangular ashtrays, a precious totem of urban excavation in that era. Beatrice, carrying her largest pocketbook, was able to snatch a souvenir while the bartender, in order to aid their obvious quest, conveniently turned his back to wash some martini glasses. They said goodbye at Grand Central and looked forward to seeing each other again in the fall.

* * *

In New York's summer heat, Jim made the acquaintance of a socially connected, young businesswoman a few years his senior named Sally Shreve. Her name appealed to him; it had that rich girl's sound he liked, and besides she had great style. She belonged to that sorority of women who meant to spend a few sparkling years in town and make the most of it prior to a well-placed marriage. They went to all the bright places—Cherio's, LaRue's and the Blue Angel—and danced all night on a variety of Roofs—the St. Regis, the Astor, the Rainbow Room—up among the towers of Manhattan.

Sally was sufficiently intrigued and curious about Jim but wondered if his good manners and thin appearance concealed any unusual sexual tendencies, so she devised a plot to test the preferences of his reproductive system. One warm evening, he was greeted at her door by a roommate, who apologized for Sally's delay, actually asked to inform him that it would be an hour or more before Sally would appear so she—Sally—had suggested that he nap on her bed because she was planning for them to attend a late night supper party and that he should take advantage of her tardiness and be well rested and raring to go by the time she arrived home. It seemed a little strange to Jim, perhaps there had been a miscommunication, but then again these were her sheets that she was inviting him to nest in, hopefully to crumple together in some wondrous wrestling event that very night. So the roommate escorted him into Sally's trap and she even pointed out to him where he could hang his trousers, and before long there he was, lying in her bed, breathing her very perfume. The light in the sky was disappearing and he was almost asleep when he heard someone at the door. Perhaps his moment had arrived.

He was disappointed to see a young man appear, with a funny look on his face, who promptly began taking off his clothes. That seemed odd to Jack but he greeted the newcomer with civility thinking that maybe this was just the resting place for all trousers. He tried to start up a conversation until the guy dropped his shorts and started to hop between Sally's sheets with Jim. Then in one sweeping motion, as the one body arrived, Jim's body departed on the other side.

What the hell was going on? He redressed aware of the other guy's interest in that activity and left the room to bump into no one else but the tardy Miss Shreve herself.

"Oh, hi," she said. "Ready for a big evening?"

"I've been using your dormitory," he said, hoping for an explanation.

She smiled. It was probably the smile that got him. If she had lied or been honest, that would have been one thing, but all she did was smile and grab his arm and begin her well-mannered chirping. He noticed her roommate giggling near the exit.

This was one of his last sieges at society's gate. Later he would chase some rich girls but his heart or theirs wasn't in it. When he re-entered the plebian world, there were a few other merchant's daughters he dated, but it dawned on him that he was not what they were looking for; he didn't have the name, the money or the patience to fish in society. He was as good a catch as groundfish.

* * *

By fall, Jim knew he would be called up into the service in the near future. His passive/aggressive acceptance of this probability worked in two ways. He mentally accepted the idea that everyone in his generation should serve; they owed that to the half-million guys who fell in the War. He didn't feel put-upon nor did he wish to dodge his responsibility. He could have easily been deferred by attending any type of school but that option felt like a copout. Still, he resented the idea that he would lose two years of his youth to a militaristic machine that appeared to have little sense of contemporary humanity and no personal creative outlet for its battalions of men except a dull, regimented survival, or the maelstrom of combat.

* * *

Meanwhile there was the new season. When the Broadway theaters shake out their curtains and vacuum the orchestra floor each September, the New York audience swells with anticipation. Eager to be the first to subscribe to unproven hits, enthusiasts scan the *Times* and *Tribune* for gossip of new productions. Showgoers are eager to re-engage in the subtle transference and shifts of plot that take the audience through a mysterious tunnel where images that were originally perceived to be true at the start of a drama are transformed into rich new feelings by the last act. The nuances engineered by these playwrights—like Miller and Tennessee now at the height of their powers—were deemed miracles on 44th Street.

If there was a theatrical season that could compare with the memorable one of '49-'50, it might be this one that followed. That prior year had seen *The Cocktail Party* by T.S. Eliot and *Member of the Wedding* by McCullers with Julie Harris, whose performance was one of the best Jim was ever to see. Also *Lost in the Stars* by Maxwell Anderson and Kurt Weil, a musical drama that opened his eyes to Africa, plus *Come Back, Little Sheba* by Inge and *The Wisteria Trees* based on Chekov with Helen Hayes. Jim had seen every one of these productions.

Now that he was able to attend nightly, Jim discovered that the '50-'51 showlist was filled with many of the names that would add to the luster of the New York Renaissance now well under way, a movement that would make the city the center of the universe for a few short years, based on the reputation of its art studios and dusty theaters and, to a lesser degree, on its poetry, music and fiction.

The ′50-‘51 season opened with a drama by Aldous Huxley and a new play by critic Wolcott Gibbs, who proved that he could write a drama with the best of them as well as dissect them. His *Season in the Sun* set in Fire Island was performed in a sea of white lights so glaring it brightened the hollows of the skull. This was followed shortly by Ethel Merman's reappearance on stage in another Irving Berlin hit, *Call Me Madam*. Jim loved the way she stood on stage, legs apart, belting out the lyrics—challenging audience members not to be seduced even though she didn't have an ounce of cuteness on her. The patter and swing of "You're Just in Love" brought down the house, Merman humbly accepting the shower of audience affection as if she had known she could win them over. She was more than pretty. She was a blooming star. Jim's love of musical comedy had begun when he had seen her summers before in *Annie Get Your Gun*. Jim missed an opera based on a Langston Hughes production but he did attend Menotti's opera double-bill, *The Medium* and *The Telephone*. He also missed a play by John Steinbeck and revivals of Hecht and MacArthur's *Twentieth Century* and Shaw's *Arms and the Man*. But he was front and center when a future film favorite leapt into the consciousness of New York audiences. Richard Burton virtually flew through an open window to make his entrance in *The Lady's Not for Burning,* a drama written by Christopher Fry, who had the audacity to write plays in verse. Fry had been one of the authors that Barbara had introduced him to during his Delavan summer.

Then along came social barnburner Clifford Odet's *Country Girl,* followed by *Book, Bell and Candle*. Then Christopher Fry reappeared as the translator of Anouilh's *Ring Round the Moon.*

When Jim saw *Guys and Dolls*, he was still in his "quality of life" phase that eschewed the appearance of lowlifes in the arts, but his ear was nevertheless struck with the opener, "Fugue for Tinhorns." And the Broadway voice of Robert Alda.

He would miss Louis Calhern's *Lear* and Ibsen's *Enemy of the People* adopted by Arthur Miller. As well as Lorca's *Bernaldo Alba* and Kingsley's play based on Koestler's *Darkness at Noon*, the book that had warned the English-speaking world of the more grievous sins of Marxism.

Later in the season, there would be Maurice Evans in *Richard II* and Tennessee's *Rose Tattoo* and an adoption of *Billy Budd* and an aging Olivia de Havilland as Juliet. Even as *South Pacific* continued its run, Rogers and Hammerstein's produced another winner, *The King and I. Kiss Me Kate,* was still running, and it was joined by a musical based on *A Tree Grows in Brooklyn*. On the list rolled. There was a failed Edmund Wilson play. Then *Stalag 17*.

The American playbook was overflowing with talent.

* * *

In September, seated in the upper balcony of the old Metropolitan Opera House in the Upper Thirties, Jim Mahoney found that his pursuit of art culminated in a radiant display of human ingenuity: The Sadler's Wells Ballet had returned for a second-year tour of America. They brought with them a production of *Sleeping Beauty,* one that owed a debt to the version that Diaghilev originated in London in 1929. They danced 153 performances over four months in more than thirty cities.

Jim reveled in the combination of music, dancing and myth. The movement of the corps re-ordered space in his mind and carried his vision into patterns that produced waves of clarity so refined in his eye that he would equate them with the highest art. The company swirled his senses in harmonic order. They uncluttered something in his brain and he would go forward with the belief that he had been transformed. Nothing could ever take away his perception that he had viewed human perfection with his own eyes. It was the most important performance that he would ever see because it gave him, for the first time in his life, the gift of total satisfaction. The flowing line, the vulnerable whiteness of her skin and the streaming red hair of Moira Shearer along with the elegance of Robert Helpmann on his final tour saturated Jim's quest for beauty. The order and harmony of the human world had been confirmed and he would no longer need to accept anything less than greatness He himself might never achieve it in his life or in his work, but he knew it existed and that belief bolstered his wandering soul for a long time.

* * *

Jim had discovered that San Remo was the current hot spot in the Village for writers. Along with McKnight, Jim drove into the city late one afternoon looking for this literary den. Even though they arrived at the 8th Street bar at an early hour, every seat and table was already occupied. They spent the next two hours on their feet, trying to rub elbows with the literary elite, or others like themselves who were on the same quest. The customers seemed to be a combination of university kids, dancers with their big cloth bags and some older folks, perhaps the regulars whose bar had been invaded by a bunch of book bugs.

A timeworn patron approached Jim and McKnight as they stood at the bar.

"Hey, young man. You look like a sensitive kid." He was directing his blurry gaze at Jim. "You might like to read some of my poetry. I have a special one just for you for only twenty-five cents."

With that, the scruffy old man pulled out at a small piece of paper from his pocket containing a mimeographed poem. The scissored line was slightly crooked.

"Ah ..." Jim began

"Max," the guy said.

"Max, you from the Village?"

"Man, I'm royalty here. They call me the King of Bohemia."

Jim, gauging his age, asked, "Were you actually here in the Twenties with Fitzgerald and O'Neil and that bunch?"

"Sure. Knew them all. I started in Chicago with Sandberg and Sherwood Anderson and all the *Poetry* and *Little Review* people. Pound thought my poetry was top-notch."

Jim knew about Harriet Monroe and Margaret Anderson's magazines and their link with subeditor Ezra Pound in Paris.

"No kidding. Sure, let me have a couple of those poems." The wandering vagrant had caught Jim's attention.

"Are you a published writer?"

The old man laughed showing a few missing teeth. "In the Twenties alone, I wrote seven books of poetry and six novels."

McKnight saw Jim's eyes expand.

Who is this guy? Jim wondered. "What's your last name?"

"Bodenheim. I thought you knew me."

"Certainly recognize your name," Jim said with a fluster.

McKnight confirmed their slippery memories. "When did you come East?"

"When the Chicago movement began to burn out. The Village was where all the action was. Worked on some poetry magazines. One day, I even wrote a poem with Gene O'Neil and that *Catholic Worker* lady."

"What are you doing now?" Jim asked.

"Me? I've been panhandling since the Thirties. Showing those plutocrats they can't keep me down."

Max looked at McKnight, "Bad scar you got there, buddy."

McKnight touched his face. "Yeah."

"Poetry," Max said, looking at his slips of verse, "is my scar."

Jim was chagrined that this was the way he had to interact with someone from the times that he had enthusiastically embraced as a model for his own future. He was caught between admiration and disgust at the condition of the old man. Is this what happens when the poetic light goes out?

They watched Max slap down fifty cents on the bar for a three-finger whiskey.

Max was everything he abhorred. Jim's sadness was complicated.

"How could you stand talking to him? He stank."

"I didn't even notice," Jim replied.

With its dusty bohemian air, Jim tried to overcome the distaste created by Bodenheim and absorb San Remo's environment. He at least felt that he was beginning to operate in the present, which is where artistically he had always wished to arrive. Disheveled as the present was.

* * *

Jim had learned that the world of the spirit and poetry can disarm the demons of childhood and that the artistic life—he defined it incorrectly as the life of the intellectual—was the correct course if one had the courage and ability to maintain its momentum, and that the coequal of religion was art and that the two were mixed together in spiritual delight. He knew that some of the friends he made would last a lifetime. And that university life with its classroom-created doubts, leaps of growth, broken relationships, genuine mature friendships, its breaking open of the world into large digestible slices and the clean sense of enlightenment—all these were the reward that parents gave their children or that their children discovered for themselves when they went off to college.

He felt that he had accomplished what he had set out to achieve. He had uncovered a body of knowledge, and though limited—lacking science—he had discovered a trove of creative gems. He had saturated himself in the arts and literature, history and politics and he looked forward to a life that would place these pursuits at the center of his existence. He would never stop learning and reading. Out of chaos, he had sought and he had found and all this treasure he intended to keep.

The dream he dreamed was not denied him.

Chapter 8
(1953 - 1954)

Six days after he had been discharged from his two-year hitch in the Army, during which time he had made the difficult choice to leave the Church and had suffered through another disastrous love affair, Jim was in Ann Arbor urging the Admissions Office to allow him back to classes. It was not a sure thing that he would be granted the privilege of matriculating again, owing to his horrible record in '50-'51. Using all his powers of persuasion, he tried to sway the normally unforgiving system in his favor, but his limited verbal skills were a deterrent. He could focus on schoolwork now, he told the administrator, a skeptic with long experience uncovering academic miscreants, a man who had been challenged by the best liars in the history of draft-dodging. It was January, 1953 and a new semester was about to begin.

"Why did you fail in your junior year?" Jim was asked.

"I was writing a novel," he replied, disingenuously.

"What makes you think you won't start a new one and face the same outcome?"

"I've spent the last two years reading," Jim said, "and I'm here to integrate what I've learned. I'm here for the academic, not personal, work. I think I'm better prepared now to fulfill my major."

The functionary, one of life's deciders, looked at Jim. He saw a thin, nervous kid who was really not a kid anymore. He looked intense. Burning inside. Maybe too intense. But since he had been able to pilot his way through the Army, he probably had the ability to deliver a few good grades.

"The fact that you've come out here on your own to reapply in person shows some initiative." The functionary hesitated, taking one last long look at Jim. "You have permission to return. But you're on probation and any slacking off, and you'll have to leave for good."

Jim felt redeemed. He had caught a break.

"Registration has already begun. Get your student papers out at the front desk. Then you'd better high-tail it over to the gym. You can check about housing downstairs."

Jim filled out the forms, reacquired his student ID and walked to the Phi Pi house.

As he crossed the Quad, he noticed that the student population had grown younger. He compared appearances between now and two and a half years ago when he first arrived. The vets had been upper classmen when Beatrice and her class arrived at college. The young ones were now seniors and the vets had moved on to their Levittowns. It was no longer a campus ruled by tales of war; it was now filled with multiple-thousands of males maneuvering to stay out of the new one. True, there were still a few vets finishing graduate studies but most underclassmen were teenagers. The intensity of purpose that accompanied the vet's posting to the university had stirred up campus life for a few years but Jim soon discovered that the driving force that the G.I.s brought was gone and had been replaced by a queasy sense of fear that accompanied the birth of the Silent Generation. Jim Mahoney vowed he wouldn't be influenced by the new conformity spreading around him. He would have none of it. He would insist on being his own man.

He would miss the vets; they were from his own "felt" time. Surviving the firestorm of WWII, there had been no time for them to relax before a series of new conflicts started up, fomented in Eastern Europe and in China through its surrogate North Korea. The Korean War—it was called a Conflict—seemed to have ricocheted off the big one. Many reservists had been forced to fight both wars.

But people hungered for peace. It was as if the Second War had been so uncontained, so universal, that now in its aftermath, citizens wanted to be left alone and ignore the significance of world events. Because the globe was not totally on fire, people could rationalize that their lack of interest in further warfare was warranted. Ex-servicemen, caught in the maw of economic competition, had been slammed into a desperate need to find normalcy. Across America, monetary rather than geo-political issues became paramount and as stiffness began to clog the country's patriotic arteries, it was jobs that became important. The vets soon discovered that if a person appeared to be different or too independent, he risked never finding a good wife, a good salary or a house with its own barbeque pit.

Everyone underestimated the worthiness of the Korean War and the effect of conflict on its participants. Who cared about a regional war after the climactic world one? Aside, of course, from the fifty thousand G.I.s and their families that actually or emotionally died in a lonely corner of Asia. It wasn't winning this new Conflict that the young Michigan male students championed or it wasn't that they accepted war's calling as sacrificial duty. It was about staying out of the draft altogether. Flunking courses was a potential death sentence. Jim was now one of the vets, a refugee from what people were calling a puny war, but he knew the avoiders and deniers hadn't asked the Marines who had fought up the snow road to China or his boyhood buddy, Jack Scanlan, who took months in Japan to mend from wounds, if combat was superfluous. There was a great national apathy regarding this new side-war.

Beatrice wasn't at the Phi Pi house, but some of her sisters remembered Jim, and made him feel welcome. Straight-shooting Threads walked into the chintz-covered living room and immediately recognized him, even though she was amazed by the change in his visage from larky playboy to serious adult.

"You're back! What a surprise. How did we ever get you out of New York?"

Threads looked more confident. The freshmen greenbeans he knew were all polished seniors now.

She said, "Bea read us some of your letters about bulldozing the Army brass. Funny stuff. She'll be so glad to see you. She's probably out with Walter."

That was a new name.

Jim said, "I was going to ask her advice about Lit courses."

"One thing to know is that we're all mad about Professor Harrow. From Harvard. Try to catch one of his sessions."

The women here were a genuinely authentic group: Adie driving around in her funeral hearse; Ginny, the southern Venus; tall Ella whose quizzical look was an invitation to test her powers;

O'Leary, who found it difficult to accept her own intelligence; Threads herself who could have fought a revolution; and Dory, the redhead, a reed in the wind—all immensely attractive and all lining up for big late-Twentieth Century lives.

After registering for classes, he spent most of the day finding a place to keep warm in the freezing winter air. He found a room across the street from the cemetery near the Arb in a share house where he would be bunking in with four grad students, a lively bunch of astronomers. Then he walked back to the Phi Pi house to see Beatrice. She was surprised to see him. They hadn't corresponded in six months and he was unaware that she had taken up with an academic specialist known to be a perennial pre-doc. She had a more serious look now that she was a senior, and he detected an edge of haughtiness in her voice. He immediately fathomed that the closeness they once shared was a thing of the past.

"I didn't expect you," she said, pulling away from his embrace.

"Didn't arrive until this morning after an all-night train ride. A week ago I was still living in the barracks."

"We'll have to get you resettled and find you some new friends." She knew as well as he did that he had burned all his bridges two years before.

They walked out and were standing on the curb where they could be alone.

"Give me a clue," he spurted out. "What happened between the two of us?"

"It just didn't work out with you gone."

And that was, it seemed, all there was to it. In time, their essential caring for each other returned and they again became friends, but it was sticky in the beginning until they faced the real reason for their break-up.

A few weeks later over coffee, Beatrice confronted Jim, "You probably don't know what happened so I'll tell you. The June after you went in the Army, my sorority big sister went to the annual Phi Pi meeting in Texas and she's sitting around the pool one day talking to this girl representing Lawrence and they start telling stories about how tough it was for some of their sisters to keep a relationship going with guys who had been drafted. And my big sister, starts telling this other woman about me—how you asked me to marry you before you left for boot camp and the girl from Lawrence tells the same story about you and Barbara Hanover."

Jim's face froze.

"How you had asked her to marry you that same New Year's weekend. Luckily, we both said no. Maybe some day you'll tell me what that was all about."

Jim was mortified. It was true what he had done. If either one of them had been willing to face overseas separation or combat injury, and to share a Quonset hut on some god-forsaken base in the middle of nowhere for a couple years and face little pay and no prospects—after giving up their own education—then he would have been ready to give up his search for himself and finally share a bed with a woman he cared for and somehow bumble through.

Beatrice nevertheless fixed him up with a couple of dates among the younger sorority girls and he began a fling with Dory, a redhead from Philadelphia.

* * *

Stationed stateside while in the Army, Jim, in effect, spent two years reading and listening to music in the Fort Bragg Post Library when he wasn't on duty as an MP. Wherever he went, there was always a twenty-five-cent pocketbook sticking out of the wide back pockets of his fatigues that were able to accommodate a four hundred page volume. His mature view of American literature was fairly integrated by now, and he was more or less current with England's contributions. He thought most of the pieces of the novels' historical development were in hand. His general overview was sufficiently rounded that he could begin to plunge deeply into the canons of his favorites. Fitzgerald he knew. Faulkner had begun to rise in his consciousness.

Luckily, he had help from Dr. Harrow, who provided a semester's course analyzing both the bard of Oxford, Mississippi and Henry James, an author for whom the professor was chief interpreter. The course on Faulkner would become the basis for Jim's explication of the bewildering South. In following semesters, the good doctor would light up the writings of Melville and Twain. The scholar, who had been exiled from Harvard, was famous on campus for inviting his grad students over to hear him play the organ. Jim was surprised at the intensity of Dr. Harrow's anxiety; his worn visage along with his stutter elicited a voice throttled in pain and subject to explosive bursts of blasted sound. In time and as the genius of his literary knowledge became clear, Jim would become unaware of the problem. Harrow's verbal suffering was like McKnight's facial scar. After a while, it wasn't there. This semester, the other subject taught by Dr, Harrow was 17th Century Poetry. Jim joined both classes.

* * *

Jim began a journal:

"Too much is written, but to the pile of broken phrases and the massive heap of alphabetical scrap, here are more words to be bundled up, towed through mortal toil and finally dumped in the yard of accumulated expression. The tangle sometimes provides originality; more often the cartman unloads an assortment of personal advertisements, neighborhood pamphlets and paperback prejudices. If the purpose for beginning a blotter includes improvement, entertainment and evaluation, and if the individual can, through memos to self, close the circuit of one's own communication, then between the hope and the realization, between the desire to make known one's impressions and having them stare back for a long time, falls not the doubt about one's earlier beliefs but a picture of a faded time.

Two years in the Army provided me with the notion that life is determined only in proportion to one's refusal to transcend dullness. As the most inept private first class in the Army, I succeeded in setting myself apart from my bored brothers so that I might retain a shred of individuality. Action as a separatist was the only way I could tolerate a routine that supported the dysfunctional and petty."

* * *

Journal — February

"The recital given by Miss Ava and Miss Mary on the twin pianos provided a good opportunity for harmless mental mischief. The piece, especially the first movement, aroused a dispute between the performers as to how the piece should be rendered. One could almost believe they hadn't bothered to practice together. The disagreement bore on whether it should be played technically and precisely, as is probably the case, or with a type of warmth imaginable only in the breasts of Jane Austen's passionflowers. I'll never know which part Miss Ava or Miss Case took in the eternal struggle between the intellectual and the passionate, but it should be noted that the frenetic runs of the one counterplayed by the grandiose style of the other made for lamentable dissonance. I fear there is strife in the Music Department."

* * *

On the first weekend that he could carve out of his schedule, Jim journeyed to see Barbara in northern Wisconsin where she was now a senior in college. In Chicago's Union Station, mindful of Fitzgerald's rhapsody on winter trips to the mythologized northland of his youth, Jim boarded an ice-crusted train, encased in steam and smeared with patches of white frost. His feelings, born in the innocence of the romantic spree he shared with his Wisconsin beauty, re-ignited. The coaches were so cold that passengers remained in their overcoats until the heat came up. Jim watched the frozen, snow-covered fields speed by and wondered what two years of separation would bring. She had told him that she had been seeing one of her classmates.

They were awkward at first but he quickly judged that the sweet insecurity of her teen years had been cured. And she noticed in him, a much darker version of his once smiling countenance.

The first thing she noticed was how frazzled he looked.

"My god, you've changed. Look at you. What did you do, lose your baby fat?"

"Can I pass it along to your feminine parts?"

"No thanks. You can probably tell that the food is good here."

"That's what you get for going to school in the breadbasket."

They found a soda shop in town and sat for two hours testing the strength of their neglected relationship.

"First I have to apologize for the findings at the Phi Pi convention the year I went in the army," he confessed. "I hear I was hoisted by my own peculiar judgment."

Barbara took a long time before she answered and finally said, "I've forgiven you under the belief that you were mad at the world for having to waste two years of your life and that you were looking for a life raft, a Mae West for your emotional system."

He was astounded, as he had always been, by her acceptance of human fragility.

"You're generous."

"You're welcome," she said in a straightforward manner. She understood him.

"You know your friends. It must be why I always knew that sooner or later, maybe we'd probably get together."

"I've always had a pretty good idea for what I was looking for in a man," she said, her eyes burning into him.

"Some guy coming at you through the dust of a small library."

"With a book under his arm and sure of nothing but his own emotions."

"Excitable as they are."

"Yes. Excitable as they are."

"They're fairly excited right now in case you haven't noticed."

"You're not alone, you know."

He reached over and touched her and she held his arm.

Later after dinner out, they sat in a guest lounge in the college by themselves and re-connected slowly.

"I've been thinking about you a lot lately," he said. "When I'm with you, I just seem to pull myself together—like you complete the circuit for me."

"I know what you mean. Connection made."

They embraced. He couldn't get close enough to her.

"It's just hard for me," Barbara said. "The guy I've been going with went crazy when he heard that I said it was OK for you to come up. Right now, he's alone doing what we do every Friday night—volunteer work at the hospital. He's down on his hands and knees scrubbing floors and scared to death about you and me."

"Just let yourself go," he said seductively.

"Oh, god, I'd like to."

"Is there somewhere else we can go?"

"In my car. Come on."

The night was freezing cold, near zero. They bundled up and half-froze before the pre-war car warmed up. They drove to a quiet path near the school and began to roam over each other's bodies.

"We've got three choices. We do it here. Or in a motel. Or elope to California."

"I'm not doing it in the car," she adamantly replied.

"And I can't afford a motel," he said. Then, lightening up, added, "Let's pack for San Francisco."

That broke the heat wave that had steamed up the car windows. They sat talking for an hour, alternatively turning on the ignition for heat and sitting nestled together as the cold seeped back in.

She re-entered his life, quieting many of his anxieties.

* * *

The astronomers living in the Ann Arbor house invited Jim to view the constellations from their observatory. The obs was located between two well-populated dorms on the edge of the campus, and Jim eagerly joined a half-dozen stargazers as they were setting up the scope for an evening's peek at the firmament. How far away the universe actually was soon emerged. Instead of pointing the lens toward the heavens, the would-be astronomers aimed their magnification at the windows of the nearby women's dorm. Excited but determined, they had trouble locating a room with naked females but soon discovered a coed in the buff pacing in front of a mirror, practicing smoking a cigarette.

He had seen girls preen before; guys too after a shower in the gym. He had noticed women checking the behavior of their hair in a mirror before leaving or entering a home. But this was drama. This was acting. This was Bette Davis with her cigarette prop.

Jim, appalled and delighted, was as stimulated as the rest of the voyeurs and soon had his turn at the eyepiece. A girl with beautiful breasts and a delicious derriere strutted back and forth across the room, swaying. Toting a cigarette and studying her movements for signs of glamour in the glimmering glass, she appeared to be carrying on an imaginary conversation.

Anatomy and astronomy had never been closer.

* * *

Journal – April

"Dr. Harrow, whose very soul trembles on the undulating lagoon that is his face, read in class today Donne's 'Death Duel Sermon,' making for superimpositions of what is conflict of great intensity in the present that was pedantic in the past. It was comparable to the emotional experience of Good Friday service when he performed as a rite, the *'Stabat Mater*.'

This afternoon, a professor from Frieburg lectured on Luther's role in Germany at present and he managed to convince no one that spiritualism and predestination are the answers to the woes of the defeated country that kept him in a concentration camp during the war. A kindly man, whose points of reference fall into the Romantic tradition, rose to a verbal pitch when he asked in different terms, 'How long, O Lord, will thou forsake us?' He earnestly attempted to be objective about his homeland. He was a loving failure."

* * *

Journal – April

Today Dory, the redhead from Philadelphia, who at present is peeved with me because I got tight and left her to shift for herself last weekend at the sorority's House Formal, and along with Threads, a sugar sweet activist, who was the object of my chasing at the party, all three of us had coffee at the Union. The redhead, who has a beguiling lip that twitches except when she's kissed and who made me incarnate Poverty by repeating, 'That's poor! That's poor!' when I wouldn't place my beer mouth on her twitch after the party, sat rather glumly today under her crimson curls while Threads kept bursting out in little fits of unexplained laughter. We began telling of our various thieving experiences as children. Threads, I suspect like myself had stolen from the dime store but when the redhead deb, who is such a prim Mainliner, told us she too had put toys under her coat in the Woolworth store, I realized, if Dory could pilfer, all humankind must be corrupt.

Beatrice sat with us until her perennial grad student arrived with his History cronies. He came over to the table and Beatrice, simple and fresh when in love, lavished and bathed him in a beautiful smile that I remember so warmly. I chuckled to see that old flash of affection and was nostalgic in that remembrance—when I turned to see my other companions watching me, knowing exactly what I was thinking, one sullenly and the other laughingly.

* * *

Journal – May

"Ormandy brought his troupe back to town today for the music festival. He is older now and more volatile; not the suave, cuff-adjusting conductor I remembered. His music, still smooth but more passionate, is destined to accompany people in their transcendental swoons. Kincaid, the beloved Philadelphia flautist with bushy white hair, still whistles silver tones. The first violin lady with the low-cut gown seems to have a new boyfriend, the chubby second violinist. They pizzicatoed together, bumping instruments; surely a type of musical flirtation. Chopin's First was well studied but lacking, and Prokoviev's machine symphony, though perfectly rendered, lectured in the Russian idiom overmuch.

Dory was there with a new boyfriend.

Next night the festival presented the *B Minor Mass* under Johnson's direction and it was almost enough to reconvert me. Kincaid got a better hand than the singers, one of whom had an irreligiously sultry voice.

A dream fragment last night involved a group of philosophers cutting pieces of a pie from a large circle. Significance being what, I can't imagine, unless it concurs with my ineptitude for piecing together a system."

* * *

Journal—May

"At my place, Kennedy's 'cross from Death's Gate, the tulip tree can be seen budding awkwardly. This is the first day the mixture of heat and high spring wafted fragrantly and the air is voluptuous in comparison to a day last week when everything merely smelled uniformly sodden green.

A letter from Barbara today, written in a beer fog, was tenderly passionate; the delicate shell she lives in grows to a deeper hue of red. No longer pink, not yet a woman, but promising full stature once her imagined inadequacies are purged. Whether or not I can assist this growth in her remains to be seen.

Last night the projected novel on authority became clearer when I thought of my Army buddies as fitting together in such a way that they become a cross-section of really bright young guys under pressure. A short novel might be finished before I graduate next January and then the Long Island history project could remain unencumbered by unfinished work."

* * *

Journal – May

"Dory told me a story about the ingenuity of one of the coeds during the 'panty raids' two years ago, the one that began the national fad. The girl, caught in the shower with only a towel available, heard the boys coming and knowing that she would be detected in the nude, wrapped the towel around her head and strolled down the hall past the males, her pride saved and her figure, common gossip."

* * *

Journal – May

"Kathy, a delightful example of what a Theta should be, one who thinks well rather than worrying about her looks, told me a story of a girl in her philosophy class, who after arguing heatedly with her instructor against determinism, was asked to leave the class. She wouldn't budge, saying that she couldn't will herself to commit such an act, turning his argument against him. I suppose the entire argument for authority could be dismantled if all was determined, leaving us irresponsible.

Dr. Harrow brought into class a Southern cook book, mostly recipes from a lady's guild, and gave us ingredients for Brunswick stew to match by analogy the complexity and involved time in Faulkner. It was as charming as the day he brought in Southern hymn recordings (he calls them 'sacreds') and beat out the rhythms with his furiously palsied arms. His thoughts must transcend in an uproar to the One."

* * *

Journal – May

"Last night a bunch of us were out learning woodsy ways in the Arb, the scholastic "hundred" set aside as much for botanists as for boozing bonfire builders. We walked through the knee-high African grass and the redhead and Beatrice absorbed quarts of water through their tennis shoes and spread out a couple of M-monogrammed blankets. Buffeting the delicate ears of our naiads from the obscene drunks cavorting through the glen, we encamped for the evening. Why didn't we build a fire like the ones we used to construct? Could it be, old fella, that the heat is out of it? It seems so today. If I'm a hung-over Romantic, and if as Mumford says, the picnic is the highest form of Romantic living, could it be that, if last night's charade lacked the late bucolic frenzy that I once enjoyed, my ideological format needs new ink? Maybe I should write with white ink. Invisible incunabulum, hiding grey shades and old regrets."

* * *

Journal – May

"Stephan Spender spoke this afternoon at the Hopwood Lecture and charmed the audience with his polish and poise. His amusing introduction, which he was long in delivering, prated against the awards that were to follow his address. His comment that a Romantic would find himself at home beneath the imitation constellations on the ceiling that electrically lit a blue firmament above us in the hall caused Dr. Harrow across the aisle to voice his thunderous, cadenced laugh. Spender's advice for young writers was that they should avoid writing realism. Called them documentaries. Suggested they should act out of the center of their artistic conscience.

Now that exams have started, I call Dory every night and read a bit of Keats to soothe her academically tortured mind. Examination time is a test of character. Judy Eastfall becomes a madwoman when she can't remember the sub-theme of a Beethoven symphony. Betsy Platter, another DG, sat bolt upright all through the three-hour Faulkner/James exam. Bre'r William would certainly compare her to the antebellum ladies who never touched the backs of their chairs. All students are bleary-eyed; most show signs of fatigue. The redhead, I think, did the most eccentric thing. She went out to a car lot and bought an old Buick. Of course, I didn't do anything strange. I always climb up on roofs.

Students tend to regress during exams. When it rains the coeds trudge barefoot along the street, juggling books and shoes. We even played 'Kick the Can' behind the Theta house the other night, not with as much zest as I remember from childhood, but well enough for consumptive college kids. Over in front of the Lutheran church, a cryptic, Gothic work, the holier students play croquet with much unchristian knocking of the ball away from the wickets."

* * *

Journal – June 6:

"Today, with exams over and seniors with over-active tear glands submitting unwillingly to their inevitable graduation, was one of those long June days that never seem to end; time relaxes its grip, and memory, as in Faulkner, moves back and forth in time, nostalgically isolating those who are still here physically from those who have already mentally transited into the outer world. If the university was more a part of life than it currently is, such a problem might not exist. The seniors leave in abjection, except for those looking forward to summer marriages, aware that college has no continuity in later life. Some everlasting sophomores never advance past this day, so it is well that the day is long and that there were such events as Beatrice's birthday celebration where we could be together for the last time.

The Bell, our half-acre tavern, offered such an opportunity, and after much pulling together of tables and isolating the minors, who can't legally be served, the party was well along by the time Mary Cambridge, who shall be studying at Oxford this summer, and I pranced in with a birthday cake. Along with weddings, summer jobs and overseas voyages were the main topics, one group antagonistic to the enthusiasm of the other. Mary and I later went to see the movie, *Red Shoes*, probably the finest ever made, and pronounced that it was the key factor in the new national interest in ballet."

* * *

Jim, who still lacked credits to graduate, decided to attend summer school so he could finish his degree requirements by the end of the fall semester, leading to a January diploma. Before the summer classes began, he attended Barbara's graduation at Lawrence across Lake Michigan.

Journal –June 7

"Mary Cambridge and I motored through the farmland of central Michigan today to her home in Grand Rapids, neither the Grand River being rapid nor the rapids grand and were feasted in the easy, informal style created by a chicken dinner. Dr. Cambridge, the local health officer, was interrupted at dinner by a frantic mother seeking solutions to a case of measles.

Mary, a lovable female who tolerates my stammering better than most of her sex, proved a good companion during our journey that was brightened by a radio version of *Amahl* from Florence and excerpts from Prokofiev's *War and Peace.* By bus, I've come as far as Muskegon where I will take the *Milwaukee Clipper* across to Wisconsin. Just north of here, the D.G.'s are holding a lakeside party. I should have enjoyed attending so as to join with my colleagues in the Blue Blazer Club whose ritual is pouring down a burning shot of bourbon. I was initiated into the club last Friday by Dory, while her sister Ally argued free will with a seven-foot med student who played "Shenandoah" badly on his uke."

Journal -June 8

"An old salt would be shocked to see the various pleasure areas offered by the *Clipper*: dance floor, bar, movie lounge. Sitting on deck reading Fitzgerald's notebooks and essays, I spent the morning inspecting the passing foundations of the young ladies aboard by surreptitiously peering over the edge of my book. I have come to a general conclusion as to the deliciousness of the Midwestern derriere. The waist towards twenty is expanding, the breasts either inordinately small or full, but the posterior is generally the same, namely in its fullness. The rears that young ladies in the East accentuate by cropping their woolen material directly below the equator appear in the Midwest not as frequently. I much prefer the yielding fullness of the country ladies. With thinner waists, the local lassies could, I believe, pour themselves into hourglass dresses to display their various parts to best advantage. The wide berth is definitely the one to applaud in this day of nervous thinness.

Milwaukee, upon arrival, was a-buzz over the formation of a National League baseball team. The train to Appleton carried an abundance of young kids on their way to summer camp in the northern part of the state. With the exception of a sour farmer who wouldn't let some lady to sit beside him, the trip was non-eccentric.

Woman, child, girl, milkmaid, queen—these and the whole catalogue and range of femininity can be applied to the most precious Barbara. Of course, I think of her as possessing both bucolic and extra-country qualities, and she laughs at my idiotic conception of her. But my excuse—probably best in the world, and really not an excuse at all—involves the honestly felt love that I have for her which is not a projection of myself, but an appreciation of her complex individuality that when linked and connected in her and run back on the same communication path to me, serves as an avenue for what is a simple melting of two natures."

* * *

Barbara was waiting for him at the Appleton station, sitting in her Plymouth, reading. She had ended her romance with a fellow classmate and was wondering if her long-time affection for Jim would provide a new starting point for them. He slid in beside her and embraced her across the transmission system.

"Gear shift gets you right in the heart," he said.

"Telling us it's time to accelerate, my dear." Hesitating, she continued, "You almost look human again."

"I've been well fed by the Omega Chi house cook and supported by Uncle Sam or Aunt Columbia, or whoever keeps sending me greenbacks every month."

"Spoiled are we?"

"Saturated in American literature."

"Good. First things are still first."

"That includes you."

He hoped their spirited affection would help carry them through the weekend.

Her social skills had always been better than his, and she knew that she would have to carry the extra burden of integrating him into her crowd, a lively group making their college farewells.

"How are you reacting to the end of classes?"

"Sentimental about leaving, I guess," as she started up the engine and headed for campus. "And a little lost. And wondering where you and I are going. Plus looking forward to Europe."

"You'll have to kiss the Blarney Stone for me."

"Sorry, O'Mahoney. Just Paris and London."

They were very careful with one another. This might be the beginning of a more fruitful relationship or, conversely, a recognition that they weren't meant to be together. Their lives had brought them to this decisive moment. She was ready to begin her next career, perhaps in Chicago while Jim was due to graduate in six months. They ate a quiet dinner alone and turned in early, she in her dorm room, he in a guesthouse a mile up the river.

The weekend was destined to be a tense group experience. With friend Peggy and her gregarious boyfriend, Jack, and three other couples, a picnic was planned on the river the next afternoon.

"On to the fast-flowing Fox," Jack commanded his forces. "Let's go exploring."

They hiked and canoed along the shore of one of the old portages that had brought settlers into mid-America. Where glacial boulders had been deposited along the shore, they jumped from one to another, with much arm waving at their individual conquest over natural impediments—the triumph of collegiate revelers and the return of summer to their northland. In the evening the ongoing beer festivities carried them along. But it was not all going smoothly.

Journal – June 10

"It's not many days of the year that the willows near the river shed their seeds in angelic hair that float up into a blizzard on the side of a hill. I find a comparison with my own over-rated being, especially after reviewing Barbara's probing last evening, to the effect that gauze enfolds me because the nature of my seed remains invisible. The question of how best to express what is within me as opposed to what appears on the façade is to solve a problem that's difficult. She says I can't get outside of myself. I'm bottled up and am my own prisoner. This after a day was spent pushing a canoe through a shallow stream and bickering with Barbara at a local tavern. Both situations were intense and a bit draining and she remained uneasy. It's the old complaint. I can't make her comfortable because she is always aware that I'm self-conscious and not participating. Yesterday, she kept touching me to try to settle me down. It wasn't spontaneous but a contrived series of gestures that she knew was affecting me. It was as if we were both trying to express an idea of love that even in its casualness was powerful. But we were not at ease and our fumbling was pathetic.

The day began pleasantly with a trip to Waupaca, which means tomorrow—the arrival date when computing Indian traveling time—and the tomorrow that Barbara and I say will lift us from our miserable uneasiness. We seek comfort and can't find it. Perhaps yesterday should have been our waupaca but the current left us adrift. But there is still the presence of love that can't be shaken loose. Set within is an opal of many hues, and in our desire to cast different lights upon it, we might succeed in refracting an entire life scheme. But because this is graduation week for her, and I am so far failing in an attempt to bridge our realities, it's became a problem of whether I should leave or not, but she'll have to make that decision.

In the morning, we motored through a series of lakes by launch. The ten of us hired five boats and with assorted meats and breads followed a shallow stream where we sometimes had to drag the boats over the rocks, a funny sight—the humanness of people, who could much more comfortably walk along the shore—but who would rather struggle. The incorrigible attempt of man to solve his own self-generated problems.

Last evening at a crowded table either too large or too small for us to fit comfortably, Barbara and I bent our heads together in a discussion that resulted in my not assimilating into the group, She took my behavior as a piece of scorn which I denied and told her that when I was with her, it was impossible to be aware of anything but her. Then we got into a conversation about the social scramble and she's lecturing me on public protocol to the point where I realized that when we were in company I plainly bored her. She has told me that she loves me, but never why she did. And when I tell her why I do, the result is a sermon that lacks feeling. Physically, I ache with the expectation of what someday might occur while her entire appearance and gesture is in communion with her necessity to please and be pleased. The man that she loves most, and one as equally talented as she, shall have to provide her a big life through which she can widely range. It's not a matter of her changing what is already an expressive personality, but there must be an allowance for her capacity. It might not be me who can give her what she needs without her changing her expansive habits, but somewhere in the larger field of her players, it has been a pleasure to serve."

* * *

Barbara's parents arrived the next day for her graduation ceremonies. They were coldly polite to Jim, wondering what he was still doing hanging around in their daughter's life at a time when her wedding bells should be tuning up.

As a graduation gift, Jim gave her a copy of a work by Samuel Hoffenstein, a screenwriter for the *Wizard of Oz.* The couple had chortled over his well-thumbed works in Delavan. She smiled when she opened the colorfully wrapped package to find a pristine edition of *Poems of Passion Carefully Restrained So as Not to Offend Nobody.* Jim included a copy of Morah's *Cinderella Hasenpfeffer and Other Tales Mein Grossfader Told*, quirky dialect humor.

* * *

Journal – June 13

"Today, we head for Delavan. The post-graduation party went on until dawn spiced up by David and Lily, a British couple. They were light and airy and full of charm. Barbara responded cheerily to both of them. She's going to enjoy England.

Three years ago, Barbara and I loved each other and sought for things we no longer seek, this in my case more than hers. We hoped that this time we could celebrate new love rites and overcome our old immature affections, though as strong now as then for me. We were good when we were young at understanding life. As Barbara says, we were more agreeable when green. This all came out when some truths filtered through the alcohol. She says she is still devoted to the younger version of this antiquity. I'm miserable."

* * *

Journal – late June

"It is a soft and terribly green evening; the campus bells chime in Burton Tower and the kids on the next block are maiming one another with 'machine gun' sounds that sputter from their lips. Of all the evenings spent in Ann Arbor, this is the blest one of the year. It isn't warm or even fragrant, but, with the exception of the children, peaceful. Deep in what's left of my soul, it would be nice to reflect the kind of calmness that's in the air. But the longing that keeps me searching disallows it. Whatever the confluence that finally arrives to satisfy me, I hope it comes on an evening like this.

Barbara left for Europe and upon her return, we shall have to make some decisions about whether or not to continue. Delavan provided us with a quiet background and an opportunity to re-set some of the injuries of the last few years. And life will have to be very long before the remembrance disappears of watching the dawn after the all-night graduation party, when standing fifteen feet apart on a dew-covered lawn, we decided to stay together.

Carl, one of the astronomers in the house, suggested we take a walk through the moonlit Arb. A fine idea it was too. The Arb always brings back memories of my old beliefs in the natural. Tonight that spirit returned for a time. Tomorrow, Carl marries. Under the same circumstances, I think I would have preferred to walk alone."

* * *

The university administrators turned creative that year and introduced a school-wide "Summer of the Popular Arts." Literature classes studied Mickey Spillane, the detective writer. Art school students pored over comic strips. Engineers got out their Erector Sets. Jim took a philosophy course that featured the views of an English writer, Collingwood. In describing the difference between art and entertainment, the philosopher suggested that art consisted of images that remained in the brain, and were discussed and puzzled over, while the delights of entertainment soon evaporated. The thought provided a simple pathway to understanding for Jim. A thing of art requires a studied contemplation, involves a higher level of thought, and is distinct from show business. It was a good enough explanation to last a lifetime.

* * *

Journal – July

"I saw the Good Humor Man fixing a flat today and thought he looked funny wrestling with an oily tire in his white suit. I also saw a serious-looking student walking down the street with a triple-decker ice cream cone (called 3-D after the new movie process) and laughed out loud.

Dr. Harrow was seen padding around town in an all-white suit—the older J.A. Prufrock.

Charlotte (another redhead) from Wellesley and I have been looking for Corona in the skies all summer. Tonight, on the island that separates the Huron River for a pace, after a tender embrace, our first in deference to her betrothed millionaire in Chicago, we immediately sighted her.

There is peace tonight in Korea but there is no ringing of bells and nobody cares. Everyone came home red from the beach."

* * *

At the end of the summer of popular arts in Ann Arbor, Jim trained home; it would be the first time in nearly three years that he would spend more than ten consecutive days in Manhasset. He now felt totally separated from his hometown's former embrace and eager to find his own place in Manhattan or Chicago. He had only one more semester to go.

The highlight of his trip home was to greet Barbara on her return from Europe. She had accepted his invitation to stay over in New York for a few days on her way back to Wisconsin. They were scheduled to see the new Rogers and Hammerstein musical and he looked forward to squiring her around Manhattan. He waited anxiously at Idlewild Airport for her plane to land after her two months abroad. She arrived in the terminal with her friend Peggy looking overtired and tense. Perhaps the flight had been exhausting.

"Hey, world traveler. Welcome home. Hi, Peggy."

"It's been such a whirl, I hardly know where I am," Barbara said, trying to avoid his embrace.

"Back in these loving arms."

She was startled and instead of lighting up for Jim, she looked anxiously at Peggy.

"I see. No public display of affection," he said. "Peggy, you'll have to look the other way." And he kissed her.

She pulled away. "Peggy's catching a three o'clock to Chicago. And Jim, I need to change my reservation. I can't stay as long as I thought I could."

They drove to Manhasset and Jim introduced Barbara to his mother and sister. Perhaps she should lie down for a while after such a long flight that included a long refueling stop in Greenland.

They sat in the living room after dinner and Barbara said, "Jim, I have something to say." She hesitated and went on, "I met an

Englishman in London and he followed me all over Europe. I finally gave in to him. I hate to tell you, but I fell in love with him."

Jim was stunned.

"He's older and from a good family in the West Country. He's sensitive and funny and I think I'm going to marry him."

He looked at her with a blank face. "What the hell . . ."

"I'm sorry, Jim."

"Sorry? I thought we could start making plans of our own."

They sat on the couch facing their separate futures. Jim turned sullen and began to dis-assemble the feelings that had begun to seem permanent.

"Permanent for a few weeks," he said, half aloud.

She tried to console him but there was no balm. She quickly escaped to the guest bedroom. As she walked up the staircase, she looked back at him with a pitying look.

For two days, they explored New York, but his heart wasn't in it and she wanted to leave. She advanced her plane reservations again and was shortly gone. The Wisconsin dream, indeed the entire Midwestern dream flew away with her.

They were all gone now. All of them. Bonnie had married some Navy guy. Lucy was about to deliver her first child. Beatrice was living in New York with her girlfriends. And now Barbara had opted for a life in Europe. The slate was clean. The question was whether he had the emotional strength to write the novel he was planning, put something bold down on paper, leave his mark on a space that felt so empty. The answer he heard inside himself was in the positive. He'd go it alone. Bloody but unbowed as his Army buddy, Gooden, would say.

Gooden was still living with his parents in Manhasset and commuting into Manhattan to work in the editorial offices of one of the large publishing houses. They were glad to reconnect during his break even though it had been a hard week for Jim. He and Gooden, while in uniform, had developed a strong bond that had finally provided Jim with a male friend. They had grown up together and had actually played on the same team at one stage. But they had run with different crowds.

The buddies had time to share some late night coffee breaks before Jim returned to school, amid promises that Gooden would come out for homecoming in Ann Arbor.

* * *

Journal – September

"There comes a certain time when each man should make peace with himself because body and soul begin to wear from combat. The sailor in his navigation knows how to come around to his destination by hauling in extra sail. As to myself, there is some tucking in to be done because my lines are snagged and my sheets are all over the ocean. To trim a sportive mind and not follow physical dictation shall be difficult, but the necessity to do so is demanding some consideration.

I've just returned from Helen's garret behind Burton Tower and can find but little use for myself after talking with her. Beautiful and bird-like, her profound intensity was lightened enough today so that I almost entered into a meaningful conversation with her. She is so exacting and questions every value so minutely that she makes me feel like a clod when I compare her advancement with mine.

A week ago, I had left a bottle of milk and a copy of Simone Weil's *Gravity and Grace* at her door with a note that said I wished to provide her with food for both her body and soul. Here were two kinds of nourishment depending on her mood. I said Weil makes for one kind of model in the case of up and coming mystics like herself. Today, she ripped into Weil saying that physical feelings and pain were not pertinent to a formulation of ideas.

Tough biscuit she is."

* * *

Jim was surprised in October when an Army buddy appeared at his front door. Bill Schneider and he had been staunch allies when Jim was working in the post stockade at Fort Bragg and where the downed parachutist, a prisoner, had been the yard boss. Schneider, interested in creative writing and sure that all authentic, young authors went to war whenever real fighting broke out, had sought a transfer to fight in Korea. He was a member of the 82nd Airborne.

The brass had turned down his request, so he refused to jump and was court-martialed and sacked from the Division. That allowed him, after a short prison sentence, to volunteer from a new outfit for the combat experience he desired. Jim had been his literary mentor but was wary of Schneider's temper and hard-core skirt chasing.

"I'll be a son of a bitch! Schneider!"

"The same, Your Excellency."

"What are you doing here?"

"Same as yourself, mate."

"What happened to you after Bragg?"

"I ended up fighting in Korea and was wounded in the leg. I just started classes."

"I can't believe it."

"I thought I might find you here."

"It's only been a year since Bragg, but what a year for you."

"Yeah. I think about how we used to muscle those jailbirds into shape."

"How you did, you mean," Jim said. "Where are you living?"

"I'm in one of those coops with a bunch of Michigan misfits."

"Welcome to the club. I can't offer you any coffee."

"I thought maybe we'd just take a walk."

They strolled out toward the Arb while Schneider talked about his wild heroics in Korea. It was a cold night and the wind was screeching.

"You know I was desperate to get into combat," Schneider said, pulling up the collar of his tight jacket and lighting a cigarette. "I arrived in Seoul eight weeks after I got out of the brig and was pushed right up into the front lines. I loved it. We'd be firing most of the day, or at least the artillery was. My specialty was at night. I'd cross the lines, all blacked up, with no equipment but a knife. I'd crawl up on their outposts, infiltrating past them, and kill those sons of bitches while they were asleep."

Jim was stunned.

"I got seven of them."

Jim could hardly believe his ears. He knew Schneider had a dangerous side but he had no conception of its murderous depth.

"Pretty strong stuff," Jim acknowledged.

"Yeah. I got all the bile of a bad Detroit life out of my system. Now I'm ready to do some serious writing. I just had to get all that hate out of me first by inflicting it on somebody else."

Jim wondered if his bitter experience might warp him and turn Schneider into a cake of ice. There had to be some place in his narrative that prized frozen emotions.

The wind rattled through the trees and the clouds rode quickly past the moon. It was an eerie night all around.

"I've never heard such a story."

"And you the big author. Speaking of which, what are you working on?"

"The novel I was hacking away on at Bragg. Trying to fit Jung, my old girlfriend and what it means to be educated into one package."

"And how's it going?"

"Not as well as I'd like."

"I'm going to write one about what mayhem combat is."

As they were walking along past the tall trees that led to the Arb, a violent gust of wind burst through the bare branches with whistling intensity. As the howling reached them in full fury, a wild gust caused Schneider to suddenly leap to the earth, flattening himself in the grass that bordered the road. He was pawing the ground, as if he were digging a foxhole. Or maybe his own grave.

"What the hell?"

Schneider said, picking himself up, "Sorry. Sounded like incoming. Knee-jerk reaction."

Jim tried to integrate Schneider into his crowd, including introducing him to some of the tougher tots on campus, but his Army buddy went about offending everyone he met and Jim finally gave up on him. They had had a special relationship in the confines of the prison, but that time had passed. They would have coffee sometimes and reminisce. Soon Schneider made his own friends.

* * *

Journal – October

"Dory and I last night went to see Roberta Peters perform at Hill Auditorium. The singing, which was pleasant, aroused a subjective state of being, namely that of feeling completely young. Fall in Ann Arbor, with its intense signs of summer's death, may seem an incongruous time of the year for such sprightly emotions, but there was such a briskness of spirit, such fullness in the environment that I caught some of its strength. Usually, I can remain quite objective and put aside the feelings of the young, but when I was immersed tonight in its over-rated abandon, I felt close to the entire childhood of life. It was extraordinary to think that the fall was perfect, the singing incomparable, and the lights of young eyes were flashing—idiot that I am—just for me. This irrepressible feeling, rather delicious, was odd enough and strong enough that I thoroughly enjoyed it. A stuffed-shirt youth to be exact, but carefree and a bit blown inside out nevertheless."

* * *

It was a totally different experience from the one with Schneider when Bob Gooden flew into Ann Arbor for a football weekend. Gooden had continued to correspond while Jim was at school, letters that were tightly phrased and funny. The pair had been part of a draft call that included a hundred or more Long Islanders. They were sworn in the same day in January of '51. They had shared some good times in the interim and some dark ones as well, especially when Jim's religious faith had been put to the test.

"Hey, Gude!"

"O'Mahoney, is it?" asked Gooden, flicking his Irish brogue. "Me mother sends her best in the form of fresh jelly rolls, warm from this morning's oven, knowing ye must be starved for real baked goods. She swears they mend all wounds, no matter that the neighbors say they're belly bombs."

"Blurp ... How are you, Grumpy? Did the stewardesses take good care of you?"

"Lavished me with their biscuits, seeing it would be indiscreet to do otherwise. Now, show me your cornfields. I'm new to the district."

"Many treats await you," Jim said as they headed toward the baggage area. "This evening you're giving your standard speech at the Omega Chi house."

"I'm what? What's an Omega Chi?"

"Sort of a women's seminary. We couldn't allow you to come all this way without dropping a few pearls of wisdom for the ladies. I told them you had a ready text on how to keep one's virginity."

"Oh, that speech. Thought I had lost it."

"Lost your virginity? For sooth!"

"What else, Lochinvar?"

"Your Friday night date is one of the leading Socialists on campus. She intends to convert you or ask you to help her blow up one of Ma Bell's telephone booths or something."

"Good. My FBI file needs some thickening." Gooden said.

"I hear they have a special section just for Republicans."

"So where is this university of yours, my bright-eyed boy?"

They rode the bus back from Ypsilanti and settled into Jim's place. They toured the campus and in mid-afternoon walked over to the Phi Pi house.

The redhead's friend, Marsha Threads, the sassy campus leader who fluently lifted her left-leaning voice in public and private, was to be Gooden's date for the weekend.

"What's this I hear? You're a Republican?" Threads greeted. "We'll have to work on you while you're here."

"Is this where the Farm and Labor party holds its blood rites?"

"That's in Minnesota. Over that way. Here we're called the Young Wobblies."

"Wobblies? I'm a little off-balance myself after riding that tin can I flew in on."

"We'll get you back your legs," she said in mock seduction.

"You know I'm not impressed by orthodox liberals like Mahoney here."

"Bite your tongue, boy," Threads told him.

"I think they'll get along fine," Dory told Jim.

"Yes. But which one will murder the other first?"

At five, Jim and Bob arrived at the sorority house where Jim had been serving lunch and dinner the past couple semesters. The cook, Miss Maggie with her troubled brow, never showed favoritism to any of the servers, thus allowing her the option of criticizing all. But she was never mean, just quietly suspicious. What was established truth along Greek Row was that she made the best Sunday roast pork in town with gravy suitable for bottling. One coed said she intended to be embalmed in it.

"Hi, Miss Maggie. This is my friend from New York. He's substituting. We came early so I could show him the ropes."

"He's OK, but no spilling."

"He's steady as a juggler," Jim replied.

"Is this where I give my speech?" Gooden asked, going along with Jim's ploy.

"Yes. You'll have to wear a speaker's gown," Jim said, handing him a long apron.

"Is this a Masonic sorority?"

"Let's make a sound check. You can inspect the venue as we set the silverware."

"About this speaking. Is there an emolument?"

"Yes. Dinner."

They had established their particular brand of banter over a two-year period while in the Army. It was not always recognizable to others.

A couple of guys from the med student fraternity next door came by—one to serve and the other to wash dishes. They sat down at the kitchen table for dinner. Their usual conversation involved the impossible requirements of the university's Anatomy class, one that kept the future doctors up all night.

Promptly at six, fifty or so girls and a few alums came down for dinner and noticed that one of the servers was new.

"Who do we have here, Jimbo?"

"Picked him up off the street." One never gave a straight answer to these women.

"In a good neighborhood, I hope."

"Yeah. The one with blinking red lights."

Gooden, neither suave nor distinguished, wore his suave and distinguished look.

"When do I give my speech?"

"Actually, I've just tricked you into serving," Jim confessed

"Tricked me, did you? Listen, smart ass, I'm giving my speech anyway."

Gooden walked along delivering plates of food and began mumbling something to the girls. Some of them looked up at him quizzically, thinking they heard some suggestive language. Others thought he was humming.

"Even in the throes of passion ..." he would begin. Or, sliding and dipping along the long tables, he whispered, "Keep your legs crossed at all times. . ."

"Jim," called the housemother, a very gray and grandmotherly woman. "What is that boy muttering about? Is he off his runner?"

"He must have a speech defect."

"Do you know him?"

"Never saw him before," Jim said with a straight face.

"Odd boy."

"Appears deficient."

Because they had set up the dining room, they left shortly after the cleanup.

"You deceived me about the speech."

"No, I heard good reports that the girls loved it. They've already set up a sub-committee to hold workshops."

"It was a quite entertaining talk if I don't say so myself."

"Don't you worry. It'll be remembered if the housemother has anything to say about it. But just because you're not invited back right away, it's probably their way of telling you that they'll plan a bigger event next time."

"Perhaps the talk will be anthologized."

"Year's best, I'm sure."

The foursome, Jim and Gooden, along with the redhead and Threads, followed the latter to an open house at the Socialist Club, a large studio downtown.

"What will me sainted mother think?" Gooden asked.

"Tell her you did it out of a new found sense of brotherhood."

They went on to the P-Bell and drank pitchers of beer. When they returned to the sorority house to drop off the girls, Jim and the redhead went into the backyard along with other couples to enjoy some smooching in the bushes.

"That Threads woman wouldn't even let me up the front steps," Gooden complained as he waited by the curb. "Beat me with a broom, she would."

"Don't worry. We'll see them later when we come back for the fertilization rites,"

"What fertilization rites?"

"We pretend we're serenading them but we'll actually be tickling their fancy."

"This better be good," Gooden said. "What's in that bag?"

"The coconut mask you sent me. You're wearing it during the ceremony. I'm anointing you Ishtar, the Egyptian god of fertility."

They returned about midnight after another drink. As they wandered, Jim gathered a few twigs and leaves. Back at the Phi Pi house, nearly all the lights were out.

"First we build a little bonfire," Jim said.

Eyeing the few twigs, Gooden said, "A very small bonfire."

Jim lit his puny fire and instructed Gooden that they had to do a little dance and sing the Michigan fight song.

"We have to evoke the gods. You want this thing to work, don't you? Think of all the rewards. Fifty hopped-up women."

Jim sang the words and Gooden played along as the fire sputtered.

"I don't see any of them hanging out the window."

"I know their toes are tapping. I can just sense it."

"Has anyone ever told you that you are very weird?"

They were as happy as two kids in a mud-slinging contest.

Suddenly, "What's going on down there, you boys. Put out that fire and quit that singing before I call the campus police."

"The housemother. Cheese it."

They took off down the street, laughing.

The next day they went to the colorful Homecoming Game and later to a reception at Phi Pi, followed by a dance that evening.

Gooden went back to New York on Sunday and left Jim with the sure knowledge that he had a bonded brother in his fire-dancing friend.

* * *

Around Thanksgiving, an article by playwright Arthur Miller, a Michigan alumnus, appeared in a popular newsstand magazine. After spending some time in Ann Arbor, he wrote a long article that focused on his alma mater. He said essentially that he found no love in Ann Arbor but a lot of fear.

* * *

Journal – December

"The guy next door has just come back to school after being in Korea. Matter of fact he was back in town sixty days after leaving the front. On the last day of the war after the armistice had already been signed and during the period before midnight when the treaty went into effect, one jet flier, in an attempt to get in an extra mission to improve his record for promotion, nosed right into the runway and died—the futility of ambition."

* * *

Journal – December

"This has really been such a pleasant fall that I should have made annotations during the period so that I could have better remembered it—not that remembering is the first function—but it would be nice to look back on such good days. As to the future, it does promise to be better. Especially should have remembered the details of Gooden's trip at Homecoming and our fertility rite on the lawn of the Phi Pi house where we only succeeded in fertilizing the housemother. Plus his guest of honor speech at Omega Chi.

For now, the Christmas season is upon us with a performance tonight of the *Messiah.* My red-headed friend hummed through most of it."

* * *

A month prior to his January graduation, James Francis Mahoney had one more youthful decision to make, whether to seek employment in Chicago, the site of his early childhood and family origins, or in the New York that took him through his teenage years. He had long ago established that he wanted to work in the publishing business and he felt a loyalty and a magnet from both cities. As a result, he chose to spend the holidays alone in Ann Arbor and wrestle with the question alone.

* * *

Journal – December 20

"A college town at Christmas is undoubtedly the most hopeless and forlorn place in the world. Yet I saw Menotti's *Amahl* on television and that has put me in a properly respectful mood, that is, if a former Catholic can respect the Christmas story. I remain in this outpost for only one reason and that is to avail myself of the opportunity, before entering the world, of making some inspection of my career directions and to review my spiritual position. The preliminaries to a business life should have been taking care of already by a twenty-five-year old like me, but this age being this age, it is rather difficult to enter the world on an automatic, stainless steel escalator. I feel I'm forthright enough now to face the world. Idealist, I am, and shall remain. I intend to appear like other people, though somewhat radical and Socialistic. I'll buy gray and blue clothes, small checked and conservative. I'm even learning to hold my tongue. In the stultifying decade that I fear is about to begin, I promise not to conform to my contemporaries, save in dress and polite conversation. How long I can remain honest about all this is for me to discover. I seriously doubt if I can remain so for long."

* * *

Journal – Christmas Eve

"Being no alien to the Christmas tradition and still loyal to some of its inner implications, I went out tonight gaily appareled in my new presents (sweater from Dory, tie and socks from me; the holiday tie, as usual to be burned on New Years morning). I went out to chase down the Christmas goose and seek the signature of

Christ. The bells were tolling and thinking that I would find the first much quicker than the second, I walked about the village seeking inn. But, alas, no room in the mercenary hearts of proprietors who flee when the students are on vacation. There wasn't a restaurant open in town except the chop-suey house, so, goose or no goose I say to myself, I'd much rather spend my evening with my Chinese friends than some fled Christians, and though there is no wishbone in Egg Foo Yong, I feasted. I didn't understand until later when consciously genuflecting to the Christ man that I was seeking a definition of the season.

I crossed campus to the chapel and observed some signs of childish playfulness. Stamped out in the snow outside the chapel by little people's feet was a large circle, the pagan symbol of fertility and in the interior, I read backward S U S E J. I went into church and quietly stood beneath the XIII Station of the Cross. I had found what I was looking for.

I have come home to listen to Dr. Harrow's 'sacreds.'"

* * *

Jim retired into the labyrinth of his decision. True, New York supported most of the publishing houses but there were opportunities in the Midwest. Manhattan had an abundance of pleasant distractions, lots of music and shows, but if one was selective and paid attention, the arts prospered just as well inland. True, one had to be more selective and willing to travel. But was it a good thing to be choked by Broadway performance choices when he was seeking the quiet of a writer's den? OK, maybe the Midwest didn't possess the political or intellectual meadowlands that were so much a part of the Eastern Seaboard. But was all the Eastern frenzy that accompanied the dog-eating competition and cutthroat coarseness necessary? He needed a job, but he also craved quiet where he could begin the work he thought he was destined to accomplish. He would have to give the question a lot of thought. For a change, there was no woman pulling him one way or the other. This was his decision to make.

Jim didn't think he was a finished product yet, but he felt that he had journeyed far from the callow teenager and irresponsible person he had been. He knew he would be interacting with the big world outside of himself, and he was ready to engage.

* * *

Journal – late December

"The dilemma appears to be: I feel better when I'm enjoying an organic relationship with the environment. It might be easier to achieve peace of mind in the countryside. But what happens to the soul in the boondocks, who knows? Sure, the good life can be achieved in non-urban areas but what happens when country life tries moving to the city? Will it bring me into harmony? Or is this the difference between the selfish and responsible man, the one who accepts the tranquility of rural life and the one that fights for urban civility? Which are the happy campers and which the flawed heroes? Still it seems that the passive intellectual is of lesser interest than the active one, though we need the thinkers."

* * *

Jim knew that he didn't want to end up in the suburbs where he had failed so poorly. He knew, in all honesty, Manhasset had saved him when he was ten, before he began his years of bad behavior. That is to say, he allowed his town to watch him corrupt himself. But the suburbs were now out. In terms of geography, he wanted to be all in or all out of the city.

* * *

Journal - New Year's Eve

"So, I choose Manhattan instead of Chicago, realizing I don't belong in the rat race, and knowing beforehand that I may bring on my own destruction. I should like to be the genial lad that could exist in either place, but I can't accept the soft way out. And yet, I'm taking a chance that I can make New York satisfying enough to remain at peace amidst all this mid-century war.

During all this, my friends have been beautiful."

* * *

It's not only Indian mystics who climb up an internal ladder seeking harmony. Jim had steadily raised the bar that measured the heights of his potential. He had started cranking out his goals six years earlier in order to monitor his intellectual/artistic progress, measuring as he went along whether knowledge and understanding allowed him to become more comfortable with life's ambiguities and himself. Having propelled himself from callow youth to creative adult, he now sealed off his school years as he prepared to find his life's work. He had used an independent social-intelligence indicator in order to qualify his friends and open their hearts. Searching for soul mates was like a person stepping across stones in a stream; the stones get smaller, more slippery and further apart as one tries to gain the outstretched arms of a true friend arriving from the far shore.

He finally came to believe that he couldn't interface with most people except in a friendly surface way. He didn't have sufficient generosity of spirit to be openly gregarious with everyman. He didn't possess that sixth Irish sense that allowed him to crawl into other people's hearts. Not that he denigrated others, except during political discussions, or thought himself superior to anyone, but he chose to limit his loyalty to a few people who engaged life the way he did. In reality, he wasn't qualified to limit his coterie to a private world of the elite. He never thought he was a member. Never one of the elect. Still he wanted to muddle at the upper level.

He wondered why he didn't have the sense to use his brain when he was young. Why didn't he engage the eternals that a young mind is capable of grasping in its imagination? Or respect and revere self-reliance and be taken seriously at the time of emerging responsibilities? Because, of course, he didn't know how and didn't have the means. Or because he was frightened and timid, and found himself confused by the diffidence of his parents, by the Church or society. Or unable to control himself. But he didn't live in a society where human reasoning counts as much as money and prestige—where the rules turn into prejudices that are the fodder for certain kinds of appetites. People conform because they're trying to please those who think they have the right to exercise power over them. We behave for our authority figures. But Jim would have none of it.

It's the young that need the most help, he thought. If they come from a safe environment and a good home, they'll have a good first half of life and most likely control the struggles they encounter. But a kid from a bad neighborhood or distressed family will have to pull him/herself up, fight all the way and, if lucky, achieve balance and have a quieter existence after thirty. After the fireworks of youth.

He felt he had to discard most of what he grew up with before he could begin putting himself together. Many opt for going the route of their parents—a treacherous way to one's own salvation, he felt. He thought, we usually have to throw off conformity and its values, even our communities and sadly, our religion. We must retreat from our families, our familiar places in order to find ourselves, because independence holds the answer.

There will be in every generation those who stand by their parents and those who escape them to form their own lifestyle. The first will be traditional, conservative and protective. Those who adventure out on their own will be the opposite, but the potential leaders of any generation will come from the latter, though the former will hold title to the land, the economy and may finally outsmart the creative and experimental.

The problem with Jim was that he never had a mentor. He had perhaps been too undistinguished to receive notice or too proud or ignorant to call for help.

He held the notion that he had become a better person. He was, after all, an adult now and should have perfected himself. But he knew that his bad behavior could still arise and sometimes overwhelm him. He knew he wasn't the authentic finished product of human reform. People might say he was a good guy, but nobody thought he was a person of good character except for a few who understood how difficult it had been to straighten himself out. But he kept making mistakes. Family friends noticed his sardonicism.

His victory was that he had learned to read the tea leaves of his culture without sacrificing his feelings—or so he thought.

What he had attained was himself. With all that, little did he know.

When he was a brand-new teenager, his body's hormones saved him and now his mind allowed him to proceed into the larger world.

Meanwhile, there was love.

THE COLUMBIAD

BOOK 1

Eagles Rising

Eagles Rising is the story of a family's struggle through the early 20th Century. The novel details the transition of the Irish-American Mahoneys from their Iowa homestead to a Chicago South Side neighborhood. The story chronicles how the family becomes unwitting participants in the city's labor, gangster and race wars.

Book 2

First Lights

First Lights is the eternal story of the struggle a boy is forced to combat as he reconciles his spiritual feelings with the requirements and enticements of the world, especially when he's energized by the bouncy trampoline of awakening sex.

Book 6

Yo Columbia!

Set in Manhattan's fast-paced publishing world of the Eighties, *Yo Columbia*! is the story of the courtship of an inter-racial couple. The pair sets out to find the lost opera of Scott Joplin. The lovers also uncover a historical black beauty that was the model for traditional representations of America.

CPSIA information can be obtained
at www.ICGtesting.com
Printed in the USA
FFOW02n1911030416
22920FF